To: Laura Marks
From: Leslie Marks

HOT NIGHT

IN THE CITY

TREVANIAN

HOT NIGHT IN THE CITY

THOMAS DUNNE BOOKS

ST. MARTIN'S PRESS 🙢 NEW YORK

THOMAS DUNNE BOOKS.
An imprint of St. Martin's Press.

www.stmartins.com

Book design by Victoria Kuskowski

Library of Congress Cataloging-in-Publication Data

Trevanian.
 Hot night in the city / Trevanian.—1st ed.
 p. cm.
 "Thomas Dunne Books."
 ISBN 0-312-24202-6
 1. United States—Social life and customs—20th century—Fiction.
2. City and town life—Fiction. I. Title.

PS3570.R44 H68 2000
813'.54—dc21   00-029679

First Edition: June 2000

10 9 8 7 6 5 4 3 2 1

TO ALEXANDRA

Without whose patience, faith, and inspired insights

this book could not have been written

CONTENTS

HOT NIGHT IN THE CITY

There were only three passengers on the last bus from down-town: a man, a woman, and a bum. The slim young man sat alone at the back of the bus because he had an instinctive mistrust of men in uniform, even bus drivers. Unable to sleep because of the heat and a relentless gnawing in the pit of his stomach, he had left the flophouse and deposited his bindle in a bus station locker so he could wander the streets unencumbered. The young woman sat close up behind the driver clutching her handbag to her lap, her knees pressed together and her gaze fixed on the nippled rubber floormat to avoid making eye contact with the old bum who sat across from her, smelling of piss and sweat and waking up with a moist snort each time the bus hit a pothole or lurched to miss one.

An oppressive heat wave had been sapping the city for over a week. Not until after midnight was it cool enough for people to go out and stroll the streets for a breath of air. In the stifling tenements that separated air-conditioned downtown from the breezy suburbs, kids were allowed to sleep out on fire escapes, sprawled on sofa cushions. On the brownstone stoops down below, women in loose cotton house dresses gossiped drowsily while men in damp undershirts sucked beers. At the beginning of the heat wave, people had complained about the weather to total strangers with a grumpy comradeship wrought of shared distress, like during wars or floods or hurricanes.

But once the city's brick and steel had absorbed all the heat it could hold and began to exhale its stored-up warmth into the night, the public mood turned sullen and resentful.

The bus crawled through tenement streets that were strangely dark because people left the lights off to keep their apartments cooler, and many streetlights had been broken by bands of kids made miserable and mutinous by the heat. But the interior of the bus was brightly lit, and it made the young man uncomfortable to be moving through dark streets in a glass specimen case with everyone looking at him from out there in the dark. All the bus windows were open to combat the heat, but the breeze was so laden with soot that it was gritty between his teeth, so he reached up and snapped shut the window in front of his seat. An advertising placard in the arch of the roof assured him that he could improve his chances of success by 25%, 50%, 75%...Even More...by Building a Powerful Vocabulary the Amazing Word-Wizard Way! Money Back If Not Totally Delighted! Let Words Unlock Your Buried Inner Potential! My inner potential must be buried pretty goddamn deep, he thought. He'd been on the drift for two years now, ever since he'd brought his participation in the Korean Police Action to an informal end.

The girl at the front tugged the slack cord, and a deformed *ding* brought the bus to a lurching stop. The young man slipped out through the back accordion doors as the girl thanked the driver and stepped down from the front of the bus. With a swirl of dust and litter, the bus drove off, carrying the snorting drunk into the night.

She walked towards the only unbroken streetlight on the block, tottering a little because she was unaccustomed to high heels. When her ankle buckled, she looked back at the sidewalk with an irritated, accusing frown, as though she had tripped over something. That was when she noticed him.

It occurred to the young man that she might think he was following her, and the last thing he wanted was to frighten her, so he put his hands in his pockets and began to whistle to show that he wasn't trying to sneak up on anybody or anything. It was the theme from *The Third Man*, a film he had seen six times in one day when he'd gone into a narrow, fleabag movie house one rainy afternoon to get some sleep but, fascinated, had stayed until the theater closed after midnight. He could recite the whole 'cuckoo clock' speech by heart, and in Welles's voice, too.

It was obvious from the rigidity of the girl's back as she increased her pace that his whistling wasn't putting her at ease. And why should it? he asked himself; she probably listened to the eerie tales of *The Whistler* on the radio. The boy got a real surprise when she reached the streetlight and turned on him. "You better not try anything!" Her voice was reedy with tension. "This is an Italian neighborhood!"

The boy held up his palms in surrender. "Whoa there, ma'am," he said in his moistly toothless Gabby Hayes's voice. "You ain't got no just cause to go chucking a whole passel of I-talians at me." But she didn't find that funny. The streetlight directly overhead turned her eyes into gashes of shadow beneath vivid brows; only the tips of her lashes shone, mascara'd with light. He smiled and said in his stammering Jimmy Stewart voice, "Look, I'm...I'm just terribly sorry if I frightened you, Miss. But I want you to know that I wasn't following you. Well, yes, yes, I *was* following you, I suppose. But not on purpose! I was just, sort of, well...walking along. Lost in daydreams. Just...just lost in daydreams, that's what I was. Look, why don't I just...just...turn around and go the other way? It's all the same to me, 'cause I'm not going anywhere special. I'm just...you know...sort of drifting along through life."

She still didn't smile, although it was a *great* Jimmy Stewart, if he did say so himself. She continued to stare at him, frightened, tense; so he made a comic little salute and walked up the street, away from her. Then he turned back. "Excuse me, my little chickadee, but you said something that tickled my cur-i-osity." He dragged out the syllables in the nasal, whining style of W. C. Fields. They were talking across a space of perhaps ten yards, but it was well after midnight and the background growl of downtown traffic was so distant that they could speak in normal tones. "Pray tell me, m'dear. Why did you warn me that this is an I-talian neighborhood. Just what has that—as the ancient philosophers are wont to wonder—got to do with anything?" W. C. Fields tapped the ashes from his imaginary cigar and waited politely for her answer.

She cleared her throat. "Italians aren't like most city people. They have family feelings. If a woman screams, they come running and beat up whoever's bothering her."

"I see," W. C. drawled. "A most laudable custom, I'm sure. But one that would be pretty hard on a fellow unjustly accused of being a mugger, like yours truly." She smiled at the W. C. Fields, so he kept it up. "You are, I take it, a woman of I-talian lineage?"

"No. I live here because it's safer. And cheap."

He chuckled. "You've told me more than you meant to," he said in his own voice...well, the made-up voice he used for everyday.

She frowned, and the steep-angled light filled her forehead wrinkles with shadow. "What do you mean?"

"You've told me that you live alone, and that you don't have much money. Now I wonder if you'd be kind enough to tell me one other thing?"

"What's that?" she asked suspiciously, but already the first spurt of adrenaline was draining away.

"Is there someplace around here where I could get a cup of coffee?"

"Well...there's a White Tower. Four blocks down and one over."

"Thanks." His eyes crinkled into a smile. "You know, this is a strange scene. I mean...really strange. Just picture it. Our heroine descends from a bus, right? She is followed by a young man, lost in vague daydreams. She suddenly turns on him and threatens to Italian him to death. Surprised, bewildered, dumbfounded, nonplussed, and just plain scared, he decides to flee. But curiosity (that notorious cat killer) obliges him to stop, and they chat, separated by yards of sidewalk that he hopes will make her feel safe. While they're talking, he notices how the overhead street lamp glows in her hair and drapes over her shoulders like a shawl of light. ...A shawl of light. But her eyes...her eyes are lost in shadow, so he can't tell what she's thinking, what she feels. The young hero asks directions to a coffee shop, which she obligingly gives him. Now comes the tricky bit of the scene. Does he dare to invite her to have a cup of coffee with him? They could sit in the Whitest of all possible Towers and while away a few hours of this stifling hot night, talking about...well, whatever they want to talk about. Life, for instance, or love, or maybe—I don't know—

baseball? Finally the drifter summons the courage to ask her. She hesitates. (Well, come on! What young heroine wouldn't hesitate?) He smiles his most boyish smile. (I'm afraid this *is* my most boyish smile.) Then the girl— Well, I'm not sure what our heroine would do. What do you think she would do?"

She looked at him, mentally hefting his intent. Then she asked, "Are you an Englishman?"

He smiled at the abrupt non sequitur. "Why do you ask?"

"You sound like Englishmen in the movies."

"No, I'm not English. But then, you're not Italian. So we're even. Well...I'm even. Even-tempered, even-handed, and even given to playing with words. But you? You're not even. You're most definitely odd."

"What do you mean, odd?"

"Oh, come on! Accepting an invitation for coffee with a total stranger is pretty goshdarned odd, if you ask me."

"I didn't say I'd go for coffee with you."

"Not in words maybe, but...say, which way is this White Tower of yours, anyway?"

"Back the way we came."

"Four blocks down and one over, I believe you said."

They walked down the street side by side, but with plenty of space between them, and he kept up a light trickle of small talk, mostly questions about her. She soon warmed to his light, smiling tone because she was lonely and eager to talk to somebody. He learned that she had been in the city only six months, that she had come from a small town upstate, and that she had a job she didn't like all that much. No, she didn't wish she'd stayed in her hometown. Oh sure, she got the blues sometimes, but not bad enough to want to go back there. At the next corner, she turned unexpectedly in the direction of the all-night coffee joint, and their shoulders touched. They both said "Sorry," and they walked on, closer now, but she was careful not to let their shoulders touch again as they approached the White Tower, a block of icy white light in the hot night.

It was pretty full, considering the late hour. The air-conditioning had attracted people driven off the street by the heat. In the booth next to theirs, a young couple fussed over three kids wearing pajamas and unlaced tennis shoes. The baby slept in the woman's arms, its mouth wetly pressed against her shoulder. The other two made slurping noises with straws stuck into glasses of pale tan crushed ice from which the last bit of cola taste had long ago been sucked. Among the refugees from the heat wave, the boy recognized several night people by the way they hunched defensively over the cups of coffee that represented their right to stay there. They were his sort of people: the flotsam that collects in all-night joints; the losers and the lost; those on the drift, and those who'd been beached; nature's predators, nature's prey.

Mugs of coffee between them, the boy and the girl talked; and when their talk waned or their thoughts wandered inward, as sometimes they did, they gazed out onto the empty street lit only by the bright splash from their window. Once he caught her examining his reflection in the glass. Her eyes saw his looking back at her and they flinched away. He hadn't had a real chance to see what she looked like out in the darkness, so he made a quick appraisal of her reflection. She was young and slim, but not pretty. Her face had a bland, peeled look. But her eyes were kind and expressive, and they were set off by long, soft lashes that were her only natural ornament. He was careful not to compliment her on her eyes, however, because saying a girl has nice eyes is an admission she isn't good-looking; it's something like describing a person with no sense of humor as 'sincere', or saying a really dull girl is a 'good listener'. Her shoulder-length hair was curled in at the ends and, with her short bangs, it made a frame that emphasized the blandness of her face. She had gone out that night in a stiff cotton frock with little bows at the shoulders, a full skirt held out by a rustling crinoline, and a matching bolero jacket. There was something odd about her clothes...like she had borrowed them from someone who was not quite her size.

Then it hit him: June Allyson!

Every major film actress had her characteristic makeup, hairdo, and wardrobe that girls imitated, each following the style of her 'favorite movie star': meaning the actress she thought she most closely resembled. For girls with too much face, there was the 'Loretta Young look'; for hard-faced girls, the 'Joan Crawford look'; for skinny-faced girls, there was Ida Lupino; for chubby-faced girls, Mitzi Gaynor or Doris Day; and for terminally plain girls there was always Judy Garland, who had to rely on her cornball, moist-eyed, hitch-in-the-voice earnestness.

This girl's scanty bangs and under-roll hairdo, together with her girl-next-door cotton dress and matching jacket, told him that she had chosen June Allyson as her 'favorite'. He thought it was sad that she'd settled for June Allyson who, with her flat face, shallow eyes, and lisping overbite, was among the plainest of the popular actresses. A real girl-next-door, for crying out loud.

"That's a lovely dress," he said with gravity.

She smiled down at it. "I got all dressed up and went to the movies tonight. I don't know why. I just..." She shrugged.

"A June Allyson movie?" he asked.

"Yes. I'd been waiting to see—" Her eyes widened. "How did you know?"

He slipped into his Bela Lugosi voice. "I know many things, my dear. I have powers beyond those of your ordinary, everyday, run-of-the-mill, ready-to-wear, off-the-shelf human being."

"No, come on, *really*. How did you know I went to a June Allyson movie?"

He smiled. "Just a lucky guess." Then he popped back into the Lugosi voice, "Or maybe not! Maybe I was lurking outside the movie house, and I followed you onto the bus, stalking my prey!" He shifted to Lionel Barrymore, all wheezy and avuncular, "Now just you listen to me, young lady! You've got to be careful about letting bad boys pick you up and carry you off to well-lit dens, where they ply you with stimulants...like caffeine."

She laughed. "Well, you're right, anyway. I did go to a June Allyson movie. She's my favorite."

"No kidding?"

"It was *Woman's World*. Have you seen it?"

"Afraid not."

"Well, there's these three men who are after this swell job, but only one of them can have it. And their wives are trying to help them get it, and..."

"...and June Allyson is the nicest of the wives? A smalltown girl?"

"That's right, and she— Wait a minute! You said you haven't seen it."

"Another lucky guess." Then back into the Lugosi voice. "Or was it? You must never trust bad boys, my dear. They may smile and seem harmless, but underneath...? Churning cauldrons of passion!"

She waved his nonsense away with a flapping motion of her hand: an old-fashioned, small-town, June Allyson gesture. "Why do you call yourself a bad boy?"

"I never said that," he said, suddenly severe.

"Sure, you did. You said it twice."

He stared at her for a moment...then smiled. "Did I really? Well, I guess that makes us a team. I'm the bad one, and you're the odd one. Riffraff, that's what we are. Tell you what: you be riff, and I'll be raff, okay?" Then Amos of *Amos 'n' Andy* said, "So elucidate me, Missus Riff. What am yo' daily occupational work like?"

She described her work at a JC Penney's where Weaver Overhead Cash Carriers zinged on wires, bringing money and sales slips up to a central nest suspended from the ceiling, and the change came zinging back down to clerks whom the company didn't trust to handle money. She worked up in the cashier's cage, making change and zinging it back down. "...but most of the stores have modernized and gotten rid of their cash carriers."

"And what if your store modernizes and gives up Mr Weaver's thingamajig—"

"Overhead Cash Carrier."

"...Overhead Cash Carrier. What happens to your job then?"

"Oh, by then I'll be a qualified secretary. I'm taking shorthand two nights a week. The Gregg Method? And I'm going to take a typing course as soon as I save up enough money. You know what they say: If you can type and take shorthand, you'll never be out of a job."

"Yeah, they just keep on saying that and saying that. Sometimes I get tired of hearing it. So, I suppose that what with your job and your shorthand classes and all, you don't get out much."

"No, not much. I don't know all that many people. ...No one, really."

"You must miss your folks."

"No."

"Not at all?"

"They're religious and awful strict. With them, everything is sin, sin, sin."

He smiled. "They do a lot of sinning, do they?"

"No, they never sin. Never. But they...I don't know how to describe it. They're always *thinking* about sin. Always cleansing themselves of it, or strengthening themselves to resist it. I guess you could say they spend all their time *not* sinning. Sort of like...well, do you remember when we were walking here and I bumped into you and we touched shoulders, then we walked on making sure not to touch again but thinking about it every step of the way? Well, with them it's sort of like that with sinning, if you know what I mean."

"I know exactly what you mean." Actually, he hadn't once thought about their shoulders touching, but to admit that would be unkind. And he admired her simple frankness where other girls would have been coy.

They fell silent for a time, then she emerged from her reverie with a quick breath and said, "What about you?"

"How do I feel about sin?"

"No, I mean, tell me about yourself and your job and all."

"Well...let's see. First off, I have to confess that I don't work in a JC Penney's, and I've never taken a shorthand course in my life. I haven't the time. I'm too busy lurking around movie houses and following girls on buses."

"No, come on! How come you talk with an English accent if you're not English?"

"It's not an English accent. It's what they call 'mid-Atlantic'. And it's totally phony. When I was a drama major in college, I—"

"You've been to college?"

"Only a couple of years. Then the Korean Police Action came along and I—" He shrugged all that away. "No, I'm not English. I just decided to change my voice because I hated it. It was so...New York. Flat, metallic, adenoidal, too little resonance, too much urgency. I wanted to sound like the actors I admired. Welles, Olivier,

Maurice Evans. So I took courses in theater speech and I practiced hours and hours in my room, listening to records and imitating them. But it turned out to be a waste of time."

"No it wasn't! I like the way you talk. It's so...cultured. Sort of like Claude Rains or James Mason."

"Oh yes, my dear," he said as Rains, "the phony speech eventually became habitual." He shifted to Mason, which was only a matter of bringing Rains a little further forward into the mask, dropping the note, and adding a touch of aspirate huskiness. "But even with a new voice, I was still the person I was trying not to be. Damned nuisance!" Then he returned to the voice he used for everyday. "For all my correctly placed vowels and sounded terminal consonants, I was still a bad boy running away from...whatever it is we're all supposed to be running away from."

"So you left college to join the army?"

"That's right. But the army...well, they decided to let me out early."

"Why?"

He shrugged. "I guess I'm just not the soldier type. Not aggressive enough. Are you cold?" She had been sitting with her arms crossed over her breasts, holding her upper arms in her hands. He reached across the table and touched her arm above the elbow. "You *are* cold."

"It's this air-conditioning. I don't know why they turn it up so high."

The refugees had been steadily thinning out, and now the family in the booth behind them left, the mother with the wet-mouthed baby in her arms, the father carrying one child and pulling a sleep-dazed little girl along by the hand, her untied shoes clopping on the floor. Soon the place would be empty, except for the night people.

She looked up at the clock above the counter. "Gee, it's after two. I've got work tomorrow." But she didn't rise to leave. He drew a deep sigh and stretched, and his foot touched hers beneath the table. He said, "Excuse me," and she said, "That's all right," and they both looked out the window at the empty street. He watched her eyes refocus to his reflection on the surface of the glass, and he smiled at her.

"What about you?" she asked. "Don't you have to be at work early?"

"No. I don't have what you'd call a steady job. I just drift from city to city. When I need money, I go to the public market before dawn and stand around with the rest of the drifters and winos. Job brokers come in trucks and pick out the youngest and strongest for a day's stoop labor. I almost always get picked, even though I'm not all that hefty. I give the foremen one of my boyish smiles, and they always pick me."

"It's true, you do have a boyish smile."

"And when the boyish smile doesn't work, I fall back on my 'look of intense sincerity'. That's a sure winner. Stoop labor only pays a buck or a buck ten an hour. But still, one thirteen- or fourteen-hour day gives me enough for a couple of days of freedom."

"But there's no future in that."

"*What?* No future? I've been tricked! They assured me that stoop labor was a sure path to riches, fame, success with the women, and a closer relationship with my personal savior. Gosh, maybe I'd better give it up and take a course in shorthand. The Gregg Method."

He meant to be amusing, but the smile he evoked was so faint and fugitive that he said, "I'm sorry. Look, I wasn't poking fun at you. If I was poking fun at anybody, it was myself. You are absolutely right! There's no future in stoop labor. I've got to start taking life seriously!" He made his eyes crinkle into a smile. "Maybe I'll start next Thursday. How would that be?"

She didn't answer for a time, then said she really had to be getting home.

He nodded. "You want me to walk you? Or do you feel pretty safe in your Italian neighborhood?"

"What about you? Don't you have to get some sleep?"

"They won't let me in. It's too late. So I'll just roam the streets. Cities are interesting just before dawn when everything is quiet, except for the occasional distant siren announcing a fire, or a crime, or a birth—which is a sort of crime, considering the state of the world. There's something haunting about a distant siren. Like when you hear the whistle of a freight train at night, far off down in the valley, and you'd give anything in the world not to be the kind of..." He stopped speaking and his attention turned inward. He seemed to be listening to a distant freight train in his memory.

She cleared her throat softly. "Gee, it must be interesting to travel around on freight trains and see things. Lonely, I suppose. But interesting."

"Yup!" he said in Gary Cooper's lockjaw way. "Real interesting, ma'am. But real lonely, too."

She pushed her coffee mug aside. "I've really got to get some sleep." But she still didn't rise to go. "You said something about not being able to go to bed because they wouldn't let you in. Who won't let you in? Why not?"

"Obviously, you're not *au fait* with the protocol of your friendly neighborhood flophouse. They're all pretty much the same. You sleep in wire cages that you can lock from the inside to protect your bindle from thieves and your body from men who— They're not exactly homosexuals. Most of them would rather have a woman. Most of them fantasize about women. But..." He shrugged and glanced at her to see if this was embarrassing her. But no. She was listening with a frown of concern, trying to understand with a total absence of coyness that he admired. "The flophouse routine is simple and rigid. You aren't allowed in until ten at night, and by eleven the lights are turned off. Early in the morning, usually five-thirty or six, the alarms go off and you've got half an hour to get out before they clean the place with a fire hose, shooting it through the wire cages. The mattresses are covered with waterproof plastic so they don't get soaked, but they always feel clammy, and the place always smells of urine and Lysol. But the price is right! Four bits a night. A dime extra if you want a shower. Tonight I took a long cold shower, then I lay on my cot, reading a paperback until the lights went out. But it was so hot! The rubberized mattress stuck to my back and made a sort of ripping sound every time I rolled over. And the sweat was stinging my eyes. So finally I decided to get out and wander the streets. But then..." he shifted to a Peter Lorre voice, nasal and lateral with dentalized consonants "...what should I see but June Allyson coming out of a June Allyson movie, so naturally I followed her. You think that was evil of me, don't you, Rick. You don't like me much, do you, Rick."

He smiled and returned to his street voice. "And now here I am, talking to a very, very sleepy girl in an almost empty White Tower. Ain't life a gas?"

She shook her head sadly. "Gosh, what a terrible way to live. And for a person who went to college, too."

He let W. C. Fields respond. "That's the way it is out there, my little chickadee. It's not a fit life for man nor beast!"

"You must be lonely."

"Yup," he said. "Sometimes a fella gets lonelier than one of those lonely things you see out there being lonely." Then he suddenly stopped clowning around. "I guess I'm nearly as lonely as a girl who gets all dressed up on the hottest night of the year and goes out to see a movie...all alone."

"Well I...I don't know many people here. And what with my night classes and all..." She shrugged. "Gee, I've really got to get home."

"Right. Let's go."

She glanced again at the clock. "And you're going to walk around until dawn?"

"Yup."

She frowned down into her lap, and her throat mottled with a blush. "You could..." She cleared her throat. "You could stay with me if you want. Just until it gets light, I mean."

He nodded, more to himself than to her.

They stepped out of the cool White Tower into the humid heat of the street. At first, the warmth felt good on their cold skin, but it soon became heavy and sapping. They walked without speaking. By inviting him to her room, she had made a daring and desperate leap into the unknown, and now she was tense and breathless with the danger of it...and the thrill of it.

He looked at her with feeling. 'This is it,' he said to himself. 'She's the one,' and he felt a thrill akin to hers. When he smiled at her, she returned an uncertain, fluttering smile that was both vulnerable and hopeful. There was something coltish in her awkward gait on those high heels, something little-girlish in the sibilant whisper of her stiff crinoline. He drew a long slow breath.

He followed her up three flights of dark, narrow stairs, both of them trying to make their bodies as light as possible because the stairs creaked and they didn't want to wake her landlady. She turned her key in the slack lock, opened the door, and made a gesture for him to go in first. After the dark of the stairwell, the room dazzled and deluded him. The streetlight under which they had first met was just beneath her window, and it cast trapezoidal distortions of the window panes up onto the ceiling, filling the room with slabs of bright light separated by patches of impenetrable shadow. His eyes had difficulty adapting to this disorienting play of dazzle and darkness because the brightness kept his irises too dilated to see into the shadows. The oilcloth cover of a small table was slathered with light, while the iron bed in the corner was bisected diagonally by the shadow of an over-sized old wardrobe that consumed too much of the meager space. The only door was the one they had entered through, so he assumed the toilet must be down the hall. The room was an attic that had been converted at minimal cost, and the metal roof above the low ceiling pumped the sun's heat into the small space all day long.

"It's awful hot, I know," she whispered apologetically. Standing there with her back to the window, she was faceless within a dazzling halo of hair, while the light was so strong on his face that it burned out any expression; she wore a mask of shadow; he wore a mask of light.

"I'll open the window so we can get a little breeze," he whispered.

"You can't. It's stuck."

"Jesus."

"Sorry. Would you like a glass of water? If I run it a long time, it gets cold. Well...cool, anyway."

"Do we have to whisper?"

"No, but I..."

"But you don't want your neighbors to know you have someone up here?"

She nodded. "You see, I've never..." She swallowed noisily.

"I understand," He didn't whisper, but he spoke very softly. "Yes, I would like a glass of water, thank you." He sat on the edge of the bed, sunk up to his chest in shadow.

She turned the single tap above a chipped sink and let the water overflow the glass onto her wrist until it got cool. He could tell she was glad to have something to do—or, more exactly, to have something to delay what they were going to do.

The harsh streetlight picked out a two-ring hot plate on the table. Its cord ran up to a dangling overhead light. The bulb had been taken out and replaced by a screw-in socket. He deduced that cooking in the room was forbidden, but she did it anyway to save money. She probably unplugged the hot plate and hid it when she left for work. There was an open workbook and a pad of paper beside the hot plate: the Gregg Method. These everyday objects were abstracted, caricatured, by the brittle streetlight that set their edges aglow but coated them with thick shadow. The room had a shrill, unreal quality that put him in mind of a bright but deserted carnival lot, and something about it made him think of a kid jolting awake from a terrible nightmare to see the shadow of a tree branch dancing insanely on a window shade.

She brought him the glass of water; he thanked her and drank it down; she asked if he would like another; he said he wouldn't, thank you; she told him it wouldn't be any trouble; he said no thanks, and she stood there awkwardly.

"Hey, what's this?" he asked, holding up a glass sphere that his fingers had discovered beneath her pillow where they had been unconsciously searching for that coolness that children seek by turning pillows over and putting their cheek on them.

"That's my snowstorm."

He shook the heavy glass paperweight and held it up into the band of light across the bed to watch the snow swirl around a carrot-nosed snowman. "Your own private snowstorm. A handy thing on a hot night like this!"

"I won it at the county fair when I was a kid. I used my ride money to buy a raffle ticket, and I won third prize. I told my folks I found it at the fairground because they're dead against raffles and bingo games and all kinds of gambling. My snowstorm's the only thing I took with me when I left home. Except my clothes, of course."

"So your snowstorm's your friend, eh? A trusted companion through the trials and tribulations of life."

"I keep it under my pillow, and sometimes at night when I'm

feeling real blue I shake it and watch the snow whirl, and it makes me feel safer and more...oh, I don't know," She shrugged.

"Back to your sentry post, loyal snowstorm." He returned the paperweight to beneath her pillow and patted it into place; then he reached up, took her hands, and drew her down to sit beside him.

"Please..." she said in a thin voice. "I'm scared. I really shouldn't of...I mean, I've never..."

He pressed her hands, clammy with fear. "Listen. If you want me to go, I'll just tiptoe down the stairs and slip out. Is that what you want?"

"...No, but...Couldn't we just..."

"You know what I think? I think I'd better go. You're scared, and I wouldn't want to talk you into anything you don't want to do." He rose from the bed.

"No, don't go!" Her voice was tight with the effort to speak softly.

He sat down again, but left a distance between their hips.

For a moment she didn't say anything, just sat there kneading the fingers of her left hand with her right. Then she squeezed them hard. She had come to a decision. She began speaking in a flat tone. "I was sitting at the table, like I do every night. Practicing my shorthand by the light of the street lamp because it's too hot to put on the light. And suddenly I was crying. I just felt so empty and lonely and blue! I wasn't sobbing or anything. The tears just poured out and poured out. I didn't think I had so many tears in me. I was so *lonely*." Her voice squeaked on the word. "I don't know a soul here in the city. Don't have any friends. Even back home, I never went on a date. My folks wouldn't let me. They said that one thing leads to another. They said boys only want one thing. And I suppose they're right."

"Yes, they are," he said sincerely.

"After a while I stopped crying." She smiled feebly. "I guess I just ran out of tears. I splashed cool water on my face and tried to work at my shorthand some more, but then I just closed the book and said, no! No, I won't just sit here and mope! I'll dress up in my best and go out and *find* someone. Someone to talk to. Someone to care about me and hold me when I'm feeling blue."

"You decided to go out and just...let yourself be picked up?"

"I didn't think about it that way, but...Yes, I guess so."

"You wanted to make love with a total stranger?"

"No, no. Well...not exactly. You see, I've never..." She shook her head.

"Shall I tell you something? I knew you were a virgin when I first saw you. Yes, I did. You had that Good Girl look. Like June Allyson. But somehow—don't ask me how—I could tell that the good girl was looking for a bad boy to make love to her. Funny, how I could tell that, eh?"

"But you're wrong. I was just looking for someone to talk to. Someone who might care about me."

"Oh. So you didn't want to make love, is that it?"

"I don't know. Maybe I did. Sort of, anyway. I didn't think it out or anything, I just took my towel and went down to the bathroom and had a long cool bath, then I put on my good dress, and out I went. Just like that."

"...Just like that."

"I took the bus downtown, and I walked around. Boys on street corners looked at me. You know, the way they look at any woman. But none of them...I guess I'm not...I know I'm not pretty or anything..." She paused, half hoping for a contradiction. Then she went on. "They looked at me, but nobody said hello or anything, so..." She shrugged.

"So you decided to go to the movies. *Woman's World.*"

"Yes." Her voice had a minor key fade of failure.

"But hey, wait a minute! You did meet someone! Not much of a someone, maybe. Just your common garden variety drifter. But you talked to him for hours over coffee. And now...here we are."

"Yes, here we are," she echoed. "And I'm afraid."

"Of course you're afraid. That's only natural. It isn't every day that a virgin sits in the dark with a bad boy she hardly knows." She didn't respond, so he pursued. "Even though you're a virgin, I suppose you know about how two people...love, and all?"

"Yes. Well, sort of. Girls used to giggle about it in the school locker room. They talked about how people...did it. I didn't believe them at first."

"I know just what you mean. To a kid, it seems such a silly thing to do. Putting your peeing equipment together. How could *that* be fun? And when you think of your own folks doing it...! It's enough to gag a maggot, as a folksy old tramp might say."

"The girls at school used to make up terrible stories about...it. Just to see me blush. I was easy to tease because I was shy, and I didn't know anything. My mother never told me anything. Once the girls played this joke on me? They gave me a folded piece of paper and asked me to write down my favorite number, then on the next line my favorite color, then my second favorite color, then—oh, I don't remember all the things; but the last question was whether I bit ice cream cones or licked them. Then they unfolded the paper and read it out loud. And there in my own handwriting I had written how many times a day my boyfriend and I *did* it, and what the color of his...thing...was when we started and what color it was when we ended, and stuff like that."

"And finally, your confession that you licked it."

She nodded miserably. "I didn't go back to school for the rest of that week, I was so embarrassed. I pretended I was sick. And then I really did get sick. I mean...that's when my periods started."

"But, of course, that couldn't have had anything to do with the girls' teasing."

"Oh, I know that, but still...coming right after and all..."

"Yeah, I understand. Kids can be rotten to one another."

"That was years ago, but I still get tears in my eyes when I think about it."

"Yeah...tears of rage. I have that sometimes. The rage just wells up in me and I blub like a kid."

"You do? Really?"

"Sure. So you saw all those embarrassing things written in your own handwriting, and now you're learning to write in a different way. In shorthand."

She frowned. "That's not why I'm taking shorthand."

"Could be part of it. Psychology is a screwy business. Like me playing all sorts of roles because I don't want to be—" He shrugged. "So you've never made love. Gee. Still, I suppose you've necked with boys. Been caressed and...you know...touched."

"No, never. I've never had a...boyfriend." She said the word in a tone of gentle awe. "Boys never found me attractive in that way." She made a dismissive half-chuckle. "Or in any other way, really. My mom used to say it was a blessing, me being plain. At least my looks wouldn't get me into trouble."

"But you've had dreams about lovemaking. That's only normal."

She didn't answer.

"And I suppose you've made love to yourself."

She didn't speak.

"I mean, you've...you know...played with yourself and caressed yourself. There's nothing more natural."

"My folks wouldn't think it's natural. They'd say it was a sin."

"Well, of course they would. But do you think it's a sin?"

After a moment she said, softly, "...yes."

"But you do it anyway?"

"...yes..."

"Hm-m. Well, that's mostly what our making love would be like. Only I'd be doing...you know...what you do for yourself. I'd be touching you and caressing you and bringing you pleasure. Unless, of course, you don't want me to."

She concentrated on the fingers she was twisting in her lap.

He took her hands and kissed them. They were rough and cold. He lifted her face by her chin and gently kissed her closed lips. They were thin and dry and tasted of cheap lipstick. When he drew back he saw that her eyes were closed, and there was a teardrop in the corner of one, so he shifted to his W. C. Fields voice. "The hardest part, my chickadee, is getting started. If we were already in bed and I was holding your dee-lightful chassis in my vee-rile arms, everything would just happen naturally." Then he changed to a gentle, understanding voice with a smile in it. "I know exactly how you feel. Even with us worldly bad boys it's always awkward. In the beginning."

"It is?"

"Yup. Look, I'll tell you what. Why don't I go stand out in the hall for a few minutes while you slip into bed. Then I'll come back and look around." He donned his Lionel Barrymore voice. "Great land o' Goshen, who's that under those blankets, Dr Kildare? Why, I do believe it's June Allyson. I'd better just slip in and keep her warm. It's my medical duty."

She sniffed the tear back and waved away his nonsense with that flapping gesture of hers.

"I'll be back in a couple of minutes." He made a broad burlesque of shushing her with his finger to his lips as he tiptoed across the room and eased the door open. Out in the dark hall, he took long, slow breaths while he listened at the door. At first he heard nothing. Then there was a sigh. Anticipation? Resignation? The springs of the iron bed twanged softly as she rose. He heard the faucet run. Then there was the rustling of her crinoline underskirt as she stepped out of it. Another silence. Then the soft twang of the bedsprings again.

"This is so..." she sought just the right word to describe the beautiful moment. "...so *nice*. Lying here like this...talking...being close." He had guided her hand to his soft penis, and she was holding it tentatively, dutifully ('politely' might be more exact) while her mind fondled the words: 'boyfriend...my first boyfriend'. Her hand on his penis was the only place their bodies were in contact because it was so hot. After bringing her to climax first with his hand, then with his tongue, he had lifted his head to find her belly wet with sweat, so he had blown across it gently to cool her. And now they lay side by side, looking up at the splayed shadow of windowpanes cast onto the ceiling by the streetlight.

"That was just wonderful," she said dreamily.

"Hm-m, I could tell it was from the way you moved. And the sounds you made."

"Gosh, I hope the neighbors didn't hear." She pulled her shoulders in and laughed silently into her hand.

"How many times have you...?" She didn't know how to put it.

"Have I what?"

"How many women have you...you know?"

"You really want to know?"

"No, don't tell me!" Then, after a moment, "Yes, tell me. How many?"

"You're my fifth."

"The fifth time you've made love? Or your fifth woman?"

"Both."

"Both? You mean you've made love only five times and each time with a different girl?"

"Exactly, Watson," he said in Basil Rathbone's arch drawl. "Five girls...five times. Curious business, what?"

"Were they like me, your other girlfri— These women?"

He squeezed his temples between his thumb and middle finger to ease the pressure. "No, nothing like you. The first one was when I was in college. She was old. About as old as my mother. I met her in a bar that was off limits to college kids. She was always there, sitting at the end of the bar, drinking gin. Her thick makeup and fake, ritzy voice were sort of a joke. People called her 'the Countess'. We drank and she talked about when she was a young woman in high society, and how all the men used to be crazy about her, but they were not of her social standing—crap like that. The bar closed, and we went walking down along the railroad tracks. I was pretty drunk. I suppose I thought we were going to her place. She had trouble keeping her balance because the ground was rough and broken. She fell against me, and I caught her, and she kissed me, a big wet kiss, and I laid her back on a muddy bank. And that, ladies and gentlemen, was my introduction to the splendors of romance! That night I quit college and joined the army to defend American Democracy and apple pie against the menace of International Communism and borscht. After basic training, I was given leave before being shipped over to Korea. It was Christmas, and I took a bus to Flagstaff, Arizona. Why Flagstaff? I had to go somewhere, and Flagstaff counts as somewhere...well, nearly. Not far from the bus station, I saw a girl in this all-night coffee joint, and from all the way across the street I could tell she was lonely. I have an instinct for loneliness."

"Like you could tell I was lonely?" she said softly into the dark.

He was silent for a moment. "Yeah, like I could tell you were lonely. Well, I joked with this girl, talking in one actor's voice after another, and the next thing you know we were walking towards her place. She was an Indian, and an orphan, and lonely, and just about as far as you can get from pretty, and...Well, anyway." He pressed his thumb into his temple, hard. "I decided not to return to the army. That meant I had to go on the drift. Casual pick-up jobs here and there, following the fruit crops north, flophouses, stoop labor, freight trains. Then there was this woman in Waco, a born-again fanatic who wanted to save me. And later a black hooker in Cleveland who'd been beaten up by her pimp. I couldn't kiss her while we made love because she had a split lip. And that's it. My total love life. Not much of a Romeo. But then, people don't like to get mixed up with someone like me. Damaged boys end up damaging other people. You understand what I'm saying?"

"Sort of. Well...no, not really."

They were silent for a time, then she said, "I thought it was going to hurt, but it didn't."

He tugged himself from his tangled thoughts. "What?"

"When we...you know. The girls at school said it hurts the first time, and you bleed."

"Well, we didn't do the part that hurts."

"Yes, I know. Didn't you...don't you want to?"

"Do you want me to hurt you?"

"No. No, of course not, but, I want you to have...you know...pleasure. I wish I knew how to..." She shrugged. "I'll do whatever you want." She snuggled her hot body to his and whispered into his ear. "How can I make you feel good? Tell me. Please."

He was silent.

"I'll do anything."

He chuckled. "Lick me like an ice cream cone?"

He felt her tense up, so he quickly said, "I'm sorry, I was just joking. No, there's nothing I want you to do. There's nothing you can do."

"What do you mean?"

"I suppose you've seen drawings on bathroom walls in school. Do you remember what the men's penises looked like?"

She shook her head.

"Oh, come on now. Of course you remember. Describe them to me."

"Well...in the drawings they're always huge. As big as arms. And sometimes there are drops of sap squirting out of them."

"Sap?" He laughed. "*Sap?*"

"Well, whatever it is. The stuff that makes—Oh, I see! You were afraid I'd have a baby. That was why you didn't..." She hugged him.

"No, that wasn't why. I didn't do the part that might hurt you because I...can't."

"You can't?"

"My penis can't get erect."

"Oh." Then, after a longish silence: "Were you hurt? Wounded or something?"

"No, I wasn't wounded." Then, after a moment: "But yes, I was hurt."

"I don't understand."

He drew a sigh. Here we go. Here we go. Here we go.

"When I was a kid (actually, it started when I was a baby) my mother used to...she used to play with me. Mostly with her mouth. That's the earliest thing in my memory, her playing with me. Of course I didn't know there was anything wrong with it. I thought it was just the way things are with mothers and their little boys...Kissing and cuddling and all that. Then one night she told me that I must never, never tell anyone what she did, because if I told, then mean people would come and spank me *hard* and put me into a deep, dark hole forever and ever. That's when I realized that we were doing something wrong. And being a kid, I naturally thought that it was my fault somehow. I used to have nightmares about being thrown into that deep, dark hole, and I..." He stopped short and shook his head.

"You don't have to tell me about it if you don't want to," she whispered.

"No, I want to. In fact, I have to, because that's the only way..." He shrugged, then he took several calming breaths before telling the shared darkness above them the things he needed her to know. "While my mother licked and sucked me, she would play with herself, and after a while she'd moan and squirm, and she'd suck faster and harder, and sometimes it would hurt, and I'd whine and tell her that it hurt, but she'd keep on until she was gasping and crying out! Then she'd lie back on the bed panting, and I'd be cold down there where I was all spitty with her licking and sucking. And sometimes it hurt real bad. Inside."

"Your mother...! She was crazy."

"Yup. She was always drunk when she did it. To this day, the smell of gin reminds me of being a little kid, and I can feel the pain inside, behind my penis."

"I'm sorry. I'm really sorry." She slipped her hand away from his soft penis, as though to avoid hurting him more.

"Then, when I was about five or six—I don't know exactly how old, but I hadn't started school yet—she was playing with me this night, tickling and sucking, and suddenly she lifted her head and smirked—I can still see the smirk—and she said, 'Well, well! Aren't *you* the naughty little boy! You want it, don't you, you bad, bad boy?' You see, my penis had got stiff. That can happen, even when a boy is too young to...well, too young to know what's happening. And from that night on, for the next couple of years, she'd make me stiff, and that would drive her wild, and she'd suck me hard while she played with herself, and she'd say I was a bad boy because I wanted it. I wouldn't get stiff if I didn't want it, she'd say, and she'd suck me until it hurt down in my testicles. Then this one night...this one night the hurt didn't go away after she stopped. It got worse and worse. And the next morning I couldn't go to school because it hurt so bad. She told me it was nothing. The pain would go away pretty soon. But I could tell she was scared. She said that if anyone found out what we did, they'd put me in that deep black hole and leave me there forever and ever. And everyone would know it was all my fault, because I got stiff, and that meant I wanted it, and they'd know I was a naughty, bad boy. By the time night came, my side was swollen and I had a fever. All night long I tossed in my bed with pain. The next morning, I found myself all alone in the house. My mother had gone. I had to pee real bad, but I couldn't because it hurt too much. I was afraid I was going to die. So I called the emergency number I found on the back of the phone book. It was the first time I ever used a phone. An ambulance came and took me to the hospital. I had ruptures. Two ruptures. There was an operation, and they kept me in the hospital for a long time. When I was feeling better, a social worker visited me in the children's ward. They couldn't find my mother anywhere. She'd run away. Abandoned me."

She turned onto her side and looked at his profile. He could feel her eyes on him, could feel the weight of her pity, and it felt good. "What about your father?" she asked. "Why didn't he stop your mother from...Why didn't he do something?"

"There was no father."

"Oh." After a silence, she asked, "Did you tell the doctors what your mother had done to you?"

He shook his head.

"Why not?"

"Because I didn't want to get her into trouble. After all...she was my mom." His jaw muscles worked, and she could hear the grinding of his teeth.

"It isn't fair!" she said.

"No, ma'am, it's not," his Gary Cooper voice agreed. "Not even a little bit fair." Then his own voice continued, "The doctor told the social worker that I had damaged myself by masturbating, and she told me I'd done a terrible thing and I would hurt myself badly if I didn't stop."

"So...what happened then?"

"They put me into an orphanage run by Catholic brothers. I got long lectures about how sinful masturbation was, and my earlobes would burn with embarrassment...and rage...at the injustice of it. Kids have a painfully keen sense of injustice. The brothers made me take cold showers, even in winter. They said it would keep me from abusing myself. The cold showers gave me an ear infection that put me back in the hospital, and that was the end of the cold showers. But not of the lectures." He fell silent, and he lightly rubbed his stomach to quell the gnawing. Then he used his Bela Lugosi voice. "And there you have it, my dear. The blood-curdling tale of...The Limp Penis!"

"I'm awful sorry."

Something in the depth of the silence outside told him they had reached that last dead hour before dawn. He'd have to leave soon.

"You must have been a real smart kid. I mean, you got into college and all." She was determined to find a silver lining in all his troubles: a Hollywood happy ending.

"Yes, I was smart. A bad boy, but a smart one. But I quit college and joined the army. Then I quit the army to become a full-time drifter."

"But a person can't just quit the army, can they?"

"Oh, the army wasn't all that happy about my taking off. They're out there looking for me even as we lie here, sharing secrets."

"Aren't you afraid they'll catch you?"

"I'm afraid of all sorts of things."

She drew a sympathetic sigh and said, "Gosh."

"Gosh, indeed. While I was in the army, I sort of went wild this one night. I ended up sobbing and screaming and beating up this Coke machine. I might have gotten away with it if it had been a Pepsi machine, but Coca-Cola *is* America, and beating one up is a matter for the UnAmerican Activities Committee, so they put me in the hospital. The loony bin. This doctor told me..." he slipped into his Groucho Marx voice "...Your problem isn't physical, son. It's psychological. That'll be ten million dollars. Cash. We don't take checks. For that matter, we don't take Poles or Yugoslavs either."

"And now you can't feel any pleasure? Like the kind you made me feel?"

"Yes, I can feel pleasure. And sometimes I need it very badly. But it's not easy for me to get pleasure. It's difficult and...sort of complicated."

"Is there anything I can do? To help you, I mean?" Her voice was thin and so sincere.

"Do you really want to help me?"

"I do. Honest and truly, I do."

"Cross your heart and hope to die?" He sighed and closed his eyes. "All right." He sat up on the edge of the bed. "You scoot over here and turn your back to me. And I'll bring myself pleasure. Is that all right?"

She slid over to the edge of the bed, awkward and uncertain. "Will it hurt me?"

"Yes," he told her softly. "But not for long."

She was silent.

"Is that all right? The hurt and all?" he asked. "I won't do it, if you don't want me to."

She swallowed and answered in a small voice, "No, it's all right."

He reached down and trickled his fingers up her spine to the nape of her neck and up into her hair. She hummed, and he felt her skin get goose-bumpy with thrill. His hands slipped under her hair and he stroked the sides of her neck up to the ears, then he reached around and gently cradled her throat between his hands. She swallowed, and he felt the cartilage of her windpipe ripple beneath his fingers. He bared his teeth and he closed his eyes and squeezed, and pleasure overwhelmed him.

After covering her with the sheet carefully, tenderly, he sat on the edge of the bed and looked up at the distorted trapezoid of bright light on the ceiling. In her struggle, she had clawed her pillow away, revealing her snowstorm paperweight. He held it up to the light and shook it, and the snow swirled around the carrot-nosed snowman...black snow in silhouette, and a black snowman. When his breathing returned to normal, he went to the sink and washed himself off. He looked back at the bed and was overwhelmed with pity for her. She had been so trusting...so vulnerable. The gnawing within him was gone, maybe forever. Maybe he'd never again have to...

But he knew better. It had eventually come back after each of the others, and it would come back after June Allyson

He dressed and tiptoed down the creaking stairs and out into the empty street where the predawn air was damp and almost cool. He walked slowly back towards downtown, hands in pockets. He would go to the public market and pick up a day's stoop labor, then he'd get his bindle from the bus station and hit the freight yards to catch a boxcar. Maybe the West Coast this time.

Over the city, the first milky tints of dawn began to thin the sky, and the morning air already felt stale and dusty in his nostrils.

It was going to be another scorcher.

MINUTES OF A VILLAGE MEETING

Ours is a small village in the Basque province of Xiberoa perched on a hillside above the sparkling Uhaitz-handia, which floods the low pastures each spring, making the earth rich again. We are neither rich nor poor; God provides enough for those who work hard and tend their flocks closely, but He protects us from the temptations of wealth by giving us land that is not excessively bountiful.

Without meaning to brag, I can say that we celebrate three traditional Basque festivals each year, while our neighboring village of Licq celebrates only one, and that only because they want to attract people to their cheese fair run by greedy merchants in direct competition to our own cheese fair, which offers far better—but enough! This is neither the time nor the place to reveal the low greed of those grasping Licquois, nor do I intend to condemn them for letting their ancient Basque traditions wither and drop away, for I understand that the old ways are easily forgotten by those who cozy up to tourists from Paris and Bordeaux, and listen to the outlander's French-speaking radio, and end up desiring his modern machines and his comforts. But the people of my upland village are sustained by those ancient fêtes and customs that have marked the joys and tragedies of Basque life since before Roland broke the mountain with his sword not so many kilometers from this very spot. (It was we Basques, you know, who thrashed that proud Roland at Roncesvalles—ancestors of mine, perhaps.)

We of Xiberoa are considered to be backwards and old-fashioned by those coastal Basque who live in the shadow of the outlander. Our accent is imitated to make jokes funnier, and occasionally people come from as far away as Paris to photograph our *lera* carts yoked to the horns of the russet oxen of Urt and piled high with the dried fern we harvest from the hillsides for animal bedding. Because we are the last people in all of France to use wooden wheels, outsiders smile on us and say that we are charming and quaint, but they shake their heads and tell us that we must inevitably change with the changing world and march to the ragtime rhythms of Paris. And perhaps this is so. Surely things are changing, even here. We are slowly becoming a village of children and old people, as our young women go to work in the espadrille manufactories of Mauléon, or go off to Paris to become maids, and our young men go to the New World to tend rich men's flocks; and they come back only at feast times, the young men riding automobiles that have radios inside of them, and the young women wearing skirts that show the bottom half of their legs.

Well, enough about the village. Perhaps it is old-fashioned, as they say, but any chance for rapid change is ruled out by our cumbersome old Basque style of government: village meetings in which every person may say his piece before he votes, even those who have only a light vote. Not all people have the same vote in our village meetings: some have heavier votes and some lighter; it depends on how much land you have inherited and how well you have done with it. We are told that in the lowlands all people are equal under the law. This seems very foolish, for any man with eyes in his head can see that men are not equal. The role of the law should be to assure equality amongst equals, and to make it possible for someone to become more equal if he works hard and has God's luck with him. Perhaps our way of seeing things is flawed, but we like it because it is our own way and, as the old saying has it, *txori bakhoitzari eder bere ohantzea.** And as the wise old Basque saying tells us: Old sayings are wise.

---

*Each bird finds his own nest beautiful.

We don't exactly 'make laws' at our village meetings; what we do is come to understandings that are written up in the minutes. And these minutes are sometimes very complicated, because we take every consideration into account and leave no loopholes that might tempt men to do things for which the village would have to ostracize them. Ostracism is a powerful penalty here, for it extends to the offender's wife, who will not be allowed to share the succulent bits of gossip that are exchanged every Tuesday down at the village lavoir where the women laugh and chat to the rhythmic splat of their wooden paddles spanking the laundry clean. A wife thus deprived of the sauce and spice of village life will make a many-faceted hell of the life of the offending husband. In this way, the wife becomes the stick for beating the man; but ancient Basque justice does not allow the ostracism to be extended to the children, for that would be unfair. Wives select their husbands, but children do not choose their parents.

What I want to tell you about is the minutes of a village meeting we held a few years ago, just before the Great War took seven of our young men away to the army, three of whom went on to God, while one came back strange in his head from the gas, and one who left as Zabala-the-Handsome came back as Zabala-One-Leg. I want to show you how careful and clever is our thinking about things—not from pride, which is a sin, but to make a record of ourselves, because I am beginning to accept that the old way of things must pass and, without a record, our grandchildren are doomed to slip into the world of the outlander where, as you know, all people are exactly alike.

But you could not understand the minutes of this meeting unless you knew something about the Widow Jaureguiberry, now gone to God, but at that time still amongst us. So first I will tell you about the Widow Jaureguiberry.

Each day the Widow Jaureguiberry would drive her small flock of sheep from our village to Etchebar, the next village up. And each evening she would drive them back. Now, tradition requires that the shepherd lead the flock so that the beasts will not stray into other people's fields. He is not permitted to *follow* the flock and allow it to blunder into other people's fields and fatten on their grass. Exception is made in the case of a sudden storm catching the shepherd out, and obliging him to drive his sheep into a field to keep them from wandering. This exception is not easily abused, for everyone knows if the bad weather could have been anticipated by looking for the signs in the sky. All mountain Basques are born with the ability to read the sky, although some are beginning to lose it by listening to forecasts on the radio.

The Widow Jaureguiberry always *followed* her flock, and her sheep were forever straying into the fields of others and eating their grass, while the widow limped after them shouting and seeming to be at her wits' end, as she managed to scatter the sheep from one pasture to the next. And she would visit each house in turn to chant her prolonged, whining apologies to the owner of the field, complaining about how hard it was to have her house in our village but to have to drive her sheep back and forth each day, because her pasture was up in Etchebar. And all the time the old woman was explaining this, her sheep were eating your grass!

Of course, God makes fools only in the Béarn, and everybody in our village knew that the Widow Jaureguiberry had no fields of her own, neither in our commune nor up in Etchebar. Her husband had not been a good peasant; he had been a dreamer and a drinker, and he had lost all his land before God invited him into His fold by letting a thunderbolt hit him during a storm in the high mountain pastures. His childless wife was left with nothing but the good will of old Aramburu, the wine merchant who had taken their land, one glassful at a time. And so it came to pass that the Widow Jaureguiberry was obliged to sustain herself by allowing her few sheep to feed on the grass of others. But she was fair about it; she let her sheep stray longer into the pastures of the richer peasants, and controlled them so that they bypassed the land of the poor. (Which proves that, in reality, she was as good a shepherd as you or I.)

You see, the Widow Jaureguiberry was a proud Basque woman who could not humble herself to request assistance from the commune. To do so would be to admit that her husband had not been a good provider—which, of course, he had not, but that was her own business, and not the world's. Also there was the matter of shaming her dead father, who had made the unfortunate match for her. She had found a way to live off the commune without appearing to do so. We all knew what she was doing, and everyone was a little proud of her Basque ingenuity. Everybody, that is, except the Colonel, who had fought the Prussians in '70, and who was the richest man in our village and therefore the stingiest, for God punishes the stingy by exposing them to the temptations of wealth, just as He protects the generous by keeping them in the safe haven of poverty—as the ancient Basque saying assures us.

All right then, that is all you need to know about Widow Jaureguiberry to understand the minutes of our village meeting. More would be prying.

The men of the village met at old Aramburu's, the wine merchant, who received us because wine is drunk at these affairs, to strengthen the wit and liberate the tongue. The problem before us was this: it was necessary to put a new roof on the infant-school, for the rain leaked through, and the teacher who came up from Licq three days each week said she would no longer come if the roof was not repaired. Of course, the men of the village would do the work themselves. We would make a fête of it and have a good time. But the tiles must be bought with money, so we decided to levy a small tax on ourselves for the purpose. It would be so many francs per hectare of land owned.

Fine. It would not cost too much, and we could never have lived down the shame of losing our infant-school, particularly as we had recently witnessed the humiliation of the people of Etchebar, who had been forced to close down their church because the priest said he could no longer come and say an additional mass every week for a mere handful of communicants. It was a sad day when two of their young men scaled the church tower to take the hands off the clock that would no longer be running. But this was necessary. They could not allow God's clock to deceive by giving the wrong time.

After this, the pious of Etchebar were obliged to trudge all the way down to our church each Sunday, and over little glasses after mass, some of us tended to commiserate with them rather more than was necessary about how humiliating it must be to live in a village so pitiable and insignificant that it didn't even have a church. So the closure of our school would mean a painful loss of face for us and a cheap laugh for them, for their infant-school, although sparsely attended, was at least watertight.

So the agreement to do the work ourselves and to purchase the tiles by levying a small tax on our land was easily arrived at...perhaps three glasses around, with old Aramburu keeping tab on his slate. Of course there were complaints from the Colonel, who was rich and stingy and who had no children and was unlikely ever to have, as he was no longer strong with women. And there was some grumbling about the Ibar family, which had very little land to tax, but which nevertheless gave God a baby every year, and the village had to school them. But such complications are to be expected. As the old saying has it: Nothing is completely fair but the Last Judgement...so much the worse for us.

It all seemed sufficiently clear-cut that we could draw up the ruling minutes in just a few hours of close reasoning and arguing.

But then someone thought of the Widow Jaureguiberry! "But wait! The widow will either have to pay her share, or she will have to admit publicly that she has no land of her own. And that would shame her!"

"But she is too poor to pay! She lives on nothing but cheese and prayer!"

"Bof!" said the Colonel. "What shame will there be? She knows that we know that she has no land!" The Colonel was bitter about the Widow Jaureguiberry because she always allowed her sheep to linger longest in his fields, as he was the richest of us all.

"Of course she knows that we know. That is not the point! The point is that no one has ever said it aloud! The shame of such things comes with admitting them, as any fool would know, if he were not so stingy that he pisses vinegar—no offence intended to anyone here, ex-army officer or otherwise."

"Oh my, oh my, oh my," said old Aramburu, rubbing his palms together. "I'm afraid this is a puzzle that will have to be untangled over several little glasses, if we are to get the wording of the minutes just right."

And so, for the next three hours, there was sharp and probing debate in the home of the wine merchant. Although as a creator of *pastorales* I am known to have a great fondness for words, and perhaps even a certain gift in that direction (I do not brag of this, lest God numb my tongue and dry up my mind), it was the oldest man of the village who was chosen to take down the minutes. It made my hands itch to see how he constantly wet the lead of his stubby pencil with his tongue as he labored clumsily over his smudged sheet, his body hunched over the table, his face not twenty centimeters from the paper, scratching out and rephrasing, scratching out and rephrasing, while the rest of us took turns speaking our minds and offering new and more precise wording.

And this is how the minutes finally read:

MINUTES OF THE MEETING ABOUT THE NEW ROOF ON THE
ECOLE MATERNELLE

It is resolved and agreed that from each farm—or from each man if there are two or more adult men living on one farm (and by 'adult' is meant over eighteen years of age, or already married, or both) but exception is made for anyone who is hoping to be admitted to study medicine at the university next year and who needs every centime his family can save for that purpose—but not excepting him if it turns out that he is not received at the university because sometimes he plays pelote against the church wall when he should be cudgeling his brains over his books—and also excepting any man who became one of God's 'innocents' when he was struck in the head by a ball in 1881, after crushing all oppostion for eight straight years at the annual jai alai competions in Mauléon, bringing great glory to our village (should there be such a person); and also excepting any old tramp who lives in the loft of someone's barn and eats only bread and onions, and who wanders about the roads in all weather, muttering to himself (and this is definitely not *a reference to anyone named Beñat, no matter how much it might seem to be)—but each and every other farm will contribute twenty-three francs per hectare (or part thereof). And the number of hectares owned by a person will not be based on what he or she claims for the purpose of his or her taxes, but rather upon his or her estimate of his land the last time he or she tried to borrow against it, and in one case upon how much land he told the potential father-in-law he had when he was trying to marry off his daughter to this trusting man's son—if any such person there be. (Note: it is understood that the Eliçabe family takes exception to this last part because*

they consider it to be dangerously close to slander and will fight any-
one who intended it to be so, particularly Bernard Irouleguy, who pro-
posed the phrasing in the first place.)

However, if any person happens to own fields in some other village
(such as Etchebar, to cite but one example), then that person (or these
persons, whoever they might be) will not have to pay the general levy,
because this council cannot find a way to make them (or her) pay
without incurring the shame of seeming to ask Etchebar to contribute
to our infant-school. And anyway, such persons probably do not have
any children in school because of her (or his) age.

But if any person (ex-officer or other) decides to buy a bit of land
in Etchebar to escape paying his share, then this exception does not
apply to him, so he might as well forget it.

Signed by the Undersigned
11th day of March, 1911

SNATCH OFF YOUR CAP, KID!

When did I get started with the carnivals?

Well, it was the summer of 1934, and down in the Kansas/Oklahoma dust bowl it was hotter than a Methodist's vision of hell, almost as dry as one of their sermons. The dust rising off those dirt farm roads would make your tongue stick to the roof of your mouth till you couldn't work up enough mouth water to swallow, let alone spit.

The Great Depression had America by the throat and it was squeezing. Everywhere up and down this blessed republic you could see men plodding along dirt farm roads, the heel-chewed cuffs of their overalls dragging up little dust eddies. It sometimes seemed that the whole country was on the move. Some were looking for work—any kind of work—but most had been on the road for months and no longer hoped to find work; they were just looking for a new place to be miserable in. Sort of like the way you toss and turn on a hot mattress.

Earlier on, back in '30 or '31, when people still had reserves of spunk left over from the good old days, local wiseacres down at the feed store would plunge their fists into the pockets of their overalls until their elbows were straight and say, "You mark my words, boys, this fine young country of ours is going to lick this depression. Yessir! It'll kick Mr Depression in the ass so hard he'll have to eat his dinner standing up at the sideboard! Pretty soon, all the Gloomy Guses who run around bitching about not being able to find work will be busier'n the official fart-catcher at a Baptist baked bean social!"

But months stretched into years, and still there was no work. Dust storms came and blew farms away; and a man's kids would look up at him with big eyes when there wasn't enough to eat; and most people couldn't remember the last time they'd laughed.

Early in the depression, carnivals and circuses and medicine shows had done lively business for the same reasons that movies showing slick-talking rich people with white telephones and tuxedos were popular: because the people were hungry for dreams. They wanted to be told that the best things in life were free, and that you could find million-dollar babies in five-and-ten-cent stores; they needed to believe that you could get something for nothing, because nothing was how much they had in their jeans. Every hayseed from Rubeville to Hicksburg wanted to forget his troubles for a while and lose himself in the blare and glare of the midway, in the oom-pah-pah of the jenny organ and the mind-numbing gabble of the pitchmen. He wanted to show off his skill to the little lady by spilling wooden milk bottles and winning a ten-cent Kewpie doll with a buck's worth of battered baseballs. But as the months and years passed without things getting any better, it was no good telling the rubes that the only thing they had to fear was fear itself, because they were scared stiff. Fear was sucking their hopes dry, leaving their spirits too brittle to bounce back. Pretty soon pickings got so slim that even rinky-dink three-truck carnivals began to offer free entrance to the shows. The rubes would shuffle around the midway, licking the rides and games with their eyes, but holding on to their nickels so tight that little drops of piss ran down the buffalo's leg. The wheels and the jennies would turn all day long under the hot sun, empty, and the guy ballyhooing the girlie show would find himself talking to a handful of kids and a couple of old geezers who'd ask wise-assed questions, then cackle and nudge one another as though they'd been around and there was no fooling them.

But no matter how bad things got, the true carnie never lost his inborn sense of superiority to any mark: the gullible local townspeople whom he viewed as an undifferentiated wad of humanity whose only purpose in Life's Great Plan was to ride the rides, gawk at the shows, lose money at the games, and gobble down cotton candy, candied apples, and all the rest of the punk junk. Oh, sure, a carnie might be down on his luck; he might not have had a square meal for three days or a bath for a week; and he might be forced to play in a stubble field to a thin trickle of rubes from East Yokelburg; but he was still a carnie, and he knew that the lowest carnie was the superior of the richest, most successful mark. Well just consider: Did you ever see a carnie play a bucket game? Or bet on a G'd wheel? Or go double-or-nothing on a roll-down? Or lose his last five-spot on three-card monty? Of course not! But marks do it all the time. All the time! What was the Crash of '29 but a bunch of marks losing their asses on some fancy-assed version of the bucket game? Eh? Well, there you are.

The difference between the mark and the carnie is as simple as it is profound. No matter how bad things get, the carnie is 'with it'. While, no matter how rich or famous or powerful the mark may become, he isn't 'with it', and couldn't be, and will never be. End of story.

I first learned about the essential superiority of the carnie over the mark from an old-timer who called himself Dirty-Shirt Red—not that he was redheaded or that his shirt was more than ordinarily dirty. I was thirteen, and I'd run away from a correctional home they'd put me into as punishment for running away from the foster home they'd put me into for running away from home. I was walking the railroad ties north when I overtook Dirty-Shirt Red, who had left the Bumpkinburg where he'd wintered over, pearl-diving in a greasy spoon, and was planning to snag the Jonah J. Jones Greater Shows as it made its swing west from the red dirt country of western Tennessee. As I overtook him, I put my head down and picked up my pace so as to pass him with no more than a grunt and a quick nod because kids on the drift soon learn to give wide berth to old men. But he laughed and said something funny, and I could tell right off that he wasn't that kind, so we fell into step and started talking. He told me he knew the country we were passing through like the palm of his hand because he'd played it with carnivals more times than a tall yellow sow's got teats. I asked him what he did in the carnival.

"Everything and anything, kid, and a bunch of other stuff, too. In my golden youth, I was a ten-in-one. You know what that is?"

I didn't.

"A ten-in-one is a one-man sideshow, a real boon for a small carnival trying to make believe it's worth going to. Oh, I could do it all. I could eat a little fire, swallow some sword, walk barefoot up your ladder of razor-sharp Cossack sabres, and juggle flaming torches while recounting the shocking mating rituals of the Fiji Islanders in word and gesture (men only, and not until midnight, to avoid inflaming young imaginations—I'm sure you understand, gentlemen). I could do magic, sleight of hand, and prestidigitation while reading the Declaration of Independence off a pinhead where it was engraved in letters so small that the marks I sold the pins to couldn't even see it—but I assured them they they'd be able to read it word for word when they got home and put the pin under a magnifying glass. (That's a last-night-in-town sort of sting, kid. You want to give them a whole year to cool off before they see you again.) Oh yeah, I did the whole scam. 'Course, I'm a little old for all that now, but I'm still worth my bed, brew, and beans. I can run a jenny, front a bottle shop, tell fortunes, belly a wheel, and sell my share of candy-candy-apple with your caramel-caramel-corn. I am what you call your genuine all-round carnie, born and bred, taught and trained, guaranteed not to rust, bust, corrode, or explode. The only original patented version. Beware of imitations."

Well, one thing was sure: he could talk. And, impressionable kid that I was, I'd have given anything to have that swinging, chanting, gabble of his: talk that was meant, not to inform, but to numb and mystify. I didn't know it, but from that moment on, I was a carnie at heart. And maybe Dirty-Shirt Red recognized this because when we had gone on for a couple of hours with that tiring not-quite-a-full-stride pace of men walking on railroad ties, he turned to me and said, "Jeet?"

"What?"

" 'Jeet' is Carnie for, have you eaten. It's the way carnies greet one another, because the state of your stomach is what matters most when you've been on the drift. So one carnie says to another, Jeet? And the other says, no or yes, whichever's the case, then he goes on with his meeting-people patter, too proud to make a point of being hungry and broke, but knowing that if he says, no, the other carnie'll rustle him up some grub first thing. So, Jeet, kid?"

"Not today, no, sir."

"That's *not* what you say! Don't you listen when I talk? Am I just farting into the wind, here? You got to blend that no in and slide smoothly on: something like no, but Lord-love-a-duck, it sure is hot. Why, a man could fry an egg on the sidewalk...and you go on with your meeting-folks patter. Just to say a naked no, then stand there with your teeth in your mouth would be too humbling for a carnie. Get it? So let's try again: Jeet?"

"No, and I sure could use a couple of those eggs you're frying on that sidewalk."

Dirty-Shirt Red laughed. "You're all right, kid. You got some sass in your ass, and that's what it takes in this world, where there're only two kinds of people, the carnies and the marks: them that takes, and them that gets took. Well, you'll be glad to hear that there's an easy mark of a widow lady at a farm up the line a bit. She ought to be good for a meal, if she hasn't curled up and died, or been dragged off to the loony bin, or done some other thing that would render her unheedful of the needs of her fellowman."

After about an hour, a dirt road bent in from the east and ran alongside the railroad until it came to the gate of a small farm: just an unpainted house and barn and a couple of sagging outbuildings. Dirty-Shirt Red stopped and wiped out the sweat band of his battered old hat. Then he pointed at one of the creosote-smelling telegraph poles that followed the tracks. "See there?"

Someone had scratched the pole with a big X and put a small x between the top arms of the big one. "Know what that means, kid?"

I didn't.

"That's a 'bo sign meaning this place is a soft touch. The little x at the top says you can get grub here. If it'd been at the bottom, that woulda meant you could sleep in the barn or somewhere. You're going to have to learn a little 'bo, if you want to follow the carnivals, 'cause life ain't always cherries and cream. Sometimes it's just the pits and the curds, and that's when you might have to live like a 'bo for a little while."

"A 'bo?"

"A hobo."

"Oh."

"So!" He took up a sharp piece of crushed stone from the ballast and gouged three deep lines through the X, then underneath he scratched what looked like a stubby arrowhead. "There! Now let's go see what the widow's got for us, kid!"

As we walked up the dusty road to the gate, I asked what his scratching on the pole was all about.

"Those lines passing through the X tell passing 'bo's that things have changed and this is no longer an easy touch. The blast sign— the thing that looks sort of like a backwards arrowhead?—that means that someone here has a shotgun and uses it."

I stopped in my tracks.

"No sweat, kid! This widow lady is a born-again, lifelong do-gooder from deepest Dogoodville. She wouldn't know one end of a shotgun from the other."

"Yeah, but—"

"I scratched that stuff over the 'bo sign to put them off the track. This great republic of ours is in a depression, in case you hadn't noticed, kid. The last thing a fella needs is competition for handouts."

"Yeah, but—"

"Yeah but's ass. Now you and me know about a soft touch that others don't know about. That puts us one up. A good carnie is always one up, 'cause if you ain't one up, kid, you're one down. Now when we get there, you just smile. Don't say a word. I'll size things up and play our cards; you just follow suit. And above all, don't help me! Last thing I need is some kid trumping my aces. You got a hat in your bindle?"

"I got an old cap."

"Put it on."

"But it's hot!"

"I ain't running no debating society here. Just do what I say."

I pulled my cap out of my bindle and crammed it onto my head, muttering, "I don't see why I gotta put my cap on."

"You gotta put it on so's you can take it off!" he told me, stressing each word like he was talking to a dimwit. "Women like kids who are nice and polite. Especially widow ladies. Now, let's go."

A big yellow-fanged dog came running out to bark and scratch at the gate and snarl through its slats, making my stomach tingle the way it does when you look down from a high place. Dirty-Shirt Red stayed on our side of the fence, but he smiled and talked to the dog in a cooing voice, calling it nice fella, nice fella and saying, "You really know how to bark, don't you, old fella?" then saying under his breath, "I'd like to kick his hairy ass into next Wednesday for him." Then aloud, "There's a nice fella! Yes, there's a nice fella!"

A gray-haired woman came around the side of the house and shouted, "Hugo?" and instantly the dog's menace dissolved into a slack, moist grin with a slippery tongue hanging out the side of its mouth and lots of whimpering and whining for attention. "No need to get scared," the old woman said when she got to the gate. "There ain't a peck of mischief in a bushel of him."

"I could tell that right off, ma'am," Dirty-Shirt said, peeling off his battered hat and elbowing me in the same motion. "But you mustn't scold him for barking, ma'am, because that's his job, and he's only doing it to protect his mistress. Ain't you, big fella? Yes, you are. Yes, you are! Fact is, ma'am, I just love dogs. It may be a weakness in my makeup, but there it is." He elbowed me again, hard, and I dragged my cap off. "Yessireebob, I've had dogs since I was knee-high to a grass snake, and I'd have one still if I wasn't on the road and didn't have any proper way to care for it."

"Say, wait a minute," the lady asked. "Don't I recognize you? Haven't you been at my gate before?"

"Gosh, I'm afraid I haven't, ma'am. This is the first time me and my boy's been in this neck of the woods."

"This your boy?" She looked at me, and I just smiled.

"Yes, ma'am," Dirty-Shirt said. "He ain't much, but he's mine."

"Looking for work, are you?" Her voice still had a certain measuring tone to it.

"That's right, ma'am. Back home, there's no work to be had for love nor money. We're hoping to find something up North."

"Just the two of you, is it?"

Dirty-Shirt's smile suddenly collapsed. He looked down at his shoes and in a thin, dry voice he said, "Yes, ma'am, there's just the two of us now. After the drought and the dust had done their worst, then the fever come along and..." But he couldn't go on. He covered his face with his hand, pushing his finger and thumb into his eye sockets until there were tears. Then he sniffed and wiped them away. "My woman was always sort of frail, and I guess she just didn't have the strength to go on, so she..." He didn't have the strength to go on, either. But he sniffed and made a brave, if pale, smile. "I'm hoping to make a new start up North. For the boy's sake."

The woman looked down at me with compassion melting in her eyes. I frowned and looked at the ground.

"Fact is, ma'am," Dirty-Shirt continued, "I was hoping your husband might have some work I could do to earn dinner for the boy and me. Now, before you say anything, I want you to know that if you don't have any honest work that needs being done, or if things are so hard that you really can't spare a couple of meals, I'd understand completely because that's just how things was with me and Maudie before she..." He couldn't go on.

"I'm a widow woman," she told us. "So of course there's always plenty of man's work that wants being done."

"True. I noticed there's a pile of wood yonder that needs stacking."

"That's right. A couple of tramps came by yesterday, and I give them each a po'boy to split that wood for me. But they left without stacking it."

"Those tramps are all the same, ain't they? We was *forever* being pestered by them back on the farm before..." He stopped again, but pulled himself together with a shake. "Now, I know as well as you do that most of these 'Knights of the Road' are nothing but bums looking for handouts, and trying to avoid honest work. But nevertheless I always used to give them whatever I could spare because, like our parson once said, you never know but what one of them might be honest-to-God down on his luck, and it would be a crying shame to turn that one hungry man away, even if all the rest of them is just no account bums. I've never forgotten those words of wisdom and guidance."

"Well, you might as well come into the yard. Today's baking day, so there's fresh bread. I can make you a couple of po'boys out of cold chicken and whatever else I find. I hope that'll do you."

"That'll do us just fine, ma'am. Down, Hugo! Ain't it cute the way he sticks his nose just about everywhere, the little...rascal?"

The widow led us to the pile of split wood and left us there while she went into the house to make the sandwiches. As soon as she was out of earshot, Dirty-Shirt told me in a quick whisper, "Now you just sit over there by the pump and press your hand to the middle of your chest, like this. See? When she comes back, you smile and smile, but don't you say a word."

"But why—"

"Why's ass. Just do what I say."

I perched on the edge of a wooden watering trough next to the pump, feeling stupid with my hand pressed against my chest like that, while Dirty-Shirt selected a small stick of wood from the stack and brought it over to the woodpile, walking slowly and stopping a couple of times to suck air in with long, painful inhalations, then push it out with breaths that puffed his cheeks.

He had managed to move three pieces to the woodpile, and he was resting, cradling the fourth in his arms like a baby, when the widow came out with a short plank on which there were two half-loaf po'boys, chock-full of chicken and tomatoes and greens, and two big glasses of milk, cool and frothy from the spring house. She gave one of each to me, and I smiled at her without a word, just like I'd been told.

"Didn't your ma teach you to say 'thank you', boy?" she asked in a tone more joshing than pestering.

I smiled even broader.

"He's a good boy," Dirty-Shirt called from the woodpile as he hoisted the split piece up onto the top with some effort, then stood leaning on the pile to catch his breath. "Yes, ma'am, he's a good boy, and a kind-hearted one, but he's a little..." He made a vague gesture towards his head and shrugged.

"O-oh," the widow said in a melting voice. "Well, that's all right, then. You just sit there and enjoy your sandwich. And when you're done, you can help your pa."

I was so embarrassed I could have kicked Dirty-Shirt in the shins. Instead, I smiled even more broadly—just like an idiot should—and I took a huge bite from my po'boy that squirted stuff out the back, and that made me even more embarrassed.

"I'm afraid I can't let the boy help me," Dirty-Shirt said as he came over to take his sandwich and glass of milk. "But don't you worry none. I'll do work enough for the two of us...soon as I finish this dee-lish-ious feast you've prepared with your own two— Get down, Hugo! God—*bless* it! Sure is a healthy, active dog you've got there, ma'am."

"I was watching you out the window while I was making the po'boys," the widow told him.

"That was very neighbourly of you, ma'am."

"Didn't seem to me you was moving around any too frisky. I think your boy'd better give you a hand."

"I just can't let him do that, ma'am," he muffled through a mouthful of bread and chicken and greens. "It's his heart, you see."

I set my glass down and pressed my hand against my chest.

"But don't you worry," Dirty-Shirt continued. "I'll do the work of two men."

"It ain't often you hear tell of a child with a weak heart," the widow said.

"That is so true, ma'am. So true. It's a rare congenital form of subacute bacterial endocarditis. But please don't let my doctor talk bamboozle you. The only reason I know the medical term is be-cause...well, I suffer from the malady myself. Have ever since I was a kid. It's hereditary. Thankfully, it ain't a quick killer...so long as you don't tax yourself none."

"But...now on earth did you ever run a farm with your subacute bactra—what it is?"

"Slowly, ma'am. Real slowly. And maybe that's why there wasn't enough put aside to care for my Maudie when the fever came and she..." He couldn't finish. I mean he couldn't finish what he was saying. He finished his po'boy and milk just fine. And seconds on the milk. But the widow wouldn't let him finish stacking the wood, no matter how much he begged her not to shame him by treating him like some shiftless bum because he was eager to give a fair day's work for a fair day's—"Is that *apple pie* I smell?"

"Happens it is. Like I said, this is baking day."

"Now you listen to me, ma'am, and don't you dare argue with me!" he said, shaking his finger at her. "There is nothing in this world that could make me accept a slice of that apple pie; not after eating your delicious sandwiches without properly earning them. But there is something I *would* accept, but only after telling you that here comes what you might call the sting. What I will accept—and the *only* thing I'll accept—is your permission for me to stand here for a minute and get my fill of that splendid aroma of cinnamon and apple all steaming and fresh from the oven. There is nothing in this whole wide world that so brings back memories of my beloved Maudie." And he leaned towards the smell coming from the open kitchen window, his eyes closed and a sweet smile on his lips as he sort of hung on the air by his nose.

Unwilling to intrude upon his silent memories, the widow turned her pitying eyes towards me, so I set my milk down again, put my hand to my chest, and smiled sort of thinly.

Ten minutes later, we were walking up the tracks, Dirty-Shirt Red carefully carrying half a pie wrapped in a newspaper, and the dog following along, criss-crossing close behind our heels. "You trip me and make me smash this pie, Hugo," Dirty-Shirt warned him, "and you'll get my boot so far up your ass you'll be able to taste the leather!"

As soon as we were out of sight of the widow's farm, Dirty-Shirt shied the dog back home with chucks of ballast, then we continued along, quickly falling into the not-quite-a-full-step gait of the tie walker.

I could tell he was pretty pleased with himself. Me, I felt ashamed, and I told him so. "It wouldn't of done us any harm to stack that lady's wood for her."

"Harm's ass. Harm don't come into it. It's a matter of principle.

The dumbest mark in the world can *earn* a sandwich. But to *score* one without working...that takes a carnie. And the sign of your top-flight carnie was the way I scored those toppings."

"Toppings?"

"That's 'Bo for desserts and sweet things, the stuff you top up on. Your ordinary run-of-the-mill carnie would of been content with just the sandwiches, particularly as she'd just about recognized me from the last time I came through and scored off'n her. I hope you noticed how when I conned that old mark out of the apple pie, I had the sass and grit to advertise the sting right out front, telling her I was about to do her down. Now that's as sweet as it gets, kid. That's the juiciest part of any scam."

"I don't see that it takes all that much grit to tell her you're sting-ing her when she doesn't even know what a sting is."

"There's no end of things you don't see, kid."

"Maybe so, but it seems real low to do down a nice old lady like that."

He stopped in his tracks and looked down at me with a deep frown. "That wasn't a nice old lady. That was a mark. And marks aren't old or young, or nice or nasty, or male or female. They're just marks, and they've got to be treated like marks. If you can't manage that, then there's no hope of you ever becoming a true carnie."

"But I admire her kindness to strangers."

"You *what?*"

"I admire it," I repeated, sort of pugnaciously because I'd just learned the real meaning of 'admire' and I wasn't completely sure I had it right. Where I'd come from, people said 'admire' to mean 'like', as in: I'd sure admire to go to the movies tonight, Ma.

"You admire a dumb mark? And yet you're thinking about be-coming a carnie?

"Yeah, but—"

"Yeah but's ass! If you're so cut up about scoring off that mark, then you don't have to eat your share of these toppings." He scram-bled down from the raised track and sat in the shade of a tree, where he opened his newspaper bundle.

* * *

Between us, we got that pie down pretty quickly, then we continued along the tracks for a couple of hours before we came to a little tank town that I thought was called Marksville until I realized that carnies call all towns Bumpkinburg or Hicksville or Rubetown, or some such. We left the tracks and took the road because anyone seen walking the tracks was assumed to be a hobo, and in some towns you'd do ten days or two weeks in the local hoosegow on a vag charge, and they'd work you as free labor, digging drainage ditches or patching up roads from dawn to dark. When things got real bad, especially in winter, men would sometimes walk right into town along the tracks, and even do a little panhandling on the main street, hoping to get picked up by the local badges so they'd have something to eat and somewhere warm to stay, even if it was only for two weeks. But lots of times, the law would be on to that scam, and they'd just run you out of town after giving you a going over with an ax handle to make sure you didn't come back any too soon.

Dirty-Shirt Red and I were sauntering down the main street, still heading north, when this big shiny black Packard passed us and pulled up in front of the town bank. The driver jumped out and opened the back door, and this real well-dressed man stepped out and went into the bank, after saying a word or two to people who took off their hats and smiled and bobbed with pleasure at his attention.

"Man, look at that," I said. "Owning a bankful of money, and having everybody sniffing up to you? I do believe I could get used to that sort of life."

"Not me," snapped Dirty-Shirt.

"You're telling me you wouldn't change places with that man and his fancy suit and big car and everybody bobbing and grinning at you like that? Get out of here."

. "Not for anything in the world. Why, I'd sooner look down and discover I was pissing blood than be that man. And you know why?"

"No, why?"

"Because for all his high-toned ways, he ain't nothing but a mark."

"Oh, come on!"

"I'm not shitting ya, kid. He's a mark. I've played this town, and I've scored on him."

"*You* scored on *him?*"

"You better believe it. Seven, maybe eight years ago, David Meeker's United International Shows played through this rinky-dink, one-dog town. I was running a merchandise wheel with a painted G that prevented the marks from winning more'n the odd Genuine 100% Celluloid Betty Boop Kewpie doll or one of those Original Beeno-Bingo Lap Blankets made from half a yard of gaudy material that stretched like toffee and would explode into flame if you set a match to it. Well, your high-and-mighty banker comes along with a couple of other yokel dignitaries, sort of slumming with the trash to show he was a regular guy, and he sees that I'm flashing hams. Southern Delight Honey Cured Slo-Smoked Virginia Hams, they were, wrapped up in fancy gold paper. 'I think our cook could do wonders with one of those hams,' he says to one of his ritzy pals. Now of course, there wasn't really any ham inside that wrapping, because we'd been flashing those same hams for half a dozen years and they'd long ago gone all green and slippery from the heat and been replaced with sawdust wrapped up in ham-shaped packages, but that didn't matter because the mark didn't have a snowball in hell's chance of winning enough points to buy one. (We didn't give money because gambling's illegal almost everywhere down here in Dixieville. We only gave out U-Redeem-M High-Value Premium Purchase Points the mark could use to 'buy' whatever it was your game was flashing. Well, your spiffy banker slaps his dime down on the counter and I give him a spin. And what do you know? He immediately racks up almost enough Premium Purchase Points to win his ham...almost, but not quite. So I explained to him how all he needed was to hit a five and a nine, or any product or multiple thereof, but not exceeding the optimal total, nor totally discounting the cube roots and the more significant fractional variations. Well, he stares at me for a minute, then he draws himself up and says, 'I'm a banker. Numbers are my business, and I'm not one bit bamboozled by your claptrap about cube roots and fractions.' Well, I smiles at him and says, 'You know, sir, as soon as you stepped up to my wheel I could tell that you were a man of mathematical inclinations and arithmetical propensities, so there's no use my trying to pull the wool over your baby blues. Let me be straight with you because in the long run honesty is the best policy. I use that patter—which mathematicians like you and me know perfectly well is nothing but a narcotic tangle of mystifying sounds—in order to tempt the passerby to stay with the game until he wins himself a ham, as the law of averages insists that he must, sooner or later. And why do I do that? Because, sir, I *want* him to win. I want him to win because I want other people on the midway to see him walking along with one of my Southern Delight Honey Cured Slo-Smoked Virginia Hams under his arm and a self-satisfied smile on his face, and that'll make them envious and bring them running to my place of business to plop down their dimes and win themselves a ham. And that's how I make my living. As you see, sir, there are a total of thirty-six numbers painted on the wheel before you. Now, with a full tip ("tip" being what people in my profession call the crowd standing in front of a game or a wheel) I would have thirty-six dimes—one per each number—riding on every turn of the wheel. And that, if I am not mistaken, would be a total of three dollars and sixty cents. It *would* be three dollars and sixty cents, wouldn't it, sir? Please feel free to test my contentions and verify my estimates. Now, I can purchase these fine hams wholesale for three dollars and forty cents each. Thus, if I manage to keep my tip full and enthusiastic, then somebody wins a ham with every spin, and I make twenty cents, clear profit. That may not seem like much to a rich man like you, but you take twenty cents and multiply it by a whole bunch, and you'd be surprised how soon it mounts up! Now, I am not going to stand here and ask you to cover every single number on the wheel just to make sure you win your ham. And why? Because you'd refuse to do it. And why *would* an intelligent man pay three dollars and sixty cents for a three-forty ham? That'd be bad business, and any fool can see that you have the clear eye, the quick mind, and the sharp appetite for a good deal that marks the American businessman (I say "marks" in the sense of "characterizes") and as Cal Coolidge said, "What's good for business is good for America." Here's what I suggest, sir. I suggest you put one dollar—one dollar—on either number nine or number seven, the choice is yours, freely offered and freely taken. Then I want you to come up here and spin the wheel with your own hands because this is a game of chance and we don't want skill to play any unjust role. If your number comes up within twelve spins—*twelve spins!*—then I'll hand over to you, free and clear and as an unencumbered gift of the establishment one of these Southern Delight Honey Cured Slo-Smoked Virginia Hams. Now, let's you and me walk through the percentages and probabilities of this offer. The chance of your number coming up in one spin would be one in thirty-six. Have I got that right? So with twelve spins, your chance of winning becomes...what would that become?' And the banker says, 'One in three,' and I frowned and struggled with the figures for a second, before I says with surprise, 'That's right! One in three! And I'm offering a prize that has a wholesale market value, not of three dollars, but of three dollars *and forty cents*, which gives you an indisputable advantage without making me seem like the fool who is soon parted from his money. Have I made any oversights or errors in working out the odds, sir?' Well, this banker ran over the figures in his head and guess what? I was right: he did have the mathematical advantage. So he narrowed his eyes and asked how come I was willing to give him the better part of the odds, and I wagged my finger at him and said, 'You see right through me, don't you, sir? You recognize that I stand to win either way. If you fail to hit your number in twelve (twelve!) spins, then I pocket your dollar. But if the international law of averages brings one of these fine hams into your possession, then every citizen of this town will see a leader of the community walking around with one of my hams under his arm, and the next thing you know, my poor wheel will be flooded with customers, and I'll be making a steady twenty cents with each spin. Like I said, I win either way. Oh, by the way, sir? You don't have to baby this wheel. You can spin 'er as hard as you want because she's been carefully and thoroughly G'd.'

"Well, the mark plunks his dollar down on the nine, and he climbs up and spins the wheel. Then he spins it again. And again. And pretty soon he attracts a tip of local gawkers, wondering what their town banker is doing, sweating in the sun, spinning that big wheel. Well, he kept on spinning, although I could see he was embarrassed by the crowd watching him. Finally his twelve spins were over without him hitting his nine, and he was a little huffy about the way the crowd was laughing and giving him free advice about how to spin a wheel; so, of course, I give him an additional five spins out of the goodness of my heart, telling him that I really wanted him to win his ham and bring me in rafts of customers. So he grunts out another five spins, but that darned nine just refused to come up. I pocketed his buck and shook my head and said, 'Ain't that the ornery way of mathematics for you? Sometimes the law of averages just doesn't work out in the short term. Say, you wouldn't want to risk another dollar, would you, sir?' He grumbles and walks away with his pals laughing and kidding him. So you see, kid. Your Mr Small-Town-Lord-It-Over-the-Little-Guy Banker turned out to be nothing but a mark after all."

"Yeah, but what if he'd hit the nine and won the ham?"

"If he'd of hit the nine, I'd of been so surprised I wouldn't of known whether to shit or go blind. Chances are I'd of compromised by closing one eye and farting. There was no way he could of hit the nine. Like I told you, that wheel had a painted G. I even flashed the G to your banker friend when I told him he could spin 'er as hard as he wanted because it was well and truly G'd."

"What's a painted G?"

"A G-wheel is a fixed wheel. Sometimes with elaborate brakes that let the practiced carnie stop on an empty number, sometimes with a slide that lets him skip a number with a lot of money on it. But the best G is the one painted right on the wheel, where the numbers are written on little triangles, half with their broad ends towards the nails around the edge, and half with their points. On that wheel, all the odd numbers had their points coming to a nail, so, of course, the flapper couldn't possibly stop on an odd number. A painted G is always better than any mechanical G, even a high-class belly-buff, because it's right out there in front of the mark's face, but he can't see it because he's concentrating so hard on complicated scams and devices. Of course, a painted G requires a word-weaver to fog their minds, which is why yours truly is one of the finest wheelman in this republic, from sea to shining sea."

I turned around and looked back down the street to the big shiny Packard parked outside the bank, and I shook my head. "Yeah, but all the same I admire the way—"

"Admire's ass, kid. He's nothing but a mark. Not worth thinking about."

* * *

When we reached the edge of town where the houses began to thin out, we climbed back up onto the tracks and walked on northward. The sun was settling into the horizon, growing big and dusty red where it had got snagged in a clump of trees that threw their long shadows across the darkening flatlands. I heard singing off to our left, where a little white clapboard church was standing next to its burying ground, its windows already lit for evening worship. On the front steps was this preacher dressed in black, and some parishioners were standing around, looking up at him with respect and admiration.

I stopped and looked down on the scene, and I felt a sort of tug in my chest. "Man, wouldn't I give a lot to be in *that* man's shoes," I said. "I can just see myself standing there and being admired and respected by everybody, and nothing to do but get up in the pulpit and lay into folks, telling them how low-down and vile and sinful they are, and how they'll sure as hell roast in eternal fire, if they don't shape up pretty goddamned soon."

Dirty-shirt nodded. "Yeah, I gotta admit that preaching's a pretty soft scam. Any fair-to-middlin' carnie could make a bindle out of, if he was willing to sacrifice his freedom and settle down in some Boobville Corners. And quite a few of them have done just that. But believe me, kid, you wouldn't want to be that particular shame merchant."

"Why not?"

" 'Cause he's the biggest goddam fool of a mark I've ever seen. And I've seen a lot."

"You know him?"

"I recognize him." Dirty-Shirt started to walk on, and I followed. "In my line of business you learn to recognize people before they recognize you and go after the law. Or their shotguns. Yeah, I recognize him from some twenty-five years ago when I played through here with Happy Elmer Holliday's Great Eastern Amalgamated Shows. He was lots younger then—but then, who wasn't? Except for you, of course. You were still part of some angel's nightmare."

"What makes him the biggest mark you ever saw?"

Dirty-Shirt shook his head. "That man...! That man threw away what most men would have given their front seat in hell to have. He passed up Loving Grace Appleby. Can you *believe* it?"

I could believe it because I didn't have the slightest idea who Loving Grace Appleby was, and I said so.

"Loving Grace Appleby was the best piece of ass that ever drew breath on God's good green earth. You can't compare her to other women, no more'n you can compare a ten-car, high-ball railroad carnival manned by top-drawer scam-mavins to a broken-down three-truck punk show run by a handful of forty-mile stumble bums."

I wasn't with the carnivals yet, so I didn't know about highballs and scam mavins and forty-milers and punk shows, but I got the idea that this Grace Appleby was something special.

He sighed and said in a voice soft with memories, "...Loving Grace Appleby...Oh, my, my, *my!* She danced the hoochie coochie with Happy Elmer's show, and believe-you-me, kid, when, she did her little appetizer in front of the show tent, those rubes would crowd around and stare up at her, their mouths open, their eyes bugging, and their imaginations chugging full steam ahead, while their wives either huffed off in disgust, or stood there stiff as stone, staring daggers towards Grace, their lips pressed together so tight they almost bit 'em off. Grace was the highest paid hoochie-coochie girl in the game because Happy Elmer made every flatman and wheel spinner on the midway give her a cut, and the scam mavins were willing to pay it because of the way she drew in the marks and left them stunned and ready to be plucked. Grace Appleby was prime stuff. And I am talking *prime* here!"

"What happened to her?"

"Oh, she went the way of all flesh, kid. She got old and sick and fat and her face got bottle cut in a fight over loving rights. But in her prime, there wasn't a red-blooded carnie who wouldn't have given his gift of gab for half an hour with Grace. I remember one man declaring that he'd willingly eat a mile of her shit just to see where it come from...and there ain't no higher praise nor loftier sentiment than that. I'm telling you, boy, Grace was *amazing!* Matter of fact, they wrote a spiritual hymn about her.

"But I don't want you to think she was a loose woman or anything like that. Nosiree, Robert. Her hoochie coochie was full of promissory notes, but she never paid off on them. Oh, sure, on the carnival's last night in town she'd do her famous Midnight Double Blow-Off Special that cost the mark a whole dollar to watch (adult males only, please, to protect women from damaging thoughts and youngsters from draining habits). And she'd flash a boob at 'em just before the lights went off and she disappeared behind the curtains, but that's the closest she ever got to Hookerville. No, Loving Grace Appleby never sold her body. But every once in a while she'd *give* it away. Some lucky carnie would catch her fancy, and she'd invite him to her wagon and we wouldn't see him again until the next morning, when he'd be found walking around the midway, dazed, his eyes glassy, and a vague little smile on his lips. We'd all gather around and ask him how it'd been, but the lucky guy'd never tell us, not because he was prudish and sin-whipped like some mark might be, but because he just couldn't find the words to do the experience justice."

"Did she ever choose you?"

"No, son, she didn't. And that's my greatest regret in life. I'd of given her my fullest attention and eager cooperation, believe-you-me, but she never chose to bestow her amazing gifts on me. But she did choose that stupid mark of a preacher!"

"What?"

"That's right! This one night after the show, Grace was having a laugh and a beer with a bunch of us in the cook tent, and in walks this Bible-pounder and says he wants to see her privately. Well, we all hooted and said sure, and the people in hell want ice water, too! He explained that several women of his parish had complained about the corruption of morals caused by this Whore of Babylon, who— We all stood up and tightened our belts and got ready to kick a little pious butt, but he lifted his hand and explained that he was just quoting the women and not making any accusations off'n his own bat. And we told him he'd *better* not be, and we sniffed and flexed our shoulders and settled down again, each hoping that Grace had noticed how he'd jumped to her defense—you know how men do. Then this preacher explained that he hadn't come to drive Grace out of town, like his parishioners wanted him to. Instead, he'd come to save her. Well, we all hooted again, but Grace stood up and said she thought it was very kind and neighborly of him to concern himself with the well-being of her soul, and she'd be pleased to hear what he had to say. And off they went to her wagon, leaving the rest of us staring and shaking our heads and saying that there's no accounting for taste.

"Well, I guess this preacher didn't have the slightest idea of what Grace had in mind because when she made her intentions clear, he came backing out of her tent, stammering and gulping and begging her not to misunderstand his mission. Then he turned and ran, and the last we saw of him he was disappearing down the midway, all elbows and heels and flapping coattails.

"Would you believe it? That butt-stupid guilt peddler had a chance to experience heaven right here on earth, but he ran off and left poor Loving Grace Appleby as frustrated as a one-armed paper-hanger in a roomful of electric fans! And you've got the brass to tell me you admire this man? Back off and give me breathing space, will you?"

I thought about all this for a while, then I said that it probably took a whole lot of willpower for him to run away, but it was the right and proper thing for a preacher to do.

Dirty-Shirt Red stopped short and turned to me. "Kid? I'm beginning to think that maybe you ain't got the makings of a carnie in you, after all."

"Well, maybe not. But I admire that widow's kind nature, the way she gave us those po'boys and pie and—"

"An easy mark. Hell, even 'bo's can score off her!"

"—and I admire a man like that banker who managed to put together enough money for a big car and fine clothes and servants and—"

"Just another mark. I told you how I scored a buck off'n him on a ham wheel, for Christ's sake!"

"—and I'd just love to be looked up to and admired, like those churchgoers were admiring that preacher and hanging on his words."

"The dumbest mark of them all! Threw away a chance with Loving Grace Appleby! Look at you, standing there with your face hanging out, telling me how you admire all those marks. What you don't seem to be able to get into your thick head, kid, is that the lowest, most down-on-his-luck carnie in the world is worth more than the kindest hearted, or the richest, or the most pious mark that ever stumbled onto a midway. That's how it is, and that's how it will always—" He stopped short.

"What is it? What's wrong?"

He was staring down the track into the evening gloom. "I'll be damned," he whispered. "I'll be god-good'n-damned if it ain't...How about that?"

I followed his stare, and there approaching us down the tracks was this...floppy thing. That's the only way I can describe this apparition. It was a man. But he didn't walk like a man. With each step, he'd lift his knee high and flop his foot out like he couldn't feel anything from his hips down. His elbows would jerk out to both sides at once, and he kept shrugging so hard I thought his shoulders would pinch his head off. He was dressed in stuff that looked like he'd robbed a scarecrow, and the way his rags were flopping and fluttering all around him didn't calm the general effect at all. His white hair was straggly and tangled, and as he approached I could hear that he was carrying on an animated conversation with someone he was plenty mad at.

Dirty-Shirt Red pulled me over to the side of the track to make room, and this apparition passed us by, jabbering and jerking, and winking and jabbing whoever he was talking to in the ribs with his elbow, and never even noticing us.

"Snatch off your cap, kid!" Dirty-Shirt told me. "If you're so hot to admire somebody, start admiring! That there is Carl 'Friendly Fingers' Boyd. He used to be the best three-card monty dealer in the game!"

THE SACKING OF MISS PLIMSOLL

M iss Plimsoll was plain.

Oh, she was loyal; you had to give her that. Totally, relentlessly, oppressively loyal. But this canine virtue was not sufficient to alter his determination to be rid of her, because, to be frank, her plainness was an embarrassment to him. Almost a personal affront.

Not only the reading public, but also the lemming swarm of academic critics proclaimed Matthew Griswald to be the Last of the Disenchanted Generation; the archetype of the moody, creative loner; a tough word merchant whose crisp, minimalist style concealed profound depths of sensitivity. And over the years he had come to share this perception of him. A snotty novelist of the New York gosh-it's-tough-to-be-me-and-misunderstood school went so far as to describe him as 'head priest of his own cult, forever burning incense at the altar of Matthew Griswald.' This was envious nonsense, of course, but, yes, Matthew did see himself as tough, heroic, virile, yet through it all deeply sensitive. And no sensitive man would fire the woman who had stood by him through the years of his Great Drought, when he couldn't write anything worthwhile, just because she wasn't a pretty little bit of sexy fluff.

But consider the way Plimsoll dealt with his guests!

She didn't openly disapprove of the cinema idols, the meteors of the jet set, and the rest of the social leeches and cultural sponges who sought to affirm their importance by casually letting it drop that they had been invited to one of Matthew's famous parties, but she was annoyingly unimpressed when he mentioned one of these beautiful people, and she would communicate this apathy by a dry, "Oh, really?" or a yet more deflating, "Is she someone I should know, sir?"

Not only was she unimpressed by those who flocked to praise him and to be seen doing so, she wasn't all that impressed by the Grand Old Man of American Letters himself. Of course, he didn't expect her to fall into ecstasies of adulation. By no means! But his four decades of literary prominence merited a certain deference, a certain...

And then there was the way she would arrive at his flat each day so businesslike and full of solemn purpose that he never dared to tell her that he had decided not to work that day because he was tired, or had a nasty hangover, or was just feeling lazy. Her busy, puritan presence forced him to grind out his daily quota of words, whether he wanted to or not.

But while these irritations of long standing constituted the background climate for his decision to give her the sack, there was no denying that the basic reason was the fact that Plimsoll was plain. Remorselessly, unrepentantly plain. Christ, she even lacked the intriguing ugliness of the *jolie laide*. Her plainness had a negative, draining weight. Her entry into a room had the same effect as three pretty girls suddenly leaving. (He liked that line. He had used it before. Several times, in fact.)

While he denied having manufactured his public image as a gruff, macho man of action, Matthew recognized its commercial advantages, and there was no denying that his he-man persona would benefit from his having a secretary others would envy: the sort they would assume he slept with when he was too busy to shop around the sexual meat market that was bohemian London of the No-Longer-Swinging Seventies. What his image needed was a secretary who would stir envy in his guests: a lissom, haughty Black, maybe, or an exotic Oriental, or better yet a cute Cockney in a miniskirt. No one could accuse Plimsoll of being exotic or cute. In fact 'cute' was the kind of word one avoided in her presence, lest the clear intelligent eyes behind her round steel-rimmed glasses rake one with icy scorn.

Griswald scrubbed his white whisker stubble with his knuckles as he padded barefoot into his living room to survey the wreckage of last night's bash. A hybrid between a sigh and a groan escaped him. He hadn't intended to throw a party; it had just happened; and before he knew it the place was full of smoke and chatter, and everybody was drinking his booze and stroking one another's egos, and butts. And now the place smelled like a Catalonian bordello, and the jagged edges of a hangover lacerated the backs of his eyes when he moved his head.

He sloughed off his thick terry bathrobe and stood in his shorts, his breasts and stomach flaccid beneath the purplish varnish of sunlamp tan that leathered his skin. To think that this sagging gut had once absorbed body blows in the ring! With a sigh, he began the torture of his morning exercises, despite the sour taste in his mouth and the shards of pain behind his eyes. The first sit-up brought a thud of blood to his head, and he lay back with a martyred moan.

"Oh, God." He covered his face with his hands. Why did he subject himself to this daily hell? Was it his fault that the reading public insisted on identifying him with the athletes, warriors, and white hunters he wrote about?

Of course it was his fault. He had milked those roles for all they were worth.

Well, let's get on with it. Thirty-five of the best!

One...uh...two...uh...three...oh, God...four...uh...five...uh...

By the time his third novel appeared—all solid adventure tales told with journalistic economy and garnished with a trick of repetition he had gleaned from an expatriate American poetess who theorized that readers felt impelled to fill perplexing repetitions with layers of subtle significance—Matthew found himself lifted into cult status by critics who praised his deceptively simple style and devoted paragraphs to his deceptively two-dimensional characters with their deceptively juvenile values and their deceptively selfish goals. This rush into fame almost cost Matthew his career—indeed, his life. He made the understandable, if lethal, mistake of believing what they wrote about him, and for the next eleven years he tried to write in the style of Matthew Griswald. And failed, of course.

Fourteen...uh...fifteen...Oh, *Christ!* Now I've lost count. Well, twenty-one...uh...twenty-two...uh...

Fortunately for his finances, if not his art, the critical and academic communities had invested too much of their reputations in him to permit him to fail; so his Pulitzer Prize came during the years when he was constipated with efforts to write like himself.

...Thirty-four...uh-h-h...thirty-five...uh-h-h. Oh, to hell with it! Enough!

Matthew had never trusted intellectuals, being himself more a man of the senses than of the mind, more a man of experiences than of experience. His male characters were all creatures of action, not of reflection; and his female characters were the stakes for which the men played, not players in the great game. In short, Matthew gave voice to the infantile ideals of the masculine America of his era. But for all his intellectual and philosophical shallowness, he had an original temperament, an eye for evocative detail, a good ear for dialogue; and he was always a stern critic of his own work. It was this critical gift that was his undoing. Late one afternoon at the height of his popularity, he stood at his writing easel, reading for a third time that day's output of self-emulation. He ended up staring through the pages, his eyes defocused, until the room darkened into evening. With no histrionics, he took the nearly-finished manuscript and dropped it into the wastepaper basket. Somewhat more theatrically, he drank a bottle of whiskey in two hours and got so sick he had to spend four days in a hospital, after an undignified session with a stomach pump. For more than two years after that he suffered what he called the Great Drought, during which he didn't write a word. Lost and scared, he made an ass of himself with drinking and scrapping and women, all to the delight of the journalists. In the end, it was fear that saved him. It was either get back to writing, or suicide.

Funny how life turns on little things: when he put the barrel of the newly cleaned and oiled shotgun into his mouth, he was nauseated by the cod-liver–oil taste of it, a taste that suddenly carried him back to a childhood dominated by a cold, demanding father whom he had spent the rest of his life 'showing'. He shuddered and gagged and put the gun aside.

As a palpable symbol of making a fresh start, he left New York for London, where he took a flat and began working. He cut down on his drinking by staying dry until dark, and he began a routine of regular meals and exercise. And every day, every day, every day, he ground out a self-imposed number of pages in which he tried to free himself from the old, monosyllabic, staccato style and the worn-out idiom of the Tough Hero with Hidden Pain. At first, things went very badly. Like the circus performer who lets go of one trapeze bar before the other is within reach, he abandoned one style before he developed another, and he fell into the void. In seeking to avoid the trivial, he found himself creating the tedious. He had never had much to say, and now he had lost the ability to say it in the old crisp yet evocative way.

But with strength of will born of desperation, he forced himself to pour out the words, turning out pages of flaccid sentences, stupid characters, and ridiculous stories—most of it going directly from typewriter to wastepaper basket, rejected by his unforgiving critical sense, the one talent that did not wither during the Great Drought. His money ran thin, and he survived on little checks his agent sent from reprint and residual rights. Fortunately, his foreign sales remained strong because the monosyllabic simplicity of his style and the transparency of his characters' motives made him easy to translate without significant loss, and easily understood by non-English speakers with fifteen hundred word vocabularies. Although his ability to write fiction had diminished, he could still sell articles on hunting and fishing and Spanish blood sports.

But the time came when he knew he must start producing fiction, if he were to prolong his fame and fashion. He decided to hire a literary secretary to free himself from the time-consuming, patience-fraying business of cleaning up copy. Someone—he no longer remembered who—recommended a copy editor at his British publishing house, a woman who had a fascination with his writing and who might, therefore, be willing to work cheap.

And that was how he began working with Miss Plimsoll, who was everything a secretary should be—everything, that is, except pretty enough to contribute to the Griswald image. Efficient and unobtrusive, it wasn't long before she was handling his correspondence with his useless agent and with those readers who still sent letters—mostly ploys to get his autograph, which still had some value in the collector's market. She also managed his flimsy finances and kept his ever-shrinking social calendar. She even did minor editorial work, cleaning up fuzzy passages, deleting inadvertent repetitions, patching up little lapses in logic and sequence, all of which freed his time and energies as he entered the most frantic phase of the Great Drought. He inflicted a yet more grueling work rate on himself which, even when it failed to recapture success, at least dulled his panic with the anodyne of fatigue.

Little by little, a new style began to coalesce. Occasionally a page would not be dropped into the wastepaper basket. His characters were still men of flesh and appetite rather than spirit and mind, more moody than deep, more hesitant than reflective, but they became a little older, a little kinder, and hitherto unknown elements began to play a part in their actions: compassion and regret, for instance...even remorse. A short story was offered and published; then another. He won a minor award for a piece about the Paris of his youth, the self-lacerating jealousies and self-inflicted anguishes of his 'lost generation' of self-imposed exiles. He started a novel. And when he went dry, the encouragement he received from his agent, together with gloomy financial prognostications from Plimsoll, made him keep working, flogging out the words, despite his grumpy complaints that nothing flowed naturally and easily, as it had done in the old days. As he licked the drafts into shape, his critical sense told him the writing was not bad, and was getting better.

The book gave the critics a chance to fill their columns with comparisons between his earlier style and this new one, and The Graying of Matthew Griswald became a fashionable topic at literary cocktail parties. The book never breached the top half of the best-seller charts, the first of his novels not to do so; but the fact was, the heroic era of American letters was passing, soon to be replaced by moist, adjective-strewn, soap-opera novels written about and by ambitious women seeking fulfillment and self-discovery through commercial success and musical beds.

An honest and therefore only moderately successful film was made from his novel; then another novel followed; and soon his stories were in demand everywhere, despite the collapse of the short fiction market in America, where the reading classes were more interested in articles on self-assertiveness, advancing one's career, getting in touch with one's inner self, and skillful money management. The Great Drought was broken, and his life routine slowly returned to its old rhythms. His flat became a meeting place for the literary luminaries of London: young talents on their way up, writers scratching to maintain their place in the public eye although they produced little beyond reviews of other people's work, society drones who viewed idleness as a sign of breeding, media creatures who, lacking any talent other than their ability to thrust themselves forward aggressively, became talk show hosts and television panelists—in fact, all the social perennials: the climbers, the succulents, the epiphytes and parasites, the delicate blossoms that flourish best in reflected light. Parties sprang up of their own volition, always at his expense, and more often than not he ended up drunk in bed with one of the literary ladies or one of the cute young things who gravitate to such gatherings. He found that he could reduce his work rate to only three or four hours a day, easily half of which was dictating answers to letters and requests into his tape recorder, while Plimsoll cleaned up the latest pages of whatever tale he was working on.

Over the next four years of relative success, his waist and eyebrows thickened, his hair thinned, his beard whitened. But Plimsoll never altered in energy, attitude, or appearance. Always crisp, always exact, always pushing him to deadlines and duties; she was a dour presence in tweed skirt and white, high-necked blouse, sensible shoes, and long, meatless legs. Her expression seemed to blend strained patience with mute rebuke, particularly when she arrived, as she would this morning, to find the flat strewn with the litter of a party. And her attitude towards the women who sometimes lingered into the morning was a politely arctic version of the reaction one might have at finding something alive in the bottom of one's soup bowl.

Naturally Matthew resented this, just as he resented Plimsoll's busy, productive proximity as a silent recrimination to his laziness. But above all he resented her being so remorselessly, so unrepentantly plain! He sometimes felt she did it on purpose.

Just last night during the party he had been stung by the persistent ribbing of one of those people who feel they must pay their way by being unceasingly clever. He had contended that all writers sleep with their secretaries (or, if not exactly 'sleep with', at least use them occasionally to relax from work tensions). Many of his guests had met the cool and proper Miss Plimsoll in passing, and they found hilarious the image of Matthew Griswald, Iron Man of Letters, reduced in his waning years to grinding away on the razor-sharp pelvis of Miss Plimsoll.

That was the last straw. It was time to be rid of Plimsoll. He could easily manage his own revisions and corrections...or whatever the hell it was Plimsoll did. All he really needed was someone to juggle his calendar and respond to earnest letters from readers, using the standard forms he had worked up to save time and thought. Any good typist could do that, even a cute young thing with no more brains than a racehorse. Yes, his mind was made up. This morning he would find an opportunity, and the courage, to interrupt their iron-clad routine and inform her that her services would no longer be required. That was it. Settled.

...Or maybe it would be better to write her a letter. Just to keep the whole thing from becoming tacky and...well, personal. No fair-minded person could call that cowardice. No, it was simply handling a nasty chore in the most dignified way....For everyone concerned.

Yes, but what reason would the letter cite for sacking her? The problem, Plimsoll, is that you have a sharp pelvis? Sorry, kid, but the roundness of your glasses and your lack of chin are beginning to affect your typing speed?

No, the letter idea was stupid! After all, he'd have to dictate it to *her*, and that would lose him the advantage of emotional distance. The best way to play this would be to find fault with everything she did for a couple of weeks so she wouldn't be surprised when he finally said that all this arguing and bickering was making it impossible for him to work! Hey, maybe if he found fault persistently enough, she'd quit of her own volition. He'd be surprised and hurt by her decision to leave him, but he'd try to understand her feelings, and he would be—

He heard her key in the door, which then closed with a precise click. She had an irritating way of *pressing* a door closed behind her, rather than just shutting the goddamned thing. Like any normal person would! Christ, she even closed doors tidily!

"Mr Griswald?" she said, as she entered, crossed to the little table that served as her desk, and dropped off the letters she had collected at his door. She greeted him exactly that way every morning, the slight interrogative lift at the end of his name serving in place of 'good morning'. She glanced at the debris of the party with infuriating expressionlessness.

"Damn it, Plimsoll..." he began. But although his irritation was genuine enough, he couldn't think of anything specific to complain about.

"Sir?" she asked, as she opened the oversized new attaché case she had begun to affect lately, drew out the retyped pages of yesterday's output, and tapped them on his desk to make the edges perfectly smooth before setting them on his desk for his pencil corrections...if any. "Sir?" she asked again. "Is something wrong?"

"Damn it, Plimsoll! I was thinking my way through a problem and almost had the solution, when you came bursting in and drove it out of my mind!"

She measured him with her frank, intelligent eyes. Then she smiled faintly and began collecting the messy pages he had ground out yesterday between her departure and the arrival of his unexpected guests. "I'm sure it will come back to you, sir," she said over her shoulder as she brought the work to her own table.

" '...sure it will come back to you, sir,' " he iterated in a singsong chant that he instantly regretted as infantile. "It frigging well *won't* come back! It's lost now!"

From her straight-backed chair she looked at him, her eyes slightly narrowed, as though she were hefting his mood. "Are you feeling ill, Mr Griswald?"

'Feeling ill' was her euphemism for hungover, and Matthew answered that he was not 'feeling ill'!

Her smile thinned. "Perhaps not, sir. But you are a little tetchy this morning." She dropped the junk mail into her wastepaper basket and began opening the other letters, reading them with her rapid, vertical scan and setting them on her desk in order of urgency. "Oh, here's a letter from Mr Gold. Details of the MCA option with which you should familiarize yourself. He'll be telephoning from New York at..." she tipped up the pendant watch that was her chest's only ornament "...at one o'clock our time."

"Yes, yes, I remember," he growled. "The bloodsucking bastard."

"That's hardly fair, sir. Mr Gold stuck by us through our difficult times."

"There's no such thing as an honest agent. Certain people have a warp in their DNA spirals that cripples their consciences and lets them become drug dealers or child rapists or tobacco company executives or literary agents. And what's all this about *our* difficult times?"

"Just a manner of speaking, sir. Shall we go over your calendar?"

"No," he growled. "Where in hell is Mrs What's-her-name? This place looks like a pigsty!"

"Yes, it does, rather," Miss Plimsoll said, in a tone so expressionless that Matthew could take it for arch. "But I'm afraid Mrs O'Neil won't be in. She telephoned me this morning to say she was feeling a little off."

"Off what?"

"Off color, presumably. And off the wagon as well, I suspect."

"You disapprove of drinking, don't you, Plimsoll."

"I disapprove of anything that prevents a person from doing his work, sir."

"But particularly the vices, eh?" He was becoming frustrated with Plimsoll's disinclination to rise to his ill-humor and his taunts.

She looked at him from behind her steel-rimmed glasses and smiled with a hint of weariness. "To which vices are you referring, sir?"

"Just the usual lot. The Big Seven. Sloth, Greed, Envy, and the rest of the gang. And their insidious cousins, the Seven Deadly Virtues: Moderation, Probity, Sincerity, Thrift, Chastity, and the rest of them. How do you stand on the deadly virtue of Chastity, Plimsoll?"

Her lips compressed slightly as she returned to making notes in the margins of the letters she would answer on his behalf. "If chastity is indeed a vice, sir, one can take comfort in the knowledge that it's the one vice modern society is struggling to stamp out, and quite successful—Ah!" She held up an envelope. "We have an invitation from Somerville, my college at Oxford. You are invited to deliver a lecture next term."

"On what?" He sat at his desk with a heavy grunt.

"Let me see...There is to be a colloquy on 'the Antihero in Literature and Society'."

"The antihero exists only in literature. The same person in society is either ridiculed or crucified. ...Or both. And anyway, academics don't know the difference between an antihero, an unlikely hero, and an attractive villain. What are they offering?"

"It appears that they offer expenses and a banquet in your honour."

"A banquet in my honor, eh? Well, screw 'em, the tight-fisted bastards."

"May I paraphrase that in my reply?"

Was she was trying to be amusing, or was she was being snide? "I never got a college degree. In fact, I was kicked out of two colleges."

"Wisconsin and Northwestern."

"Right! And I never majored in *literature!*"

"I am aware of that, sir." She smiled. "I recall a letter to an American academic in which you expressed your view that studying literature is, for a real writer, what analysing horse droppings would be to a stallion."

"I never said *droppings!* No, I never studied literature, but *you* did."

"Yes, sir. In fact, I published a stylistic analysis of your early work which, if I say so myself, was widely praised as a—"

"But for all your literary study and insight, you ended up a typist. There you are, Plimsoll. Some people lay the eggs; others just nibble at the omelets."

She lowered her eyes. "Well...I'll confess to nibbling my share of omelets, sir, if you'll confess to laying your share of eggs."

With a grunt and a frown he buried himself in Plimsoll's neatly typed transcript of yesterday's output, while she dashed off answers to the morning mail. She was able to type replies in so close an imitation of his style that he could get away with just signing or, in rare instances, adding a P.S. in his own scrawl.

"Well, what about you, Plimsoll?" he asked out of a long silence.

"Sir?" Her tone was distant, her attention on the letter she was typing.

"We were talking about the deadly virtue of chastity."

She was used to the non sequitur vectors his thoughts often took when he was working. "Are you asking what I think of chastity, sir?"

"I'm asking if you're guilty of it."

She was silent for a moment before pointedly changing the subject. "Have you decided what you're going to say to Mr Gold when he calls?"

"Bloodsucking ten percenter!"

"Mr Gold has proved himself a devoted friend."

"Devoted to profit. Let's get back to your chastity. What shape is it in, Plimsoll? Unassailed? Assailed but well-defended? Assailed but not within the last decade?"

"I see no reason to discuss my chastity, sir." There was an edge to her voice.

Ah! A chink in her frosty armor. At last.

"Don't think I'm asking on behalf of my own inquisitive libido. I'm working up a character not unlike you, and I was wondering how she would respond to a sexual advance."

She turned from her work and looked directly at him. "Why on earth would you want to introduce a character like me, Mr Griswald? You usually populate your novels with women of a more obvious and functional sort."

"Contrast, Plimsoll. I want to establish a character alongside whom the ordinary woman would seem to be a passionate houri."

"...I see."

"Well?"

She drew a sigh and folded her long, thin hands over her lap. "Very well. To begin with, I believe that chastity—which in my view flows from a sense of self-worth—is a most desirable quality in any person. It has been my observation that the promiscuous are either seeking to deny an unstated accusation of sexual inadequacy or attempting to find companionship at its most biological and least compassionate level. One might say that for them coitus is a prelude to handholding; fornication, an avenue to conversation. But I do not equate chastity with sexual abstinence. I see nothing unchaste in making love when one loves...even when that love is only an ephemeral flood of feeling, and neither the product nor the precursor of an enduring relationship. Have I responded adequately to your question, sir?"

"My frigging cup runneth over!" He returned to scanning yesterday's work. But after a minute he lifted his head. "How old are you, Plimsoll?"

She emitted a slight sigh that seemed to ask if she were ever to be allowed to get on with her work. "I am forty-six years old, sir."

"Forty-six. Fifteen years younger than I am. And already you're standing aside from life. You've become an observer rather than a competitor."

"I have never wanted to be a competitor, sir. Which is not to say that I don't want to be a participant."

"You can't participate unless you're willing to compete. Life is a contact sport." He liked that, so he scribbled it into in the little notebook he kept for collecting orts of colorful or apt phrasing. When he looked up, he found Plimsoll watching him.

"May I ask what is wrong, Mr Griswald?"

"Wrong? In what way wrong?"

For a moment her gaze remained on him, unblinking. Then she lowered her eyes. "You seem to be bristling with antagonism this morning, sir. And I find it difficult to ignore the feeling that you're intent upon embarrassing me...even hurting me."

"Nonsense! That's one of your problems, Plimsoll. You're hypersensitive." He sensed this was the moment to list her other flaws and faults, and to tell her he had decided to give her the sack. But he recoiled from the unpleasant task.

"Is it really nonsense, sir?" She lifted her eyes and measured him for a moment, then, with a slight lift of her shoulders, she returned to annotating the day's mail.

Shit, he thought. His chance to get this business over with was slipping away. "Ah...actually, Plimsoll, there *is* something on my mind."

"Really?" Her eyes remained on her work, but not her attention.

"Yes, I...well, to tell the truth, I've decided to..." He knew he was going to lie, as he usually did in awkward social circumstances. More for the sake of the other person's feelings than for his own comfort, of course.

She left her finger on the paper to mark her place and looked up at him, her eyebrows raised. "You've decided what, sir?"

He cleared his throat. "Look here, Plimsoll. This routine of work, work, work is beginning to burn me out. I'm sick of cranking out a couple of thousand words every day, every day, every day. I need a break. And I've been thinking about the south of France."

"What a splendid idea, sir! And perhaps you're right. A change of scene might do you a world of good. But, of course, you mustn't stop writing altogether. We both know the danger in that. The juices stop flowing and your style becomes heavy, and—"

"Never mind my goddamned juices!"

"The season's already begun, so I'll have to get cracking to find us someplace pleasant but not overrun with tourists." She smiled self-deprecatingly. "I'm afraid I have only schoolgirl French: accurate enough in grammar, frightful in accent. But still—"

"Hold it! I didn't say *we* were taking a vacation. I said *I* was."

"Oh," she said, with a soft catch. "Oh, I see." A slight flush reddened her long throat. "I didn't mean to...But I naturally assumed that..." She smiled bravely, but Matthew could have sworn her eyes were damp. Then she took a quick nasal breath and continued in a businesslike tone. "And what do you have in mind for me to do while you're *en vacance*, sir?" The bit of French just slipped out. "I assume I shall act as a letter drop, unless you want to deal personally with all the trivia of—"

"Listen, Plimsoll, the fact is...Well, I'm not absolutely sure I will be coming back to Britain. This damned weather and...everything. And even if I do return to London, it won't be the same as before. I plan to reduce my work rate permanently. I can afford a little more leisure. I mean...well, goddamnit, I've earned it. In any case I won't be needing a...well, it would be a waste of talent to use a person like you just to answer a few letters and...that sort of thing."

As he spoke, her eyes slowly widened, her spine straightened, and she seemed to grow taller in her chair. "Are you letting me go, Mr Griswald?"

"I wouldn't put it that way."

"How would you put it, sir?"

"Well, it's not as though...You know, funnily enough, just the other day I was talking to someone from Piper and Hathaway, and he said they were dying to have you back," he lied with his usual glibness. "In fact, I wouldn't be surprised if they gave you a—"

"I am not interested in returning to copyediting, sir," she said firmly.

"Oh? Well, that's your business, of course. I just thought you might—"

"Excuse me for interrupting, but would you mind terribly if we didn't discuss this further just now? I have a lot of work to get out this morning. And I confess that I find this subject rather... unsettling."

He shrugged. "Whatever you say. But it's something we have to face sooner or later."

She closed her eyes and took a deep breath before returning to the task of responding to a devoted fan from Seattle who suggested, not at all obliquely, that if the Great Man ever found himself in the Pacific Northwest, she would be delighted to be of service.

An hour passed in taut silence broken only by the staccato click of Plimsoll's typewriter in counterpoint to the loose clatter of his old portable, which he loathed because it was forever breaking down, but it had become so much a part of the Griswald mystique that every visitor wanted to have a look at it. Another sacrifice he made to his image. He kept his head down, pretending to be absorbed in work. He couldn't understand why she was reacting in this childish way. This unexpressed resentment! This accusing efficiency! This hysterical silence!

"I need a drink," he grumbled, as he rose to get himself a glass of burgundy. He didn't really feel the need for a drink, but he wanted to let her know that this wasn't easy for him, either. "Look at this place! I don't know why that goddamned Mrs What's-her-name can't manage to get here and clean up. God knows I pay her enough!"

Plimsoll did not respond. She rolled the last of the morning's letters from her typewriter and added it to the stack for his signature. Then she turned her chair towards Matthew's desk and folded her hands in her lap. "There are one or two things I should like to say to you, sir."

Here it comes, he said to himself. "All right, let's have it." He was glad she wasn't going to accept being fired without complaint, because exposing himself to her angry vitriol would diminish any sense of guilt he might feel over this business. He carried his glass to the desk and sat down heavily. "Fire away, Plimsoll," he said with a martyred sigh.

"Before I 'fire away', sir, I should like to remind you again that Mr Gold will be calling from New York in..." She tipped up her pendant watch. "...in approximately two hours."

"Forewarned is forearmed...the frigging bloodsucker."

"Your unjust evaluation of Mr Gold provides us with a useful starting point for what I have to say."

"Just so the starting point isn't too far from the finish line."

"I'll do my best to be succinct, sir." She composed herself for what he feared would be a lengthy tirade. "I should begin by telling you that I have always considered you to be one of the most gifted writers of our age."

"I have seldom heard a set-up line more pregnant with its 'however'."

She smiled. "However...I also find you to be the most self-centered and ungrateful man I have ever met. Mrs O'Neil serves as a case in point. She has cleaned up after your silly, profligate parties for six years and you've never even bothered to learn her name. Mr Gold carried you through your most difficult period, and yet you constantly refer to him as a parasite. And I, who have worked with you and supported you for these many years...Tell me, Mr Griswald, do you even *know* my first name?"

"Your first name?"

"My first name."

"Well, it's...All right, so I don't recall it at this moment! But I'm sure you have one. Coming, as you do, from generations of C of E freeloaders, I have no doubt that your bishop father lavished every inexpensive luxury on you, including a first name. Indeed, I wouldn't be surprised if, in an orgy of nomenclatural prodigality, he didn't bestow a middle name on you as well! He might even have— What are you smiling at?!"

"Nothing important, sir. I've always been amused by your habit of retreating behind barriers of 'sesquipedalian obfuscation' when you're stung with a sense that you're in the wrong. It's a charming tic, really. Particularly in a man noted for the leanness of his style. Don't you agree?"

"No, I do not!" He bit off each word.

"Pity. One of your saving graces has always been your sense of humor. Without that, you would often have been...well, frankly in- sufferable."

He stared at her. "You're certainly making it easier for me to give you the sack without remorse. What did you mean when you said that Gold carried me through the Great Drought?...If anything."

"Mr Gold would never tell you himself, but I think you should know. Do you recall how you managed to survive the lean years when you were unable to produce material you considered—and quite rightly—worthy of your name?"

"Of course I do. I lived on a trickle of residuals, foreign rights, reprints—that sort of thing. A trickle from which Gold wrung his percentage, you can be sure. So what?"

"There *were* no residuals."

"What? What the hell are you talking about?"

"No residuals, no foreign rights, no reprints. You were, not to put too fine a point on it, a drug on the market."

Matthew was silent for a long minute. "Are you trying to tell me Gold sent that money out of the goodness of his heart?"

"He sent it because he had faith in your talent. And because he was sorry for you."

"*Sorry* for me?" He stood up, and thick hangover blood thudded painfully behind his eyes. "That presumptuous son of a bitch was sorry for *me?* Well, I'll give him something to be sorry about. When he calls this afternoon, I'll fire his ass!"

Miss Plimsoll tilted her head to the side. "No...I don't...think so."

Matthew's face stretched with mock wonder. "I beg your pardon?"

"I don't think you're going to give Mr Gold the sack, sir." A ghost of a smile creased the corners of her eyes. "Any more than you are going to give it to me." She rose and opened her oversized attaché case. As she drew out a large stack of manuscript, some rumpled and old, she said, "Perhaps you have wondered why I began carrying about so cumbersome a case a couple of months ago."

"Frankly, I hadn't spent much time worrying about it."

"No, I suppose not. To do so would imply an interest in others."

"If you're accusing me of not staying awake nights, pondering the hidden implications of the weight and size of your attaché case, then I plead guilty. And I assure you that— O-oh! Wait a minute! I get it. You've written a novel! And you want me to help you get it published, as conscience money for giving you the sack. Don't believe that crap about everybody having a novel somewhere inside them, Plimsoll. There are two kinds of people in the world: the storytellers and the audience members. And you, Plimsoll? You're an audience member. You are, in fact, the prototypic audience member. No, I don't want to read your manuscript. I'm not interested in the refined wordsmithery of someone who has never lived, never sinned, never loved!"

"Oh, I have loved, sir," she said, as she carefully evened the pages of the manuscript by tapping them on her desk.

"No! Don't tell me! Plimsoll in love? It's an image as arousing as a hip bath in ice water. And what poor bastard was the recipient of this uniquely modest gift?"

"You, sir."

"*Me?*"

She drew a shallow breath. "But that's neither here nor there. What I want you to do now is to read at random from this material. I think you'll find it very—"

"*Me?* You've been in love with...?" His eye fell on the top sheet of the manuscript. "Wait a minute! What's going on here? This is *my* work!" It was indeed two drafts of his latest novel: his own, full of X-ings-out and penciled marginalia, and Plimsoll's neatly typed copy. She had evidently disobeyed his instructions to burn his originals after copying them, to protect his reputation as a natural stylist whose first draft was practically galley perfect—a facet of the Griswald myth that he had not originated, but one he perpetuated.

"Now, Matthew, why don't you sit down and read through some of this manuscript while I make us—"

"*Matthew?*"

"—while I make us a nice pot of tea."

"I don't drink tea!"

"Well, I'll make some for myself, then. No, on second thought I'll have a glass of your excellent burgundy."

"My burgundy?"

"Just read the manuscript, Matthew. Whatever limitations you may have as a man of compassion, I have complete faith in you as a critic."

While Plimsoll sat at her desk, sipping the wine, her long legs crossed at the ankle, Matthew read, scanning at first with impatient irritation; but his frown deepened as he read with growing—and chilling—fascination. She had made many small deletions and adjustments, an adjective pruned here, a more precise verb substituted there, no one change significant in isolation, but in the mass they made a lean paragraph out of one that had been merely thin, or converted a redundancy into evocative foreshadowing, or transformed the obscure into the ambiguous. He could not quite put his finger on the overall change brought about by her culling and honing, but it had to do with increased celerity. If a minute spent reading his original draft were taken as a norm, compared, for instance, to a heavy, eighty-second minute spent wading through Faulkner's glutinous word-bogs, or stumbling through Henry James's involute parentheticals, then Plimsoll's revision could be said to have swift, light, forty-second minutes. In sum, what the world recognized as the Griswald style existed in Plimsoll's copy and was absent from his original.

He set the manuscript down and stared out the window, his eyes defocused, his stomach cold. For years he had half-known, if never really faced, the fact that he lacked most of the qualities he admired in his characters. He had never really been devoted to the political causes he so pugnaciously espoused, he was too wrapped up in self to care about the anonymous Wad; even his lovemaking was based more on tactic than emotion; and as for his much-vaunted physical courage? He had climbed those mountains with the aid of guides; he had shot those lions with a backup man covering him with a Holland and Holland; he had made sure he was often photographed, rough and unshaven, with guerrilla fighters, but he had written his famous war coverage at secondhand, closer to hotel comforts than to battle-field dangers. For years he had admitted to himself that if he were not a good writer, he was nothing at all. And now...

"I think I know what you're feeling, Matthew," Miss Plimsoll said softly.

"Do you? Do you really? What a consolation it is to realize that Plimsoll knows how I feel."

"This is something you must understand. I could not have written those novels and stories alone. It's you who have the creative imagi-nation, the experience, the sense of pain and laughter, the pantheon of unique and fascinating characters."

"I'm delighted to have contributed a little something."

"Yours is the voice. I am merely the interpreter. What you lost during the Great Drought was merely...style. And that's the only thing I have provided: just style. Please don't feel miserable, Matthew. We have been a team for some years now, a *belle équipe*, but it's always been you who possessed the inspiration and the dynamic energy, and I've admired those things in you...loved them, actually."

"I don't want to hear about it," he said wretchedly.

"I know this is unpleasant for you. You've never been exactly avid to face the truth about yourself. So it's inevitable that this truth comes with pain...as it comes to the heroes of our novels."

He reached forward and rubbed his palms along the sides of his battered old typewriter in a kind of tactile farewell.

"I was content with my invisible role," she continued. "I even cherished helping you the more for the knowledge that you were unaware of it, and happy to be so. And I had every intention of going on like that forever. But I have seen something growing in your at-titude towards me for the past month or so." She smiled thinly. "You're nothing if not transparent, Matthew."

"Please don't call me by my first name."

"But I've always called you Matthew...to myself. I've known for some time that you were steeling yourself to be rid of me. At first I was sorely stung by the unfairness of it. But then I realized that you were as helpless in this as you are in other things. You've been a slave to your image for years now, and getting rid of me would have been yet another service demanded by that image. So I decided to take matters into my own hands, for your good as well as mine."

"I don't want to hear about any of this. Nothing matters anymore. It's all over. I suppose you intend to do an exposé? 'Matthew Griswald's Secret Collaborator'? You'll make a bundle with it. It's the kind of scandal the journalists salivate over."

"Nothing could be further from my mind, Matthew."

"What *is* on your mind, then?"

"I propose that we continue our association."

He looked at her out of the corners of his eyes, with chary mistrust. "You're saying that you're willing to go on just like before?"

"Well...not *just* like before."

"Ah! I knew it. What is it you want?"

"I have reached an age when one must consider one's future."

"So it's money."

"Security rather than money. Our mutual security. Which I believe would best be assured if we were to marry."

His eyes widened. "Marry? You and me?"

"Your shock is not terribly chivalrous, Matthew. It's a solution I've considered in moments of reverie for many years."

An almost unthinkable possibility grew in Matthew's mind. "You *are* speaking of a marriage of convenience, aren't you? A marriage that ensures your financial future and gives you the social advantages, the parties, the media events, and all?"

"Actually, I don't foresee all that many parties. They're not good for your health, to say nothing of your work habits. And I must tell you that I have no intention of entering into *un mariage blanc*, a sham union confected for purely financial reasons."

"Whoa. Let me get this straight. Are you saying that we—that you and I would...?"

"I foresee us working together, tackling problems, and reaping successes together. We shall cherish one another, and we shall...satisfy one another."

"...Satisfy. And I suppose this relationship is to be monogamous?"

"Oh yes, indeed, Matthew. Most strictly monogamous. You will never know how I have been hurt by the mindless women I've found here in the mornings, all rumpled and smelling of sleep."

He nodded slowly, still dazed. "So...if I want your help, I have to buy the whole package. Brains, crotch, and all. That's the deal, is it?"

"That is the deal."

He turned again to the stack of manuscript on his desk. He reread two pages of his first-draft work, then the same passage in her revision. Then he tossed the papers aside and looked again at Miss Plimsoll in frank appraisal. Well, she has a nice complexion. And her hands aren't all that bad...

"It's true, isn't it, what you said about the characters and the situations being mine and mine only. All you do is tighten and polish a little. What you might call 'stylistic packaging'."

She smiled faintly. "That's all I do, Matthew. Just packaging."

He puffed out a long sigh and shook his head as though to clear it. "Tell me, Plimsoll. Are you...well, are you any good in the sack?"

Miss Plimsoll glanced down and smiled into her eyelashes. "I take it you use the word 'sack' in a sense different from the sack you were intending to give me?"

"Ghm-m!" he growled. "Well, are you? Good in the sack?"

A slight flush blossomed on her throat. She tipped up her pendant watch and glanced at it. "We have an hour and twenty minutes before Mr Gold calls. That gives us sufficient time to investigate the matter, I should imagine."

HOW THE ANIMALS GOT
THEIR VOICES

AN ONONDAGAN PRIMAL TALE

Europeans moving westward across America collided with Iroquois press-ing eastward to maintain contact with the Algonquin tribes that they fol-lowed as a shepherd follows his flocks, for raiding was an important part of their economy. The Europeans found the Five Nations to be the most advanced tribes in North America, both culturally and politically. They also found them to be fierce and ruthless fighters of a caliber they would not meet again until, a hundred years and half a continent later, they encountered the Sioux and the Apache.

Occupying the center of the Five Nations of the Iroquois Confederacy, the Onondagas were neither so warlike as the Senecas nor such crafty traders as the Mohawks, but their role was essential to the union, for they were the conveners of inter-tribal meetings, and they acted as mod-erators in disputes, as befitted the tribe of Hiawatha who, with Dekana-widah, had molded the warring tribes into a peaceful league centuries earlier.

In addition, the Onondagas were custodians of tribal memory, guard-ians of tradition, and tellers of the ancient tales until, most of their war-riors fallen in battle against land-hungry Europeans, the women, children, and old men were driven north to the haven of New France, where they settled on poor, stony farms. Lacking young men, they inter-bred with the French who had left their women behind in their pursuit of riches. My grandfather was a child of Onondaga/French parents.

In the early years of this century, the Onondaga gift for story-weaving was still alive here and there in pockets of their diaspora. It was from her formidable aunts that my mother learned tales of the sort ethnologists call primal myths. All the stories began by describing the creation of the world by Crayfish, Buzzard, and Wind working to the plan of She-Who-Creates-by-Speaking-Its-Name: always the same words spoken in the same rhythm...those repetitions that children find so enchanting and reassuring. After being attached to the origin of things, each tale would go its own way, each carrying a moral message meant to elevate and to guide.

When I was very young, my mother put me to bed with these stories, told in the harsh, old-fashioned French patois of her aunts, a sound that I associated with the stern-voiced chants of the Onondagan story-tellers who used similar cautionary tales when they sought to persuade recalcitrant rebels to bend their will to that of the Confederacy. I remember only three of those stories: one that explains why maples lose their beautiful leaves in autumn and is a warning against pride, another that tells how North Star volunteered to remain in the cold northern sky to direct lost people and is about the virtues of service, and the story I'm going to tell you now, my childhood favorite because it involved many animals acting badly. Its message is obvious, but it was one the Indians failed to heed.

In the beginning, and for more than half of the Allotted Time there was no dry land, only sky and water and a thin mist where they met. Then She-Who-Creates-by-Speaking-Its-Name asked, "Who will make Earth for me?" Now Crayfish was bored, so she said, "I will make Earth for you." And Crayfish went down to the bottom of the water and rolled balls of mud with her tail and piled them up, one upon the other, one upon the other, until the mud rose higher than the water.

Then She-Who-Creates-by-Speaking-Its-Name said, "Yes, but this Earth is all flat and dull to the eye. Who will make it lively and diverse for me?" And Buzzard, who was bored, said, "I will make it lively and diverse for you." She flew over the vast expanse of soft mud, and when she flapped her mighty wings down, valleys were pressed into the land, and when she drew her mighty wings up, mountains were lifted from the land, and when she soared and glided, the great plains and plateaux were left flat.

Then She-Who-Creates-by-Speaking-Its-Name said, "Yes, but this Earth is all soft and wet. Who will make it dry for me?" And Wind, who was bored, said, "I will make it dry for you." And she breathed over the hills and valleys and plains for a very long time until they were dry and hard. The fish of the sea wondered what possible use this dry hard place could have, for fish have no under-standing of dry places, just as they have no experience of rain.

Then She-Who-Creates-by-Speaking-Its-Name spoke out the names of all the plants and all the animals, and each appeared as its name was spoken. Some went to live in the valleys, some in the moun-tains, some on the plains. And when Crayfish and Buzzard and Wind saw all this, they were very proud of themselves, believing that these plants and animals had been wrought from their own imaginations, for the power of She-Who-Creates-by-Speaking-Its-Name is not per-ceived as a waterfall is perceived; rather, it is perceived from within, as a dream is perceived. In their pride, Crayfish and Buzzard and Wind strutted and swaggered and sang of their wisdom and skill. And this is why old men dance the comic dance of Crayfish, Wind, and Buzzard to this day, strutting and swaggering and chanting those bragging songs that make children laugh at their foolishness.

Yet for all their strutting and bragging, in their hearts Crayfish and Buzzard and Wind were vexed because their fine work could not be seen and admired, for the world was wrapped in eternal darkness, as it shall be again at the end of the Allotted Time.

Now, Coyote, the most guileful of the animals, took up the cause of Crayfish and Buzzard and Wind, saying it was a shame that no one could see to admire their fine creation, but in fact Coyote's reason for despising the darkness was that she was a daylight hunter. Hearing Coyote's complaint, She-Who-Creates-by-Speaking-Its-Name whis-pered into the darkness, saying, "Who will make light for me?" And Star whispered back, "I shall make light for you." And she turned and shone upon the land with all her might, but her glow was feeble, so Coyote still complained that it was not light enough, although Rabbit and Prairie Dog thought things were just fine as they were, for they are daylight prey. Coyote pouted and sulked and wheedled and whined until she got her way, so Star made children upon herself until they were many and many in the sky, and they all shone down with all their might, glittering and twinkling with the effort, but still Coyote grumbled that it was not light enough. So Moon said, "I will help you, Star," and she turned and shone upon the world. But Moon is fickle and inconstant by nature: sometimes only half of her shines, and sometimes only a quarter, and sometimes no part at all, so Coyote pouted and sulked until She-Who-Creates-by-Speaking-Its-Name went to the cave of Sun and begged her to go up into the sky. But Sun loved her splendid pink-and-gold cave and was loathe to leave it, so She-Who-Creates-by-Speaking-Its-Name bargained with Sun, saying that she would not have to shine all the time; she could return to her cave when she was tired of shining, and the darkness she left behind her would be called Night. But still Sun was reluctant to leave her cave, so She-Who-Creates-by-Speaking-Its-Name bargained further, promising Sun that after the Allotted Time was spent, she could return to her cave and leave the land in darkness forever. Finally Sun agreed to go into the sky for half of each day, leaving at dawn and returning at sunset. The growing pink-and-gold you see at dawn is Sun slowly rolling the stone away from the mouth of her glittering cave, and the pink-and-gold of evening fades as Sun slowly pulls the stone back in behind her. But although she had allowed herself to be persuaded to shine on the land, Sun was sad to leave her splendid cave and bitter that Coyote's pouting and sulking had forced her to do it, so she wept sad tears and bitter tears on the morning of that first day, and where her sad tears fell upon the ground they became women and her bitter tears became men, and thus humans became the eternal enemies of Coyote, and sought forever to thwart and destroy her; but, alas, Coyote is too clever.

Now the women and men of the tears made children together, and some of these children went to live on the mountains, and some in the valleys, and some on the prairies, but the bravest and the truest of them came to live in the woodlands, and these called themselves the People, but the pale-eyed ones who came to buy furs and steal land called them the Iroquois.

As you have seen, in the Early Time all things—stars, wind, buzzards, animals—spoke the language of She-Who-Creates-by-Speaking-

Its-Name, a language that was called the Tongue. Well, so did all the women and men born of Sun's tears. But in punishment for misdeeds too vile to be told, most humans were made to forget the Tongue and were obliged to speak instead many nasty babbles. But the Iroquois people had not indulged in these misdeeds, so they were allowed to continue to speak the ancient and beautiful language of animals and stars and wind and of She-Who-Creates-by-Speaking-Its-Name. In time all the animals, one by one, lost their ability to speak the Tongue, some out of foolishness, some out of naughtiness, and some just from bad luck. There was a story about how each animal lost the Tongue, and these were useful stories meant to teach us the dangers of Carelessness and Greed and Rage and Disobedience and such things, but, alas, these stories have fallen from the tribal memory and now we must learn the harm of Carelessness and Greed and Rage and Disobedience the hard way, by suffering their effects.

Thus did the People come to be the only creatures who could understand She-Who-Creates-by-Speaking-Its-Name and speak to stars and winds and storms and ghosts. And among the People, the tribe that used the Tongue to greatest effect was your own Onondagas, the children of Hiawatha, for we wove the Tongue into tales meant to amuse on top and to teach underneath. Like this one, for instance:

One day, She-Who-Creates-by-Speaking-Its-Name was gazing back across time, reflecting upon the glories of the People, when out of the corner of her eye she saw something in the other direction, towards the future, that made her gasp in dismay. She saw that all living things would soon be threatened by pale-eyed enemies from across the sea. Dispatching Turtle to watch for the invaders' arrival on the shore of the eastward sea, she commanded all the animals to meet for seven days in a great lodge, there to discuss ways of dealing with this menace.

But how, you ask, could all the animals meet together if Turtle was absent? Well, at that distant time, Turtle was not counted among the animals because of her shell's resemblance to a rock.

To avoid the chaos of all the earth's animals meeting in one lodge, She-Who-Creates-by-Speaking-Its-Name ordained that each clan send one representative of its essential nature. Dog would represent all vulgar things, for instance, and Crow all complaining things; and there was greedy Bobcat, and slippery Otter, and sly Coyote, and ill-tempered Bear, and nervous Ground Hog, and haughty Frog, and bewildered Mole, and placid Tree, and many, many others. But why, you ask, was Tree invited to a meeting of the animals? Well, at that distant time, Tree was accepted as one of the animals for a very good reason which, alas, has fallen from the memory of man. Without offense, let me say that we shall move more quickly if you keep your questions to yourself.

At first, no humans were invited to sit in the Great Meeting, for She-Who-Creates-by-Speaking-Its-Name felt that the animals represented the various elements of human nature adequately, be it vulgarity or greed or guile or ill-temper or pride or stubbornness or any other thing. But a senior storyteller of the Onondaga, a man who was called Old because of his age, was commanded to preside over this gathering because he possessed three necessary skills: first, being of the People, he still spoke the Tongue, so he could interpret She-Who-Creates-by-Speaking-Its-Name's will; second, the Onondaga were experienced at smoothing out quarrels and settling disputes; and third, Old understood the many voices of the animals, for he used them in telling stories to the children of his tribe. The first thing Old did was to ask She-Who-Creates-by-Speaking-Its-Name to allow the animals to understand one another, just for the time of the Great Meeting; and so She visited each animal's ear as a soft-voice-that-tickles, and lo, they could understand one another.

Now you should know that the seven days of the Great Meeting lasted for many, many years, for in those distant times a day was as long as it needed to be, and thus many generations of the People were born, grew up, found mates, became old and feeble, and returned to enrich the earth while the Great Meeting was still going on. Late in the first day of the meeting—a day devoted to greetings and to exchanged hopes for the triple blessing of luck in mating, brave death in battle, and immortality in the songs of one's descendants—Turtle, who had been sent to keep watch on the distant shore of the Great Water, opened her sleepy eyelids and was startled to see a huge war canoe bearing down on the shore, its vast oar-cloths filled with wind. Now, Turtle's heart was not a bold one, for stones do not

strengthen their spirits through battle, yet she resisted her impulse
to flee until she had watched warriors wade ashore from the vast war
canoe and thrust their spears into the sand, claiming the land as their
own. Peeking out from beneath a bush, Turtle saw that these men
had the pale eyes of bloodless ghosts. At the sight of them Turtle
swallowed hard and was sore afraid, yet still she stood her ground
while the pale-eyed ones celebrated by pointing their long firesticks
into the air and making them roar and belch out smoke and flame.
Then one of them pointed his firestick at a deer who was standing
at the edge of the forest, frozen by curiosity. The firestick shouted
its smoke and flame at the deer, and the deer fell, an invisible arrow
through its heart. At this, Turtle turned and rushed back towards the
meeting lodge, eager to tell She-Who-Creates-by-Speaking-Its-
Name of the frightening wonders she had seen; but rushing for a
turtle is not what rushing is for other creatures, so twice ten times
ten summers would pass before Turtle came panting and gasping to
the lodge of the Great Meeting...

...where, alas, nothing had yet been decided because the assembled
animals were squabbling over matters of precedent and ancient privilege, and many used this occasion to air old disputes, rake up old
wrongs, and exchange new insults, all the animals shouting at the top
of their voices...voices very different from those they use today, as
you will see. Old pleaded for calm, but he failed to quell the deafening
babble.

"I have the right to sit closest to the fire," yapped haughty Frog,
"for I am distantly related to Crayfish who made the land."

"I refuse to accept the pipe of reconciliation after vulgar Dog has
soiled it with his spittle!" growled fastidious Snake.

"What compensation will I get if I surrender my rightful place to
Beaver?" purred litigious Turkey.

"When do we eat?" gobbled vulgar Dog.

"I refuse to share anything with anybody!" croaked greedy Bobcat.

"Who said she would not share with anybody?" asked bewildered
Mole, who was almost blind. "Who? Who?" And her neighbour whispered that greedy Bobcat had said that.

All the animals cried out either for preference, or against old
wrongs, or for advantage, or in simple ill-temper, each louder than

the others, until the din and confusion was more than Old could stand.

"Please be quiet," he begged. "I must have silence if I am to hear within me the soft voice of She-Who-Creates-by-Speaking-Its-Name and pass her message on to you!"

But the angry clamor increased until evening, and thus passed the first day of many, many years, and still Turtle was desperately rushing towards the meeting place at her slow pace.

When Old arrived at the meeting lodge on the morning of the second day, he found the animals already entangled in argument with Crow hissing at full voice, and Tree barking away, and greedy Bobcat croaking her head off, and Dog gobbling loudly into the ear of Frog, who yapped her annoyance to squeaking Bear and purring Turkey. Try though he did, Old was unable to bring order out of the chaos. And in like manner did the third day pass. And the fourth. And the fifth. And thus was the time for deliberation and preparation squandered in squabbles and petty pride.

On the night of the fifth day, Old began a fast to make himself calm in his deepest parts, so that he might hear the silent voice of She-Who-Creates-by-Speaking-Its-Name. He continued his fast through the night to weaken his body so that wisdom could slip past the barriers of knowledge and enter him, but he heard no voice. All the next day he chanted until his words lost all their common meanings and were free to take on universal meanings, but still no voice came. So he commanded the young men of his clan to prepare the sweat lodge with two fires, and he sat alone in the heat and smoke of the sweat lodge, fasting and chanting and sipping a wooden cup of the juice of the mushroom-that-pours-light-into-your-mind until he suddenly felt the presence of She-Who-Creates-by-Speaking-Its-Name growing within him. He asked her how he could hush the blustering delegates so that they might receive her warnings and her advice. And her silent voice whispered into his bones, telling him how to silence them with a woven basket, and he smiled at her crafty ruse.

And while all this was going on, Turtle continued to dash towards the meeting lodge, as she had for scores of years. But now her neck was stretched far out from her shell in an effort for speed, because Pale-eyes had followed her towards the setting sun and was gaining on her every day.

The animals were in full babble that morning of the seventh and last day of the Great Meeting when Old entered carrying a woven basket which he placed near the entrance. He then walked slowly to the center of the circle and sat on the ground, while all around him swirled snarls and banter and taunting and boasting. But the talk staggered and faltered, first here, then there, as one by one the delegates noticed the elsewhere stare in Old's eyes and his deathly pallor caused by long hours of fasting and by sipping the juice of the dangerous mushroom. They could all see that his spirit was with She-Who-Creates-by-Speaking-Its-Name.

Speaking through Old's hollow, eerie voice, She-Who-Creates-by-Speaking-Its-Name told the gathering of the menace of Pale-eyes, who would chop down the forest (Tree winced), and foul the swamps (Beaver blanched), and slay the game (many gasped), but who would do his greatest harm to the People, against whose arrows he would turn his firestick, and the People would fall in vast numbers. But his firestick was not Pale-eyes' most dreadful weapon. He would also cough upon the People and they would suffer fever and pain and whole families would die, whole clans, whole villages, and few would be left to chant of their ancestors' glorious deeds. But illness was not Pale-eyes' most dreadful weapon. He would also give the People dreamwater, which would daze them and make them believe they could hear the silence and see the invisible, and this was most alluring for from the moment they were wept upon the soil the People have yearned to hear the silence and see the invisible. They have sought it through taking strong tobacco water into themselves, through drinking the juice of magic plants, through fasting until the body is too weak to imprison the imagination, through dancing until the spirit is spun off from the body—anything to bring themselves to that dream place where silence speaks and the invisible reveals itself. Pale-eyes' dreamwater would steal the dignity of the People and make them fools and braggarts. But even his dreamwater was not the most dreadful of Pale-eyes' weapons. He would also give the People his

Book, which would teach them to be meek, to accept insults, and to wait for justice after death. And the bringers of the Book would ridicule the teachings of She-Who-Creates-by-Speaking-Its Name and mock the ancient truths and ways. Our fierce courage would be sapped, our inner voices would be silenced, and we would become pliant, obedient, and foolish.

"But why does Pale-eyes hate the People so?" Coyote cawed in mock sympathy, secretly pleased that his eternal enemies would be made to suffer.

"Who asked why Pale-eyes hates the People?" wondered bewildered Mole, "Who? Who?" And four or five of her annoyed neighbours spoke harshly, saying, "Coyote asked it. Now be quiet!"

Speaking through Old, She-Who-Creates-by-Speaking-Its Name answered Coyote's question. "Pale-eyes hates the People because he has in his belly a terrible hunger to own their land."

"Own land?" gobbled vulgar Dog. "But how can one own land?"

"Absurd!" scoffed Tree in an outraged bark. "Whoever heard of owning land!"

"One cannot *own* land," growled Snake. "You might as well say that one can own the air, or the waters, or the clouds! Such things cannot be owned. They can be enjoyed, or used, or sung about, but they cannot be owned."

Bobcat croaked in agreement, but deep in her greedy heart she could understand the sinful pleasure Pale-eyes must feel at having something for himself alone and not having to share it with anybody.

Each tried to out-scoff the other at the silly idea of owning land or air or clouds or water, and it wasn't long before everyone was purring and barking and hissing and meowing and croaking and gobbling and snarling until none could hear Old's soft voice; so he rose up and stared at them with terrible eyes, and ordered them to be still! Be still!

And there was a sudden silence in the meeting lodge.

"There now," growled Snake softly. "You must all be silent. Serves you right."

"Oh, shut up!" cawed Coyote.

"*You* shut up!" snarled Owl.

"Everybody shut up!" commanded Bear in her thin, high squeak.

"Don't you dare tell me to shut up!" yapped haughty Frog.

And again the Great Meeting was a-roar with the noise of everyone silencing everyone else, while bewildered Mole turned around and around, asking, "Who said we must be quiet? Who? Who?" Exasperated by her constant confusion, everyone in the meeting turned and shouted at Mole, "Old said it! Old said it!" And Mole sat down, blinking and chastened.

Then Old rose up and glared about him with a terrible wrath. "You petty things!" he roared. "You small-hearted things! You have no command over your passions! We shall never learn how to stand against Pale-eyes with all your babbling and spatting. Therefore, I command you to take the voices out of your mouths and put them into yonder woven basket until the meeting is over. Do as I say, and do it now!"

And meekly did all the animals, even ill-tempered Bear and haughty Frog, pluck the voices from their mouths and drop them into the woven basket. Crow dropped in her hiss, and greedy Bobcat her croak; Dog put in her gobble, and haughty Frog her yap; Coyote gave up her caw, and placid Tree her bark; Bear surrendered her thin, high squeak, and Turkey her purr, and Owl her snarl.

Then they all sat humbled before Old, who quelled his rage with long slow breaths before saying to She-Who-Creates-by-Speaking-Its-Name, "It is clear that the People must fight Pale-eyes and drive him away."

Speaking within his heart, She-Who-Creates-by-Speaking-Its-Name said, "You will fight Pale-eyes, but you will not have victory. The People are brave and resourceful, but they are few, for all the Five Nations are but two thousand warriors, while Pale-eyes is ten thousand, and again ten thousand, and ten thousand more and more and more, all flowing across the Great Water without end."

Old sighed deeply. "Then we have no choice but to learn to live beside him," said Old.

"You cannot live beside him," responded She-Who-Creates-by-Speaking-Its-Name, "for he will destroy the land. The People are few and they tread the land lightly, staying at one place only until Earth is weary, then moving on so that she can rest and recover. But Pale-eyes is many and he will tread the land heavily, forcing Earth to bear until she is so warn and fatigued that she crumbles into the streams and is swept away forever."

"Is there nothing we can do?" cried Old.

"There is a way to save yourselves," answered She-Who-Creates-by-Speaking-Its-Name. "You can—"

But if there was an answer it was never heard, for at this moment Turtle stumbled into the meeting lodge, out of breath and panting from her centuries-long dash to bring the terrible news. "Pale-eyes is coming!" she cried. "Pale-eyes is coming! He is right behind me!"

All the animals jumped up in alarm and opened their mouths to cry out in terror...but no sound came. They looked like ghosts in horrid nightmares, with their wild eyes and their mouths open, screaming in silent panic. They rushed to the woven basket, pushing and shoving to get at their voices, and in their frenzied haste they snatched out whatever voice came to hand, clapped it into their mouth, and ran off into the forest crying, "Pale-eyes is coming!" Pale-eyes is coming!" Crow took the caw of Coyote; Dog grabbed the bark of Tree; Frog snapped up Bobcat's croak; Bear hooked out Snake's growl; Owl seized the Who? Who? of bewildered Mole, who took Bear's thin, high squeak, while Coyote snatched out Frog's yap and Turkey popped Dog's gobble into its mouth. Snake was beginning to swallow Crow's hiss when greedy Bobcat snatched most of it away, leaving Snake with only a little hiss, while Bobcat has a lot. Not content with most of Crow's hiss, greedy Bobcat also took Owl's snarl and Turkey's purr and ran out with all three in her mouth. Tree was last to get to the woven basket for, then as now, trees moved more slowly than other animals, and when she felt around the bottom of the basket there was no voice left for her, because greedy Bobcat had taken so many. So vexed was Tree that she swore to have nothing further to do with the animals and she became a member of the plant family, where she remains to this day.

Old went forth to face Pale-eyes and fell before his firestick.

As a reward for her heroic two-hundred-year-long dash to warn of the coming of Pale-eyes, Turtle was adopted into the animal family, an honor that she accepted for fear of offending them, but deep down she regretted forsaking her honored position as swiftest of the rocks to become slowest of the animals. But as she became an animal after all the animal voices were used up, Turtle still speaks the silent language of the stones. Listen very carefully to her someday, and you will hear it.

AFTER HOURS AT RICK'S

L ast call was announced by Sam One and echoed at the far end
of the bar by Sam Three. In obedience to the phoney traditions
of Rick's Café Américain, a scratchy disk of *As Time Goes By*
was put on the turntable to signal the end of the drinking day.
The clock read two-ten, which meant it was five minutes before two.
It is another tradition at Rick's to set the bar clock ahead fifteen
minutes to create a little leeway for moving drunks out. All the regulars know this gimmick, so it doesn't work; but that doesn't prevent
it from being one of Rick's instant traditions, like playing *As Time
Goes By* and hanging huge blowups of stills from *Casablanca* on the
walls, and calling all the barmen Sam. This last had a particularly
precious embellishment: the barmen are known as Sam One, Sam
Three, Sam Five, etc., because some wag once described them as an
odd lot.

Rick's has been the city's most popular meat market for the past
four months, and four months hence, it will surely be out of fashion
and probably no longer even in existence. That is the mutable way
of things in Dallas, city of glass, Naugahyde, chrome, and Tomorrow.

I had drunk enough to feel surprisingly sober and to regret having
wasted money on hooch that failed to dissolve the crust of my dev-
ilishly attractive bitterness. I tipped back the last of my scotch-and-
milk and asked Sam One for another before last call. When he told

me that last call had already gone, I opened my eyes wide and demanded to know why nobody had advised me of so significant an event. He sighed operatically and made up another, taking care to label it 'a quick one'.

I surveyed the bar with that dolefully sardonic expression I effect. Nothing but losers left at this hour. Two men sat arguing with hooch-blurred intensity: young, hard-charging sure-to-succeed types wearing the uniform that made mid-Seventies Texas businessmen look like ticket agents for minor airlines, white belts and white shoes, double-knit polyester slacks, and jackets in centennial primaries. Spaced out along the bar were three single males staring into their glasses, trying to figure out why they had failed to make out, not realizing that they were Darwinian rejects from the mating process—the kind who drive Volvos. At the end of the bar was a boozy, buxomy gal with big hair and an eyelash that had come unstuck at the corner. She was still waiting for the guy who had excused himself to go to the men's room half an hour ago. And two stools up from me was a woman in her mid-thirties, 'dressed for success' in a feminine version of a man's business suit. She had come in an hour ago when the action was peaking, and now she seemed a little embarrassed to have missed the tide of lust and ended up beached and alone.

A sad lot, I evaluated. The culls, the losers, the shucks. And yet, there was I—*me*—sitting in their midst. Ironic. Ironic!

An hour earlier, the bar had been full of action, with its clientele of mercantile types of both sexes, all playing it for more interesting than Nature had designed them to be, all hunting for crotch in this pasteboard jungle of music, laughter, hooch, and single-*entendre* jokes that elicited loud guffaws, not because the *mots* were *bons*, but because the laugher wanted to show that he had got the joke and was—if only to that modest extent—with it.

I had hooked an easy fish early in the evening, but I let her off the line—off my dizzyingly clever line, that is—out of fatigue and boredom and age. Age looms large with me. Lots of men have trouble with the arrival of male menopause, but with me it's worse; I just cannot accept the idea of being forty; and that's awkward when you're almost fifty.

I downed my scotch-and-milk, pushed myself off the stool, and signaled Sam One for my tab.

"That'll be thirteen-fifty, Mr Lee."

"You took care of yourself, Sam?"

"I always do, sir."

"Wonderful. I have it on excellent authority—one Virgil, an Italian tour guide who works the rings of Dis—that the most attractive feature of hell is that the *service* is *compris.*"

Sam One guessed from my tone that this was supposed to be clever, so he made a weary effort towards a laugh but produced only a slight nasal sigh.

Slight though it was, this sigh had an astonishing effect: the lights went out, and Rick's was plunged into darkness.

A crash of thunder seemed to split the tarmac of the parking lot, then the lights flickered and came back on. All the drinkers were startled and frightened, so they laughed.

I went to the window and looked out. A storm had broken over the city; hailstones the size of moth balls clattered onto the parking lot and bounced up to a height of three feet. The tinny rattle of the hail obliterated the sound of *As Time Goes By*, now playing for its second and last time.

The only warning of an oncoming storm had been an odd greenish light at sunset, a kind of bathospheric afterglow. I had noticed it as I dropped into Rick's at six-thirty on my way home from the university.

By the time the other customers joined me at the window, the diagonal streaks of rebounding hail had stopped and rain was drilling down, rapidly melting the hailstones almost before they stopped bouncing and rolling.

"O, mutability!" I muttered.

"Oh, shit!" muttered the woman at my side, the 'dressed for success' thirtyish one I had noticed up the bar.

"No, just rain, I think," I said.

One of the customers called back to Sam One, telling him that no Christian barman would send customers out in shit like this.

"You see?" the woman said to me. "I told you."

As everyone drifted back towards the bar, Sam Three was quick to explain that he couldn't sell any more drinks without risking his license.

Fine, someone said. Don't sell us another round. *Give* us another round.

And because most of us were regulars, Sam One shrugged and nodded to Sam Three, who, with cheerless fatalism, began to make everyone another of the same.

"I hope you realize," I said, taking the barstool next to hers, "that the fact that these yahoos agree with you about the rain being shit does not constitute proof. The vox populi is almost always the voice of ignorance, which is why democracy is the least efficient thing since early experimental substitutions of waxed paper for toilet paper in an effort to reduce time wasted in the john. In the case of that particular guy, it was his inability to distinguish shit from Shinola that ruined his career as a television meteorologist."

"He wouldn't make much of a shoe-shine boy, either."

"True. Except in West Texas, where a wedge of dung under the heel of the boot is a symbol of status."

"To say nothing of rural chic."

"You're fun to banter with, lady. You have a well-developed sense of the ridiculous and a firm grasp on the whimsical. And what is more, you're quick on the uptake. I like the cut of your gibe, sailor."

"Thanks, mister. What's that you're drinking?"

"Scotch-and-milk."

She made a dubious face. "Is it good?"

"I've never thought of it as a moral issue."

"You seem to have a low opinion of our fellow drinkers, stranded here in this Casablancan hailstorm."

"Oh, they're all right in their way. Just a pack of moonstruck kids who sit all night on barstools in the hope of striking up a relationship that occupies that satisfying middle ground between romance and getting a quick lay."

"Yeah, I know the type. Pitiful."

"Yes, pitiful."

And the conversation lay there for a while, as she pushed ice around in her drink. Mentioning getting laid by its name often has a stunning effect on the social flow.

"What's your name?" she asked, without looking at me.

"Marvin Lee. And yours?"

"Martha Zinberg."

"You don't look like a Martha."

"Fifteen years ago, I didn't look like a Martha, maybe. But I'm afraid I'm growing into it. But you, you *really* don't look like a Marvin."

"Thank you. It's unfair that Marvin Lee should be so patently wimpy a name, while Lee Marvin sounds all sinew and balls."

"Poetry's a funny thing."

"True. I remember giggling all the way through *Paradise Lost*." She smiled. "Do you come here often?"

"And what zodiac sign was I born under?"

"Hey, give me a break. I'm new at this sort of business."

"Ah, the cry of the Sabine women. All right, yes. I come here often."

"To pick up women?"

"Certainly not! Or, to be more precise...why else? And how about you, Martha? Did you come here to get picked up?"

"I thought so an hour ago. Now I'm not sure. It's my first time."

"Your first time at Rick's?"

"First time anywhere."

"Married?"

"Divorced."

"Recently?"

"Very."

"Children?"

"None. You?"

"Which?"

"Any of the above."

"Married, yes. And I have produced an F-1...she who just yesterday was a little girl, all sugar and spice and unanswerable questions, but who will soon be entering Yale as what the acceptance letter called a 'freshperson'."

"How do you earn your money, Marvin?"

"I don't actually *earn* my money. I'm a university professor. 'History of Western Thought.' Creating faculty positions is our culture's way of providing for brilliant people who are emotionally underdeveloped."

"That has the sound of a rehearsed line."

"Just what it was. What about you, Martha? How do you earn your money?"

"I'm a lawyer. My husband and I were in practice together."

"Zinberg and Zinberg?"

"No. Just Zinberg."

"Ah! And was that the problem? Insufficient recognition for your contribution?"

"...No, that was more a symptom than one of the problems. You want to hear about them? The problems?"

"Nope."

"Oh." She blinked. Then: "Well then, do you want to tell me about your problems?"

"Sure. My wife is a wonderful human being. My daughter is a blend of beauty and wit. I got tenure eight years ago. And I publish articles in the major journals of my field with machinelike regularity."

"These are your *problems?*"

"Seen from the inside, yes. You see, I always wanted to be captain of a tramp steamer on the South China Sea. Or a novelist. Or a movie star. Or a apple grower in Vermont. And instead? Instead, I have a departmental committee meeting in the morning. Now there's excitement for you. What about you, Martha? Did you ever want to be an apple-growing movie star adrift in the South China Sea?"

"No. All my life I wanted to be a lawyer."

"Well then, you've won life's great battle! You've made out."

"Not tonight, I haven't. My first shot at the swinging singles scene wasn't a screaming success. I realize that zaftig isn't in this season, but still...I mean, come on! This place was steamy with libido earlier on, and some of the boys were too drunk to discriminate. And yet...here I am. Still sitting here. Advise me, Marvin. What should I do? Offer green stamps?"

"Do I understand you correctly? Are you asking me for guidance on how to get yourself laid?"

"I think I am. I'm not sure. After all, this is my maiden voyage...if a matron can have a maiden voyage. This is my first time out since the divorce. Maybe I just want to talk. Share ideas, dreams, insights, wisecracks." She tilted back her head and looked at me narrowly. "Come to think of it, maybe you're not the person to ask for advice. I mean, you're obviously no hotshot at the business of seduction."

"I resent that!"

"Well, you're still here, aren't you? You didn't find anyone for tonight."

"Yes, well...that's the part I resent."

She laughed. "You're sort of fun."

"Fun? Wow! Like a barrel of monkeys? Gee! Actually, Martha, I *did* make out tonight. I ran my patented, all-purpose, never-fail Switch Routine on a girl, and she fell like the Roman Empire. So you see, when you assume that I am here, rather than sweating on the belly of some highly desirable chick, because I lack persuasive skills, you are full of shit up to your pink, shell-like ears—if you don't mind my waxing poetic."

"Wax away. Are you drunk, Marvin? You sound pretty drunk."

"Only my mouth is drunk. My mind is perfectly pellucid. Hey, if I had slurred that 'perfectly pellucid', *that* would have been funny. So? Do you want to learn how I made out, or not?"

"Is it still raining?"

"Like a cow pissing on a flat rock, as wits say in the Big Bend country."

"In that case, teach me, Marvin. I'm all ears...pink, shell-like ears, that is." She crossed her legs and assumed an acutely attentive look.

"All right, here's how it went. I approached this fish, dangled my classic 'switch' line in front of her, and pow! She was on the hook. All we had to do was down our drinks and in half an hour we'd have been in her apartment, making the beast with two backs."

"So why weren't you?"

"Well, you see, once the bait is taken and the hook is well set, my interest in landing the fish evaporates. I'm more a hunter than a killer. It isn't the tickle and squirt that attracts me. It's the constant reaffirmation that I can still harvest young flesh. Does that make any sense to you?"

"Sure. In fact, it's transparent. Even trite."

"Trite?"

"So how does this classic 'switch' sting of yours work?"

"Like most landmark discoveries in mankind's slow rise from the stone axe to the atomic bomb, The Switch is based on simple principles. All these bumbling butchers around here run standard, banal dodges. They grope the fish's emotions by telling her she's beautiful; or they grope her mind by saying she's interesting; or they grope her self-esteem by faking a common interest in the Rolling Stones or Fellini or art nouveau. Me, I cut through all this tedious persiflage and do a complete switch—hence the name—on those worn-out ploys. Playing it for bittersweet, burnt-out, and tragic, I frankly admit that both she and I are here to get ourselves laid. Then I shake my head and say what a sick and silly thing that really is. Here we sit...so much finer and more sensitive than these animals sniffing each other all around us...and yet we find ourselves shopping in the same meat market as they, victims of corporal impulses that we can't fight, even though we know how stupid and ultimately unsatisfying it all is. I sigh and say that at least we can preserve our dignity by not conning each other with shams of tenderness and affection. We can call a spade a spade. (Note of caution for potential switch users: The 'call a spade a spade' line is a little dodgy when the target fish is Black.) And there you have it, Martha. My sure-fire switch scam...patent pending. After it's been run, the two of us finish our drinks while raking those around us with glances of superior scorn. We're a team now. We've both accepted reality, both admitted we're there to get laid. Ergo...let's get to it."

"And that really works, Marvin?"

"More often than not."

"Hm-m. It doesn't sound very romantic."

"We're not talking about romance. What we're talking about is more like giving blood, or taking a vitamin capsule, or pissing—which are, as a matter of fact, excellent analogies for the three major impulses that drive us towards random sex."

Martha probed the bottom of her glass with a plastic swizzle stick. "Would you mind telling me something? Why didn't you take a shot at me? Didn't you notice me sitting here?"

"I noticed you."

"And?"

"Well, you see...I've got this problem. I only target young fish, sprats. Lurking in the corners of my mind there is this notion that youth is a communicable disease that one can catch through direct contact."

"Does it ever work, this chasing after youth?"

"It *always* works...for about thirty minutes."

She took the swizzle stick out and licked it meditatively. "I don't think your sting would work for me. Too complicated. Too devious."

"Don't lick that. Plastic causes cancer." I must have swallowed too much hooch that night, because I found myself feeling something like compassion for her. So I decided to play it straight with her. "Martha? I told you about the switch game where the angler lays it right on the line with the fish. Well, there's a more advanced version of the ploy, one I call the Double Switch. That's where I tell some intelligent fish at the bar all about the switch game."

She was silent for a couple of beats. "You're saying that I've just been a victim of the double switch?"

"That's it. But remember...it's reserved for the smartest fish."

"And that's a compliment, eh?"

"Indeed it is."

"Hm-m. But what about your taste for young flesh and all that business about youth being a communicable disease?"

"Martha! Do you really think I have so little imagination that I am incapable of lying?"

"...I see."

"Like everybody else, I take what I can get. But because you're bright and witty, I thought I'd warn you. Particularly as this is your first night out on the hunt. Seems only sporting to give you a chance to get away."

"I'm not all that sure I want to get away. Do you mind if I ask—do you love your wife?"

"Sure."

"But then...why?"

"It's all about being fifty and not being a captain on the South China Sea or a farmer in Vermont. You're parked out in the lot?"

"Yes. A cream Mercedes."

"Convertible?"

"Yes."

"How did I know that? When this rain breaks, I'll follow you to your place."

"Ah..." She put her elbow on the bar and her cheek in her palm, so that she was looking sideways up at me. "May I use the confessional now?"

"Sure. I was almost through anyway. Confess away."

"We can't go to my place."

"Roommate?"

"Sort of. There's my husband and my children. I don't think they'd understand."

I looked at her, and suddenly I felt very tired. "You're not divorced."

"Nope."

"And this isn't your first time out cruising the meat markets."

"Ah...no. Say, could there possibly be such a thing as a triple switch?"

I rubbed my face. "So the Master Stinger got stung, did he? Well, how about that? Not bad, Martha. Not bad at all. Especially for a woman who found my crotch-scam too devious." I pushed off the barstool and went to the window. The rain had thinned to little more than mist, and streetlights were reflecting in shallow pools faintly opalescent with automobile filth. I couldn't tell if the hail had done any damage to my battered old Avanti, but I was sure it had harmed her Mercedes, and that was a comfort.

"Marvin?" She joined me at the window. "One morning a woman who has been a good wife and a busy mother lifts her head from life's tasks, blinks and looks around, and she realizes that she's forty and the parade has passed her by while she was making plans for others. You know what I mean?"

"Please don't batter me with this truth and sincerity stuff. I can't handle it. My whole life has been a celebration of artifice. Down with meaningful relationships! Up with the psychological barriers? Bring on the colorful hang-ups!"

She was silent for a moment. Then: "I see. Well, at least we could console each other by making—what was it? The beast with two backs? I have enough money for a motel."

I sat heavily in a chair by the window. "I'm sure you have, Martha."

She sat across from me. "Your ego's hurt, isn't it."

"Sure. Of course. But that's not really it. It would be pointless for us to make it in some motel with 'Genuine Western Oil Paintings' on the walls. In the morning, our strongest desire would be to shower until the scent of the other person was flushed down the drain. We'd be obliged to make up stories for people who no longer believe us. And a week from now, we wouldn't even remember each other's names. We don't have anything to offer each other, Martha. There's nothing we even want from each other. All there is between us is a low background fever of sexual curiosity."

While I spoke, she smiled at me with amused patience that made it difficult for me to keep my eyes on hers. I felt burned out, vitiated.

Sam Three started up the worn record of *As Time Goes By*, and Sam One went along the bar telling everyone that the storm was over and he really had to close.

Martha continued to look at me, her eyebrows arched calmly.

"It would be absolutely pointless, Martha. We probably wouldn't even perform very well."

"So what happens now?"

I sighed and stood up. "I'm going to take a walk."

"And me?"

"It's a big night out there. There's room for you to take a walk, too."

"But not together."

"But not together."

She narrowed her eyes and evaluated me. "Marvin, you're really a washout, you know that?"

"Yes, I know."

I left Rick's Café Americain and walked around the empty streets for a couple of hours; then I decided I had to get away...go to someplace new and fresh! Canada, maybe. Or the South China Sea. I found my car standing alone in the lot, and I got in and drove north, with the rising sun glancing and glittering through the passenger side window.

But about ten miles out of town, I ran out of gas. I took that as a sign—hey, maybe even a metaphor for my life!—and I managed to get to my committee meeting at the university, unshaven but only a little late.

THAT FOX-OF-A-BEÑAT

The people of my village share with all Basque peasants an in-born reluctance to give out any information that might be used to our disadvantage, or, if not actually to our disadvantage, then at least to some other fellow's advantage, which must ultimately be the same thing, for God in His wisdom has seen fit to fill His world with fewer desirable things than there are people chasing after them, and so what the other fellow gets, I don't.

Nowhere is our disinclination to burden others with accurate information more evident than in financial matters. It is common for a shepherd with a fruitful flock to complain long and bitterly, not only because God hates a braggart, or to prevent relatives from asking to borrow money, but also because the posture of poverty gives one moral leverage when selling one's cheese to the traveling wholesalers. The only peasants who do not claim to be impoverished are the truly poor, who seek to avoid the scorn of their neighbors and—even more galling!—the pity of those who might assume that their poverty is God's punishment for wrongs committed by past generations of their family.

No one in my village is fooled by the conventions of speech and behavior that oblige the fortunate to minimize their possessions and the miserable to pretend they haven't a care in the world. Oh, those dim souls from Licq, our neighboring village, might be fooled by such dodges, but not us. We all know that those who pretend to be content with their lot are probably as poor as stones (and perhaps deservedly so, within God's Great Scheme of Retribution), while those who bemoan their poverty most shrilly are secretly well-off, like the Colonel, who became our village's richest man from his practice of snapping up land from the feckless and the unlucky, but who was so tightfisted that he even resented having to pay his share to repair the school's roof. But the Colonel no longer worries about collecting other people's land, not since God reached down last winter and collected him.

Oh yes, we all know how the rich moan while the poor sing, but the glory of the Basque mind lies in its capacity to see subtleties within subtleties, so it is accounted a great gift to be able to judge just *how* rich are those who complain, and exactly *how* poor—and therefore vulnerable in commercial dealings—are those who walk about lighthearted and smiling, like an idiot stunned by a loose tile falling from a roof.

But a wise old Basque *dicton* tells us: Every rule has its exceptions, even this one. Such an exception was the case of old Uncle Arnaud, who never complained about losing his best sheep to wolves and the lightening and never cursed the rich merchants of Paris (known collectively as 'the government') for depressing the price of wool so they could steal it from us. He accepted these strengthening Trials of God with a resigned shrug and a calm smile—exactly as though he were poor, while all the time he was as rich as a tax collector! But even the sly and subtle Uncle Arnaud was not so admired for craft and obliquity as the man who came to earn the title, 'that Fox-of-a-Beñat'.

Beñat was our village idiot (or 'village innocent' as our parish priest insisted we call him, reminding us that the Treacherous Apple was the fruit of knowledge, and that those who know the least are often—indeed, almost always—better Christians than those burdened with facts and understanding). Every village in those days had at least one village idiot—save for Licq, of course, where nearly everyone could lay claim to that title—and it was not uncommon for dark and dire histories to be attached to these poor souls. Our Beñat attracted more creative biography than most, for he lived in the loft of the late Widow Jaureguiberry's barn, where he sustained himself on bread and raw onions—no doubt in penance for some (probably unspeakable) sin. Equally suspect was Beñat's custom of taking long walks—not walks such as some lazy dunce of a Licquois might take—but *long* walks from which he would return with muddled tales of Saint Palais, fully forty kilometers away down the valley, or of Saint Jean Pied-de-Port, half again as far, and over the mountains! Sometimes people encountered him on the road as he slouched along in his awkward, jerky gait, muttering and grinning to himself in that mysterious way of his, and there was no mistaking our Beñat, with his wide, crooked mouth and his huge ears, and eyes set not quite at the same level, to say nothing of the baggy, low-crotched trousers he had worn from longer ago than the collective memory of our village stretches. There were even rumors that Beñat had walked all the way to Paris and back, and the fact that he never spoke of Paris lent a certain credibility to these rumors; for isn't it just like an idiot to imagine he has only been to Saint Palais, when in fact he has been in Paris?

The widespread suspicion that he had visited Paris was finally substantiated. Each fall, foreigners from Paris and Bordeaux appeared in our village, dressed in crisp new hunting costumes and filling our café/bar with talk of their prowess as hunters of the *palombe*. The money these northern hunters spent was important to our narrowly balanced economy, and it was a source of some puzzlement and distress to us that many of them were so stupid as to allow themselves to be seduced away from simple, clean accommodations in our honest village by the tarted-up restaurants and overdecorated hotels of Licq.

These northerners sometimes mistook us for quaint rustics and amused themselves by imitating the chanting music of our speech, though they could never achieve the melody of our expression because they were crippled by the Parisian's inability to pronounce final e's. Naturally, we repaid their discourtesy by renting them only the worst bird blinds in the valley, while we ourselves shot and netted the *palombe* from the best positions and always had a few extra to sell to them, so they could support their boasts of manful skill when they returned to whatever Paris or Bordeaux they came from.

One day several of these northerner 'hunters' were in the new café/bar that Monsieur Aramburu had made out of his father's old-fashioned wineshop by the simple expedient of changing its name and keeping a pot of filter coffee on the back of the stove. Aramburu was also our mayor, as he had the village's only telephone. Well, that Fox-of-a-Beñat (though he had not yet earned that title) came shambling past the window in his ragged old clothes, grinning and muttering to himself as always. One of us asked the tableful of boasting Parisians if they had ever happened across old Beñat on the road to Paris. The loudest and best-equipped of them (the ones with the fancy costumes never bag the birds, as Basque *palombes* are not so stupid that they cannot recognize a hunting jacket) winked at his companions and told us that indeed he had often seen our village innocent in Paris, riding through the park in a fancy carriage filled with young and beautiful girls. Well, of course none of us missed the wink, and we knew better than to think that any young and beautiful girl would ride about with a man who ate mostly onions, but we could discern a seed of truth in this story, nevertheless. Any man who was such a fool as to be unable to tell a good hunting blind from a miserable one would be perfectly capable of passing within ten meters of our Beñat without recognizing him. So here was this Parisian trying to ridicule us by pretending to have seen Beñat in Paris, when in fact he *had* seen him and was too stupid to know it! The laugh was on him!

But it was not only because of his enigmatic wanderings as far as Saint Palais and Saint Jean Pled-de-Port (and now even to Paris!) that our village innocent attracted so many stories to himself. There was rich fodder for gossip in Beñat's very peculiar drinking habits.

Beñat didn't drink. Never. Not a drop.

It is true, of course, that our village priest (a man who had been educated both in Pau and in Bayonne, and who therefore knew something of this world, unlike that simpering simpleton who babbled from the pulpit of the Licq church) had often reminded us that good Catholics drink only in moderation. But who can claim that never touching a drop is 'drinking in moderation'? It is quite the opposite! There were two bodies of opinion concerning Beñat's strange immoderation in the matter of drink. Some suspected that perhaps the old idiot was not a Catholic but a Jew or a Saracen—or, worse yet, a Protestant!—and was therefore not obliged to drink in moderation like the rest of us. Others dismissed this view as ridiculous, pointing out that Beñat spoke excellent Basque—for an idiot—and all the world knows that speakers of Basque must be Catholic, for Basque was the language of the Garden of Eden and is currently the language of heaven, although there have been efforts by French-speaking bishops of Paris to suppress this historical fact. The most widely accepted explanation for Beñat's suspicious refusal to take a little glass now and then was that in result of some grave sin committed while drunk during his youth, he had made a vow to give up the pleasure of wine forever. His great sin was understood to have involved you-know-what, and this meshed nicely with the newly uncovered reports of beautiful girls in carriages in Paris!

When teased about his abstemiousness, old Beñat used to grin and say that he didn't drink because he was too poor. And this always elicited guffaws as men tugged down the lower lid of their eyes with their forefingers and nudged one another, because it was universally understood that Beñat was very, very rich. Not just rich as some miserly old piss-vinegar of a Licquois might be rich, but *rich!* As rich as an *Amérloque!*

The evidence of his wealth was overwhelming. For one thing, following the rule that everyone who is poor pretends to be comfortable and everyone who is rich pretends to be wretched, it was obvious that old Beñat was wealthy beyond the dreams of a coin-biting merchant. Also, here was a man who was older than the church tower and had in all those years spent nothing on clothes and eaten nothing but bread and onions and the occasional blood-of-Christ apple 'borrowed' from the village's most famous apple tree. How could such a man fail to be rich? And what about all these mysterious voyages to Paris...and perhaps even beyond! Do poor men travel in search of poverty? No. Rich men travel in search of yet greater wealth. Poverty is something you can enjoy at home.

Oh, yes, the evidence of Beñat's wealth was overwhelming. And it must be confessed that his hidden riches (in search of which the boys of my era spent many afternoons, digging in all the unlikely places a fox of an idiot might bury his gold) were a source of concern among the men of the village. You must not think that we envied him his good fortune. It is not within the Basque character to be envious—save for the grasping people of Licq, where it is understandable, as they have everything to be envious of. No, it was not envy that our people felt, it was a keen sense of the injustice of it all. We rankled at the knowledge that when poor old Beñat died, his fortune would pass to his family, the Hastoys, those rich and haughty owners of an espadrille factory in Mauléon. It twisted a man's heart to think that all those good gold francs scraped together throughout a long life of eating onions and wearing tattered old clothes would end up in the pockets of people who were already too rich to pass, as some camels are said to do, through the eyes of needles, particularly as one of the Hastoys had recently lost a chance to marry a plain, honest girl from our village and had ended up marrying a dolled-up strumpet from Licq, and we all know the circumstances under which *that* occurs.

It was widely accepted that old Beñat was a distant and maybe oblique member of the snooty Hastoy clan, their overweening pride being the reason they had cast him out and now denied him. After all, what family likes to admit being related to an idiot, even a rich one? To be sure, whenever anyone suggested to Beñat that he was a Hastoy, he denied it with a grin. But what credence is to be given to the word of an idiot? And what significance must one give to that grin? Eh? Eh? And whenever a Hastoy was confronted with the question of relationship, he denied it with an angry vehemence that would make anyone suspicious. Obviously a sore point.

One afternoon, some men giving themselves a little rest from life's cares at Mayor Aramburu's café/bar saw old Beñat pass the window with his jerky, uncoordinated stride.

"Eh-ho!" the witty and teasing Zabala-One-Leg called out. "Come join us for a drink, Beñat!" And everybody laughed.

"No thank you, sir," old Beñat responded, grinning and nodding as idiots do on such occasions.

"Don't you like wine?" another wag asked, winking at his fellows.

"It is too expensive for me, sir," the idiot answered, standing at the entrance but not entering, for he was shy of the company of gentlemen with fine work clothes.

Everyone laughed and several eyelids were tugged down at this well-known bit of cupidity.

"Say, where have you been, Beñat?" a young shepherd asked. "I've not seen you for a week."

"Ah, sir, as for that, I have been walking."

"Oh? Whither?"

"As the road took me, sir. From stone wall to stone wall."

"All the way to Paris?"

"Paris? Paris? Well...I suppose that's possible, sir."

"On business, were you?"

"Business, sir?"

"Harken, old man. Don't make *too* many sous. They will only end up in Hastoy pockets."

"My sous? In the pockets of the Hastoys? But I don't understand. Why will that be so, sirs?"

"It is ever so. The family inherits. Unless you make a will with Maître Etchecopar to the contrary. What's wrong, Beñat? Don't you want your money to go to the Hastoys?"

"Well...no. No, I need my few sous."

"For what?" the young wit cried. "To buy onions?"

Everyone laughed when old Beñat said, "Just so, sir. To buy onions."

"Well, Beñat," Mayor Aramburu said from his throne behind the bar, "if you don't want your money to go to the Hastoys, you'd better make your will with Maître Etchecopar next Thursday."

"If you say so, sir. But...what is a will?"

"A will is a thing you make with a lawyer when you think you are going to die," informed the mayor, who not only had a telephone, but who also read the newspaper all day long behind his bar and therefore was—after our priest, of course—the most knowledgeable man in the village.

Old Beñat's face twisted with the effort to comprehend this. At last he said, "Then, yes, I must make a will. For I have a feeling I shall die soon. Well, thank you, sirs. I must be off."

"I'll say you're off! 'Way, 'way off!" cried Zabala-One-Leg as Beñat left the doorway and departed for his nest in the barn of the late Widow Jaureguiberry—God comfort and reward her.

The ambience in the mayor's bar became suddenly heavy and morose, and men sat staring into their glasses. It is not wise to speak of death, for it is widely known that mentioning bad things beckons them.

"Hm-m-m. Could it be that he *is* going to die soon?" the mayor wondered aloud. "It is possible, my friends, that idiots know things that others do not, for idiocy is largely a matter of the mind."

The men nodded gravely as they silently hefted this morsel of insight.

Now, those envious, backbiting Licquois always try to make much of the fact that our village does not have a full-time lawyer, and that Maître Etchecopar comes over from Licq only one Thursday a month to attend to our legal business. The truth be known, we are a peace-loving village and our men are brave, so the few disputes we have are settled honorably with fists, unlike those thieving cowards from Licq who are forever at one another's throats in the safe, cowardly way of litigation and are therefore obliged to have a full-time lawyer.

Thus it was that old Beñat had to wait until Thursday to consult Maître Etchecopar in his ad hoc office in the sitting room of the priest's house. And when the idiot shambled out of that office, grinning and muttering to himself, all the men at the window of the bar and all the women watching from behind their curtains experienced a satisfying sense of justice done, and the pleasure of knowing that those haughty Hastoys had been cut out of his will. Now the new Hastoy wife, that strumpet of a Licquoise, would not be lording it over us with money that belonged to the village in which it had been hoarded for more years than there are loafers in the government!

That afternoon the men giving themselves a little rest from life's rigors in Mayor Aramburu's café/bar were more than usually silent as they sat over their glasses of strong emerald green Izarra. (The weaklings in Licq drink the milder urine yellow Izarra.) After a time, one of them drew a sigh and gave voice to what everyone was thinking, "But then...if not the Hastoys, who?"

The mayor stopped wiping his glass and scowled at the bigmouth, for he had been considering that very thing for several hours, and he could see no advantage in everyone in the village troubling themselves over the issue of Beñat's inheritance.

"Ah-ha. I think I know who'll get it," said a man standing by the window. "Regard." He gestured to the church across the square where Beñat was walking down the stone steps with the village priest. All the men gathered at the window and looked across the square with fatalistic shakes of their heads. To be sure, it was the priest's duty to grab for the Church as much as he could from old people who, approaching death, seek to assure their places in heaven through acts of charity. And we were proud to know that our priest, who had studied both at Pau and Bayonne, could grab more in a day than the bungling old fool of a priest at Licq could grab in a year. But there were so many things a man could do with those piles of buried gold. Useful things. Enjoyable things. Perhaps...who knows?...even good deeds.

The men shrugged and sighed, then returned to their tables and conversations. It was evident that the Church would have old Beñat's gold, and there was no point in weeping over a stillborn lamb. But our mayor pondered the matter at greater depth, for people with telephones listen and learn things, and they become craftier than others. The mayor reasoned that old Beñat had seen the priest *after* he had visited the lawyer. Therefore, it was not necessarily true that the Church had the old idiot's gold firmly in its holy fist. And while there is time, there is opportunity.

A week later, the men who gathered at the mayor's café/bar to discuss plans for the fête of the village's patron saint were surprised to find old Beñat installed at the table by the window, drinking a pressed lemon as he listened to our long arguments and debates with his vague grins and friendly nods. We learned that the mayor had employed the idiot to do light chores about the café, and in return for this labor he received a nice little room overlooking the mountain stream that runs through our village. Also, Beñat took his meals with the mayor's family, sitting between his host's two plump and pretty daughters, who were solicitous of his comfort and often put the choicest morsels on his plate. The work required of Beñat was minimal, so he passed most of his days sunning himself on the bench in front of the café/bar, or sitting in the shade of the plane trees, and he was grateful to the benevolent God who had brought him to such ease and comfort in his last months on this earth. The mayor told him it was right and just to be grateful to God—even a little dangerous not to be—but he should not be too grateful, and not *only* to God. From time to time, Beñat would disappear from the village, off on one of his mysterious walks, and during such times his new family would worry and fret over his safety, as he had not visited the lawyer since their first meeting, so his affairs were still unsettled.

In every way, the old idiot's life was gentle and pleasant, save that he sometimes missed his raw onions, for the mayor's plump and pretty daughters had insisted that the raw onions must go if he were to sit between them at table. To mitigate his disappointment, they sometimes brought him one of his favorite blood-of-Christ apples, those crisp juicy ones with little flecks of red in the white meat.

While it is true that a village innocent is given to understand things that are hidden from those whose vision is confused by intelligence, and may therefore feel the approaching shadow of death, it is also true that Beñat was an idiot, so it is not surprising that he misread the signs of his end by a little.

In fact, he misread them by a bit over eight years.

After Beñat's burial in the mayor's family plot (his headstone boldly carrying the name Hastoy, to the great chagrin of those haughty merchants), a decent respect for the dead required the mayor to let some time pass before he looked into the matter of Beñat's will. It was not, in fact, until later that afternoon that he found himself sitting in the once-a-month office of the lawyer from Licq, discussing the subject.

"But of what money do you speak?" Maître Etchecopar asked.

The mayor eyed him narrowly. There is no trusting these Licquois in matters of honor. "What money? Beñat's fortune, of course."

"I don't know what you're talking about, Monsieur Aramburu."

"But the old idi—the Departed One—visited you to arrange his will. Don't you remember?"

"Ah, yes! I recall now. But that was years ago. He came to see me because he felt he was dying, and a friend had told him he must make a will."

"Exactly. I was that friend. And...?"

"And?" The maître laughed. "Well, I had to explain to him that there is no point in making a will if one has no money."

"No money?"

"Not a sou."

"But...but all those years! He lived to be a hundred at least! And had a vigorous appetite to the very end, I can assure you! Surely he saved *something*."

"The little money he earned repairing stone walls around the countryside was spent in buying his bread and onions. He died with nothing."

"Nothing?"

"Nothing."

That evening found the mayor in close conversation with our village priest.

"And you say he visited you only to make his confession?"

"Just so. He wanted to cleanse his soul because, he said, he could see his death coming. It appears he was a bit farsighted. Ha-ha."

"Some things are funny, Father. Others are not."

"Ah, to be sure, to be sure." The priest dried his eyes on the sleeve of his cassock. "The kindness of your family to our departed brother has been a lesson to all the village."

"Hm!"

"Without breaking the confidence of the confessional, I can tell you that he had fewer sins on his soul than a little girl at her first Holy Communion. I am sure that at this moment he is sitting joyfully in the blessed presence of God, if that makes your grief easier to bear."

"Oh, yes. Much, much easier. But...but what of his long walks to Paris and beyond!? If he was not attending to his riches, what was he doing?"

"I too was curious, so I asked him about that."

"And...?"

"He told me he took long walks because he liked to see things."

"Liked to see things? *See* things! What kind of a reason is that, I ask you?"

The priest lifted his shoulders. "An idiot's reason, I suppose. After all, dear Beñat was...well, innocent."

"Innocent? Innocent! Like a fox he was innocent!"

Our mayor never completely lived down the little chuckles and casual comments made by his customers on the subjects of Christian charity and how some people's sly and subtle tactics sometimes mis-fired. And it was widely shared throughout the village that one of the great dangers of having a telephone was that electricity harms a man's brain and makes him so dense that even the village idiot can trick him out of eight years' bed and board. But although he winced be-neath the jibes, even Mayor Aramburu felt a grudging pride that our village had produced this Fox-of-a-Beñat who, idiot though he might be, was still slyer than the most intelligent of those dolts from Licq.

MRS McGIVNEY'S NICKEL

I passed the greater part of each day incognito. It used to make me laugh inside to realize that bypassers seeing me on my way home, dressed in worn-out sneakers with many-knotted laces, last year's school knickers patched at knee and butt, no socks to cover skinny, bruised shins, my cap skewed around to the side, mistook me for an ordinary kid, little suspecting that in fact I was a daring and resourceful leader of a team of hardened mercenaries.

It was our assignment to defend North Pearl Street from the Germans who, having gobbled up Czechoslovakia that March, now set their sights on Albany, which they planned to infiltrate by way of North Pearl. The U.S. high commander in chief of everything had called me into his lavish secret office to explain that if North Pearl fell, Albany was doomed, and if Albany was lost, what hope was there for America? So the fate of the country was in my hands and those of my band of loyal followers. Ranged against us were several thousand heartless, highly trained Nazi Strong Troopers.

Like many children, I lived an intense and secret playlife, and thought I was unique in this. So complex, so theatrical, so absorbing were my story games that I remember each summer between the ages of six and ten in terms of the game that dominated it. With Europe's slide into war a constant theme on radio news broadcasts, it was inevitable that the story game of the summer of 1939 would have to do with Nazis.

My scalded lungs rasping for air, I pressed back against the weathered siding of a boarded-up stable that dated from the era of horse-drawn wagons. Slowly...slowly...I eased my eye around the corner of the stable to locate the snipers concealed in the—they spotted me, and a bullet splintered the wood near my cheek! I drew back and hissed at my followers, "We'll make a dash for the shed. It's our only chance!" Uncle Jim exchanged a worried glance with Gabby Hayes, who raged, "Goshdarn those dang-nabbed, lop-eared, low-down, pigeon-toed, no-account..." He sputtered off into mutters of indignation. I used to let my followers blow off steam now and then, knowing that when the chips were down they would obey my instructions because I knew best how to avoid being picked off by those dirty Nazi Strong Troopers with their itchy fingers curled around the triggers of high-powered automatic shooting devices. Gail looked at me, her eyes glowing with admiration, while Reggie nodded crisply in his stiff-upper-lip British way. I kept up a spitty covering fire with my Thompson submachine stick as my band dashed across the alley one by one and dove for the shelter of the shed. Both Reggie and Doc got hit on their way across, and Kato, my faithful Japanese valet, had to drag them the rest of the way. Then it was my turn. After emptying my last five-hundred-round magazine into the German trench-bunker-wall-fortification, I scrabbled across the alley on all fours, getting a slug in one shoulder and another in my leg and another in my other shoulder and scratching my knee on a broken bottle as I skidded into the shelter of the doorway and gathered my team around me. Gritting my teeth to conceal the pain, I drew a situation map on the ground with the map-making stick that also served as a pistol with an inexhaustible clip, a telescope that could read the enemy's plans at half a block, a radio that translated German into American, and a stick of dynamite that you lit with your snapped-up-thumb cigarette lighter and threw at the enemy, or rather, at the base of a huge rock outcropping that overhung the enemy's position and came crashing down on them, crushing them to a pulpy mass that your eyes flinched away from, but you told your followers that sometimes war wasn't a pretty sight, but you had to do what had to be done

and that was that. Throwing your dynamite was a desperate last re-
sort, considering the huge expenditure of war material the loss of this
versatile stick constituted...or would have constituted, if you didn't
always have the remarkable good luck to find another such stick
lying close to the body of a fallen (or crushed) Strong Trooper. (All
right, so I mis-heard 'Storm Troopers' on the radio. Is that a crime?
Jeez!)

My band of intrepid followers included Uncle Jim from the week-
day radio adventure *Jack Armstrong, All-American Boy!*, which also
provided my admiring tomboy of a cousin, Gail, who mostly said,
'Wow!' or 'Whatever you say, Chief.' In addition, there was Gabby
Hayes, toothless, bearded sidekick in innumerable grade-Z cowboy
movies; then there were Jack, Doc, and Reggie from *I Love a Mystery*.
Since Reggie was British, I had to use my 'English accent' so he could
understand my instructions. Finally there was Kato, my faithful valet.
This last character I borrowed from *The Green Hornet*, without being
exactly sure what a valet was, but if Kato was Britt Reid's 'faithful
Japanese valet', he'd do for me. (A couple of years later, right after
the attack on Pearl Harbor, Kato became overnight a 'faithful Filipino
valet', but by then I was no longer playing story games.) Each of my
seven followers, Gail, Gabby, Jack, Doc, Reggie, Kato, and Uncle
Jim, had a distinct personality and role that I remember clearly to
this day: Gail was always astonished and admiring, Gabby was full of
folksy wisdom and given to long strings of curses, Reggie always knew
the polite thing to do, Jack and Doc were brave but headstrong and
rash, Kato was faithful, and Uncle Jim was always worried that I was
taking on tasks harder than any one man could hope to accomplish.
This mixed bag of followers might fret and squabble and occasionally
let their hot heads carry them too far, but when the chips were down
they were all courageous and, what was more important, obedient.
Oh, it's true they often got into trouble that called for quick reactions
on my part, but I was fond of them, even if they sometimes tried my
patience.

I always muttered aloud as I played all the characters in my story
games; and there in the alley that late summer afternoon I was muttering harder than usual as I questioned a snide, sneering German
officer I'd captured. Because my story games were always tense and

emotional, the volume of my muttering and the vigor of my gestures tended to increase unless, as sometimes happened, I glanced up and blanched to find someone looking at me. I would quickly convert the dramatic monologue into a song (with gestures), because although talking to yourself is a sure sign of being nutty, there is no shame attached to singing to yourself. But I never felt the ploy had really worked, so I would wander away, furious with the eavesdropper for spoiling the game.

Well, I was muttering hard, explaining our desperate situation to my followers, having ordered Doc to blindfold the German officer so he couldn't see the map I was scratching on the ground, when my concentration was snagged by a sharp tapping sound. Annoyed by the interruption, I looked around, but I couldn't see anybody, so I started explaining that we had to stop those Germans from advancing another inch, even if it meant laying down our—again I was interrupted by the *tap-tap-tap* of metal against glass. I looked up and down the alley. Nothing. I was all alone. Then a movement at the edge of my peripheral vision caused me to lift my eyes, and there looking down at me was Mrs McGivney, our block's crazylady, smiling in that soft, sweet way of hers. Immediately my followers vanished, as did the four or five thousand Nazi Strong Troopers dug in at the far end of the alley, and I was left all alone, the leader of men suddenly shriveled into a skinny little kid caught talking to himself.

The block's belief that Mrs McGivney was crazy was based on her peculiar shopping habits, her excessive shyness, and the long, old-fashioned dresses she always wore. She was never seen on the street except for quick trips over to Kane's Grocery, always at closing time. Even if other people were ahead of her, Mr Kane would serve her as soon as she came in, because she was very timid and would slip away and not come back until the next evening rather than risk being noticed or, yet more upsetting, spoken to. Respecting her sensitivity, Mr Kane never spoke to her. He would just smile and raise his eyebrows above his thick glasses, and she would quickly mutter off her shopping list, which he would fill, toppling cans from their high stacks with his can-grabber gizmo and catching them in his apron with that theatrical brio of his, or scooping macaroni or rice from one of his tip-out bins and hissing it into a little sack on his scales, always bringing the weight up to just a bit more than you asked for, or slicing cheese off the block in the hand-cranked slicing machine.

After filling her order, Mr Kane would tell Mrs McGivney the total cost as he marked it down in the dog-eared book he kept under the counter, a book that was called his 'slate', although it was made of cardboard and paper. Mrs McGivney would take her sack and scurry back across the street to her apartment, never looking up for fear of catching someone's eye. Once a month, she came in with a check, which he cashed for her, subtracting the cost of her groceries. Everyone knew that Mrs McGivney received a small monthly government check for 'disability', which the street understood to mean because she was a nut, but Mr Kane once told me that in his opinion she was just painfully shy. But her reputation for insanity was an element of received street tradition and therefore impervious to evidence or reasoning. Even the modest check she got from the government was taken as proof, if any were needed, that she was insane. How else could a crazylady stay alive? She could hardly get a job...except maybe at a nut factory! And there was the suspicious way she would appear from time to time at her window giving onto the back alley and look down at the kids playing there, not bawling them out for making noise like any sane person would, or shouting at them for throwing stones that might put somebody's eye out. No, Mrs McGivney just smiled down on us sweetly...exactly like a crazylady would do.

And now there she was, standing at her window, smiling down at me after having scattered both my followers and my enemies to the recesses of my imagination.

She beckoned to me. She'd never done that to any of the kids before! I made a broad mime of looking around to see who she could possibly want before pointing at my chest, my eyebrows arched in operatic disbelief. She smiled and nodded. I lifted my palms and tucked my head into my shoulders to say, but what did I do? She tapped the window again with a nickel—so that's how she'd made that sharp noise—then she pointed to the coin, then to me, clearly meaning that she intended to give the nickel to me. She beckoned again and made a big round gesture, which told me to go to the end of the alley, around to the street, and to her apartment building. I really didn't want to; my worst nightmares were about being pursued by crazy people. But I was a polite kid, so I went. Even the wildest and toughest of us kids, several of whom ended up in prison and one on death row, would be accounted polite by today's standards. Then too, if there was a chance to earn a little money, I could hardly let it pass me by, considering how my mother regularly risked her health for just a few extra bucks. Resentful of losing my game and dreading my encounter with a crazylady, I left the alley—but not before rubbing out the map with my heel, so the enemy couldn't find out my plans.

The staircase of 232 was dark because the hall windows meant to illuminate the stairs had been blocked up when the slum landlord divided the buildings up into small apartments and put a narrow bathroom into the front of each hall. Although it was dark, I ascended the staircase with a sure step because 232 was identical to 238, where I lived.

I tiptoed up to the top floor landing and stood there in the dark, uncertain. Maybe it would be best to sneak back down and out into the light and bustle of the street, but as I turned, the door to the back apartment opened and Mrs McGivney stood there, smiling.

"Would you mind going over to Mr Kane's for me?" she asked in a little-girl voice. "I'll give you a nickel." Her voice went up on the first syllable of 'nickel' in a kind of sing-song temptation.

"Well, I don't...All right, sure, I'll go." I was relieved that she only wanted me to do a chore for her and not something...crazy.

She had a list written out, and she said Mr Kane would put it on his slate.

When I returned with the small bag of groceries she was waiting at the head of the stairs and she gave me the nickel she had tapped the window with.

"Thanks." I put the nickel in my pocket and patted it to make sure it was there. The year before, I had lost a quarter. It must have just fallen out of my pocket on my way to the Bond Bread bakery to buy a week's worth of what was euphemistically called 'day old' bread. Until it got too dark, I walked back and forth along my path, hoping to find the quarter. No luck.

"Just bring the bag in, would you please?"

I followed her into her parlor, where she took the bag and brought it into the kitchen, leaving me standing there. On a round table by the window that gave onto the back alley there were two glasses of milk already poured out and a little decorated plate with four home-made sugar cookies on it. The room was filled with frilly old-fashioned furniture and it smelled of furniture wax and recent baking...the sugar cookies; and in the corner an old man sat facing the other window. His eyes were pointed towards the buildings across the alley, but I could tell he wasn't seeing anything. I said he was old, but the only old thing about him was a soft halo of fine white hair that held the sunlight like the lace curtains did. His face was unlined, his skin was tight, and he sat there in a straight-backed chair, staring through the curtains out across the alley with an infinite calm in his unblinking, pale blue eyes. Spooky.

Mrs McGivney returned from the kitchen and stood beside the little table, holding the back of her chair, waiting for me to sit down.

"Gee, thanks a lot, but I think maybe I'd better..." But she smiled sadly at me, so I sat down. What else could I do?

There was a heavy linen napkin on each plate. Mrs McGivney took hers and put it on her lap, so I did the same, only mine slipped onto the floor. She smiled again and pointed her nose towards the plate of cookies, indicating that I should take one. I did. She took a tiny bite out of hers, and I tried to do the same, but two bits broke off, one falling onto the floor and the other getting stuck in the corner of my mouth so that I had to push it in with my finger, and I wished I were somewhere else...anywhere.

She smiled a little pursed smile that didn't show her teeth. "You live three houses up, don't you."

I nodded.

"And you're Mrs LaPointe's boy."

I nodded again, wondering how she knew, considering that she never talked to anyone.

"What's your name?"

"Luke. Well, it's really Jean-Luc, but only my mother calls me that. I like to be called just Luke."

"John-Luke. That's foreign, isn't it?"

"French. My mother's family is French Canadian. And part Indian."

"John-Luke's a nice name."

"Only my mother calls me that."

"I've noticed that you always play alone."

"Not always. But mostly, yeah."

"Why is that?"

"Why do I play alone?" I glanced past her towards the old man, wondering if we were supposed to pretend he wasn't there. "Well, mostly because I make up my own games, and other kids don't know the rules or the names of the people or, well...how to play."

"And you read an awful lot, don't you."

How did she know that I read a lot...then it hit me. I always cut through the alley on my way home from the library, not because it was the shortest way, but to avoid the little kids who, whenever they saw me with an armful of books, would chant 'professor, pro-fes-sor, pro-fes-sor', which was one of my street names. My other street name was 'Frenchy' because of my name, which was even more French-sounding when my mother reverted to her maiden name, LaPointe, but with a Mrs so as to justify us kids I suppose. On my first day at P.S. 5 my teacher said how *interesting* it must be to have a French name. I hated teachers who tried to be palsy and modern. So far as I was concerned, they could forget the social worker crap. All I wanted from a teacher was information. No sincerity, no affection, no concern, thank you; just information. She wrote Jean-Luc on the board, and for the first couple of weeks I had to deal with being called Jean, a girl's name. There was teasing and a couple of fights after school—the usual trial by ordeal that every new kid on the block had to face. I was prickly and quick to go to Fistcity, always getting my first couple of shots in while the other kid thought we were still in the Oh yeah?...Yeah! preliminaries. Most of the kids at P.S. 5 were bigger than I was, but I had an edge over them: I never gave up. Bigger kids could throw me down or knock me down, but as soon as they let me up, I always plowed into them again; and although I'd come home pretty messed up, they never got away without at least a few marks and some blood, so after a while they gave up the teasing and bullying because there wasn't much glory in being able to beat up a smaller kid, and I made sure there was always a ration of pain in it for them. I never became a leader or even anybody's best pal, but my existence on the block came to be accepted and 'the professor' was left alone. In return, I concealed my bookishness, pretending not to know the answers to teachers' questions, and occasionally making wisecracks in class, or pulling funny faces behind some admiring teacher's back after she had complimented me.

"That's right, ma'am. I do read a lot. I get some of my games from books."

"Games?"

"Like Foreign Legion. Or Three Musketeers. But mostly I get them from radio programs."

"We don't have a radio," she said with neither complaint nor apology.

I had noticed this on my first glance around the room, and I wondered how anyone could do without a radio. So totally was my understanding of life linked to our second-hand Emerson that I couldn't imagine not having *The Lone Ranger* or *The Whistler* or *I Love a Mystery* for excitement, or Jack Benny and Fred Allen and Amos 'n' Andy for laughter, or advice from Mr Anthony for getting an insight into everyday problems. My favorite moment of the day was the delicious anticipation of those ten or so seconds of hum while the tubes warmed up; then there was the deep satisfaction of a rich, familiar voice announcing one of the kids' adventure programs that my mother let me listen to for one hour every evening before home-work. I would stand on one leg in front of the radio, my head down, my eyes defocused, totally mesmerized by what I was hearing and seeing. Seeing, for old-time radio was profoundly visual; the scenes were painted by and upon your imagination. For me, radio was *real*. Splendid and enthralling, but less real, were the worlds I glimpsed in books and movies. The life I lived on North Pearl Street was certainly not splendid, but neither was it real to me; just a grim limbo I would escape from as soon as 'our ship came in'. Until then, I could find solace in my story games.

"I'm afraid of them," Mrs McGivney said, offering me a second cookie, which I politely refused, then reluctantly took.

"You're afraid of radios?"

"Of everything electric," she admitted with a little smile of self-disparagement.

Only then did I notice that she didn't have electric lights. All the houses on our row still had their gas installations in place, but the gas had been cut off except for kitchen stoves. In some rooms the gas pipes had been used as conduits for the electricity, so naked bulbs dangled from stiff, fabric-wrapped wires that sprouted from the ceiling rosettes of former gas chandeliers. In our bathroom and kitchen the disused gas pipes had fancy wrought-iron keys, but you couldn't turn them because they'd been painted over so many times. But Mrs McGivney still had fancy cut-glass gas lamps on her walls, with bright brass keys to turn them on.

"Mr McGivney just loves the gaslight," she said. "He's always glad when it gets dark enough for me to turn it up." She smiled at the unmoving old man, her eyes aglow with affection.

I looked over at him, sitting there with his pale eyes directed, unseeing, out the window, his face expressionless, and I wondered how she could tell he liked the gas light. Could he speak? Did he smile? And what was wrong with him anyway? Was he crazy or something?

I felt her eyes on me, so I quickly looked away.

"Mr McGivney is a hero," she said, as though she were explaining something.

I nodded.

"My goodness! Do you know how long it's been since we've had a little boy come visit us?" she asked.

"No, ma'am." I didn't really care. All I wanted was an opening to tell her that I'd better be getting home.

"It's been a long, long time. Michael—that's my nephew?—he used to visit us sometimes. I don't think he much liked coming up here, but Ellen—my sister?—she used to make him come. And every time he came, I'd give him some of my sugar cookies. *He* used to like my sugar cookies, unlike some little boys I could mention."

"I like your sugar cookies, too, Mrs McGivney. I think they're... nice. *Real* nice. Well, I guess I'd better be going. My mother's been sick and—"

"Mr McGivney is a hero," she said again, sticking to her own line of thought and ignoring mine. I could tell she wanted to talk about him, but I was uncomfortable with the waxy-clean smell of the place, and with that smooth-faced old man staring out at nothing, so I told her that my mother would be wondering where I was, and I thanked her for the milk and cookies. She sighed and shrugged, then she opened the door for me, and I escaped down the dark staircase.

I sat for a while on my stoop before going into our apartment where I knew my mother would be in bed, bored with her most recent siege of lung trouble and smelling of mustard plaster and Baume Bengué. Kids were playing stickball in the street, blocking traffic and exchanging insults with an impatient truck driver who wanted to get through. The game broke up when second base drove off, and the kids clustered around Mr Kane's corner store for a while, then drifted down Livingston Avenue towards the docks. I knew they'd end up wandering through the deserted warehouses down by the river, snooping around in the rubble-littered, piss-smelling, water-dripping vastnesses. They'd probably use their slingshots to shatter the few windowpanes that remained tauntingly intact, then, bored, they'd wander back and cluster again in front of Mr Kane's until someone thought of some other trouble to get into.

Kids had been playing stickball that day back in June 1936, when my mother, sister, and I first found ourselves sitting on the front stoop of 238 North Pearl Street, our clothes and bedding in cardboard boxes on the sidewalk, and our few pieces of furniture looking shamefully worn and shoddy in the unforgiving glare of sunlight. I was six years old, and my sister four. She was hungry and sleepy and close to tears after the long trip down to Albany from Lake George Village in our uncle's rattletrap of a truck. My mother looked anxiously up and down the street for my father. She hadn't seen him in five years, not since the morning he went out to look for work and didn't come back, leaving her pregnant with my sister and only two dollars and some change in her purse. Then a letter arrived saying he was sorry he had run away from the family he loved, but he just couldn't stand not being able to support us, and he knew that her family would give us a hand if he was out of the way. Mother's family hadn't approved of him because he was a gambler and a con man—

fair enough reasons. Then, after five years without a word from him, a letter came out of the blue, saying he had found a job and an apartment in Albany, where we could make a new start. My uncle had had us on his hands since my father abandoned us, and he made no bones about resenting the time and money it cost him to bring us down to Albany, so when my father wasn't there in the street to welcome us, my uncle just unloaded our stuff in grumpy haste and left us there, hoping to make it back to Lake George before nightfall because his old truck had no headlights. Leaving my sister to watch over our things, Mother and I went into the red brick building to look for our apartment. That was my first experience of that medley of smells—boiled cabbage, mildew, Lysol, other people—that I would come to recognize as the smell of the slums, the smell of poverty and hopelessness, cold and eternal in the nostrils. There was an envelope stuck into the crack of the door of apartment #2, and in it there was the key and a note from my father saying that he had gone to buy something special for a party, and he would be back in a jiffy. We went back outside and sat on the stoop, waiting for him. We never saw him again.

For the next seven years we lived on North Pearl Street, a typical slum block of the Thirties. Shoals of dirty brats with runny noses, nits, and impetigo playing noisy games of kick-the-can or stickball in the street while unshaven out-of-work men in stretched, sweaty undershirts talked in loud voices from stoop to stoop on hot summer nights as they sucked at quart bottles of ale. They scoffed at those who had managed to get jobs. "You won't catch me kissing up to some boss just to get a job pushing a broom or digging a ditch!" Clearly, they were above that sort of thing. Only a handful of men on our block had regular jobs, a couple with the Bond Bread bakery on the corner, and a few doing part-time work on the loading platform of the Burgermeister brewery. North Pearl was predominantly Irish, ghetto Irish, who were content to live on handouts in the slums generation after generation, bullying their cringing wives and beating their rebellious kids, while the more ambitious Irish worked their way into the mainstream of America, finding jobs in the first generation and professions in the second. The men of North Pearl lived off of transient WPA jobs and Child Benefit checks. Of Albany's poor, only the Irish ever got those cushy WPA jobs that consisted of leaning on a shovel and looking with judicial interest into a hole that someone else had dug weeks before. This was because the political machine that ran Albany was the O'Conner Gang.

The Irish families on our block had received welfare for so long they had come to consider it a basic civil right, but my mother writhed in shame that circumstances had reduced her to living on public charity. Her! Ruth Lillian LaPointe who, like all the LaPointes, had always worked for everything she got! But she had been buffeted by repeated blows. First her charming, handsome, glib husband deserted her, leaving her to provide for two babies just when the Depression was at its deepest and darkest. Then her father, who had stepped in to help to the best of his limited resources, died in a car crash. Then her always fragile lungs gave out, so that she got ill every time she tried to work, as she stubbornly insisted on doing every Christmas.

Although North Pearl Street was a sump for society's lost, damaged, and incapable, I never felt inferior to anyone else, not even to those lucky kids in the Mickey Rooney movies who lived in small towns with big lawns and Sunday dinners, and had wryly benevolent fathers who remembered that they, too, had been rascals when they were young. I didn't feel inferior because my mother wouldn't let me. Okay, so the chips were down for us at that particular moment; she admitted that. We were going through a rough patch, no denying it. But she made it clear that, unlike our neighbors, my sister and I didn't belong in the slums. And not only did we not belong there, but we weren't going to stay. No, sir! One of these days our ship would come in, and when it did...we'd be out of there in a flash. Boy-o-boy just you watch our smoke!

Between bouts of lung trouble, my mother was energetic, doggedly optimistic, and full of laughter and games; and unlike the haggard, drained mothers of other kids on the block, ours was young and slim and pretty. My sister and I were proud of her, but always a little apprehensive too. Our pride flowed from the fact that this resilient, courageous woman was unfailingly supportive of us, encouraging the slightest glimmer of talent or gift, and assuring us that only a dirty trick of Fate had dumped us into the poverty of Pearl Street, where we didn't belong. (But we'll be out of here just as soon as our ship comes in, you mind my words!) Our apprehension had to do with Mother's hairtrigger temper which flashed out at the least, often imagined, slight to her dignity—an oversensitivity common among those who know their ethnic background is viewed with derision or disfavor and who, in aggressive compensation, feistily boast of those despised roots. Mother boasted about being French-'n'-Indian, the first ethnic strain accounting, in her view, for her refined taste, and the second making her a dangerous person to cross.

One manifestation of my mother's bristly pride was her refusal to accept that, poor though she was, her kids couldn't have what she called a 'decent Christmas', which involved her finding part-time work as a waitress in some cheap restaurant that needed help over the holiday season. She would get back from work late at night, having walked all the way through the cold and slush to save money for our presents, and inevitably her lungs would give out by Christmas morning, which she would spend lying on the living room couch, fevered and coughing, watching my sister and me open presents that were too expensive for our condition of life. Several times she ended up in the hospital with pneumonia, and once she was put into a sanatorium for two months, during which my sister and I were sent to a Catholic orphanage, a grim prisonlike institution set in wintry fields of corn stubble that seemed infinitely bleak to city kids. The first day, a brother took me aside and told me that I should pray every night for my mother's recovery. That night I alternately prayed and cried into my pillow, because it had never occurred to me that she might die, leaving Anne-Marie and me there forever.

The boys wore gray canvas uniforms, and we marched in silence to meals, classes, and prayer, our lives punctuated and dictated by clamorous electric bells. We showered in cold water and slept in an unheated cavernous dormitory that was supposed to 'harden us up' against the rigors of life, but it only kept us in a permanent state of drippy noses, sore throats, and ear aches. Discipline was rigid and hierarchical, the older boys being in charge of the younger. This led to bullying and illegal late night beatings with wet towels carried out in the shower room within a ring of older boys.

Anne-Marie and I were separated upon arrival at the orphanage, and she was sent to the girls' wing where, only five years old and having no idea where I was, she cried herself to sleep every night and reverted to bed-wetting, for which she was both ridiculed and punished. She was picked on because she was pretty and vulnerable, and bigger girls yanked her around by her long, blond hair. One afternoon a couple of weeks after we arrived, I was in the tangled mass of boys that ran and hooted and screamed wildly during the pandemonium of our unmonitored recess periods, when I thought I heard Anne-Marie's voice within the chaos. I searched for her among the tight-packed shoal of blue-uniformed girls who used to watch the rampaging boys from their side of the high chain-link fence that separated us, but before I found her the bells rang and we had to run back inside and leave the exercise yard for the girls. I later learned that I had walked right past her while she vainly called my name. I couldn't hear her through the din, and I failed to recognize her because a nun had cropped her hair in an effort to save her from being tormented by envious girls. She cried all that night. But the next day I walked up and down my side of the fence until I found her, and we held fingers through a chain link while she sobbed with a mixture of relief and misery. And that's how we spent the rest of our recess periods until the day we were called into the director's office and told that we were being sent home. Our mother was well again.

It wasn't until we were home that Mother told us how the social workers had decided that she was not in good enough health to be a 'fit mother', and that we kids would remain in custody at the orphanage until we were sixteen, old enough to get jobs. Mother had used the formidable weapon of her furious French-'n'-Indian temper to browbeat the astonished social workers into letting us live together again. But next time...

To avoid there being a next time, whenever Mother had to go to the hospital, Anne-Marie and I did everything we could to conceal the fact that we were at home alone, so the social workers wouldn't send us back to the orphanage. I would wash our clothes in the bathtub, and Anne-Marie would try to keep the house clean, awkwardly wielding a broom twice her height. When I did the shopping at Mr Kane's, I would mention that my mother had told me to get this or that, or that she was feeling just fine, thank you...anything to deceive any welfare spies that might be lurking around.

My sister and I came to dread the approach of Christmas. Mother never seemed to realize how frightened we were that our fragile family would be broken up again, and permanently this time, all because of her hard-headed determination to give us 'Christmas presents every bit as nice as those rich kids get, come Helen Highwater!'

For years I thought of Helen Highwater as some sort of avenging she-devil who descended upon people who were trying to get things done. You see, my mother had a flawed ear for idioms and adages, which she often twisted around, like accusing someone or something of being 'dull as dishwater', or her life-long assumption that the 'hoi polloi' were the snobbish upper crust of society. When she said the word she always used to push the tip of her nose up with her finger to illustrate the snootiness of the hoi polloi. I suspect that she was sustained in this error by the similarity between 'hoi polloi' and 'hoity-toity'.

The welfare agency gave us $7.27 a week, and through careful buying, extreme self-denial, and great imagination in the planning of meals, my mother managed to feed and clothe us on what worked out to a little less than thirty-five cents per person per day. The welfare paid our rent directly to our faceless slum landlord instead of giving us the money and letting us find our own accommodations. They paid much more for our three-room apartment than people with money in hand would have been asked, but then as now the Lords of Poverty didn't trust the poor not to squander or drink up their money.

So the welfare system gave us basic shelter and food, but we were on our own when it came to those little extras that made life more than a daily grind of survival: birthday and Christmas presents, or going to the movies once a month, or buying my sister a nice dress 'once in a blue noon' to give a little variety to her wardrobe of ill-fitting hand-me-downs provided by the nuns at Saint Joseph's Convent, or buying a pound of the coffee that was my mother's only hedonistic vice (just two cups a day), or for the special holiday celebrations she used to make for us, like our long-awaited and much-appreciated Easter treat of 'Virginia Baked Ham' that she confected from two cans of Spam, a can of pineapple and a small bottle of maple syrup. Mother used to shape and score the Spam and arrange the rings of pineapple, then bake it so that it looked exactly like a miniature glazed ham, and we used to have yams with margarine and maple syrup, which was cheaper than sugar in those days because Vermont sugarbush owners were suffering badly from the Depression. It was my job to color the margarine, putting the white block of grease into a bowl, then sprinkling the orange coloring powder over it and mixing it in with a fork until it looked like butter...though it still smelled like grease. It would not be until the war came along and absorbed all the produce of America's Dairyland that the powerful butter lobby allowed precolored margarine onto the market.

These little life-enhancing pleasures could not be had on thirty-five cents a day per person, so extra money had to be made either by my mother or by me, shining shoes or running errands. And sometimes we just had to do without. But even when things seemed their grimmest, Mother used to assure my sister and me that one of these days our ship would come in and carry us far, far away from the slums to some Easy Street out West where we'd never again know the helplessness and hopelessness that is the worst part of poverty. When I was little, I envisioned Mother's metaphorical ship pulling in at one of the Hudson River piers, and my mother and sister and I would walk up the gangplank, and never look back. But one night we were sitting at the kitchen table and Mother was dreamily describing the splendid house we would live in one of these days, when I became rich and famous...and with a shock of ice at the pit of my stomach I suddenly realized that *I* was the ship my mother was waiting for, and it was *my* task in life to rescue us from Pearl Street. The weight of responsibility was staggering, and it was soon after this recognition that I began to lose myself in my story games.

Evening came as I sat on our stoop, thinking about the day we arrived in Albany with our boxes of stuff and our bits of battered furniture standing on the pavement for everyone to see. I got up from the dirty step that left a gritty mottle on the backs of my bare legs and went in. As I passed through our kitchen I dropped the nickel Mrs McGivney had given me into our Dream Bank, which was an empty box of Diamond kitchen matches we hid on the shelf under the real box of matches to baffle any thief who might come snooping around. The Dream Bank was money saved up from Mother's occasional part-time jobs and from my rounds of the bars and taverns downtown on Friday nights, carrying my hand-made shoeshine box on my shoulder and asking men if they wanted a shine (black and brown polish only, no two-tone shoes), which only the occasional drunk or some guy trying to impress a woman ever wanted, although sometimes they'd give me a nickel or even a dime to get rid of me. Like selling apples on the street corner, shining shoes during the Depression was a way of begging without total loss of dignity. The Dream Bank was supposed to be for special things that would bring color into our lives...we bought our second-hand Emerson radio with the cracked Bakelite case from it, paying twenty-five cents a week for over a year...but more often than not, it got emptied out for dull, soon-forgotten things, like food or clothes.

That evening after the last of my radio programs, I tugged myself back to reality and went to sit on the edge of my mother's bed to play two-handed 'honeymoon' pinochle with her, while my sister cut out and colored dresses for her paper dolls. To save the cost of new paper doll books, my mother would buy one then trace the clothes, tabs and all, onto paper she gleaned by cutting open brown paper bags and ironing them flat. In this way, one paper doll book did the service of half a dozen, lasting until the cardboard dolls got too limp from handling to stand up. My sister would spend hours drawing her own designs and coloring them in, then hanging them onto the cardboard dolls in a series of 'fittings', all the while twittering animatedly as she played both the dressmaker and the customer, usually a rich, spoiled, very demanding actress. Anne-Marie loved to create styles from what she saw in the movies or in magazines, but her games were burdened, and to some degree spoiled, by my mother's need to see everything we did in terms of its potential as the ship that was sure to come in and rescue us from Pearl Street. That summer, Mother was sure that Anne-Marie would become a famous costume designer for the movies and bring us all to Hollywood, just as she viewed my bookishness as a sign that I would become a university professor and take us all to live in some nice college town upstate.

...Or maybe a doctor. As my mother was often in and out of charity hospitals, I guess it's natural that her romantic ideal was The Doctor, just as her implacable enemies were The Nurses, particularly the impolite or dismissive ones who were, my mother was sure, jealous of the interest the doctors took in her unique 'lung condition', which never did receive a specific name like bronchitis or emphysema or pleurisy. So one of the ways she proposed for me to lure our Ship of Hope close enough to shore for us to slip on unnoticed, was by becoming a doctor. For one whole winter, I wove and unraveled games in which I was a famous doctor who somehow managed to save the lives of rich patients without having to come into physical contact with them. Even in my games I was too squeamish to deal with people on the level of blood and pus and...other liquids.

I always felt relieved when the honor, and responsibility, of bringing our ship in was bestowed upon Anne-Marie, if not as a famous fashion designer, then as a dancer. Even as a little kid, Anne-Marie loved music and used to sing and dance around to our Emerson. Some neighbor told my mother that she had talent, 'a born professional, believe you me!' and overnight it was decided that she would be the girl chosen to replace Shirley Temple, who, after all, couldn't remain young and cute forever, could she? The next day Mother put Anne-Marie's hair up in bouncy sausage curls like Shirley's (we called her by her first name now that we were all in show business). The sausage curls would help talent scouts from Hollywood to spot her, and the next thing you knew, we'd all be in sunny California, living, as my mother with her tin ear for idiom put it, 'on the flat of the land.'

...As differs from the slippery hillside?

But for this dream to come true, Anne-Marie would need to have tap-dancing lessons, and that was out of the question, because group classes cost $1.50 per session and she would need at least two a week, which would have been more than a third of the $7.27 we received from the welfare people. So the Shirley Temple dream was put on the shelf for a while, and we went back to daydreaming about the things we would own and do when I became a rich diagnostician, famous for my unique 'hands-off' technique.

Mother's bouts of illness always followed the same pattern. She would come down with a fever and she'd hack and cough, gasping for breath as she hung over the edge of her bed to help the phlegm 'come up', a process that tested the limits of my squeamishness. I would sit on the edge of her bed late into the night, trying to relieve her wracking cough by making and applying mustard plasters and by rubbing her back with Baume Bengué. (As a little kid I had marveled at how Dr Bengué managed to sign all those tubes. Each and every one! And later I was embarrassed at having been so gullible.) As she dozed, worn out by her ordeal, I would read library books she got for me because I was too young to have a card for the adult section. When I woke at dawn, having dropped off over my book, I would be sweaty and my clothes would be all twisted. The apartment would smell of mustard and eucalyptus, but usually her coughing would have abated and her temperature would have dropped enough that we could go to school. But the next evening the fever and coughing would begin again until the attack had run its course, leaving her wan and thin.

While I was shuffling the pinochle cards, I mentioned that I had made a nickel doing Mrs McGivney's shopping for her.

"Mrs McGivney?" Anne-Marie asked, shuddering at the thought of getting close to a crazy lady.

"How did you happen to run into Mrs McGivney?" my mother asked, and I told her how I was playing in the back alley, and she got my attention by tapping on her window with the nickel.

"And you went up to her apartment?" Anne-Marie asked.

"Sure."

"You weren't afraid?"

"Nah."

"You didn't go in, did you?"

"Sure. She gave me a cookie."

"And you *ate* it?"

I asked Mother about Mrs McGivney, but she didn't know much: just that she had lived in that same house for as long as anybody could remember. "It's nice of you to run errands for her," she said. "The poor old thing." She patted my hand. "You're a good boy, Jean-Luc." I had the feeling I was being pressured into visiting Mrs McGivney again. My mother had a good-hearted desire to do things for people, and when she couldn't manage it herself, she would volunteer me. I didn't like that, but I never complained because, as she said, I was a good boy. A resentful good boy.

The possibility of a game began to take shape in my mind. "Ah-h, do you know anything about Mrs McGivney's husband?" I asked casually, dealing out the cards.

Mother said she'd never heard anyone mention a Mr McGivney. She was pretty sure Mrs McGivney was a widow, or maybe an old maid that people just called 'Mrs' out of courtesy.

Glimpsing the intriguing possibility that I just might be the only person on the whole block who knew about Mr McGivney, I shifted the subject away from them and, with the part of my mind I didn't need to play cards, I began a story game of detective in which my followers and I helped radio's *Mr Keene: Tracer of Lost Persons* track down the mysterious Mr McGivney, famous hero. Meanwhile Anne-Marie sat on the floor, muttering complaints on behalf of her actress paper doll about how dull, dull, *dull* all the clothes in the shops were, then she gasped with astonished delight when Anne-Marie's newest 'creation' was revealed.

The next day after school I climbed over our back fence into the alley to play my new game. I sat in the doorway of a shed with my back to 232 and a book up in front of my face as though I were reading it, but in reality I was keeping watch on Mrs McGivney's windows, looking over my shoulder through a small mirror I had borrowed from my mother's handbag. I could see nothing through the lace curtains. My followers complained about being bored with this no-action game, but I reminded them that the stakeout was an important part of detective work. All right, so maybe it wasn't all that much fun! But it had to be done, and we were the ones chosen by Mr Keene to do it. They could quit, if they wanted to, but me, I'd stay at my post until hell froze over, if that's what it took! I turned my face away and refused to listen to their apologies, until Uncle Jim and my faithful Japanese valet, Kato, pleaded with me to forgive them for complaining. But my admiring young niece, Gail, continued to whine about this being a dull game, so finally Tonto and I (sometimes I borrowed Tonto from *The Lone Ranger*) began a careful examination of the ground, using a magnifying stick to look for clues. We found what might be part of a footprint, and there was a very interesting piece of broken glass, and a half-covered cat turd that Tonto said had been dropped since the last full moon, but that was all. Searching for

Lost Heroes was beginning to lose its zest as a game, and I was considering changing back to driving the Nazi Strong Troopers out of their bunkers with my blasting stick, when I heard three crisp clicks of metal on glass above me and I looked up to see Mrs McGivney smiling down from her window, holding a nickel up for me to see and motioning for me to come up. At first I felt bad: it's pretty shoddy detective work when the suspect spots the stakeout; but then I realized that maybe I could get into the apartment in the guise of a kid willing to run an errand, and do some undercover snooping around. I told my followers to wait for me there. I'd report back after I'd grilled the old dame.

If they got bored, they could blast Nazis.

Mrs McGivney met me at the top of the dark stairs and I followed her into the apartment, where her husband still sat straight backed at the window, looking out over the alley, his pale eyes empty She told me that she had forgotten to write 'pickle' on her list, and she knew that Mr McGivney would just love to have one of Mr Kane's big plump dill pickles.

I couldn't be sure to get a big plump pickle, because Mr Kane's practice was to roll up his sleeve and reach down into his barrel and give you the first one he touched. If it was little, he wouldn't drop it back into the brine and try for a bigger one because, as he explained, he'd pretty soon be left with nothing but little pickles, so people would go somewhere else to buy pickles where they had a chance of getting a big one. When I returned with an average-sized pickle wrapped in white butcher paper I found the little round table by the window set up with napkins and little plates and sugar cookies and milk for two. I told Mrs McGivney that I really couldn't accept the nickel she was trying to press into my hand, not for buying something that had only cost a nickel; but she said I had walked the same distance as if I'd been sent for a whole bagful of groceries, and therefore I had earned the nickel; but I said no, I hadn't really earned it so I couldn't take it; but she continued to hold it out, standing there with her head cocked and giving me one of those ain't-I-the-cutest-thing glances out of the corners of her eyes, the kind of look Shirley Temple used when she wanted to get her way. Adults thought Shirley was just too adorable for words, with her dimples and her pouting sideward glances, shaking her pudgy finger at people she thought were being naughty, but every red-blooded American boy yearned to kick her in the butt. Hard. In the end, I took the damned nickel. Jeez!

Those sugar cookies had something against me. They didn't get caught in the corner of my mouth this time, but I had just bitten one when Mrs McGivney asked me how my mother was, and when I tried to answer through the cookie, I coughed and sprayed crumbs and ended up feeling stupid and clumsy. Not much of a start for a slick detective.

I was curious to know what was wrong with Mr McGivney, but I didn't think I should ask. Instead, I told her I'd have to be getting home before long because my mother was sick.

"Still? Oh-h, I'm sorry to hear that."

"She's almost over it."

"Is she often ill, John-Luke?"

"Only my mother calls me John-Luke. Yes, I guess you'd say she's sick pretty often. She's got weak lungs."

"And you take care of her?"

"My sister helps."

"What about your father?"

My sister and I knew our father only from a photograph taken during their two-day honeymoon in New York City in 1929: a handsome man in a linen summer suit, his jacket held open by a fist on one hip to reveal his waistcoat, a straw hat tipped rakishly over one eye, his disarmingly boyish smile both knowing and mischievous. "I don't know anything about him."

"Oh...I see. Well...the important thing is to always be a good boy and take care of your mother."

I couldn't think of anything to say and Mrs McGivney seemed content just to sit there, smiling at me vaguely, her head tipped to one side. I glanced over at Mr McGivney, but he was still staring out the window. And I remembered a scary episode of *Lights Out* about zombies and the living dead.

I felt Mrs McGivney's eyes on me, so I turned to her quickly and asked her the first question that came to mind, so she wouldn't guess that I had been thinking her husband might be a zombie.

"Ah...ah...what was your nephew's name again?" I'd just ease into this interrogation. You know, like smart detectives do.

"My nephew?"

"The one who used to visit you, but doesn't anymore? You told me his name, but I forgot it." Out of the corner of my eye, I watched Mr McGivney. I'd never seen anyone sit so still before. Even his eyelashes didn't move. I watched to see if he'd blink.

"Do you mean Michael?"

"Michael? Who's Mi...Oh, yes. That's right. Michael." No, he didn't blink. Was it *possible* not to blink? I looked at his neck, then his wrist, but I couldn't see any throbbing of a pulse. It was almost as if...

"He's dead," she said with a sigh.

"What?" An icy wave rippled down my spine.

"Michael was killed in France. Poor, dear boy."

Oh...the nephew. I took a deep breath, and tried to get back to my interrogation. If the nephew died in France during the Great War, then he hadn't visited them for about twenty years. "Uh...Don't you have any other relations?"

She smiled a faint, sad smile. "No, no. My people are all gone, and Mr McGivney was an orphan, so no, we don't have any relations." She shrugged, and sudden tears filled her eyes but didn't fall. "No one at all."

"I'm...I'm sorry."

"Are you, John-Luke?"

"Only my mother calls me...Look, Mrs McGivney, I'd better be getting home." I rose from the chair and went to the door. "Thanks a lot for the cookie." Then I did something risky. I turned to Mr McGivney and said, "Good-bye, Mr McGivney."

"He can't hear you."

"Is he deaf?"

"No, no, he's not deaf." She opened the door for me. "Mr McGivney is a hero."

"Oh." I looked back at him. "...I see, well..." I left.

Uncle Jim, Gabby, Tonto, Jack, Doc, and the rest were in the alley, anxiously awaiting my return. "Michael!" I whispered hoarsely out of the side of my mouth. "Killed in the Great War. Write it down, and don't forget it!"

A week or so later, I was cutting through the back alley with an armful of books about birds that I was returning to the library. I no longer remember why I suddenly decided to make our ship come in by becoming a rich and world-famous ornithologist, but I wouldn't be surprised if I had just stumbled across the word 'ornithologist' and taken a fancy to it. It was a period when I lurched from one eventual profession to another, often on the basis of small clues to my destiny I found while reading the encyclopedia in the library. This idea of becoming an ornithologist lasted longer than most...a week or two, maybe. I had even begun my first book, *Meet the Warbler*, which I wrote *as a book*, with sheets of paper folded in half and stapled together so you could turn the pages and read my careful printing, which I justified right and left by spreading or cramming the final words. The cardboard cover had a crayon picture of a yellow warbler on it, and at the bottom: Written by Jean-Luc LaPointe, author. It was dedicated to 'my best friend, My Mother'. Working on the worn, fingernail-picked oilcloth of the kitchen table, carefully wiping the tip of my nib on the edge of the ink bottle after each dip to avoid blots, I painstakingly produced half a dozen pages of this seminal study, scrupulously altering a word here and there from my research sources to avoid being a copycat. Then something went wrong; I don't remember what. Maybe I misspelled a word, or miscalculated the room necessary to fit a word in, or made a blot. At all events, my effort to erase the error made a huge smear, and my attempt to erase the smear converted it into a hole, so I abandoned the profession of ornithologist and began to look for yet another career that might bring our ship into port. I found the aborted scholarly effort many years later, when I was going through my mother's things after her death. She had underlined the dedication: To my best friend, My Mother.

I had stopped in the alley to shift the heavy bird books from one arm to the other when three sharp clicks on a window above made me look up. Mrs McGivney was gesturing for me to come up. I indicated the books I was carrying and tried to mime the complicated message that I had to bring them to the library before it closed. But she just smiled, tilted her head in that little-girl way of hers, and beckoned me up, so I reluctantly returned the books to my apartment and went down the street, up her stoop, and up the staircase to the top floor.

Again the cookies and milk, again her wistful smiles, again Mr McGivney sitting perfectly still in the evening sunlight. But this time I was determined to uncover the facts about his heroism. I decided on a deceptively direct approach. "Mrs McGivney, how did Mr McGivney become a hero?"

She seemed pleased that I was interested enough to ask. "Mr McGivney was a soldier. He fought the Spanish in Cuba."

Now we were setting somewhere! A war hero! I had read something about the Spanish-American War, but I couldn't place it in history. It wasn't a war that inspired novels and movies, like the Civil War and the Great War, which we didn't think of as World War I because the trouble brewing in Europe wasn't yet called World War II. "When was that, Mrs McGivney?"

"He left to join his regiment the day after we were married. He looked so grand and handsome in his uniform!"

"Yes, but *when* was that?"

"I'll bet half the people on the block came to our wedding. It was up at Saint Joseph's. Do you know Saint Joseph's?"

Of course I knew Saint Joseph's. It was our parish church. Within two years, I would become an altar boy there, but at that time my only religious distinction was my ability to get through the Stations of the Cross faster than any other kid on the block. None of us would have dared to skip a single word of the five Hail Mary's we said at each stage of the Passion, nor would we have failed to bow our heads at the word 'Jesus', but we saw nothing wrong in saying the prayers as fast as we could, rising from one Station while still muttering nowandatthehourofourdeathamen, then sliding to the next on our knees and beginning its string of Aves before we'd come to a complete stop. And we would never have dreamed of failing to genuflect as we crossed the central aisle to get to the second half of the Stations, but we did it so quickly that sometimes a kid would get a bruised knee.

"Sure, I know Saint Joseph's." I made a mental note of where they got married. It didn't seem important just then, but in an investigation of this kind the smallest bit of information might turn out to be the key that unlocks...

"We stood there at the altar, him in his uniform and me in my mother's wedding dress. It was all so...beautiful. I was just seventeen, and Mr McGivney was twenty-one."

"And this was...when?"

"September. September weddings are good luck, you know."

"Yes, but what year! I mean...what year were you married, Mrs McGivney?"

"1898. That's when our boys went to Cuba."

1898. Another century! But then...let's see...if she was seventeen in 1898, and this was 1939, that would make her about sixty. That was pretty old, sure, but not impossible. Still, it seemed strange to me that this old man had been in the war *before* the Great War. The Great War had started when my mother was about *my* age, for crying out loud.

"So he was wounded while doing something brave in Cuba?" I asked.

"No, he wasn't wounded. I don't know exactly what happened. And, of course, he wasn't able to tell me after he came..." She shrugged. Then she continued in a distant voice, tenderly fingering the old memories. "I moved into this apartment right after I came back from seeing him off at Union Station. All the boys in uniform...bands playing...people waving and cheering. I made this little nest for Lawrence to come home to." She rose and started to walk around the room. "I ran up the curtains myself, and found furniture in second-hand stores, and my father helped me paint—he was a house painter, you know—and I chose this paper for the parlor...like the color?...Ashes of Roses, they called it." She took her husband's hairbrush from the sideboard and stood behind him, lightly brushing his white hair, while he sat, bathed in the westering sun that filtered through the lace curtain, looking gently out at nothing. "I wrote to Lawrence every day, telling him how our apartment was coming along. He wrote every day too, but his letters used to come in clumps—nine or ten at a time. That's how they do mail in the army. By clumps. Then...then his letters stopped coming, and there was no word for a long time—more than a month." She stopped brushing and looked down upon his fine hair. "I was so worried, so frightened. I asked Mr O'Brien if he could find out why the letters weren't coming through. Mr O'Brien the mailman? Then this letter came from the government, and I was afraid to open it. Everybody on the block knew I had this government letter because Mr O'Brien told them. My mother and father and sister came and asked what the news was. I told them I hadn't dared to open the letter. My father said I was acting silly; there was no point in putting it off. I might as well know one way or the other. But I didn't want to, so my father said he'd open it for me, but I said no! No, Lawrence was my husband, and it was my duty to open the letter. ...when I was ready."

Tears stood in her pale blue eyes, and her voice had gone tense and thin as she relived standing up to her old-country father, probably for the first time ever, telling him that Lawrence was her husband and she would open the letter when she was ready.

Then she blinked and looked across at me. "You know what? I believe that was the first time I said the word 'husband' aloud. I always called him Lawrence, of course. And we'd only been married four months, and I'd been busy fixing up our home, so I didn't see many people or get much chance to talk about him. My husband...husband." As she savored the word, she began brushing his hair again.

As I sat watching her brush his hair while he gazed, empty-eyed, at the roofscape beyond his window, his pale cheeks suddenly trembled! Then his lips drew back in an unconscious rictus that revealed long, yellow teeth, but the eyes remained dead.

A sharp breath caught in my throat. "Mrs McGivney...he just...he...!"

She nodded. "I know. He sometimes smiles when I brush his hair. Lawrence just loves having his hair brushed."

Well, it didn't look like a smile to me. It looked like a man in terrible pain hissing out a silent scream through his teeth. Then, with a slight quiver, his cheeks relaxed, the grin collapsed, and the teeth disappeared.

It was a moment before my heart stopped thudding in my chest. I wanted to get out of there, but a private investigator working for

Mr Keene, Tracer of Lost Persons doesn't turn tail. I drew a deep breath and asked, "What about the letter? It said he was a hero?"

"Yes, a hero."

"What had he done?"

"It was from his commanding officer. Captain Frances Murphy? He regretted having to tell me that Private Lawrence McGivney had contracted an illness in the performance of duty. He was in a military hospital and would soon be shipped home so he could get every care and comfort—I remember the exact words. Every care and comfort. That's what I've tried to give him. Captain Murphy went on to say that Private McGivney was a cheerful and willing soldier and that he was well liked by everybody in the regiment. Think of that! Everybody in the whole regiment."

Wait a minute. Being liked by everybody then getting sick didn't seem to me to be the stuff of heroism. But I didn't say anything.

And for a while Mrs McGivney didn't say anything either. She stood there brushing her husband's hair, a fond smile in her eyes as she seemed to reread the letter from his captain in her mind. Then she blinked and focused on me. "You know what I'd bet? I'd bet dollars to doughnuts you'd like another cookie. Am I right?" She looked at me out of the sides of her eyes in that coy Shirley Temple way.

"No, thanks, I—"

But she shook her finger at me. "Now don't you tell me you can't eat another cookie. A boy can always make space for another cookie."

As she went for the cookie jar on the counter I asked, "What was Mr McGivney sick with?"

"Brain fever," she said from the kitchen. "He ran this terribly high fever for days and days, lying in his bunk, sweating and shivering, sweating and shivering. The doctor at the veteran's hospital over in Troy—Dr French?—he told us that most men would have died." She brought back one of her little decorated plates with a cookie on it and set it before me. She still had the hairbrush in her hand. The long white hairs entangled in its bristles made me shudder. "Dr French said that Lawrence had fought a long, heroic battle against the fever, and survived!"

Oh. So *that* was the kind of hero he was.

"But..." She sighed. "It was the fever that left him...well, like he is."

"And you've taken care of him ever since?"

She smiled. "I wash him and feed him and...everything. He likes it when I brush his hair. He doesn't say anything, but I can tell by the way he sometimes smiles."

So she had lived alone with him up here for more than forty years, cleaning him and feeding him and brushing his hair. Forty years. So long that the existence of Mr McGivney had dropped out of the collective memory of the block, which now thought of Mrs Mc-Givney, when it thought of her at all, as just a shy old crazylady. But she thought of herself as the bride who had made a cozy nest for her soldier bridegroom.

I started to ask if she didn't get lonely, up here all day without anyone to talk—but a child's instinct for social danger stopped me short. Of course she got lonely! That's why I was sitting there, eating cookies. That's why she gave me a whole nickel for buying a pickle that only cost a nickel. I could feel the jaws of the trap closing. I should never have asked her about her husband. Now that I knew how lonely she was, I'd feel obliged to come whenever she tapped at her window with that nickel and sit with her and listen to her talk about how her husband liked it when she turned the gaslight on. Another responsibility in my life. And sometimes when I dared to glance over, he'd be grinning his silent scream of a smile. Right then and there I decided I'd have to be careful about going into the back alley too often. I'd stay out of the alley altogether for at least a week to get her used to not seeing me and depending on me.

It was during that week of emotional weaning that my life toppled out of balance because of an incident that might seem trivial: a tube burnt out in our radio. There wasn't enough money in the Dream Bank to buy a new one, so I had to do without the daily hour-long dose of reality-masking adventure programs essential to my well-being, just when all the stories were at their most exciting and dangerous moments—or so it seemed to me, and all because we didn't have the dollar and a quarter for a new tube.

Mother was furious because we'd only had the radio for three years. I reminded her that the radio was second-hand when we bought it, but she said we'd been robbed and she'd be goddamned if she was going to let them get away with it! She was sick and tired of everybody doing her in! Sick of it! Sick of it! Her famous French-'n'-Indian temper carried her out of her sickbed and down to the pawn shop on South Pearl where we had bought the radio. I went with her, trying to calm her down all the way, but she stormed into the shop and slammed the radio down on the counter. I winced at the possibility of additional damage. The old Jewish man who owned the pawnshop came out from the back room and I smiled a feeble greeting, embarrassed by the scene I knew would follow. He had been good enough to let us have the radio for nothing down and only a quarter a week because we looked like 'good people'. Mother said the tube had burned out and what was he going to do about it? He shrugged. "Tubes burn out, Missus. It happens." Well, she wanted him to put in a new one and right now, because her boy was missing his programs! The pawnbroker said he'd end up in the poorhouse if he gave everybody tubes every time they burnt out, but here's what he could do. He could give us a new tube for a quarter down and a quarter a week until it was paid for. How was that? Mother snatched up the radio and said, "To hell with you, mister! This is the last time we do business with your sort!" And she stormed out. I smiled weakly at the man. He thrust out his lower lip and shrugged, and I had to run to catch up with my mother, who was steaming up the street towards home, muttering in a rage that she'd be damned if her boy would go without his radio programs because of a lousy buck and a quarter. She'd get a job in some goddamned hash house to pay for the goddamned thing! I reminded her that she was still weak from her last lung attack, but she said she knew how much that radio meant to me, and that her kids had just as much right to listen to the radio as the kids of those snooty hoi polloi bastards! She'd get that tube, and she didn't care if it killed her! Then I got angry. So it would be my fault if she got sick and died and Anne-Marie and I ended up in the orphanage! I told her to forget the radio. I didn't want the radio! I was sick of the radio! I didn't care if I never heard a radio again! And we continued home, walking fast in the hot silence of a double rage.

When we slammed into our apartment, Anne-Marie knew things had gone badly. She shot me a scared look and begged Mother to get back into bed and rest so she wouldn't get sick again. Mother started on the "I'll be goddamned if my kids..." routine, but I interrupted her, saying that she didn't have to worry about the damned tube anymore. I had a plan for getting the money. She wondered what I had in mind, but I told her it was a secret. With one of her sudden mood lurches, she took Anne-Marie onto her lap and started rebraiding her hair. I went into the bathroom and sat on the edge of the tub, the only place in our little apartment that I could be alone to think. Now that I had succeeded in shutting Mother up, all I had to do was figure out some way to get the money.

When I came back into our kitchen I had a plan...well, sort of. Pretty soon Mother and I were playing pinochle while on the floor beside the bed Anne-Marie, dressmaker-to-the-stars, murmured soothing assurances to a flustered movie star who needed something really spectacular to wear that night. Mother's rages were brief, and I think she knew how stomach-wrenching they were for us because afterward she always tried to be lighthearted and fun. That night she told us about the wild stunts she'd got up to when she was a kid, and Anne-Marie and I laughed harder than the stories deserved, because we were so relieved.

A red-and-gold sign above the new store read: The Atlantic and Pacific Tea Company, which called up images from books I had read about the South Seas and planters and dangerous natives and tall-masted sailing ships. The new A & P was what they called a 'neighborhood store', not much bigger than an ordinary corner store, but its prices were a little lower and you were allowed to walk around and pick out your own cans and fruit and everything, which was novel and interesting at that time. Also, there were intriguing new foods, like maple syrup that came in a can shaped like a log cabin. You poured it out of the chimney and when it was empty you could use the cabin as a toy or a bank. And there were three kinds of coffee that they let you grind for yourself in machines where you could choose between drip grind and 'regular' and that coffee gave off so delicious an aroma that you closed your eyes and just breathed it in. The most expensive coffee was called Bokar, a name redolent of Africa so it was right that the bag should be black; the middle-priced one, Red Dot, came in a yellow bag with a red dot; we always bought the cheapest coffee, Eight O'Clock, which came in a red bag. I used to wonder if the Bokar tasted as good as it smelled. But then, no coffee tastes as good as it smells, an apt metaphor for the gap between anticipation and realization. The cheaper prices and wider selection attracted everyone for blocks around, but you couldn't charge things there so, in the end, Mr Kane's slate won out over the A & P's novelty and economy, and it closed within the year.

The morning after our Emerson blew its tube, I was standing outside the A & P with my sister's battered old cart and a cardboard sign with red crayon letters that informed shoppers of my willingness to bring their groceries home for a nickel. That first day and the next, half a dozen old ladies used my services. I walked home beside them, pulling their bags of groceries in Anne-Marie's cart, chatting in the polite, cheerful way I thought might inspire them to tip me a couple of cents in addition to my nickel, but none of them did. And every one of those women lived blocks and blocks away from the A & P, and I had to lug their bags up to apartments on the upper floors, leaving the cart in the first-floor hallway so nobody would steal it. I pondered the rotten luck of *every single one* of my customers being an old woman who lived far away and on the top floor. And each of them too cheap to give a friendly, smiling guy a tip. What were the odds? It took me awhile to work out that this wasn't a matter of singularly bad luck. Only women who were so poor they couldn't afford to give a tip would go blocks from their homes to save a few pennies at one of the new supermarkets; and only those who lived on the upper floors would be willing to part with a nickel to have their stuff carted home and carried up to their door. Still, after two days I had earned thirty cents towards the tube, even if my sister did complain bitterly that I'd worn her red crayon down to a nub making my sign, so she couldn't make any red clothes for her paper dolls, just when red was all the rage, and her movie star customers were complaining that...

Oh, shut up, why don't you?

You shut up!

You shut up?

Copy cat, eat my hat!

Oh, shut up!

No, you shut up!

(From the bedroom) *Both of you shut up!*

The next morning I arrived at the A & P to find another boy standing there with a wagon and sign—a bigger boy with a bigger wagon and a bigger sign. And he wasn't even from our block! Well...we had words. He said he had as much right as I did to be there because I didn't own the sidewalk, so who the hell did I think I was to...

I hit him while he was still blabbing and got two more shots in while he was wondering if this was a fight or not, and then we really went to Fistcity, rolling around on the pavement, him mostly on top because he was bigger, but me getting some pretty good face shots in from below, but the manager of the A & P came out and snatched us around by our collars for a while, then he told us that if we didn't behave ourselves he'd send for the cops. When I tried to explain that I had been there first, he told me that he'd seen me start the fight. Of course I started the fight! A smaller kid has to get his shots in first or he doesn't stand a chance. Jeez! But I promised not to fight anymore, so this copy-cat interloper and I ended up standing on opposite sides of the store's door, glowering at one another until some old lady came out carrying groceries, then we'd try to out-smile and out-nice one another. I was at a disadvantage because my smile was sort of one-sided because I had a split lip. It was a scorcher of a day, and time passed slowly standing there in the sun, especially since I got only one customer that day, and that only because this other kid was away on a delivery. I could see what was going on in the women's heads. They didn't like having to pick one kid and leave the other behind, so most of them carried their own bags home, and the others chose this bigger kid because they didn't want to make a skinny little kid lug those bags all that way. Yeah, sure! Give money to the big healthy kid, and let the skinny little one go without! That makes lots of sense, you stupid old...

That night as I walked home, hot and sticky, dragging the wagon behind me, I was too tired and disheartened to remember to avoid the shortcut through the back alley. I knew I should go straight home, but I wanted desperately to play some kind of story game for a little while because without my nightly dose of radio, there was nothing to carry me away me from my life and refresh my soul. Then too, I wasn't all that eager to arrive at home with a split lip and only a nickel to show for a day's work. I was always a lot better at playing the modest hero than the brave failure.

There was only one old-fashioned streetlight in the back alley that hadn't been slingshot out. Its dim, dirty light fell at a sharp angle over the façades of the abandoned stables, texturing them and leaving pockets of deep shadow in the entranceways...a perfect setting for scary games. I slipped into a space between a shed and a stable, one side of my face lit and the other in shadow, knowing how scary I must look as I whispered to my followers that there just *had* to be a rational explanation for the Murders in the Back Alley. "I shouldn't be a bit surprised to learn that Professor Moriarty had a hand in this, Watson." (A blend of clipped speech and Peter Lorre nasality did for my English accent.) I told them that the only way to discover the insane killer was to expose ourselves to the same dangers that those poor, bloody, axe-chopped, heads-ripped-off, faces-bashed-in women...

...I just about pissed myself when that sharp tap-tap-tap on the window made my voice squeak and sent my followers vanishing into the darkness, leaving me to face the danger alone. I looked up to see Mrs McGivney beckoning to me, and her husband silhouetted in the other window by the soft gaslight of their parlor. I *knew* I should have gone straight home! Drawing a peeved sigh, I inserted a mental book-mark into my game so I could remember where I was next time, and I trudged to the end of the alley, around past my own stoop, where I stashed Anne-Marie's wagon in the basement, then down to 232, and up the stairs, the air getting thicker and hotter with every floor I climbed. It was really hot in the McGivney top-floor apartment directly under the lead roof, and their gaslighting made it hotter yet. That was the only time in my life I experienced the effect of gaslight, which was softer and more golden than electric light and didn't seem to descend from the ornate gas fixtures on the wall, but rather to come from within the things and people lit, making them sort of glow with an inward radiance...like I imagined life must be for people in the movies, or rich people.

With an edge of grievance in her voice, Mrs McGivney asked me where I'd been the last few days, and I explained that our radio had blown a tube and I had been trying to earn money to replace it. She made a tight little nasal sound, like that was no excuse, so I curtly asked what she wanted. It was late and Mr Kane's was closed. But it turned out that she just wanted to give me a glass of milk and some of those cookies that 'little boys love so much'. I didn't tell her that this particular boy would rather be allowed to pursue his game than be dragged up there to spend time with a boring old lady and a scarecrow. Instead, I sat across from her and nibbled grumpily. But she just smiled at me, then looked over at her husband and signed with satisfaction, as though everything was all right, now that we were all back together again.

I noticed that when she drank her milk she looked into the glass, like little kids do. And that's when it struck me that, like her husband, she was strangely young. She had white hair, sure, but her skin was smooth and her eyes bright. It was as if, living as they did, without hopes or fears or work or play, time had flowed lightly over them, without eroding their features, and they had remained eternally young and oddly...ghost-like.

As I left, she pressed a nickel into my hand. I protested that I hadn't done anything to earn it, but she just squeezed my hand around it, so I left thinking how nice people can be worse than mean ones, because you can't fight back against nice people.

I found my mother and sister sitting on our front stoop to get a breath of cooler air, and I joined them. I told them about the McGivneys, and Mother was surprised to learn that there was a Mr McGivney. Anne-Marie rubbed the goose bumps that had risen on her arms at the thought of sitting in the same room with a crazy man who just stared out the window all the time. I told her he wasn't crazy, just sort of...well, damaged, but she said damaged men were just as scary as crazy ones, and she didn't care how many nickels they gave me. Mother said I shouldn't accept money unless I did some chore to earn it. Otherwise it was like accepting charity, and La-Pointes didn't do that; they worked for everything they got. But she was glad I'd made some new friends, and she was sure I'd be a big help to them...poor lonely old people. I almost told her that I resented being made to feel responsible for them, but I didn't because I was afraid she'd realize how often I felt the same resentment about having to get us off Pearl Street some day.

The next morning, there was a *third* boy outside the A & P, and he had a brand-new cart and a sign with professional-looking lettering that offered to carry groceries for 4¢. You could tell from his clothes that he wasn't poor, just a regular kid lucky enough to have a new cart and somebody—probably a father—to help him paint his sign and to advise him about undercutting the competition. I could see right off that offering to carry the groceries for four cents was a smart scam, because most of the women would give him a nickel, and they wouldn't ask for their penny change back because that would make them seem too petty; so he'd get the job by underbidding us, then he'd end up getting as much as we did. I'll bet his father was a salesman with a slick line. Well, I drew this new kid aside and had a little talk with him, explaining that there wasn't enough business for three kids, and this had been my idea in the first place. Then I put on a concerned look and told him that I was worried about how sad his mother would feel if he came home with no front teeth and his fancy wagon all kicked in and— Out of the corner of my eye I could see the manager watching me from inside the store, so I just pointed at the middle of the rich kid's chest and skewered him with squinted-up eyes, which on my block meant 'You're standing real close to the edge, kid!' then I swaggered back to my battered old cart.

But he stayed, and I didn't get a single customer that day, bracketed as I was by a bigger competitor and a more attractive one. I stuck it out until the A & P closed that night. But I didn't bother to come back again. What was the use?

That Friday our weekly $7.27 welfare check came, so we were able to buy the tube, although it meant having potato soup every night that week, rather than the usual two. But I liked potato soup and still do, despite the gallons of it I consumed as a boy. That evening I stood in front of the Emerson on one leg in a narcotic state of deep soul-comfort, my head bowed, my eyes half-closed, totally absorbed in the exciting worlds of *Jack Armstrong, The Green Hornet,* and *The Lone Ranger, Masked Rider of the Plains.* The world was right again.

After my sister and I did the supper dishes, the three of us sat in the front room, listening to Friday night's run of suspense programs. We always turned off the lights and listened in the dark, with only the faint yellow glow of the radio's dial because it made the stories deliciously spooky on such programs as *Suspense* and *The Inner Sanctum*, and *The Whistler*, a man who walked by night and knew many things. He knew strange tales hidden in the hearts of men and women who had stepped into the shadows. Yes, he knew the nameless terrors of which they dared not speak!

I awoke one morning to the chilling realization that summer vacation was almost over and, what with trying to earn extra money and spending time up at the McGivneys', I hadn't gotten enough good out of it...sort of like a Popsicle that melts while you're obliged to talk politely to a nun, and you don't get to suck it white before it falls off the stick. Next year I would be ten, and I felt that advancing to a double-digit age was significant...the end of childhood, because once you get into two digits, you're there for the rest of your life. And another thing: all my life it had been nineteen-thirty something, and nineteen-thirty had a solid, comfortable sound, but next year would be nineteen-*forty*. And that 'forty' looked funny when you wrote it down and felt awkward in your mouth when you said it. Everything was changing. I was growing up before I was finished with being a kid! This would be my last summer before I had to give up my story games and start in earnest doing what I could to get us off Pearl Street.

All right, I accepted that bringing my mother's damned ship into port was my responsibility. But I couldn't take care of Mrs McGivney, too. I intended to play as hard as I could for the next two weeks until school and my burdensome adulthood started, and that meant I needed all my time for myself, for my games, for listening to the radio, for wandering the streets in search of mysteries and adventures, and there just wouldn't be any time to waste sitting around with the McGivneys.

I avoided the back alley for a week, during which I revisited one by one all the story games I had ever played so I would never forget the exhilarating fun of them. That week I fought off Richelieu's swordsmen, ran cattle rustlers off the streets of Albany once and for all, and led an expedition to the Elephant Graveyard, where we almost lost Reggie and Kato. On Sunday, I changed into play clothes right after six o'clock mass and went off to spend the morning playing one of the best games of all: Foreign Legion, which involved not drinking anything after supper the day before so I'd be good and thirsty by the time I had crossed Broadway towards the river, passed through the tangle of still-sleeping all-Negro streets that was called Blacktown, and scrambled over the high wooden wall of an abandoned brickyard that had huge piles of sand and gravel. I staggered through the endless sand, stumbling and slipping as I climbed the pile, blinded by the glaring sun, suffering terribly from thirst made worse by the fact that I was weakened by half a dozen spear wounds inflicted by perfidious Arabs whom I had always treated well, unlike some of my brother Legionnaires. My throat was parched, and I muttered to myself that the pools of icy water I saw all around me were only mirages. Must...keep...going. I wanted nothing more than to give up the struggle and just lie down and let death overwhelm me, but I couldn't. No, I must go on! There was a standpipe with a spigot by a watchman's hut, and it was part of the game to hold the vision of that cool, clear water in my mind as I crawled on my hands and knees over the piles of sand and gravel, dragging my wounded leg behind me (sometimes both legs) but determined to carry the message from what was left of my decimated company besieged in the fly-blown outpost of Sidi-bel-Abbès to the colonel of the regiment stationed at our headquarters in the noisy, bustling city of Sidi-bel-Abbès. (All right, so I knew the name of only one desert city! Is that a crime?) By taking the least direct path possible and weaving my painful, half-conscious way over the great central sandpile again and again, I could drag the game out to past noon, by which time my lips were crusty and my tongue thick with thirst. When at last I arrived at the standpipe, I put my head under it, ready for the blissful shock of its cool dousing, my fingers almost too weak to turn the rusty spigot. In a hoarse voice I cried out to Allah to give me strength. Give me strength! And I gave the spigot a desperate twist with the last of my fading strength...

...but no water came out. They'd cut off the water since last summer! Anything to spoil a game! Jeez!

By the time I got back to my block, I was *really* thirsty, so I cut through the back alley to get to my apartment as quickly as I could.

Three sharp clicks of a coin against the window above me... Oh no! And there she was, gesturing for me to come up. Nuts! Nuts! Double nuts!

But this time it would be different. As I trudged glumly up the dark stairs of 232, I confected a plan to free myself of this lonely old lady and her loony husband: I would mope and be rude, so she wouldn't want my company any longer. But first...

"Could I have a glass of water, Mrs McGivney?"

"Why, of course, John-Luke!"

I gulped it down, rather than sipping it slowly, savoring the life-saving sweetness of it, as I would have done in the dramatic last scene of the Foreign Legion game, if those idiots hadn't shut off the water!

"My goodness, you *were* thirsty. Want some more?"

"No, thank you." It was hard to remember to be rude.

"You're sure?"

She sat across from me at the little table set for two. "Here, before I forget it." She placed a nickel beside my napkin.

"No, I don't want it," I said, pushing it back to her.

She cocked her head. "Don't try to tell me that a little boy can't find something to do with a nickel."

"No, my mother said I wasn't to take money from you unless I did an errand or something in return."

"Oh, I see. Well...you just put the nickel in your pocket."

"No, I don't want it."

"Now, you just keep it until I think of something you can do later." She pushed the nickel back to me.

I didn't touch it.

She held out the plate of cookies to me, and I lowered my head and stared at the tabletop. Finally she put one on my plate. I didn't look at it.

"Would you like to wash up, John-Luke?" she asked.

"Only my mother calls me that."

"What?"

"Only my mother calls me that."

"Oh...I'm sorry. I...Well, would you like to wash up? You look a little...dusty." She smiled sweetly.

I touched my forehead and felt the grit of the sand through which I had crawled all the way back to Sidi-bel-Abbès. Having someone who wasn't my mother tell me that my face was dirty embarrassed me intensely—something left over from the time two young, syrup-voiced social workers swooped down on our apartment to see if my mother was taking proper care of us. They asked Anne-Marie and me if any men had been sleeping at our house, and one of them made me stand in front of her while she checked my hair for nits. I was so outraged that I snatched my head away from her and told her to go to hell, and the two do-gooders made little popping sounds of surprise and indignation and said they'd never seen such a badly brought up child. After they left, Mother told me that I had to be polite to social workers, or they'd write up a bad report, and the three of us would have to run away to avoid their taking us kids away from her. So it was all right for her to lose her temper and give social workers hell, but I couldn't do it. Was that it?

I got up and went over to the McGivney's kitchen sink. In the little mirror over it, I could see that my face was dirty and streaked with rivulets of sweat. I was embarrassed, so I snatched the faucet on angrily, and the water came squirting out of a little flexible thing at the end of the spigot and splashed onto my pants, making it look as though I had pissed myself, and then I was *really* embarrassed. To cover my discomfiture I quickly soaped up my hands and scrubbed my face hard, then I splashed water into my face, but I couldn't find anything to wipe it on, so I just stood there at the sink, dripping, the soap stinging my eyes, like some sort of helpless thing. Like her husband. Jeez!

Then I felt her press a towel into my hand. I scrubbed my face dry and sat back at the table, hard, *very angry*.

"You're not going to eat your cookie, John-Luke?"

"I don't want it."

"Suit yourself. But they're sugar cookies. Your favorites."

"Oatmeal cookies are my favorites. The kind my mother makes."

"...Oh." There was hurt in her voice. "I just thought you might be hungry."

"My mother feeds us real well."

"I didn't mean to suggest...I'm sure she does."

Actually, I was still thirsty enough to down that milk in two glugs, but I sat there in silence, frowning down at the little embroidered tablecloth I supposed she had put on just for me.

She made a little sound in the back of her throat, then she said, "Poor boy: You're unhappy, aren't you."

"No, I'm just...awful busy." I meant, of course, with my games, trying to get my fill of games before school started and I became two digits old and had to start looking for work, but she took it a different way.

"Yes, I was talking to Mr Kane, and he told me how you're always doing odd jobs to help your mother out. She must be very proud to have a good boy like you."

I said nothing.

"I hope you don't mind if I ask, but...your father, John-Luke. Is he dead?"

I don't know what made me say what I said then. A desire to shock her, I guess. "No, he's not dead. He's in prison." It would be more than twenty years before I discovered that I had unknowingly told her a truth that my mother had kept from us.

She drew a quick breath. "Oh! Oh, I'm sorry. I didn't mean to pry. I was just...oh, that's too bad. You poor boy." She reached towards me, but I twisted away.

"No, we're proud of him! They put him in prison because he was a spy against the Redcoats! They're going to hang him next month, but he doesn't care. He's only sorry that he has but one life to give for his country!"

"...Wh...what?"

"Look, I'm going home." I started to rise.

"No, please don't go." She stood up and hugged me to her. I turned my head aside, so as not to have my nose buried in her soft stomach. "You poor, poor boy. You've had lots of troubles and worries in your young life, haven't you? No wonder you're all nervous and worked up. But I know what will calm you and make you feel better." She opened a drawer and took out the brush that had white hairs trailing from the bristles, her crazy husband's hair, and she started towards me. I jumped up, snatched the door open, and plunged clattering down the stairs, the stair rail squeaking through my gripping hand.

By the Labor Day weekend that marked the beginning of school, I had squeezed the last drops of adventure and danger out of that summer's game of single-handedly defending Pearl Street and, by extension, the world from Nazi invasion. As a sort of farewell tour, I was mopping up the last of the Strong Troopers at the end of our back alley, where I had not been since the day I had fled down Mrs McGivney's stairs to avoid the touch of that repulsive hairbrush, the squeaking handrail rubbing the skin off the web between my thumb and forefinger and leaving a scab that took forever to heal because I kept popping it open by spreading my hand too widely: a child's curious fascination with pain.

Wounded though I was in both legs, one shoulder, and the web between my thumb and first finger, I managed to crawl from the shelter of one stable doorway to the next, making the sound of ricocheting bullets by following a guttural *krookh* with a dying *cheeooo* through my teeth, as Nazi bullets splintered the wood close beside my head with a tap-tap-tap sound of a coin against glass—what? I almost looked up, but I converted the glance into a frowning examination of the space around me, searching for snipers, as I didn't want her to know I had heard her summons. Satisfied that there were no Nazi snipers on the rooftops, I made an intense mime of drawing a map on the ground. Again she tapped her three urgent taps, and I could imagine her looking down on me. I hunched more tightly over my map. She tapped again, but this time there were only two clicks, then she stopped short. That missing click told me that she suddenly *knew* I could hear her, and I was ignoring her on purpose. I kept my head down, knowing that if I looked up I would see her there, her eyes full of sadness and recrimination.

Miserable, and angry for being made to feel miserable, I pretended to see an enemy soldier down the alley. I shot at him with my finger then ran off in pursuit until I was out of Mrs McGivney's sight.

For the rest of the time we lived on Pearl Street, I kept out of the back alley that had been the principal arena for my story games. A couple of times I caught a glimpse of Mrs McGivney scuttling across to Mr Kane's late in the evening, but I always avoided her. I never saw her hero husband again.

That next week I went back to school: a new grade, a new teacher, a tough old overdressed orange-haired bird of the no-charm, no-nonsense school who saw through the indifferent, wise-guy posturing I had assumed for self-defense. She arranged for me to take a series of IQ and aptitude tests that led to special tutoring and, in time, to a pattern of scholarships and an academic career that eventually carried us out of Pearl Street. My mother's ship came in at last.

I am now considerably older than Mrs McGivney was when I first responded to the rap of her nickel against the window. For many years I have lived and worked in Europe, as far away in space, time, and culture from Pearl Street as one can be this side of death. And yet, on those nights when the black butterflies of doubt and remorse flutter through a sleepless *nuit blanche*, I still sometimes hear that broken-off summons, those two clicks, and the recriminating silence that followed them; and my throat tightens with shame as I remember the lonely old woman that I didn't have time for because I was too busy trying to save myself.

SIR GERVAIS IN THE
ENCHANTED FOREST

Know you that in those distant days the good King Arthur did entreat his knights of the Table Round to sally forth in quest of the Holy Grail for the benefit of their souls, the glory of his reign, and the serenity of the court, which would be much enhanced by the absence of those feisty brawlers. But although each of Arthur's doughty warriors was eager to earn Man's acclaim for lofty deeds and God's forgiveness for base ones by devoting himself to the search for this holiest of relics, there was no general haste to fulfill the king's behest because, the shameful truth be known, not one of those noble warriors was certain in his heart of hearts exactly what a *grail* was...save, of course, that it was a holy thing and the right and proper object of quests. But none durst confess his ignorance for fear of ridicule, and because no other knight ever admitted doubt in this matter, each assumed himself to be alone in his shameful want of learning. Therefore, each would nod and suck his teeth knowingly upon any mention of the Grail, and when he glanced about and saw all his fellows nodding and sucking, his suspicion was confirmed that the nature of a grail was known by all save himself.

Now of all that high-born company, none was prouder of his ancestry than Sir Gervais, and for this reason he felt the shame of ignorance most sorely of all. Twice had he gone forth in search of fame and recognition, but never had he come across a grail...not to his knowledge, anyway. What most galled him was the thought that he might have seen the Holy Grail, but passed it by unknowingly, and thus lost the credit for finding it. So he confected a cunning stratagem to ferret out the exact nature, function, and shape of a grail so that he might recognize it should he come across one in the course of some future quest. One evening, as all that noble host sat around the Table, Sir Gervais said, in the most off-hand tone imaginable, "Ah...tell me, fellow knights, have you ever considered what you might do with a grail, were there one sitting upon this table at this very moment? I speak not, of course, of the Holy Grail, but rather of your common, everyday sort of grail."

"Huh? What? A grail? Here? On the table?" asked Sir Bohort, whose father's loin-strength had gone so totally into making his well-muscled body that nothing was left over for his brain.

Immediately did the proud Sir Gervais grow pale with the fear that a grail might be too vasty a thing to be placed upon a table, and that his ignorance was in danger of being revealed. "Nay, did I say a table?" he asked, laughing at his slip. "I meant to say a *courtyard*. Oft and again do men—even men of impeccable lineage—confuse tables with courtyards, for are they not both...ah...things?"

"Yea, but tell me, Sir Gervais," asked Sir Gawain, hoping himself guilefully to discover just what a grail was, "why wouldst thou put this grail of thine in a courtyard? And just what wouldst thou do with it, once thou hadst it there?"

Now did Sir Gervais hotly rue that he had introduced the matter and opened himself to accusations of stupidity—if not impiety. "And why should I *not* put a grail in a courtyard, brother knight, so long as it be a proper courtyard for the receiving of a grail? Prithee, why art thou so quick to challenge my understanding of the nature of things?"

"Nay, brother of the Table Round, wax not huffy. I seek only to understand how thou intendest to use...or wear...or admire...or perhaps punish?...this grail, once thou hast it in thy courtyard."

"Use? Wear? Admire? Punish?" asked Sir Gervais, now confused and ashamed, and therefore sore wroth. "Thinkest thou I be the low-born sort of fellow who must use and wear and punish his grail just because he has it in his courtyard? May not a man of highest parentage and pedigree put a grail into his courtyard without having any such base designs upon it? Challenge me one word further in this matter, sirrah, and thou shalt feel my boot far up thy fud, thou base, French-loving, dung-munching, host-spitting, sheep-foining bastard!"

"...French-loving? *French-loving!* O-o-oh, now has thou brought thine o'er-bred, chinless face into jeopardy from my steel-gaunted fist, thou scrofulous, leprous, lecherous, stenchy, title-licking, back-stabbing, hag-swiving..."

...Allow me to draw a curtain over this scene before it descends into incivility. No doubt the perceptive reader wonders at Sir Gawain's last epithet and asks why a knight so proud of rank and breeding as Sir Gervais would go about swiving hags, for scant is the joy and meagre the reclaim to be gained from applying one's love-tool to ancient crones.

The explanation of this slight flaw in Sir Gervais's otherwise irreproachable gentility is to be found in the true and instructive tale of Sir Gervais in the Enchanted Forest, wherein the attentive reader will learn how that noble knight earned the title by which history remembers him: Gervais! Swiver of Crones!

Know ye that it was upon a soft and fog-laden morning in autumn that bold Sir Gervais, bedecked in his richest armour, rode forth from Camelot in quest of the Grail, and of such encounters as might add to his reputation and his purse. Nor was it long before he found himself deep within a dark and dire forest where his stallion's hoof made no sound upon a thick mat of leaves as man and mount glid past ghosts of trees that emerged from the mists before, then were swallowed up by the mists behind. Overhanging boughs brushed and hissed upon his helmet, the plumes of which drooped limp with the damp.

Now, Sir Gervais was a brave warrior of lofty blood, so we are obliged to assume that if his eyes darted from side to side, it was only to seek out the adversary, and if he whistled thinly and dryly, it was only to announce his presence to any foe who might dare to face him, and if his palms sweated, it was only because they itched to grasp his sword in combat, and when he suddenly decided to turn his horse and quit that dark, dank, ominous forest, it was only to go in search of yet greater and more dangerous adventure; and surely the yelp that escaped from his throat was a sort of war cry, when he suddenly espied an ancient crone of surpassing laidliness standing beside the path, beckoning with a gnarled finger.

His voice tight in his throat, Sir Gervais addressed the hag, saying, "How now, beckoning crone of surpassing laidliness, canst direct me out of this forest? I wit thee rare gifted in the craft of telling directions, for one of thine eyes doth scan to the left whilst t'other scans to the right in such wise that their paths do intersect some few inches before thy hooked nose."

And the crone did cackle with pleasure and turn her face aside modestly. "Nay, good knight, think not to weaken the barriers of my chastity with cozening praise, for I do perceive that thou hast penetrated the mystery of this enchanted forest."

"Sayest what?"

"Nay, feign not, shrewd seducer. Well dost thou know that in this enchanted forest all things appear the very opposite of what they are."

"How's that?"

"Nay, nay, noble knight. Do not pretend ignorance."

Sir Gervais stood stiff in the saddle, his dignity bristling. "Thou dost accuse me false, rank hag! Ignorance is no pretence with me! And woe betide the base defamer who claims it so!"

"Be not wroth, good knight. For know ye that even *my* senses are sometimes bemused, though I have long lived here. Forgetting for a moment the other-seeming enchantment of this place, I thought at first that I was addressing a scrawny beggar astride a pig, his knees scrubbing the muddy track, and his feet dangling behind."

The proud knight looked about for the person thus limned.

" 'Tis of thee I speak, fair—if ugly-seeming—knight."

"Art thou plotting to get thy scabby head bashed in, ugly—*and* ugly-seeming—hag, in the hope that a bashing might work improvement on thine appearance?"

"Nay, stay thy wrath and be informed! What I have described is only thine image as it *appears* to be, here in a forest where all things do seem the very opposite of what they truly are. Seeing thee ugly, trembling, deformed, puny, and graceless, I know that thou must, in fact, be a brave knight, puissant and fair of visage."

"Crush-m'-cullions if thou hast not limned me to the last jot!"

"And I have no doubt, brave warrior, that my own grace, my delicacy, and my blushing beauty have, in thine enchanted eyes, taken on some other appearance."

"They have, Madam. Oh, indeed they have!"

Upon hearing this, the crone (or seeming crone) drew a great whimpering sigh, and a tear slowly toiled its way down the ravines of her wrinkled face to drip, at last, from the tip of her warty nose. This long and tortuous passage gave Sir Gervais season to ponder what mysterious thing had befallen him in this Forest of Enchantment. He did conclude that there stood before him a deserving target for amorous dalliance, provided, of course, that her seemingly low rank was, in fact, as high as her seemingly ugly aspect was, in fact, beauteous. For know you that Sir Gervais would not—indeed, could not—bring himself to foin a woman, however lush and frick, if she were not of noble birth, for he possessed the overweening pride of his class in such full measure that his member shrank from the debasing task of swiving low wenches, however toothsome, but it ever stood to pert attention in the presence of any woman of high title, however loathly, sere, or harsh-featured.

"But I forget form and duty," the seeming hag said, her tear having completed its lenghty course. "Surely thou art weary from thine adventures and wouldst share the comforts of my castle."

"Thou art most gracious, fair maiden."

"Princess, actually."

"Princess? Princess? Oh, forgive me, desirable Princess! May I offer thee to ride behind me?"

"Gladly would I, though I have never sat astride a pig."

"A pig?"

"Oh, la, what am I saying? Even I do sometimes err and accept the evidence of mine eyes, though I know better."

And with this, the seeming crone scrambled up behind Sir Gervais, hitching her skirts high and wrapping her seemingly scrawny and scabby legs about his.

As they rode along, Sir Gervais did exercise his courtly speech, saying, "Knowing, as now I do, that in this forest all things are the reverse of what they seem, fair Princess, I trow that the enticing bouquet rising from thee—this seeming stench—must, in fact, be the very essence of all spices rare and flowers fragrant."

The maiden blushed and wrapped herself closer to him, and his eyes did smart with the beauty of the moment.

Not far along, they came upon a fetid bog on the verge of which a crude hovel sagged upon rotting beams.

The maiden laughed a seeming cackle and said, "See how my castle's drawbridge is down, as though in anticipation of thine entrance? Oh my, I hope thou dost not take this to be a metaphor for my highly prized and well-defended chastity, you naughty, naughty, naughty man!" And with her bony knuckle she delivered him several coy knocks on the helmet that made his ears to ring.

"Drawbridge?" he said in confusion. "Castle? Ah! Of course! Know ye, Princess, that upon first glance I mistook your drawbridge for a slippery log laid across a sluggish swamp!" And Sir Gervais did laugh heartily at his error.

It became evident that thoroughbred horses, no less than highborn men, were victims of the forest's enchantment, for in attempting to cross the drawbridge, Sir Gervais's noble steed slipped as it might have slipped from a narrow log, and precipitated both riders into the moat, out of which they clawed their sputtering way, and beside which Sir Gervais stood at last, stenchy bog-water draining from his armour.

"I fear thou wilt attrap thy death of cold," the lovely princess said. "Quickly into the castle, and out of that damp armour. A good roasting before my vast hearth will regain thy temper."

Soon the knight stood beneath the soaring vaults of the castle's great hall that the uninitiated might have mistaken for a low, filthy chamber with rush-strewn dirt floor below and rotting thatch above. He shivered, all nude, before the roaring hearth that had the superficial aspect of a feeble twig fire the smoke of which coiled and recoiled beneath the roof in search of chinks and gaps.

Know you that the maiden had, for the good of her health, doff'd her sodden garments and now stood before him clothed as Eve had been when she harkened to the snake's twisted counsel.

"My God!" the knight cried. "How comely thou must, in reality, be! For if each perfection doth appear a blemish, then thou art Beauty itself, from thy balding pate to thy gnarled toes! I can no longer contain my ardour! Have at, then!"

At great length and with much invention did they tangle and roil among the seeming sodden rushes of the great hall's floor in every use and pose of amour. When finally exhausted and empty of essence, Sir Gervais rolled off, panting and clutching at a rag to cover his shivering nudity withal, while the seemingly foul crone crooned and sighed her affection as she strove in many coy and clever ways to reaffirm his lance for the lists of love.

For a year and a day, Sir Gervais languished in this enchanted castle, his body nourished by luscious joints of stag and boar that had the delusive appearance and taste of nettle soup, and his ardour nourished by an inner vision too strong to be extinguished by the evidence of his senses. And in this, he was not unlike the rest of us, each in our own personal enchanted forests—or so the sages would have us believe.

On the morning after the year-and-a-day, the seeming crone challenged Sir Gervais to offer proof of his undying love by going forth against her enemy, a neighbour baron in whose oak patch her swine did envy to snout about. At first Sir Gervais was loath to wreak hurt upon a knight with whom he had not exchanged those introductory insults that usage and breeding require, but when the seeming hag described the evil baron as a frail old man full of years and feeble of body, then did the knight recall her many kindnesses and his chivalrous duty. And thus it was that, after another dampening mishap upon the drawbridge, Sir Gervais rode forth to avenge the insults borne by the princess who clung to his back.

They soon encountered a woodcutter of great girth and so tall that he looked at the knight eye to eye, though he stood upon the ground and Sir Gervais sat astride his charger. The peasant's beard was gray, but he was sturdy as an oak and so broad of chest that he, in rough cloth, was wider than the knight in his armour.

"Tell me, hefty varlet," Sir Gervais said, "knowest thou the hiding place of the evil, if puny, baron who has given insult to this dainty, high-born maiden behind me?"

"Dainty maiden?" cried the woodcutter, and he laughed until tears ran down his cheeks and he was obliged to hold his sides in ecstatic pain.

The princess whispered into the ear hole of Sir Gervais's helm that the scoffer who stood before them was the very baron they sought.

Then spake the knight behind his hand, asking, "But lacks not this stout fellow the qualities of frailty and decrepitude thou hast ascribed to the baron?"

"Ah, my love, hast thou forgot that all things here are other-seeming?"

"Uh-h-h-h-h...Ah! Of course! Aye, but art thou certain sure that yonder laughing giant is, in fact, a puny and feeble thing?"

"Seems he not otherwise?"

"*Most* otherwise," the knight confessed with an uneasy glance at this huge ox of a man.

"Well then! There's your proof!"

Sir Gervais struggled to digest this, saying, "Uh-h-h-h-h...Ah! Of course!" Whereupon he addressed the seeming giant, saying, "Leave off thy laughter, uncivil cur, and hear my demands! Grant the swine of this princess of passing beauty the use of thine oak patch, or risk a passage of arms with Gervais, knight of the Table Round!"

The woodcutter dried his eyes upon his sleeve and said, "Hast taken leave of thy senses, lad? Were we to grapple, thee and me, I would crumple thine iron suit in my hands in such wise that thou wouldst be unable to get out when the need to shit came upon thee."

Sir Gervais whispered over his shoulder, "How is it, Princess, that this varlet does not tremble at my high rank and martial prowess?"

"Why 'tis clear as my maiden conscience, lover. Just as he appears to thine enchanted eyes to be vast and well-proportioned, so dost thou appear to him to be a scrawny thing of slight danger. Such is the way of other-seemingness."

Sir Gervais blinked and bent his mind to this complex matter. After a longish time, he cried out, "Ah-h-h! Of course!" Then he chuckled to himself. "What a dolorous surprise will be his, should we meet in harsh combat." Then to the peasant he shouted, "Enough of this petty parley! Do as I bade thee, churl, lest thy brittle old bones be brast by this hand!"

"Nay, nay," the seeming giant said, waving away the glowering knight's threat. "Do not require that I bash thee, lad, for I am as gentle of humour as I am stout of limb. Know ye that yon stenchy hag has oft and again sent befuddled fools to wrest my oak patch from me, and each of those simple fellows has earned damage most woeful. But I had rather deal with thee than dent thee. Let us bargain. Forsake that crone clinging behind thee and let me welcome thee as my son. For know ye that my daughter is a frick, lusty-tempered lass of rutting age and the need to swive and be swiven is hot and hasty upon her. But there are no men in this damned forest but we two." And with this the peasant gestured to the side of the path, where stood a maiden ripe and moist, with breasts that strained the fabric of her bodice, with hair fresh-spun of gold, fair of face, clear of eye, slim of waist, comfortable of haunch, and whose pink tongue did flicker between teeth of purest white.

Seeing her, Sir Gervais's pulse did quop in his temple, and elsewhere the restraints of his armour did irk him.

But before he could spit on his palm and cry, "Agreed, done, and double-done!" the seeming hag rasped into his ear hole, "I perceive, brave hero, that thou dost pant and drool and quop and bulge, but remember that all things here are other-seeming. To unenchanted eyes this maiden is revealed to be the very lees and slag of womanhood, ugly beneath description, diseased to the marrow, so repulsive that passing toads do retch and gag." And she went on to confide that the source of her discord with the scrawny baron was that he could not marry off his flawed and blemished daughter because his neighbour's beauty diminished the wretched little thing by comparison.

After a very long silence devoted to trying to unsnarl this, Sir Gervais said, "Uh-h-h...You mean...Wait a minute...She's not...While you're...Hm-m-m. Ah-h-h, of course!" Nevertheless, his manhood continued to pulse and quop of its own will until the crone mentioned that the seeming frick and juicy girl was not of their class. Her vowels! Her aitches! No, no, not at all one of *us*. The knight almost swooned with relief at his narrow escape from the disgrace of foining beneath his station. "Without thy guidance, Princess, I might have fallen victim to this knave's low plot! Prepare to suffer, varlet!" And with this, he drew his sword with the intention of cleaving the woodcutter's pate down to his saucy grin.

But the seeming giant grasped the hilt in midair, brast the blade over his knee, and tossed the pieces into the brook.

"Oh-ho!" cried the knight. "*Now* hast thou precipitated my wrath upon thine aged and brittle back!" He leapt from the saddle and clutched at his adversary's throat.

But the woodcutter lifted the grasping hands from his throat as easily as if they had been placed there in caress, and he slapped those steel gauntlets together until the knight's palms stung with his vigorous applause. Then he turned the knight upside down and swung him so that his head played the clapper to the bell of his helm.

"There now," he said, setting Sir Gervais again upon his feet. "Let that be an end to it. If thou wilt not have my daughter to wed, so be it. Go and pester me no further."

Dazed, his ears ringing, his palms throbbing, the knight staggered to his horse and clung to the pommel, his knees buckling.

But the seeming hag leaned down from the saddle and whispered, "Prithee, be more gentle with this frail old baron, my champion! Though I would see him punished for his insults, I do not want the sin of his murder upon thy soul!"

"Sayest what?" Sir Gervais muttered, half senseless.

"Thou hast done him great and telling hurt. Sure, he must yield after another such chastisement."

"*I* have wrought hurt upon *him?*"

"Joy-o'-my-nights, hast thou forgot that here all things are other-seeming?"

"What?" The battered knight frowned in deepest thought. "Uh-h-h-h." He squinted at the sky in intense concentration. "Er-r-r-r-r." He squeezed his eyes shut and marshalled all his powers of reasoning to the problem. "Uhn-n-n-n-n." And finally, "Ah, of course!" And with that, he flung himself again at the seeming giant's throat.

Annoyed by this fool's persistence, the woodcutter grasped him by his shoulders and shook him until his limbs dangled and flopped loose, then he forced the knight's helmet into the fork of an oak and left him hanging by his chin, his body swaying gently in the breeze. And with this, he strode away, taking his daughter with him.

Tossing the fig after the departing woodcutter, the seeming hag growled bitterly that Sir Gervais was useless to a poor girl seeking to affirm her swine's snouting rights, and she departed to her castle to await the arrival of a stouter champion.

Night fell; the forest darkened; nocturnal creatures scuttled and scurried; and still Sir Gervais hung in deepest melancholy, wondering what magic had transported him to this high tree and lodged his neck in the crook of this branch after he had so sorely punished the feeble old baron that enchantment had disguised as a stout woodcutter.

He was lost in these philosophical speculations when a soft voice called from the forest floor. Bending his eyes downward—for nothing else could he move—the knight espied the seeming lush and juicy daughter of the seeming giant, the moonlight shining upon her golden-seeming hair and her bulging, ripe-seeming breasts.

"I'll have thee down in a trice, handsome knight," she called up.

"Thank...you," he muttered between clenched teeth.

"But first, thou must promise me a boon."

"What...boon?"

"Before I dislodge thee from yon forked bough, thou must promise—" And here the maiden blushed and turned her fair face aside. "Oh, how can I say it with modesty?"

"Get...on...with...it!" muttered the distressed knight.

"Well, then. As my father told thee, I am of swiving age and humour, but there is no swiveworthy man in this forest. Hence, ere I dislodge thee, thou must promise to teach me the ways of swiving. There, I have said it!" And she hid her face with her hands and blushed modestly.

"Agreed," Sir Gervais rasped between his locked teeth.

Whereupon the seeming sumptuous maid armed herself with a stout stick, then hitched her up skirts so high that both fud and ecu were cooled by the night breezes, and scaled the tree. Jamming the stick in behind the knight's helmet, she heaved with such good will that Sir Gervais was pried free and fell with a stunning clatter to the earth, where he sat all a-daze.

Before his swirling senses settled, the maiden was upon him, clawing at the lacings of his armour that he might serve her as he had pledged to do. So willing was his brawn to redeem his promise that often he did mount her to this end, but upon each instance, his imagination warned him that this moist and panting maid was, in truth, a low-born person the swiving of whom was beneath his dignity, and this realization instantly made him all limp and unable.

For many and many an hour was he, by turns, stiffened and shriveled until, near the dawning, he was sorely cramped with dog's cullions caused by the flowing and ebbing of ardent blood.

Then did the maiden draw aside and pout and sniff and stamp her little foot. "All this fumbling and prodding, then fading and shriveling, surely this cannot be the swiving that I have heard so widely praised!"

In his shame he attested that, yes, they had done the most and the best of swiving.

"Nay, then," cried the maiden. "This swiving is a sport most treacherously o'er-famed! If it be for this that maidens dream and sigh, and in consequence of which they grow great and make babes to dangle from their teats, then no more of swiving shall I have! If God protect me from increase upon this occasion, I vow me to a nunnery, there to do His will and work 'til my flesh ages beyond yearning."

And Sir Gervais did gravely affirm her in this choice, saying that if she drew not pleasure from his swiving—which was the best and highest of that delectable art—then surely no man could ever please her. And he did feel some pride in the knowledge that he was serving God by assisting a maiden to a nunnery where she would pass her life to the leeward of temptation.

So it was that, in the fullness of time, the Maid of the Enchanted Forest rose from nun to abbess, and at last was hoisted to the high rank of saint in reward for abjuring the joy of men for all the six-and-eighty years she passed on this earth. For celibacy is rightly accounted a miracle in one so beauteous, lush, moist, and frick as she; while in the generality of nuns it is but a petty accomplishment, as it is no great feat to defend a fruit rendered forbidding and unpluckworthy by Nature.

As for Sir Gervais, he did return to the Table Round, there to regale his comrades, recounting how he had passed a year and a day in the arms of a most desirable—if other-seeming—princess; and how, out of due consideration for the aged, he had let himself be bested by a pitiable and scrawny old knight, who had tried to disguise himself as a puissant woodcutter; and how he had come perilously close to being seduced by an ugly, all-rotted hag who had pretended to be a moist and frick maiden eager to swive and be swiven. And his amazed listeners were filled with wonder and envy

For the rest of his days Sir Gervais was so affected by his term in the Forest of Other-Seemingness that he would take to belly none but crones and hags full of years and distort of feature. And although some envious knights belittled his choice of lust-targets, they were obliged to admit that he was much more successful plying his lance in the romantic lists than he had been before his enchantment.

Thus came it to pass that the knight's fame was sung down the corridors of time by bards and minstrels, in whose lays he was ever after clept: Sir Gervais! Swiver of Crones!

EASTER STORY

Now then, young man, what have you been getting up to?" my master asked, smiling. "You have certainly managed to draw the wrath of the religious establishment down upon your head. Mind you, perhaps it does them good to have their noses tweaked occasionally, if only as an exercise in humility." I translated this into the Koine dialect of Greek, the marketplace lingua franca understood throughout the Levant. During his years of diplomatic administration on the barbarian frontier my master had developed a method for communicating on a comfortable, personal level to those whose language he did not speak: while I translated in a rapid undertone, he would hold his interlocutor's eyes with his own. This had the effect of removing me from the scene and allowing my master to make closer contact than one would imagine possible between a highly civilized aristocrat from Rome and a rustic Jew from this dusty, fly-blown outpost of Judæa. As I translated the Procurator's words I tried to imitate his amicable, even jocular tone, but the bound prisoner kept his eyes lowered, making no indication that he had heard. I looked up at my master and lifted my shoulders.

Pilatus's smile faded; he spoke in a graver, sharper timbre. "You'd be well-advised to cooperate, young man. You're accused of blasphemy towards their god—your god too, I suppose. I cannot help you if you won't speak to me."

After I translated this, the accused lifted his head and settled his calm, deep-set eyes upon my master, and it was then that the Procurator saw his bruised cheek and cut eyebrow, evidence that the man's interrogators had tried to beat a confession out of him. His eyes winced away, and he glared down the long flight of stone steps to the waiting knot of priests and scribes. Their nervous shuffle revealed that they read angry displeasure in my master's stern features. As the embodiment of Roman rule in Judæa, the Procurator was often obliged to order, or at least condone, such punishments as were necessary to keep the passions of this quarrelsome, litigious people under some semblance of control, but he had an innate horror of physical cruelty. It was not that he held strong moral views against physical punishment in principle; it was more a matter of his refined sensibilities. As he once explained to me, the fact that he dined on meat did not mean he chose to witness the slaughter of animals.

As it happens, he had been dining when the request came for him to adjudicate in yet another of these local religious squabbles. The truth be known, I doubt that he minded being interrupted, as he was bored with the company of the rough soldiers of his personal guard. A young centurion officer had just ruined the climax of his story by being unable to stifle his own anticipatory laughter, but weak though the joke was, his fellow officers barked out their guffaws and pounded the table in applause. Even the highborn Claudia Procula lifted her chin and showed her small, white teeth in a polite, if minimal, mime of mirth. The corners of her eyes were still crinkled in what her husband called her 'I'm-having-such-a-good-time' expression when she glanced across to see if, for once, he was playing his role as the congenial host, or at least feigning a little interest in his guests. Her smile hardened when she saw that he was engrossed in conversation with me, a humble slave who shouldn't have been sitting at the same table with officers of equestrian rank, much less at Pilatus's side, leaving her to entertain these course border soldiers whose idea of witty chat seldom rose above the scatological. Daughter of a patrician family, she accepted that one must make do in this least desirable of all colonial posts, one that Rome bestowed only on men who lacked important patrons or who, like her husband, had earned the displeasure of Tiberius. Even before marriage had united their ancient families, she had feared that young Pilatus's caustic tongue and cool intellect might prove lethal flaws in Rome, where advancement depended more upon a facile smile and flexible ethics than upon ability. But he had been young then and handsome, and the danger lurking behind the acid irreverence of his wit had thrilled her. Who could have predicted that his cynical observations and wounding slights would ultimately maroon them on this twilight rim of the civilized world? Judæa, of all places! Land of superstitious goatherds and wild-eyed mystics, of jealous priests and suicidal zealots. What was it that Valerius Gratus had said when they arrived to replace him as Procurator? "I don't envy you, my dears. They say that if the Gods ever decide that the world needs a purging, they'll inject the warm oil at Judæa."

Claudia resented not even being allowed to entertain the officers in the relative comfort of their official residence at Cæsarea. No, they had been obliged to accompany reinforcements to this crowded, smelly, provincial backwater of Jerusalem to show the long, muscular arm of Roman authority in the hope of forestalling the civil disorder that invariably accompanied their primitive religion's principal annual festival, this...this...."What do they call this celebration?" she asked the table in general.

A grizzled, battle-worn officer sitting two places down (a risen ranker from the vulgar slackness of his vowels) offered the information that the locals called this period 'Passover'.

"Passover? And what is that supposed to mean?"

"Damned if I know, ma'am. But it's obvious that these poor bastards were *passed over* when the Gods were handing out homelands worth having."

"Quite," Claudia Procula's clipped diction was meant to remind the ranker of the social distance between them. "But why would they celebrate having been passed over?"

The old soldier shook his head. "Who knows? They're a queer people, ma'am, and that's the truth of it!"

At that very moment, at the far end of the table, I was expressing the same view, albeit with somewhat greater elegance. "As my master knows better than anyone, it is pointless to attempt to understand the Jew in rational terms. For all his cleverness and intelligence, in his deepest essence the Jew is a creature of passion who draws energy from his enthusiasms and his delusions. An example of this is the fact that, although they have been conquered and enslaved by every people who have blundered into this dreary land, they confidently believe they are the chosen people of their god. Despite all evidence, they maintain this ludicrous belief. And they are maintained *by* it." I smiled to myself, pleased with that turn of phrase.

"Hm-m." Pilatus lifted his chalice, only to find it empty. But when the serving girl stepped forward to refill it, he waved her away with an annoyed gesture. He had been drinking too much of late. Out of boredom, he told himself. "When first I arrived, I sought to understand their beliefs and superstitions. I discovered that in common with other Levantine cults, their god was originally a battle god. In fact, they still call him a 'God of Hosts', despite their many defeats. This war god consumed and replaced the rest of the pantheon to become their sole deity, but although there is no competition, he remains a jealous god, so uncertain of his power that he requires constant reassurance, praise, and glorification. Proof—if additional evidence were needed—that we make our gods in our image!" He chuckled.

I chuckled along, as befits the servant of a master of prickly temperament. "Indeed, sire, their mythology contains a tale that illustrates your point. Once upon a time, their god, being in a particularly grumpy mood, decided to destroy a licentious city and all its inhabitants unless this prophet could find a certain number of good men among the inhabitants. There follows a passage in which the prophet and the god haggle about exactly how many good men would be required to save the city, the old prophet slowly whittling the god down! How delightfully Semitic a god! A god you can negotiate with! God as market stall merchant! But for all his touches of Levantine humanity, the Jewish god is a bloodless confection, compared to the colorful heroes (and rogues!) of our own pantheon."

"Maybe, but he's not bloodless enough for me," Pilatus said. "He's a passionate god. A jealous god. A god of vengeance." He half closed his eyes. "Perhaps that's why I find these people so difficult to deal with. So opaque. So oblique. And so intriguing, too...in an irritating sort of way. Roman to my marrow, more Roman than our beloved emperor, I am a creature of reason and logic."

I diplomatically ignored this reference to the emperor. Descended from the Sabine clan of the Pontii (hence his name), Pontius Pilatus's ancestors had been aristocrats when the forebears of Tiberius were still brawny sharecroppers, a historical fact my master seldom had the tact to conceal.

"I'm a creature of reason, and rational thought is Rome's greatest strength," he insisted.

"And perhaps it's her greatest limitation, as well?" I suggested, with a tentative smile that would let me pretend I was merely playing the fool, should he take offence.

"Yes, a need for the rational can be a limitation as well. I admit to being uncomfortable when faced with illogical passion. I can cope with the aggressive man, the cunning man, the subtle man, the duplicitous man, the stubborn man, the stupid man...but the insane man? No. The madman and the zealot confuse and confound me." And, after a pause: "...and frighten me, as well."

"Certainly Judæa is a difficult post for one who is unable to deal with the zealot," I ventured.

"Perhaps that's why the honor of governing Judæa is always bestowed upon those who are out of favor. We, the expendable ones." His soft chuckle was not without bitterness.

I smiled noncommittally and lowered my eyes. I was familiar with the events that had brought my master to this wretched post. Although his high birth and native capacities should have destined him for power and privilege, he was constitutionally incapable of concealing his scorn for fools and hypocrites, a serious flaw for a politician in any form of government, a disaster in a tyranny. Some wondered why a man who so obviously lacked the thick skin and the accommodating conscience of the successful politician had entered government service in the first place. The answer was deceptively simple: Pontius Pilatus had been brought up to believe that it was a gentleman's duty to serve his country. Oh, he recognized that his view of duty was romantic and old-fashioned in this era of the professional politician with the ethics of a merchant and the tactics of a whore, yet he cleaved to the values of his class.

But being highborn and gifted did not protect him, for when the ambitious mediocrities who had felt the lash of Pilatus's scorn and ridicule managed to sniff and snivel their way into power, they took their revenge by dissuading Tiberius from assigning the haughty Sabine to any posts of importance. Finding all paths to fruitful service closed to him, Pilatus considered retirement to his country villa, a prospect that chilled the heart of Claudia Procula, for her husband's political connections afforded those social and romantic amusements that absorbed her time and energy, and kept her from brooding over the passage of her youth. She persuaded Vitellius, Legatus of Syria, to nominate her husband for the Judæan post. It was rumored that her 'persuasion' involved bargaining from a position of strength: the horizontal. I, of course, dismiss such rumors. It is my duty to do so.

As you might imagine, Tiberius's sycophants did not oppose Pilatus's appointment to Judæa, that garbage pit of lost careers. Serves him right for poking fun at those who are doing their best to serve their beloved emperor! Let the haughty Pilatus sneer at camels for a while! See how he likes that!

My master soon discovered that Judæa was not only the least honored of posts, it could also be difficult and nasty, for these people deeply resented Roman occupation, and they had long ago forged their natural gift for shrill complaint into a formidable weapon for wearing the opposition down with incessant whining and whinging.

Aware of Judæa's reputation as the dullest outpost of the empire, soon after his arrival Pilatus sought out a Greek slave-scholar trained in sophistic sleight-of-mind, hoping that intellectual exercise might serve as an anodyne for boredom. This was my humble entry into the noble household, and I trust that I have been of some small value to my lord Pontius, for I have lived many years among these people and I know not only the Koine dialect but also both Hebrew and Aramaic, the language of the Aramaeans that is widely used throughout the Levant and even appears here and there in Jewish sacred writings, part of their Book of Daniel being written in it, for instance, as is their prayer for the dead, the Qaddish, and also—But there I go, parading my erudition! Shame on me! Please forgive a poor old scholar the sin of intellectual pride, remembering that pride is the

only sin the poor can afford, and the only one the old can still
manage.

From the first, Pontius Pilatus revealed a fascination (a morbid
fascination, in his wife's view and, I confess, my own) with the plague
of wild-eyed, self-proclaimed 'messiahs' that infest this stressful moment in Jewish history. Almost every day another rabble-rousing
preacher staggers in from the desert, followed by a ragged retinue of
zealots drawn from the unwashed, the unwanted, the lost, the desperate, the gullible, the vulnerable, and the discontent—all seeking
to magnify their miserable existences by association with things eternal and miraculous. This epidemic of rustic rabbis, with their sim-
plistic philosophy and folksy adages, gives the Jewish religious
establishment and the Roman occupiers a rare opportunity for cooperation, for the priests resent the devotion and enthusiasm that the
uneducated Wad lavishes on these fanatics, and the Romans see them
as foci for social unrest in a population already dangerously unstable.
Have you not noticed how shared dislikes and fears bind men much
more tightly than do shared interests and affections? Something to
do with Human Nature, that catchall term for our baseness of appetite and paucity of spirit.

But for all that Pontius recognized the danger in these fanatics,
he was fascinated by them. He once likened this blend of fascination
and repulsion to a time when, as a child, he had seen a dog crushed
under a wagon wheel. The sight had disgusted him, yet he could not
tug his eyes away. These zealots risked being crushed by those in
power, both Roman and Jewish, yet they faced the prospect eagerly,
with a ghastly appetite for martyrdom. I pointed out to my lord the
logical inconsistency of a man who took pride in the cool rationality
of the Roman nobleman, yet who was attracted to the passionate, the
insane, the seething cauldrons of the emotions. He laughed this off,
but I wondered if there were not, at some depth within him, an envy
of these 'messiahs'...a desire to feel something so deeply, to want
something so much that he would suffer and even die for it.

He had ample opportunity to indulge his morbid interest in these
fanatic preachers soon after our arrival in Jerusalem, for zeal and
sedition seethed in every corner of the city. He had come to stiffen
the small garrison with his personal presence, making a more telling

show of his entry into the city by thickening his handful of reinforcements with his wife and her handmaidens and slaves, and his own retinue which included concubines, servants, scribes, and your humble servant, an aged rogue-philosopher who served, depending on his master's mood, as his adversary in rhetorical exercises, his confidant, his entertainer, his adviser, and his clown. Keeping the peace in Judæa (or rather, keeping disorder within acceptable limits, for my master well understood the need for a periodic controlled release of steam, lest the cauldron explode) required no small portion of bluff and nerve, for he had only three thousand Roman soldiers to control more than three and a half million Jews. Adroit political navigation would be required if his minute show of force were to restrain the hundreds of thousands of pilgrims who visited Jerusalem during Passover each year, all smouldering with religious fervor and tinder-dry for insurrection.

It is little wonder that my master was depressed and thorny-tempered this evening and little able to endure the company of gruff, shallow-minded soldiers. Shifting from my role as counselor to that of entertainer, I sought to lift his spirits. "My lord is weary with the burdens of state. Working with these Israelites is particularly sapping, for nothing is more draining than pushing against an immovable boulder. Perhaps I could arrange something refreshing? Something young and...ah...rejuvenating?"

"No, no, I'm not in the mood."

"They can be amusing, these local women. Eager, flexible, inventive, and above all grateful, for their men are often too occupied with quarreling over minor points of scriptural interpretation to gratify their not inconsiderable appetites. Perhaps this explains why so many of them seek sapphist consolation. Or perhaps it is merely—"

But the Procurator was not to benefit from my insight into the causes of this tribadistic proclivity, for there was a disturbance at the great doors connecting the Prætorium of the Castle of Antonia to the temple of Jerusalem, and the officer-of-the-guard strode across the stone floor with a hard-heeled gait, his body armor rattling with self-importance. He came to attention before the Procurator. "Sir!"

Pilatus looked up wearily. "Can you not see that we are dining?"

"Yes, sir! I see that, sir!"

"Then, if this is something that can wait..."

"They're demanding to see you, sir!"

Pilatus's eyes widened slightly. *"Demanding?"*

"Well...that is...they are *requesting* to see you, sir. It's a delegation from the San-hed-rin." These last syllables had just been memorized.

The Procurator raised his eyebrows at me.

"A religious high court of sorts, my lord," I explained. "Rome has allowed them a certain amount of self-government in matters of slight importance: religious rituals, local festivals, dietary peculiarities, marketplace customs—that sort of thing."

"Hmm. And what does it want of me, this Sanhedrin?"

"They've brought a prisoner for you to judge, sir," the officer-of-the-guard said. "It has to do with one of the 'oiled ones'."

"The 'oiled ones?" Pilatus said. "How long have you been out here, young man?"

"Too long, sir."

"Like all of us. But evidently not long enough to be familiar with one of the most common phenomena of the streets. They are called the 'anointed ones', not the 'oiled ones', although it's true that they're anointed with oil. That's what gives us the Greek word for them: the 'cristos'. I believe there's also a word in Hebrew." He glanced towards me.

" 'Messiah', sire. It means the same thing: an anointed one."

"Ah yes, 'messiah'." He turned to the officer-of-the-guard. "Very well, you may tell them I shall consider their petition after I have dined. They may come back in two or three hours."

But the guard officer hovered. "It...ah...it seems to be a most pressing matter, sir. They deman—request to speak to you right now."

Pilatus released a martyred sigh. "Oh, very well. How many are there?"

"A whole gaggle of them, sir."

"A gaggle, eh? Well, that *is* impressive. Inform your...gaggle...that I will receive a deputation of three of the cleanest of them."

The guard officer shifted uneasily.

"What now?" Pilatus asked, his patience thinning.

"I'm afraid you will have to go to them, sir. They await you on the steps leading down to the temple."

"*I* must go to *them?*"

"Yes, sir. It has to do with...well, with bread, sir."

"Bread?!"

The guard officer stared straight ahead, only a shift of his eyes betraying his nervousness.

I cleared my throat. "I believe I understand the problem, my lord. They hold us—and indeed even this room in which we dine—to be 'unclean'."

"We are unclean? Now there's the pot slandering the kettle! These Jews never had two baths in the same year before we arrived to set them an example."

"Unclean in the ritualistic sense, my lord." Pulling a comically grave face and dropping my voice to a theatrical tremor, I said, "You see, sir, we are guilty of harbouring—dare I speak the horrid words?—*leavened bread* in this place."

"Leavened bre—! The Gods grant me patience!" Then he chuckled. "Oh, very well, tell them this unclean eater of leavened bread will join them shortly."

"Sir!" And the officer-of-the-guard departed with martial clatter and stamp.

"Oiled ones!" Claudia Procula said with a shudder of distaste. "Filthy, hollow-eyed fanatics holding the mindless masses in their hypnotic sway. I am told that the desert fairly teems with them. To what do we owe this sudden infestation of...what is it the locals call them?"

" 'Messiahs', my lady," I informed her. "But, alas, there is nothing new or sudden about this plague of messiahs. They appear spontaneously out of the body politic, like maggots on diseased meat, whenever political unrest, economic deprivation, or religious reformation stalks this unhappy land. But over the last ten years or so there's been a spate of them. Hardly a day passes without some new 'cristo' entering the city with his handful of fanatic followers, curing hypochondriacs, slipping red powder into water and calling it wine, hypnotizing away the pangs of hunger, and claiming the hungry host has been fed, raising the dead—the dead drunk, usually—in short, all the usual ruses and shams."

"But why do all of them truck out the same tired old stunts? Sheer lack of imagination?"

"Not quite, my lady. They have no option but to perform the same 'miracles' because all Jews are familiar with the writings of their prophets who, down through the ages, have described the long-awaited Messiah. Each would-be messiah knows what utterances and acts and 'miracles' he must perform to fulfill the prophesies. I should be very surprised if there were not half a dozen of them out there in the streets at this very moment, all performing their miracles, all preaching, all thumbing their noses at the religious establishment, each one claiming to be the fruit of a virgin birth and descended from the obligatory family of Jesse, each followed by his coterie of bemused disciples."

"But how can it be that Jews, famed the world over for their intelligence, are taken in by these rabble-rousing charlatans?" Claudia Procula asked. "In the long catalogues of opprobrium heaped on the heads of the Jews, one never hears the word 'gullible'!"

"Ah, but they are a uniquely gullible people, my lady! Both devious and gullible."

"Is there not a logical contradiction there?" my master wondered.

"Of course there is, my lord. Contradiction is the distinguishing essence of all Levantine peoples but Jewish gullibility has a particular character of its own. The Jew is too quick-witted to be duped by others; but he often dupes himself. And how can this be? Because the Jew is a constant and willing victim of Hope."

"The Jew as a victim of Hope? Well, there's an interesting concept...if somewhat fanciful," my master's wife said.

"Fanciful if you will, my lady, but..." I began, but she had turned away to bestow her attention on other guests, so I continued to my master, "...but, sire, this addiction to hope explains why the most grasping, materialistic merchant will sacrifice everything for a chimera, a gesture, a phantom, a promise writ in sand...in short, a hope. The hope implied in his calling this arid heap of sand his 'Promised Land'. The hope enshrined in his famous deal with his god: the Covenant. Threaten his treasured hopes, and overnight the plodding, prudent Jew becomes a fanatic. An enthusiast! A rhapsodist! A zealot!"

"I'm perfectly aware of the contradictions in the Jewish character, Greek. And know what traps and snares those contradictions pose. But I am curious, and curiosity is a powerful lure for a bored man. Above all, these 'oiled ones' fascinate me, both as individuals and as a general phenomenon."

"I hope my lord recalls how the asp fascinates its victim before stinging him to death. Above all, never for a minute forget that the Jew is always willing—nay, eager!—to become a martyr, for the Jew has a marrow-deep appetite for martyrdom, and for martyring others with his martyrdom. Therein lies a great danger to you."

"To me?"

"Well, to Rome, if you'd rather. But in this place and at this time, you *are* Rome."

"May Rome admit to being confused?"

"I should be distressed if you were not, my lord. After all, it is my role to amuse by dazzling with the complexity of my insights."

"It is also your role to share your insights and unravel those complexities. I perceive a certain archness of tone that ill becomes a slave...even the most complex and insightful one."

"I am warned, my lord. And most thoroughly chastened." I lowered my eyes and retreated into a respectful silence.

"Well?"

"I beg your pardon, my lord? Did you speak to me?" I asked, all innocent wonder.

"Damn it, Greek! First you wound with your superiority, then you punish with your humility! Are you sure there's no Jewish blood in you?"

Although my smile did not desert my lips, my heart stopped for an instant. Had he inadvertently stumbled upon the truth of my origins? (If you think, dear Reader, that only Gentiles harbor anti-Semitism, then you don't appreciate the complex and involute reactions a person can have to years of scorn, ridicule, and humiliation.) When I realized that he had only meant to be amusing, I recovered smoothly with, "Ah, but I was merely warning my master that in dealing with these messiahs one must be wary of the Jewish tendency to martyrdom...a martyrdom the Jew's adversary might get to share with him, if he is not careful, for when the Jew throws himself off a cliff, he is usually holding the tunic of his enemy in his iron grip."

Pilatus chuckled. "I'll keep my tunic close wrapped. Now, then! I believe we have made the priests of the Sanhedrin wait long enough to give them a sense of their relative insignificance. Let us have a look at the captive messiah." The Procurator rose from his couch and lifted his hand to arrest the rising of his guests. "No, no. Continue your festivities, gentlemen. I'll return in a few moments. Claudia, I know I can rely on you to entertain our guests." She communicated her annoyance with an almost imperceptible compression of her lips, but old diplomatic hand that she was, she dutifully began to tease an oft-heard story out of the senior officer present as Pilatus and I stepped out onto the landing at the top of the wide staircase that led from the Praetorium down to the Judgment Hall.

Below us stood a knot of chief priests and scribes surrounded by a gawking crowd eager to witness pain and punishment. And there before the religious leaders, his head down, was a young man in a dirty, travel-stained gown of cheap cloth. They had brought him from Caiaphas after accusing him of blasphemy in that he claimed to be the Son of God. They had bound his arms and blindfolded him; then they had struck him on the face and asked, "If thou art indeed the omniscient son of the omniscient God, then say which of us it was that smote thee." And when he would not, or could not, they had mocked him, saying, "And yet you claim to be the Messiah! The anointed one that our people have so long awaited!" The prisoner had answered only, "No matter what I told you, you would not believe me, nor would you let me go," so they brought him to be judged before the Procurator.

Upon the appearance of Pontius Pilatus at the head of the stairs, the priests and scribes brought their prisoner halfway up the stairs leading to the Praetorium—well, to be exact, they brought him one step less than halfway up, so they could avoid any accusation of having entered a place wherein Gentiles were desecrating the Passover by eating leavened bread.

Pilatus looked down upon them and spoke, and I can remember his words exactly, because I was obliged to repeat them in translation. For the smoothness of my account, I shall henceforth assume you understand that everything that was said passed through me. Pilatus said, "What accusation bring ye against this man?"

"He has blasphemed, calling himself the son of God!"

The Procurator shrugged. "Is that so serious? Are not all of us the children of our gods, in a way of speaking? But if you feel that he has offended your cult, then take him and punish him according to your customs."

Seeing that Pilatus had no intention of accepting the responsibility of punishing this poor fellow over some trivial matter of local cult sensitivities, the chief priest took another tack. "This man has been perverting the nation, claiming to be King of the Jews and forbidding the people to give tribute to Cæsar. We would punish this treason against your worship and against Rome, but you have made it unlawful for us to put any man to death."

Now, it was true that the Romans had found it necessary to deny the Jews the right to put one another to death over their endless internecine religious spats, so Pilatus said, "Oh, come now! Surely preaching some political nonsense to a pack of illiterate malcontents is not a matter deserving of death." His dismissive, cajoling tone might have been used for speaking to quarrelsome children, but when he saw from their determined, thin-lipped expressions that they had no intention of letting their prey off lightly, he drew a long weary sigh and said, "Oh, very well, bring him up for me to question."

I cleared my throat to remind him of their terror of proximity to bread-eaters. "Send him up alone, then! The rest of you can wait there below!"

When the accused was standing before him, Pilatus said, "Now then, young man, what have you been getting up to? You have certainly managed to draw the wrath of the religious establishment down upon you. Mind you, perhaps it does them good to have their noses tweaked occasionally, if only as an exercise in humility." He smiled, but the prisoner made no indication that he had heard.

The Procurator's smile faded and he spoke in a graver, more urgent tone. "You'd be well-advised to cooperate, young man. You're accused of blasphemy towards their god—your god too, I suppose. I cannot help you if you won't speak to me."

The prisoner lifted his head and settled his calm, deep-set eyes upon my master without answering

"Did you, in fact, claim to be King of the Jews?" the Procurator pursued. "Before you answer, I should warn you that Cæsar is the only ruler here, so it would be possible to interpret any claim to being king as treason. Do you understand that? Now then. Are you King of the Jews?"

The prisoner responded, "Those are your words, not mine."

Pilatus looked at me, and I lifted my shoulders. We had met this phenomenon with all the 'messiahs' we had been obliged to interrogate: this peculiar reluctance to admit to their specific offenses, although they seemed perfectly willing—indeed determined—to achieve martyrdom by suffering for them. It was as though their impulses towards life and towards the diseased ecstasies of martyrdom were tugging them in two directions.

"So you're denying that you claimed to be King of the Jews? Is that it?" Pilatus said, trying to prompt him into the right answer.

The young man responded, but, typically, not to the question posed. He said, "To this end was I born, and for this cause came I into the world, that I should bear witness unto the truth. Everyone that is of the truth heareth my voice."

My master and I exchanged a glance. This business about coming into the world to bear witness to the truth had been said by every messiah we had questioned over the past year or so. Indeed, even the phrasing was almost identical. Shifting to Latin so that we could not be understood, my master said, "Another one who has learned his part perfectly. Are they just rogues and charlatans, after all?"

"Many of them, to be sure. Probably most. But not all. Some are deranged enthusiasts who really do hear voices and who clearly remember things that never happened. But the most interesting of them are honest, rustic teachers who assume the guise of the Messiah to give weight and impact to their teachings among the uneducated masses. Alas, sometimes these teachers find themselves entangled in the net of their little subterfuge when they are questioned by priests and religious functionaries and are obliged either to renounce their claims to deity, and thus lose their followers and the fruits of a life's work, or face punishment for blasphemy, which, of course, can mean death."

Pilatus nodded. "Difficult choice. Glory and death, or life and ignominy. But I'll tell you what confounds me, Greek. I cannot understand the appeal of these 'cristos' to the ignorant masses. What do they offer them?"

"Nothing."

"Nothing?"

"Well, something more profound and more attractive than nothing, Nothingness! They prophesy that the world will come to its end in a very short time. Total destruction! Final judgment! Apocalypse! And that's a very tasty prospect for the lost, the crippled, the lonely, the impoverished, the frustrated, the incompetent, the ignorant, and the powerless who constitute their followings. And even more tasty is the prospect that this total and final annihilation will sweep up the rich as well, together with the clever, the strong, the pleased, the life-embracing, the informed, the liberated, the powerful—all those whom the underclasses envy and hate."

"An end of misery for themselves, and harsh punishment for the rest of us, eh?" my master mused. "A heady and attractive mixture. Both surcease and revenge. Hmm."

"Yes, and each of these 'cristos' dangles this promise before all those who will listen. They promise that the poor and the meek and the downtrodden will reign in heaven, while the rest of us will suffer all the torments of Dis. I view these messages as so many embers thrown onto dry grasslands. While most of them will smoulder, then die out, there is a danger that the promises of one of these messiahs—it hardly matters which one—might catch and flair into a great conflagration that will sweep across the world. And that will be a dark day for all men of culture and refinement, for we shall become the despised minority in a tyranny of the ignorant underclass."

Pilatus half closed his eyes and nodded to himself, then he turned and spoke down to the awaiting priests and the eager rabble. "I have

interrogated this man that you brought before me, accused of perverting the people. I have examined him before your eyes, and I have
found no fault in him."

The chief priest stepped forth and said, "We have a law, and by
our law he ought to die, because he claims to be the Son of God."

"Die because he's an uneducated, superstitious fanatic?" Pilatus
said with scornful disbelief. "Die because he suffers from a terrible
longing to be noticed, to be 'someone'? Come, come, my friends.
What harm can he do? He's but one among the many who wander
the desert with their little bands of followers, working sleight-of-hand
miracles and preaching comfortable, rustic home truths. Why not just
take him out and give him a good flogging. Surely that will serve to
dissuade the others."

But one of the scribes stepped forward and said, "If you let this
man go free, you are not Cæsar's friend, for whosoever claims himself
to be a king speaks against Cæsar."

I threw my master a warning frown. Was he aware that by shifting
their accusation from religious grounds to political ones, they were
transferring the responsibility for his punishment from their shoulders to his? If the man were guilty of blasphemy, he would be punished by the Sanhedrin and the Procurator's only role would be
granting or denying them recourse to the penalty of death; but if he
were guilty of treason, then Rome's representative in Judæa would be
obliged to punish him, so all the responsibility would devolve upon
Pilatus. It was obvious to me that they meant to skewer my master
on the horns of a dilemma, giving him a choice between permitting
the execution of this simple man or seeming to condone his treason-
able claims.

But the Procurator had experience of the duplicitous Levantine
mind; he sidestepped the trap without seeming to notice it had been
laid in his path.

He spoke to the priests, saying, "And if he now recants his claim
to be King of the Jews? Surely then you must let him go." Pilatus
turned to the prisoner and said in an undertone, "Consider your answers very carefully, son." Then he asked in full voice, "Are you the
King of the Jews?"

The accused one made no answer, but only looked upon Pilatus with that gentle, but utter and intractable stubbornness I remember so well in my own mother's eyes. It was obvious to me that this one intended to find his martyrdom, but my master would not let him destroy himself so easily. "Aren't you going to answer? Don't you hear the crimes they accuse you of? They say you call yourself King of the Jews, and that you preach against paying tribute to Cæsar! These are very serious matters, son. It's your life that's at stake."

But still the prisoner refused to speak.

"Are you King of the Jews?" Pilatus asked, clipping off the words in a dry tone that clearly proclaimed this to be his last chance to recant.

Seeming to realize this, the young rabbi lifted his head and said, "My kingdom is not of this world."

"There!" my master said triumphantly. "Did you hear that? His kingdom is not of this world. He denies being king of anything real and substantial. He no longer claims to be King of the Jews!"

But the tenacious scribe had no intention of losing his prey. "But he has stirred up the people throughout all Jewry, all the way from Galilee to here!"

"From Galilee?" Pilatus said, suddenly seeing a way to slip between the horns of his dilemma. "You say this man is a Galilaean? Well then, he falls under the jurisdiction of Herod Antipas, who happens to be here in Jerusalem to celebrate your Passover. Bring your prisoner before Herod, for I find no fault in him."

With a gesture, he commanded the guards to escort the accused man down to the awaiting throng, then he turned and strode back into the Prætorium followed by his guards. After watching the priests and scribes take their prisoner and, with angry growls, push him roughly before them out of the Judgment Hall, I followed my master into the feasting place.

When I approached, Pilatus was receiving a cup of wine from the hands of Claudia Procula, whose countenance revealed deep concern. I stood near, my eyes lowered and my face turned aside in a way I have of becoming nearly invisible while not missing a word.

"...but you mustn't worry," Pilatus told his wife. "It's nothing serious. Just another of those cristos."

"You say don't worry, Pontius, but I can't help it. If they're so unimportant as you claim, I cannot understand why you take the risks involved in dealing with them yourself."

"It's my job, my dear. And, to tell the truth, they intrigue me, with their eagerness to sacrifice everything for notoriety, even their lives. It's the professional actor's disease writ large."

"Pontius, I beg you. Please have nothing more to do with this affair. All last night I was tormented by a recurring dream about these wild-eyed fanatics, a dream that you were being destroyed by them, your reputation annihilated."

Pilatus chuckled. "My reputation in Rome is already in tatters, as you know."

"Don't joke, Pontius. I have a very strong, very dark premonition about this evening."

"Now, now, go back to our guests, Claudia. I'll join you soon."

"You are such a *fool* sometimes, Pontius."

"Mm? Yes, yes, I suppose so."

She turned angrily and went to the guests, and for a moment my master sipped his wine meditatively. "There's something that's been tickling my curiosity," he said, almost to himself, but knowing that I was nearby and listening.

"And what is that, master?"

"You suggested that one of these messiahs might someday gain a great following from among the world's unwashed and unwanted, and you used some sort of muddy metaphor about embers and grassfires to describe the spread of the messiah's cult."

"...Muddy?"

"But how can that be? Surely when posterity looks back upon this plague of messiahs it will harbor grave doubts that one among them could have been the true son of god, while all the rest were rogues or fools."

"Oh no, sire. Future generations will not wonder about the scores of unsuccessful cristos, because they will not know about them. History is always written by the winners, and if my doleful prediction comes true, the tale will be written by the followers of the successful messiah—whichever one that turns out to be. And you can bet that these disciples will make no mention of the other messiahs, because to do so would diminish their own importance as the followers of the one true voice out of the wilderness. The scores of forgotten messiahs of my 'muddy metaphor' will fall from the memory of man, and the successful messiah will shine forth without blemish or defect. His doubts will be glorified into philosophical questions while his weaknesses—if any are admitted—will be lauded as proofs of his humanity. He will be presented as perfect, pure of spirit and body. A virgin, like his mother. If he had a wife in life, his disciples will debase her or deny her existence. No, master, the successful cristo will have neither flaw nor competitor."

Pilatus had listened to me with an air of thinking of something else, something dark and deep, and this made me uneasy, for I was sure he needed his wits about him now more than ever.

"Sire, may I speak?" I asked.

"You do little else," he muttered.

"I fear there may be something to your noble wife's premonitions of danger. When dealing with these messiahs, you might quickly find your neck in a forked stick. If you decide in favor of the rustic preachers, the priests and scribes are sure to protest loudly enough to be heard in Rome. If you decide in favor of the priests and scribes, then you can expect scores of fanatical disciples to bare their chests to Roman spears and clamber up onto crosses to inflict their public suffering on you."

"You're saying there is no way I can win?"

"Once they start hurling the corpses of their 'oiled ones' at your head, it will no longer be a matter of winning, just a matter of not losing too much, and not losing it too publicly. Your salvation lies in doing nothing, while seeming to understand and sympathize with the rights and fears of both sides."

The Procurator nodded thoughtfully. Then he said, "I wonder how our lad is doing with Herod Antipas?"

"What do you plan to do, should he be dragged before you again?"

He closed his eyes and pressed his fingers deep into the sockets in weariness. "I shall do what I can to save the poor fellow's life, and if that fails, I shall try to give him a dignified death. Perhaps I can satisfy the priests by merely chastising and mocking him publicly, hoping they'll let it go at that."

"And if they won't let it go at that?"

"Then I'll offer to exchange the life of this harmless preacher for that of one of the condemned murderers we have in custody. Surely that will satisfy them."

"Surely? Have you forgotten that you are in Judæa?"

"What do you suggest I do?"

"If your efforts to placate them by chastizing and mocking this poor fanatic fail, and if the blood lust of the mob will not be satisfied by throwing them a murderer, then there is only one thing you can do. Publicly wash your hands of the matter and let the priests punish the man for blasphemy."

"But the penalty for blasphemy is stoning."

"It's *their* penalty. Their tradition. Your hands will be clean. Rome will not be responsible."

"Have you ever seen a stoning? I have. The first year I was here, I forced myself to witness one of their ritual lapidations. The spectacle of the vicious mob was more revolting, more frightening, than the gruesome fate of the victim, a poor woman taken in adultery. If you had seen the way they all joined in to deliver the punishment...tentatively at first...one small stone taken up and thrown listlessly, more a gesture of disapproval of the sin than a punishment for the sinner. But then a second stone was thrown, and a third, and suddenly the madness was upon them. Their eyes shone...little yapping cries escaped them as each encouraged the others...flecks of foam at the corners of their mouths. And the victim. The poor woman! Pleading...weeping...trying to reason with them as the stones struck her, knocking dust puffs from her robes. She tried at first not to show pain, because she sensed that pain would stimulate their frenzy...then she panicked when she tasted the blood running down her face. She fell, and the stones rained down upon her. She staggered to her feet, but the storm of stones continued. The stones they use are small ones, too small for any one blow to kill. This has the double advantage of freeing individual members of the mob from the guilt of murder and prolonging the victim's torment. She fell again and lay unmoving, and the mob waited, silent and panting. She quivered, then moved, then slowly rose and stood there, weak and swaying, blinded by her own blood, muttering words of gratitude as best she could through broken teeth, thinking that they had decided to show her mercy after all. The crowd listened and watched in tense, tingling silence. Then, as though stirred by a single urge, they began pelting her again. Finally...more than two hours after the thing began...a pulpy mess lay in the middle of the panting, sweating circle. The occasional stone made a thick plopping sound as it hit the amorphous bog they had created out of a woman. Then the crowd moved away in silence, chastened, satisfied, and no doubt many of them expressed to their families their disgust at the animal nature of their fellowman." My master's eyes focused again upon the here and now. "And the worst part was that no one was responsible. No individual citizen had killed her. It was the anonymous, snarling mob that had done this terrible thing." He looked at me, his eyes haggard from having reseen the horrors of the stoning in his memory. "Have you ever noticed, Greek, that when I am obliged to punish some rogue everyone says: 'Pilatus had the poor devil whipped', or 'The Procurator crucified three murderers'. But when they speak of a stoning, they always use the passive voice, saying: 'The criminal was stoned to death', as though the stones themselves had done the deed, not those who cast them? No, I will not let them stone this poor fanatic whose only crime is a terrible lust for fame and significance. If there is no option but to execute him, I'll oblige them to use a more humane way."

"Crucifixion?" I asked.

"It's the quickest and least painful of the public methods available to me."

"But stoning is the established punishment for blasphemy. You cannot change that."

"No. But I can change the charge. I can order him executed for treason to Rome, rather than for blasphemy."

"But, sire! That will shift the responsibility for this fellow's death from the shoulders of the priests to your own!"

"I'm aware of that. But my mind is made up. If he must be killed, it will be for treason, and he'll be crucified. I'll see to it that they use nails to shorten the suffering. Those who are only tied onto the cross with rope can linger, suffering, for days. And I'll order a guard to give him a coup de grâce with a spear. But...but let's hope it doesn't come to that. Let's hope that Herod Antipas finds a way to subvert the will of the Sanhedrin. He's a crafty old devil."

"Crafty enough to dodge his responsibilities and send the decision back to you, master. And you will ultimately harvest most of the blame in this matter."

He nodded, resigned.

At this juncture, the officer-of-the-guard came stamping in again, announcing a delegation of priests awaiting the Procurator down in the Hall of Judgment. They had a prisoner with them.

"So soon?" Pilatus said, setting his wine cup down. "Has Herod already managed to slither out of the trap?"

I offered to go first and speak to the scribes, then advise Pilatus of their intentions and mood. I had decided to reason, to bargain, to plead with the priests...anything to extricate my master from their snare. When, having made the priests wait for a quarter of an hour, Pilatus appeared at the top of the stairs I met him with a smile, relieved to be able to inform him that the prisoner they had with them was not, thank the Gods, the poor devil we had questioned earlier.

"Yet another suicidal messiah?" Pilatus asked, looking down upon the bound prisoner standing surrounded by priests and scribes. "Two in one day. Is there no end to them?"

"Apparently not, my lord."

"And I suppose this one also claims to have been born of a virgin, and to have descended from the family of David, and fled to Egypt to avoid persecution, and taught in the wilderness, and performed miracles and—all the rest of it."

"No doubt, my master."

Pilatus sighed. "Ah, well." He gestured for the prisoner to be brought to him. "Who knows? Perhaps this one will allow himself to be saved."

"Let us hope so, sire. This messiah's name is Joshua. Joshua of Nazareth. But he affects the Greek version of his name: Jesus."

POSTSCRIPTUM FOR THE CURIOUS

The historical spore left behind by Pontius Pilatus is surprisingly faint, considering that he is the most famous Roman of them all—more widely known than even Julius Cæsar. We only have two passing mentions of his name in official records, and one rather dodgy inscription on a long-ago-vandalized tomb. He must be regarded, therefore, as a figure in church history, rather than Roman history. And even within church history, the sources are few and unreliable. Among the spurious, quasiapocryphal writings of the Pseudoepigraphia we find accounts of Pontius Pilate by Josephus and Philo, and in the thoroughly apocryphal "Letters to the Emperor" and "The Acts of Pilate," Eusebius tells us that Pilate was eventually ordered back to Rome to explain his inability to calm and quell the Jews; but by the time he arrived, Tiberius had died (that would be in March of A.D. *37) and Pilate was not reappointed as Procurator of Judæa. Eusebius goes on to recount the tradition that Pilate became a Christian in result of his encounter with Joshua of Nazareth and subsequently committed suicide—presumably in a paroxysm of guilt and grief.*

Those with a taste for irony can reflect on the fact that Pilate's wife was eventually elevated to the rank of a minor saint of the Orthodox Church (because of her prophetic dream?), and Pilate himself is a saint of the Coptic Church.

THE ENGINE OF FATE

It was an outrage! Earlier that afternoon he had interrupted his hectic preparations for returning to his native village, and he had rushed all the way down to Telephone Central, where he had been obliged to stand for half an hour with his ear pressed to the listening tube, groaning with impatience while the woman sitting before her infernal tangle of wires and plugs struggled to keep him in contact with the Lafitte-Caillard travel office. He had subjected himself to the mysterious complexities of the 'phone because he knew that the usual New Year rush for places on the night train for Hendaye would be intensified by holiday makers wanting to mark the arrival of the new century in a special way, so to avoid any delay he wanted to make sure his tickets would be ready and waiting for him when he showed up later that evening. But after arriving at the Lafitte-Caillard's at the last minute, jumping out of his fiacre, shouting orders to the driver to wait there for him, dashing through the snow and, spurning the slow elevator, running three stairs at a time up to the third-floor office, intending to slap his money down on the counter and snatch up his tickets, what did he find? He found himself at the end of a queue of last-minute travelers, that's what he found! It was an outrage!

He chewed the ends of his new moustache in frustration while the incompetent fools in front of him bumbled their way through their trivial (but *interminable*) business, collected their tickets, examined each leaf of them to be absolutely sure there were no mistakes, then waddled off to take the elevator down to the line of black fiacres waiting in front of the building, their horses fidgeting and snorting jets of steam into the night air while the drivers huddled on their high seats, collars turned up against the first snowfall of the year.

He had timed his arrival at the ticket office so as to allow himself enough time (none to spare, it's true, but enough, enough!) to get him and his sister to Austerlitz station and settled into their sleeping car before the train pulled out. Who could possibly have anticipated this clogging wad of last-minute travelers? Oh. He had, come to think of it. That's why he had ordered his tickets in advance. Well then...who could possibly have known that the company wouldn't have a separate line for those prescient enough to order their tickets in advance?

Rocking from his toes to his heels to burn off some of his anxiety, he suddenly realized that the minute hand of the clock above the desk had not moved for at least—then it made a *click-thunk* as the hand lurched forward to the next minute. Oh, *that* kind of mechanism, was it? He might have known! *And* he might have known that the booking company would have only one clerk on duty. Typical!

After several aeons, he advanced to become third in line, but when the elderly couple at the desk turned back to ask the clerk to clarify some muddled, complicated matter, our hero sighed so loudly that the old man, embarrassed and flustered by making someone behind him so impatient, lost track of his question and began at the beginning again. A glance at the clock told the suffering Basque that there remained only a quarter of an hour for the fiacre that awaited him below to make it across the river to Austerlitz station—barely enough time, assuming they were not delayed by some fool in an automobile tooting his klaxon and frightening the horses.

The worst of it was that he could see his name on an envelope on the clerk's desk. There were his tickets, only a meter away! And his money was in his hand! His bones fairly twisted within his body from impatience.

The clock lurched to the next minute, and the young man cleared his throat to speak to the large man ahead of him, a professional person, judging from his expensive black broadcloth coat and the stiff dignity of his manner. "Excuse me, monsieur. I am traveling on a mission of the utmost importance, so I'm sure you wouldn't mind if I just handed over my money and snatched up my tickets. It wouldn't take a second, and I would be eternally—"

"My business, monsieur, is also of great importance," the blond-bearded giant said, turning to him. "So I'm afraid you will just have to wait your turn."

"But, monsieur, my business is a matter of life and death!"

"And mine, monsieur, is a matter of honor."

"Next?" the clerk said in a small voice, not wanting to get involved in what was beginning to sound nasty.

"If your business was so damned pressing," the young Basque said, his black eyes darting dangerous fire up into the pale blue eyes of this recalcitrant stranger, "then you should have made your reservations in advance by the telephone. If you'd had an ounce of foresight, monsieur, we'd both be out of here by now!"

The clock *click-thunk'd* one of their precious minutes into eternity, and the clerk risked another timid, "Next?"

"I don't believe in the 'phone," Blond-beard informed his tormentor. "It is my professional opinion as a doctor that excessive use of this invention might lead to deafness."

"And it is my opinion, as a man of common sense, that your view is mindless quackery."

"Quackery, monsieur?"

"*Mindless* quackery."

"If I were not in a great hurry, I would treat you to the thrashing you deserve!"

"*You* thrash *me?* You, a fat northern slug, thrash me, a pure-blooded Basque of the race that kicked Roland's behind for him? Ridiculous."

"I will remind you that I am considerably bigger than you, monsieur."

"Larger, yes. Bigger, never!"

"Next?"

"Monsieur, I don't mind telling you that—But no. I can't waste more time listening to your infantile Gascon rodomontade."

And the doctor turned to the desk and began arranging for tickets to Biarritz.

"Gascon?" the young man muttered, stunned that anyone could mistake a Basque for a Gascon. "*Gascon?* I'll teach you to call me—" But he smothered his outrage (albeit with Herculean effort) because he owed it to his family's honor to get home to Cambo-les-Bains as quickly as possible. And arguing with this uncivil, stubborn, mound-of-meat of an opinionated, thick-headed northern quack would only delay him and—Ah, at last!

The blond doctor brushed past him on his way out to the elevator, and the young man stepped up to the flinching clerk, slapped his money on the counter, snatched up the envelope containing his tickets, and ran out of the office.

"Wait!" he shouted.

But the doctor pushed the button for the ground floor, and the elevator slid down through its ornate wrought-iron cage into the darkness below, its occupant smiling in nasty victory.

"Bastard!" the young man muttered. He threw his overcoat over his shoulder and rushed down the marble staircase that spiraled around the cage within which the elevator descended so slowly that he beat it to the floor below, where he pushed the call button, then continued his flying descent.

There! Now Dr. Blondbeard de la Sassymouth would have to open the inner accordion door and the outer wrought-iron door, then close them again and push his 'ground floor' button again to continue his descent. Our Basque knew this routine well because there was a newly installed Otis 'safety' elevator in the newspaper office where he occasionally sold scraps of drama criticism, and the journalists could never resist playing childish elevator tricks on one another.

As he continued his spiral dream, two old gentlemen flattened themselves against the wall to make room. On the next floor, he again pushed the elevator button in passing—ha!—and he plunged on down, his feet a blur, his overcoat flying behind him. Halfway down the last flight, a scrubwoman heard his clattering approach and fled downward, and he nearly came to grief over the bucket and brush she left behind, as he heel-slipped down half a dozen wet stairs, barely managing to keep his balance. As he charged into the entrance foyer, his brains a-reel, he heard the scrubwoman say something most un-ladylike, but he slammed the front doors open and broke out onto the pavement, where footsteps of passersby were revealed in an inch of fresh snow.

Oh, no! The cab wasn't where he had left it. Damn the perfidious cabby who had promised to wait until he—

Oh...there it is.

It had moved down towards the head of the rank, which had short-ened to just two cabs with the departure of the infuriating slowpokes who had been ahead of him in the queue. He ran through the whirl-ing snowflakes towards the glow of the cab's side lamp. "Cabby!" Then he reduced his voice to a hoarse croak, so as not to disturb his sister, who had finally fallen asleep in the cab after a terrible night of worry about the foolhardy actions of their irresponsible brother back home in Cambo-les-Bains. "I'll double the fare if you get me to the station in time for the seven-twenty."

He jumped in as the driver took a long swig from his flask, applied the whip to the dozing horse, and they lurched off. The young man carefully spread his overcoat over the curled-up form of his sister on the far side of the cab; then he twisted around to catch a last glimpse of the Lafitte-Caillard travel office through the isinglass rear window, and he was gratified to see the doctor burst out through the double doors, stumbling and skidding, and rush towards the last remaining cab in the rank.

Serves him right!

The cabby threaded through the snarled and snarling traffic at breakneck speed, exchanging with offended drivers those dire threats that satisfy the Frenchman's yearning to be manfully aggressive with-out actually risking physical confrontation. Fearful that the jolting and pitching of the cab might rob his sister of her much-needed rest, the young man reached into the darkness, put his arm around her, and drew her firmly against his side. She murmured a vague, drowsy, nest-ling sound, then her eyes fluttered open and she looked up

They both screamed....Although he managed to lower the end of his scream into a more manly baritone.

"Get out of this cab!" she commanded, recoiling into the farthest corner.

"But, mademoiselle—"

"Get out immediately! Out. Out! *Out!*"

"But we're in the middle of traffic."

"Get out or I'll scream."

"You *are* screaming."

"If you think that was screaming, wait until you hear *this!*" She opened her mouth, threw back her head, and drew a deep breath.

But she didn't scream, so baffled was she by his question: "What happened to my sister?"

"...Your what?"

"My sister! I thought you were my sister, but you're not."

"Thank God."

The cab lurched around a corner made treacherous by slush, and the two passengers were thrown against one another.

"Oh no you don't," she warned. "None of that."

"I assure you, mademoiselle, that I had no intention of—"

"Stop this cab."

"I can't."

"You *can't?*

"*Won't*, then."

"Oh, you won't, won't you? We'll see about that!" She reached up to rap against the roof and attract the driver's attention, but he forced her back into her seat and firmly held her there by her wrists.

"Release me, you...brigand! You...you...white slaver!"

"I assure you, mademoiselle, that I—"

"Stop assuring me of things and let me out of this cab!"

"I will not! This cab will continue at full speed to the Gare d'Austerlitz. It's a matter of life and death!"

She suddenly stopped struggling and stared at him in deepest suspicion. "The Gare d'Austerlitz? But...but *I'm* going to the Gare d'Austerlitz."

"Yes, and there's nothing you can do about it, so you might as well accept it. But as soon as we arrive I'll jump out, and the cabby can bring you wherever you want to go."

"Let go of me."

"What?"

"You're holding my hands."

"Wha—? Oh yes, of course. Sorry."

"How did you know I was going to the Gare d'Austerlitz?"

"I didn't know." He pressed his palm to his head. "This is turning into the worse night of my life."

Giving him an oblique glance that searched for signs of insanity, she was silent for a moment before asking, "What made you choose me as your kidnap victim?"

"Kidnap vic—? Oh, for the love of— Listen. I thought you were my sister. What I mean is, I thought this was my cab. They all look alike, after all. And if it *had* been my cab, then you'd have been my sister. It isn't and you aren't, but that's not *my* fault. If it's anyone's fault, it's the fault of that ill-mannered oaf."

"...I see. Ah...what ill-mannered oaf was that?" she asked, keeping her tone light and conversational, because she thought it would be best to humor him until she could find an opportunity to get away.

"The ill-mannered, stubborn, pompous oaf in front of me in the queue! If he'd had the common decency to let me pick up my tickets, I wouldn't have been late, and I wouldn't have had to rush, and I wouldn't have jumped into the wrong cab, and I wouldn't be *explaining all this to you now.*"

"I...see..."

"If only he'd ordered his tickets in advance, like I did. But no. No, no, no. The superstitious boob doesn't realize that we're on the eve of the Twentieth Century. Do you know what he told me?"

"Ah...no. No, I don't. What *did* he tell you?"

"He said that using the 'phone would make you deaf. And he calls himself a doctor."

"My brother!"

"What?"

"That was my brother! He's a doctor."

"He's also an ill-mannered, stubborn, pompous—"

"I was waiting for him while he went to get our tickets."

"My sister was waiting for me."

"I must have dropped off. I've been so worried that I haven't slept properly for two nights."

"Neither has my—"

"Now I see what happened. You've made a terrible mistake."

"I *told* you it was a mistake, but you wouldn't listen."

"Why should I listen to a self-avowed brute and brigand?"

He blinked. "I beg your pardon?"

"Oh, no, it's too late to beg my pardon. We have to decide calmly and intelligently what to—"

"Oh, my god! My sister is in the clutches of that pompous, stubborn, imbecile of a—"

"My brother may be stubborn—even pompous upon occasion—but at least *your* sister won't be obliged to defend herself against unwanted advances."

"*Advances?*"

"When I woke up, you were holding me in your arms. Do you deny it?"

"I was merely protecting you."

"From what? Brutish brigands?"

"The cab was lurching through the traffic. I didn't want your sleep to be disturbed."

"So you protected me by making sure that when I woke, I'd find myself in the arms of a strange man? A *very* strange man."

"Look, I am sorry if I upset you, but I haven't got time to chant my apologies all evening long. Listen, mademoiselle. Your brother is following us. I saw him jump into what I now realize was *my* cab, and no doubt he—Ohmygod, he's got my sister! And they're sure to arrive at the station too late to catch the train! I'm going to make it only by the closest of shaves, if at all. My sister's going to be furious. But at least your brother will be able to take care of you. All you have to do is wait at the cab rank for him."

"Where will you be?"

"On the train, of course. I absolutely must get to Cambo-les-Bains by noon tomorrow to stop my poor dunderhead of a brother from falling into the clutches of a calculating temptress. A dreadful error that would destroy his future, leave him heartbroken and—But there's no time to explain. When you see my sister, tell her what happened, and tell her to return to my flat and await news from me. She'll be all alone there, I'm afraid. She knows no one in Paris. But that can't be helped. Will you do me that favor?"

"In return for all the favors you've lavished on me? Like kidnapping me, for instance? And stealing my brother's cab? And crushing my hands in your brutish grasp?"

"I'm sorry if I hurt you."

"You didn't hurt me. I'm much too strong for that."

"Then what's all this about crushing you in my brutish grasp?"

"Just a—a sort of metaphor."

"Metaphor? That wasn't a metaphor; it was a barefaced lie."

"Well, maybe it— So what? Who are you to decide what is a metaphor and what is not? Do you think you're the only one who has to save someone from making a dreadful mistake that will ruin her future?"

"Wh—? Surely that's a non sequitur."

"And I suppose that's even worse than a metaphor? Don't you realize that my brother and I were going to Cambo-les-Bains, too?"

He squeezed his eyes shut. "What are you talking about?"

"I'm telling you that the 'calculating temptress' you're intending to save your brother from is my poor love-sick sister! And the heartless cad who's trying to trick my sister into a foolish marriage is your guileful, brutish brigand of a brother. It would appear that brutish brigandry runs in your family!"

"My brother is no brigand."

"And my sister is certainly no temptress."

"Well, I intend to make sure she doesn't get her 'poor love-sick' hooks into my brother!"

"And I mean to save her from the clutches of your 'poor dunderhead' of a brother!"

"Good!"

"Very good indeed!"

They withdrew into their separate corners and stared furiously out their respective windows. She absentmindedly drew his coat over her knees against the cold draughts that flowed in through the rattling window; then, suddenly realizing what she was wrapping around herself, she pushed the despised rag from her and let it slide onto the floor.

Snow melting from the top of the cab rippled over the panes, causing soft slabs of buttery gaslight from shop windows to alternate with harsh rectangles of cold, white, electric light from the newly installed street lamps. The young man took mental note of this lighting effect. He might use it in his directions to a set designer some day. He pulled out his watch, fumbled in his waistcoat pocket for a matchbox, struck a light, and groaned. "I'll never make it!" he muttered miserably.

"Serves you right," she said.

He despised the mean-minded sort of people who say, 'Serves you right'. By the light of the match, he saw her face for the first time, and her intelligent, somewhat haughty eyes returned his frank examination, but their color was a fascinating— Ouch! He dropped the match onto his coat, which he then snatched up and slapped until he was sure it was not burning.

"I see you take your frustration out on inanimate things as well," she said.

He lit another match, and now he could see the terrible danger facing his brother. If the sister also had that creamy complexion and those violet-blue eyes...his poor brother!

The match went out, and they experienced a moment of blindness until their eyes dilated again to the darkness of the cab, which swayed and jolted around a corner onto the Pont Sully that crossed the river at the upstream tip of the Ile St. Louis. The harsh glare of the bridge's new electric street lamps played over them in rhythmic succession, then, with a lurching turn to the left, they were following the Left Bank quay towards the Gare d'Austerlitz.

As the driver was making a daring pass, the fiacre's wheel got caught in the track of the horse-drawn omnibus line, jouncing the passengers into one another's arms. They immediately recoiled into their corners, whence they regarded one another with ruffled indignation and no small amount of suspicion.

After a brooding silence, she spoke, her voice flat with icy determination. "I've decided to go with you."

"What?"

"I don't trust you to prevent this preposterous marriage. My sister is a child. Barely eighteen."

"My brother's only two years older."

"That's evidently old enough to lure an innocent girl into marriage in the hope of getting at her dowry."

"If anyone's guilty of setting traps, it certainly isn't my brother. He doesn't need your sister's paltry dowry. He owns a flourishing establishment in Cambo."

"I daren't think what kind of establishment."

"A hotel, if you must know. One of Cambo's best. It was my father's and my grandfather's before him. But my father died, and it was obvious that my talents ran more to the literary than the commercial, so we agreed that the hotel should be my brother's. He runs it with my mother."

"Your mother's in on this too, is she?"

"Now just a minute!"

"I'm going to Cambo, and that's final! I don't trust any of your wild clan of Basque brigands."

"I take offence at your— How did you know we're Basque?"

"Everyone in Cambo is Basque—except for the poor patients who go to take the waters and end up being tricked into marriage. Then too, there's the matter of your eyes."

"My eyes?"

"Yes, your eyes. Those notorious 'melting brown' Basque eyes that feature in so many cheap romantic novels."

"I know nothing of romantic novels."

"But my sister does. She devours them. And that's why I'm going to Cambo-les-Bains with you."

"Oh, you are, are you?"

"Yes, I am."

"How?"

"*How?*"

"Do you have a ticket?"

"Of course I have a— Well...no, actually. My brother has our tickets."

"Ah! Then how do you propose to get on the train?"

"Well, I'll just have to— Wait a minute. *You* have a ticket! For your sister."

"O-o-oh, no, you don't!"

"Oh, yes, I shall! And if you don't let me use her ticket, I'll follow you onto the platform, and I'll cry and sob and accuse you of...of running off with some tart and deserting me and our children! Our *seven* children."

"You wouldn't dare."

She lifted her chin and regarded him coolly.

And he had the sinking realization that his adversary was not inhibited by the slightest sense of fair play.

"I'd do anything to save my sister from the fate worse than the fate worse than death: a bad marriage."

As though to punctuate this declaration, the carriage lurched to a stop, bringing them once again into a contact that had a brief physical—but only physical—resemblance to an embrace. The cab door was snatched open, and light from an ox-eye lantern flashed in their faces. "Train for Hendaye?" the porter asked. "You'd better hurry, m'sieur-'dame. They're closing the gates to the platform now."

The young man sprang out onto the pavement beside the impressive mass of the Gare d'Austerlitz. She descended, pointedly ignoring his proffered hand, as the porter seized two valises (the young woman's and her brother's) from the box of the cab and hastened into the station. They followed him to the turnstile, where the young man fumbled for the tickets for an eternal ten seconds before he found them in the first pocket he had checked. They slipped through the gates as they were closing, and they ran for all they were worth. She soon fell behind with a little cry of dismay, and he swore under his breath but he grasped her hand and drew her along behind him at a speed that not only cost her the last semblance of grace but even endangered her balance as they sped down the platform to where their porter stood beside the portable steps at the door of their car, making frantic signs for them to hasten. As they passed the dining car, the young woman glimpsed faces looking out upon their hectic race with expressions of unfeigned amusement blended with...something else, something that she would not identify until later, when recognition would make a tingle of embarrassment and outrage rush up the back of her neck into her hair.

With all the flair of gesture and oiliness of manner that mark the veteran tip-seeker, the steward showed them to their chambrette, deposited their valises in the racks, and turned up the gaslamp that displayed the 'new art' Guimard impulse to create foliage out of glass and metal. After the coin had been pressed into his hand and he had glanced down upon it with a thoroughly Gallic blend of resignation and disdain, the steward said that service in the dining car would begin in fifteen minutes, and he would make up their beds while they were dining. As he put his hand on the door handle to leave, he winked at the young man and tipped his head towards the young woman with a lift of the eyebrows.

She caught this yeasty, man-to-man communication in the mirror as she was taking off her Trilby fedora, and she spun around. Raising one hand to stay the steward's departure, she asked the young man, "Did you tip him?"

"Well...ah...yes, of course."

"Give me that tip," she ordered the steward.

The steward recoiled and stammered, "But, mam'selle, but...but..."

"Give it to me!" She held out her hand, and with a grimace of genuinely heartfelt pain, the steward turned his hand over and let the coin drop into her palm.

"Now get out of here! And if we push one of those buttons for a steward, you'd better not be the one who comes tapping at the door. Do you understand me?"

"But, mam'selle, I..."

"And what makes you so sure I'm a mademoiselle?"

"I'm terribly sorry, madame. I thought—"

"That's a lie. You've never had a thought in your life—other than filthy ones! Out. Out!"

The steward vanished, closing the door behind him with a thoroughly miffed click, followed by a defiant snap of his fingers, a dental mutter of outrage, an incensed extension of his neck, a petulant out thrust of his lower lip, and a disdainful flare of his nostrils, which catalogue of manly outrage he displayed only after he was sure he was safe from her.

"You were pretty hard on him," the young man said, not without a certain astonished respect.

"And you were pretty compliant. What did you think his little wink meant?"

"Oh, he didn't mean anything. Not really. That's just how men are."

"Exactly!"

"Well...after all..."

"*What?*"

"Well, what *should* he think? You're young and attractive...in your way...and you're not wearing a wedding ring. And then there's the matter of your—"

"What makes you think I'm not wearing a wedding ring? I haven't taken my gloves off yet."

"No, but naturally I assumed...Are you? Married, I mean?"

"As it happens I am not. And then there's the matter of my...what?"

"I beg your pardon?"

"After that twaddle about my wedding ring, you said, 'And then there's the matter of your...' My what?"

"Well, your dress, to be frank."

"And what about my dress?"

"I will not be cross-questioned in that imperious tone."

"You shall! What about my dress?"

"Well, it's very...ah...modern."

"Modern?"

"Short, then. It's short. Short!"

"My dress comes to exactly three inches from the ground. I refuse to obey the dictates of fashion that oblige a woman to drag her dresses in the mud—and much worse than mud—just to assure men that her reputation is sufficiently unassailable to make her worthy of their attentions...attentions that are, of course, designed to urge her to do something that will damage her reputation."

"I wouldn't dream of denying any woman her right to wear what she wants to wear. But if a woman shows three inches of ankle to every passerby, then she must accept—"

"I accept nothing! And it's not three inches of ankle. It's three inches of tightly buttoned shoe."

"Ah, so you say. But when you stepped down from the cab, there was a bit of leg visible above the shoe."

"An inch or two of stocking. Of thick, black stocking."

"Are you sure it's not a *blue* stocking? And are you sure it's a stocking, and not a bloomer?"

"Oh, so you have something against bluestockings and against the courageous Miss Bloomer?"

"I am a thoroughly modern man, and if I had my way, every woman would be as liberated as the bluest of the bluestockings, and God bless them all. But you can't blame the majority of men for—"

"I certainly *can* blame them. And I do! And as for you...Ha!"

"Ha?"

"You claim to be a modern man. And yet, even while rushing to save your brother from the clutches of the sweetest, gentlest little romantic fool in the world, you took time to notice exactly how many inches of ankle I revealed while alighting from the cab. How like a man! Men like you are the reason I became an actress."

He blinked and pressed his hand to his chest. "I am the reason you became—?"

"I'd rather not discuss it further." She turned away from him and looked fixedly out at the horizontal blur of snow streaking across the patch of gaslight. She focused back to the surface of the window and saw his reflected face, his eyes looking at her with intensity.

"Well? What is it?" she asked the window.

"Are you really an actress?"

"Does that seem so impossible?"

"No, but...I'm in theater myself. I'm a playwright. And also," he added with a dismissive shrug, "an occasional critic for newspapers."

"Critic, eh? I might have known."

"Meaning?"

"That I might have known."

"Where have you worked? Perhaps I have seen you. I may even have reviewed you."

"I am with André Antoine's Théâtre Libre," she said with pride.

"Oh," he said with a falling note. "Strindberg, Zola, Ibsen, all that lot. Plays of 'social significance'." There was a shudder in his voice.

"You disapprove of social drama? Or is it significance that frightens you?"

"I disapprove of the phony realism. Of the way the actors mutter and scratch themselves and turn their backs on the audience. That's every bit as affected in its way as the most smoke-cured of the hams rolling their 'r's' and tearing a scene to tatters with their bare teeth. What have you appeared in?"

"Oh...lots of things."

"Such as?"

"Well, I was in *Hedda Gabler*, for one. And *A Doll's House*. And *Thérèse Raquin*."

"I saw the Théâtre Libre production of *Hedda Gabler*. In fact, I wrote a review of it. But I don't remember you."

"I didn't say I played a major role in *Hedda*."

"Even in a supporting role, I'd remember that splendid mane of cupric hair, and that sassy uptilted nose."

"Well, my part was... well, actually, the director wanted me to concentrate on the *internal* aspects of my character. On what was seething beneath the surface so powerfully that to express it in words would be redundant."

"I see. You're saying you didn't have any lines."

"I'm saying that I played an intensely sensitive young serving girl who was aware of the family's innermost suffering. I reflected my sensitivity and awareness to the audience, and I believe they felt my....ah...my..."

"I see. Have you had *any* speaking parts?"

"Well...no. Not *as such*. I'm still learning my craft. It's my first season with André."

"Great heavens! Your brilliant career with 'André' is barely off the ground, and yet you're willing to let it slump while you run off to the Pyrenees to save your poor consumptive sister from the fate you claim is worse than the fate worse than death."

"I find your snide comments neither amusing nor illuminating. I can see why you chose to become a critic."

"I write reviews only to broaden my knowledge of theater...and to earn a bit of money. As I told you, I am a playwright."

"Oh? And what have you written?"

"Oh...dozens of things."

"Such as?"

"Well...for instance, I permitted the Gaieté Theatre to perform one of my pieces just last month."

"The Gaieté? But they do nothing but low farces."

"I'm not ashamed to admit that my play was a farce. A tightly written, uproariously funny farce, as a matter of fact."

"And you have the cheek to turn your nose up at social realism. You who offer nothing but asinine romps, improbable coincidences, mistaken identity, and trite screen-scenes featuring wayward husbands caught hiding from avenging wives, all this crammed into three frantic acts of babble and confusion!"

"That shows how much you know! My play was only one act!"

"Ah, so you write one-act curtain warmers to get idiot audiences in the mood for the *real* farces that will follow. And you dare to sneer at plays that deal with human suffering and social issues and the criminal oppression of women! Humph!"

"Actually, nobody really says humph. It's just a literary convention."

"Well, I say humph. Especially when I'm talking to writers of trivial..." She frowned. "My sister is not consumptive. What on earth gave you *that* idea?"

"Er-r-r-r," he struggled to catch up with this lurch of subject. "Oh, I see where you are. Well, I deduced that your sister had weak lungs because the waters of Cambo-les-Bains are famous for improving two conditions: consumption and what are euphemistically called 'Woman's Problems'. Since this latter tends to befall mostly women of 'a certain age' with little to occupy their overactive imaginations, I naturally assumed that—"

"That would be Aunt Adelaïde."

"...Aunt Adelaïde?"

"My father's sister. She came to look after him after our mother died. But lately she's become a little...none of your business. Sophie accompanied Aunt Adelaïde to the spa for a course of the waters to treat her...ailments."

"Sophie being your sister?"

"Aren't you listening? My father could hardly let his silly sister go down there all alone. She's an even greater romantic than our Sophie. You know, I'll bet anything that Aunt Adelaïde is in on this plot of your brother's to snatch poor Sophie from her family. I'm starving."

"Er-r-r-r." That lurch again. "Ah! Well, the steward said that they—"

"Don't mention that insinuating, low-minded worm to me."

"All right, but the Unmentionable Invertebrate said that they would begin serving in fifteen minutes, and that was..." he fished out his watch and snapped it open "...twenty minutes ago. I assume you'd rather not dine with a crass purveyor of trivial farces, so I'll await your return before—"

"Nonsense. We'll dine together."

He was surprised...but oddly pleased. "So, I guess I'm not all that bad after all."

"Your badness has nothing to do with it. I have no money."

"Oh."

"Shall we go?"

"Ah...by all means."

They were conducted to a table at the far end of the 'American' dining car, which obliged them to walk a gauntlet of frank curiosity mixed with...something else. She called up a mental snapshot of these very faces peering out at them as they dashed frantically for the train, and suddenly she recognized what this something else was: complicity. Benevolent complicity! As we foretold it would, a tingle of embarrassment rushed up the back of her neck into her hair at the realization that these romantic busybodies took it for granted that they were eloping lovers rushing off to their honeymoon. Probably leaving irate parents and jilted fiancés in their madcap wake. Oh, the humiliation of it! Actress that she was, it was not having an audience that she minded, it was the absurdity of her role in this vulgar farce.

Man that he was, he had noticed nothing.

She sat in rigid dignity, her lips compressed, her attention riveted on the menu, but painfully conscious of smiles, whispers, and nudges out on the defocused edges of her peripheral vision. She looked up to see him nod politely at two smiling women sitting at the table opposite, beaming at them. Sisters, obviously; unmarried, probably; and nosy without a doubt. His social smile dissolved under her disapproving frown. "What's wrong?"

She leaned forward towards him and smiled an actress's smile: all in the lips and cheeks, nothing in the eyes. "Don't you realize that everyone is looking at us?" she asked in a honeyed whisper, though there was asperity in her tone.

He looked around. "Why, yes, now you mention it. They seem a friendly enough lot. The old gentleman down there just waved and winked at me."

"If you wink back," she whispered sweetly, "I'll kick your shin so hard that you'll limp the rest of your life." She smiled and patted his hand.

"I don't understand."

"I believe that. They think..." she beckoned him with her finger, and he leaned over the table towards her. "They think we're newlyweds."

"But that's ridiculous!"

"Keep your voice down."

"But why should they think—? I mean, what right do they have to imagine that I'd—"

"Keep your voice down!" she rasped. "The last thing I want is for them to think we're having a lovers' quarrel. That would be meat and drink to them."

He looked again over at the two maiden sisters. The plumper one pursed her lips and shook her head in a gesture that said: naughty, naughty (but adorable) children.

"Ohmygod," he muttered.

"Exactly," she said.

"Well, you need have no fear for your reputation, mademoiselle. I'll see to it that it suffers no harm."

"My reputation is no concern of yours. I'm perfectly capable of defending it myself."

"Perhaps so, but you will have our chambrette to yourself. I'll spend the night sitting up in the smoking car. Staring out the window...alone...cold."

"You'll do nothing of the kind! You—" She controlled the intensity of her voice and forced herself to smile on him as she whispered, "You will *not* feed their gossip with the choice morsel that we've had a spat and I've made you spend our wedding night sitting up in the smoking car. You will spend the night sitting up in our chambrette, staring out the window, if you wish, cold perhaps, alone certainly, while I shall be sleeping not a meter away, totally undisturbed by and totally indifferent to your presence. And now, dearest husband, I believe I am ready to order."

"I've lost my appetite," he said petulantly.

"You will, nevertheless, order a full meal. And you will eat every crumb of it. I'll not have these people thinking that we are rushing through dinner so that we can— That we're rushing through dinner."

The waiter's smarmy solicitude extended to placing a bud vase on their table: a single white rose of chastity, soon, presumably, to be dutifully surrendered. She acknowledged the vase with a dry, "How *very* kind," uttered without unclenching her teeth.

They were halfway through their soup (large bowls only half full, in consideration of the swaying car) when, after a brooding silence, he spoke out in midthought. "It's not as though I were unaware of— or indifferent to—the social injustices that women face every day. Quite the contrary. It's just that...Oh, forget it." He shrugged.

"It's just that...what?" she wondered.

"Well, if you must know, I don't believe that heavy-handed 'social drama' does any good. It may rub the audience's nose in their flaws and failings but it doesn't solve anything. For one thing, social drama preaches only to the ladies of the altar society, and—"

"The ladies of the altar society?"

"That was a figure of speech."

"I *hate* figures of speech."

He stared at her. "How can anyone harbor a general antipathy against figures of speech?"

"Nothing easier. I've done it all my life. What's all this about the ladies of the altar society?"

"The only people willing to sit in the gloomy Théâtre Libre and let themselves be bludgeoned by great chunks of 'message' are those who already agree with those messages. If you want to persuade the indifferent masses, you've got to put your message into a form that most people enjoy."

"Like your farces, I suppose?"

"Exactly. Now in my last farce—"

"...A mere one-act curtain opener..."

"...*In my last farce*, I ridiculed the men who consider lonely, unappreciated wives in search of love and understanding to be 'fallen women', while husbands out on the town are thought of as gay blades and sly old rogues."

"Well...maybe." Hm-m, perhaps there was more to this fellow than a handsome face, and that thick curly hair, and those liquid Basque eyes, and that mouth with its upward— "But I'll bet anything that your women are transparent stereotypes, as in all farces: the Domineering Wife; the Pert, Desirable Soubrette; the Volcanic, Seething Femme Fatale; the Innocent, Empty-Headed Ingenue; the Flapping, Fluttering—"

"It's true that playwrights use stock characters to—"

"Don't you try to wriggle out of it by claiming they're just figures of speech!"

"Figures of speech?"

"All right, all right! So I've never grasped just what figures of speech are. Is that a crime? Is it a disgrace not to know the difference between a metaphor and a hyperbole and an anagram and a litotes and a—?"

"An anagram is not a figure of speech."

"Thank God *something* isn't."

"Sh-h-h. They'll think were having our first quarrel." He smiled.

"You think this is all very funny, don't you."

"I think it's good material for a farce. A *social* farce, of course. A farce of Impelling Social Significance. I could have a character like you: charming, determined, fiery, spouting all your suffragette stuff. While the dignified, understanding, oddly attractive playwright looks calmly into her flashing eyes and—"

"...My suffragette *stuff?*"

"Well, you know what I mean."

She was prevented from telling him that she did not know what he meant, and didn't care to learn, when the waiter came to replace the soup tureen with a large platter of steamed oysters, for it was almost New Years, the traditional season for oysters.

He applied himself with dexterity to liberating the delicious molluscs from their shells, but after the first three, he suddenly realized she was not eating.

"What's wrong? I thought you were hungry."

"I'm *famished.* I haven't had a decent meal since we received that telegram from Sophie, announcing her intention to marry the brother of an ink slinger who churns out low farces."

"Well, if you're so hungry, why aren't you eating?" He leaned forward and smiled into her eyes as he whispered in his most 'new-husbandly' voice, "You wouldn't want people to think you can't eat because you're all fluttery with anticipation, would you?" He pumped his eyebrows.

Her eyes hardened and she whispered, "I am not eating because one cannot eat oysters with one's gloves on."

"In that case," he said in a caressing tone, but separating his words carefully as though speaking to the village idiot, "why don't you take your gloves off?"

She laid her hand over his and smiled up into his eyes. "I don't take them off because..." she pinched that particularly excruciating spot on the back of the hand known only to girls who have had to learn to avenge the teasing of older brothers "...because, stupid, I'm not wearing a wedding ring. And if there's anything I'd find more repellent than these people thinking I'm your wife, it would be their thinking I'm your *mistress.*" She hissed this last word as she twisted the pinch, hard.

"Ai-i-i!" He snatched his hand from beneath hers and rubbed the back of it, mute accusation in his wounded eyes. "So it's the old she-can't-take-off-her-glove-because-she-isn't-wearing-a-ring problem, is it? All right, I'll show you what a clever farce writer can do. Hm-m-m." His focus seemed to turn inward as he ransacked his imagination for a ploy that would—ah!

"Take off your gloves," he said.

"But, I—"

"Please just do as I say. Take off your gloves."

Reluctantly, she drew off first her right glove, then the revealing left.

"Now just follow my lead," he whispered; then aloud, he said, "Goodness gracious me! Where is your ring, darling?"

Her eyes narrowed. "If this is some vicious stunt meant to embarrass me..." She lifted her forefinger and pointed at his heart.

All around them, ears that had been straining in their direction since they sat down (and particularly since his heartfelt 'ai-i-i!') now fairly vibrated, as bodies leaned towards them, although no one was so obvious as to actually turn and look.

"I told you, darling heart," he continued aloud, "that Grandma's ring was too large for your dainty finger. But, impatient little imp that you are, you couldn't wait until I had the jeweller...ah...smallen it, could you?" He wrinkled his nose at her as he picked her gloves up from the table.

"*Smallen* it?" she echoed, promising herself she would pay him back for that 'impatient little imp' business. And as for his nose wrinkling...

"Now what am I going to tell Mother? She'll be heartbroken to learn that Granny's ring has been— Well, I'll be hornswaggled!" He was pinching the ring finger of her left glove. "Here it is! It slipped off with your glove. You silly billy, you."

"Silly billy?"

He 'milked' the nonexistent ring down the finger of the glove, then he reached inside and pinched the air between his thumb and forefinger and stuffed the bit of captured nothing into his watch pocket, which he patted protectively. "And there it stays, snookums, until I have a chance to...uh...smallify it. Hubby knows best," he said, wagging his finger at her, and he could almost feel the silent applause of the entire dining car. She, with her actress's instinct, was even more aware of the silent applause than he...and she hated it. And as for that wagging finger...!

He slipped back into their now-habitual undertone. "Be honest and admit that I have the gift of invention necessary to be a successful playwright."

"If all it takes are the instincts and tactics of a confidence trickster, then maybe so."

"I've given myself three years to make it in Parisian theater."

"It might take longer than that with lines like 'I'll be hornswaggled!' And if you don't 'make it' in three years? What then?"

"Well, in that case, I'll...I don't know. It's risky to consider failure. It puts dangerous ideas into the mind of the goddess of Fortune. What about you? How long have you given yourself to make it as an interpreter of terribly, terribly significant social dramas?"

"As long as it takes."

"There's the girl! Now, to build up your strength for the long climb towards fame, riches, and social impact, perhaps you'd better start on those oysters."

No longer burdened with gloves, she dug in with undisguised gusto; but now it was he who seemed suddenly to lose his appetite.

"What's wrong?" she asked, manipulating her oyster fork with address.

"These oysters make me think about my sister."

"A pearl of a girl, is she? Or sort of slimy? Or all steamed up over your leaving her behind?"

"She adores oysters. And she hasn't eaten a thing since we received my brother's telegram telling us that he had succumbed to the wiles of...well, that he had fallen totally and eternally in love with your Sophie, and intended to marry her immediately, whether or not the family approved. Here it is, after eight, and my sister can't even go to a restaurant. I am carrying our traveling money, naturally."

"Naturally? Why is it 'natural' for men to carry the money? But I wouldn't worry about your sister." She finished her fourth oyster and fell upon the fifth. "I'll bet that at this very minute she's sitting across from my brother, demolishing a platter of oysters. Dieudonné would surely—"

"*Dieudonné?*"

"Don't bother, I've heard them all. Dieudonné would surely have insisted that your poor abandoned sister join him for dinner. My brother always does the correct thing. He is the perfect embodiment of all things conventional—even down to conventional standards of kindness and compassion...so long as it's towards 'the right people'."

"You sound as though you don't like your bother."

"Oh, I love him, of course. But, no, I don't like him very much."

"That's exactly how I feel about my sister!"

"Who's probably right now sitting across from him at a fashionable restaurant (he patronizes only fashionable restaurants and dumps them as soon as their popularity begins to pale). I can see him sitting there, looking around to see who's looking at him as he regales your sister with details of the punishments he intends to wreck on you tomorrow, when the next train brings him to Cambo-les-Bains. And your sister is probably demurely dabbing her oyster-stained fingertips with her napkin and trying to defend you."

"That shows what you know. She'd be the last person in the world to defend me. Ever since she came to 'visit' me in Paris, totally uninvited, she's been making my life a hell."

"Good girl."

"She spends all day squandering her share of the family inheritance on clothes, then all night complaining to me about my failure to introduce her to any 'nice' people. ...What do you mean, 'good girl'?"

"Then why don't you?"

"Why don't I what?"

"Introduce her to 'nice' people."

"I don't know any 'nice' people!"

"I believe that."

The waiter replaced the depleted platter of oysters with *poulet Marengo* for her and a wine-rich *daube* for him. As she began eating with artless zest, she asked, "So your sister's a snob, is she? Well, she and my brother should hit it off famously. He would like nothing better than to limit his patients to the fashionable *gratin* of Paris. The two of them could rise through the ranks of polite society, advancing side by side from dull dinner parties with 'correct' people, to even duller dinners with 'important' people—great lavish feeds in which each course costs enough to keep an Armenian village from starvation for a week, and there's at least one liveried servant for every guest with his snout in the golden trough, and— What are you doing?"

"I'm just scratching down a note or two. I have a pretty good memory for dialogue, but you rattle on at a terrifying rate. Still, if I can capture your basic energy and melody, I can flesh you out later."

"I'm not sure I want you fleshing me out. I have all the flesh I— stop writing and eat your stew. It'll get cold." But he continued scribbling.

People at neighboring tables would have given anything for a peek at what the bridegroom was writing in that little notebook of his. A love message, I'll wager. Something he'd be embarrassed to have us overhear. Oh, the young, the young! Well, at least he's eating his stew now. It would have been a shame to let it get cold, just as she told him. She's the sensible one. She'll wear the trousers in that house, you mark my words.

She looked off into space, her eyes defocused, a temporarily forgotten piece of chicken balanced on her fork. Then she said half to herself, "I don't really blame her."

"Er-r-r-r... No, no, don't tell me. Let me work it out. Let's see...ah-h...you don't blame my sister for not defending me against your brother's assaults on my character? Right?"

"Wrong. It's *my* sister I don't blame. The poor little fluff-head is in love...however unworthy the object of her affections may be."

"Well, I don't blame my brother, either. He's a victim of the romantic traditions of our family. My great-grandfather, my grandfather, my father—each of them fell in love at first sight, and each of them snatched up the woman who had captured his heart and carried her away—in two cases, to the shock and scandal of the village, as they had been promised elsewhere."

"And do you intend to shock and scandalize your village one of these days?"

"If my ideal, irresistible, heaven-wrought woman were to come along, family tradition would oblige me to sweep her off her feet and carry her off to be my cherished companion forever."

"And what if she didn't want to be swept off her feet? What if she'd rather retain her balance? And her dignity? And her free will. And her sense of independent worth."

"Well, it's obvious that your sister has none of those petty inhibitions against being swept off her feet."

"No, I'm afraid you're right. She's just let herself be carried along on waves of joy and rapture and..." She noticed the bit of chicken cooling at the end of her fork and ate it meditatively, watching the snow streak past the window. Then she said in a voice soft with awe, "...the Century of Woman."

He blinked, trying to close the à-propos-de-*quoi?* gap. But he couldn't. "All right, I give up."

"In three days we shall enter the Twentieth Century, which will be the Century of Woman."

"Ah, yes, of course. Except that the Twentieth Century doesn't begin in three days. It begins in a year and three days, on the first of January 1901."

"I've heard that, but I refuse to believe it. It may make some sort of petty mathematical sense, but poetic logic is all against it."

"There's no such thing as 'poetic logic'."

"Not for you, maybe. Just think...my daughters and granddaughters and great-granddaughters will be born in the Century of Woman. Maybe one of them will become president of France."

"Only president of France? Empress of all Europe, surely."

She nodded, accepting the additional responsibility philosophically.

"Funny, isn't it?" he said, after a short silence, during which she separated the last of her chicken from the bone with surgical finesse.

"The thought of my great-granddaughter becoming empress of Europe?"

"No, that thought is more sinister than funny. What's funny is that now that we've had time to time to recover from the shock of those letters announcing that my brother and your sister intended to elope, he with a scheming vixen, she with a Basque brigand, all we really want is for them to hold off for a few weeks—a sort of cooling off period. After that, if they are still determined to launch themselves into the stormy seas of matrimony, they can have a proper wedding, with your family and mine gathered to see them off on the long voyage down the stony road of life."

"I think you just launched their vessel down a stony road. Isn't that what's called a jumbled metaphor?"

"Mixed. I thought you didn't know anything about metaphors."

"It would appear that neither of us does. But, all right, I'd be willing to let them marry, if, that is, I find your brother to be worthy of my sister"

"Oh, you will, you will. He's so very...well, frankly, he's just like me."

She made a low, growling sound. Then she asked, "Aren't you going to finish your *daube?*"

"Hm-m? Oh, no. No, I don't think so."

She exchanged her empty plate for his half-full one. "Do you really imagine that when the snobs arrive on the next train, they'll be as solicitous and understanding as you and I are?"

"Certainly not. They'll pout and stamp and huff. But I can deal with my sister. And I have no doubt that you can manage your brother."

"That's true. So the upshot of all our panic and desperate rushing off to Cambo will be to provide you with material for a cheap farce?"

"Cheap? Not at all cheap! I envision a lavish production. A practical, lurching train interior is no cheap thing, you know. And I'll have the smell of cooking food coming into the theater through the heating vents—real Dion Boucicaut stuff—and an endless diorama canvas of countryside rolling past the windows."

"Even though it's night?"

"Uh...all right, we'll save the production costs of the diorama and just sprinkle a little water on the darkened windows and cast the occasional light over them to indicate a passing village. And the last scene? Ah, the last scene! A lavish multiple wedding. It will be spectacular. And very funny, of course."

"A multiple wedding?"

"Of course! The situation cries out for it! First to come down the aisle will be the headstrong, romantic young scapegraces who caused all the trouble in the first place. Then come the snobbish doctor brother and the social-climbing sister, who will pledge themselves to struggle upward and dullward until they achieve the highest and dullest ranks of society. (We can have some great slapstick stuff when the old eccentric they ridicule because they think he's the village idiot turns out to be the eccentric trillionaire Viscomte de Fric von Gottlot.) Then comes the touching moment (dim the lights; handkerchiefs at the ready, Ladies!) that touching moment when, inspired by the happiness of young lovers all around them, the lonely older couple (my mother and your father) decide to fill one another's autumnal years out of respect for their departed spouses. And there it is! A triple wedding with a grand— Oh-oh, wait a minute! I forgot someone."

"I was wondering when—"

"I've got to find someone for your Aunt Adelaïde. Hm-m. Ah! I have a crusty old bachelor uncle, Hippolyte. The meeting and mating of your Aunt Adelaïde will provide us with a comic subplot: the love-sick spinster and the quaint-but-loveable codger who by sheerest co-incidence happens to—"

"That's exactly what's wrong with farce! It's all based on cheap, trumped-up *coincidences.*"

"But coincidence is the means by which Fate influences the lives of mortals."

"No, I don't accept all that nonsense about coincidence being 'the Engine of Fate'. That's just an excuse for story weavers to use hackneyed conventions. Like the convention of the happy ending, and the old ploy of mistaken identity, and the toad that turns out to be a prince, when in life—in grim, hard, real life—the prince more often turns out to be a toad, and probably a toady as well."

"Yes, but life—even grim, hard, 'real' life—teems with coincidences. Take our meeting tonight in the cab. If that wasn't a coinci— Say, that's not bad." He took out his notebook and scribbled 'toad— toady' as the waiter took their dinner plates and waited until he had their full attention before chanting the dessert menu.

They chose crème brûlée, the waiter left, and she said, "What about our meeting?"

"You'll have to admit that our meeting involved a veritable medley of coincidences."

"I admit nothing of the sort. Given the fact that my sister and your brother sent telegrams announcing their intention to hurl themselves into an ill-considered marriage, there was nothing more natural than that you and my brother would rush to Cambo-les-Bains to make them listen to reason. No coincidence there, just the natural way of things. And, of course, you both went to the Lafitte-Caillard agency because that's where everyone makes their travel arrangements. Again, no coincidence. While you were dawdling up in the travel office, the cabs moved to the head of the line, as they always do, and all Paris fiacres are the same design and color, so it's hardly a coincidence that you, childishly miffed over an encounter with my brother and desperate to catch your train, should jump into the wrong cab. The fact that I was asleep in the corner of the cab was no coincidence, either. It was the natural result of my not getting a wink of sleep last night, worrying about poor Sophie."

"That wasn't a twist on the old farce dodge of mistaken identity, eh?"

"Not in the least. And it's no coincidence that you and my brother had the train tickets, while your sister and I didn't even have money for dinner. It's a result of stupid, unjust, oppressive attitudes about what men can and ought to do and what women can't and shouldn't. No, no, there was no 'Engine of Fate' operating in our encounter. It was just the logical working out of a set of givens."

"And what about the fact that you and I are both in theater? That's no coincidence, I suppose?" He knew he had her there.

"Well-l-l, in a way it's a coincidence."

"Ah!"

"But in another way, it isn't."

"Oh."

"Consider this: Take any two people meeting anywhere in the world. Many things about their meeting will be incidentally identical—and that's not the same thing as being coincidental."

"It isn't?"

"No. For instance, they would have been walking on the same street, or else they would not have met. So that is a condition of their meeting and not a coincidence. You see what I mean?"

"Hm-m."

"Also, it's likely that both had coffee that morning, that they both glanced at the newspapers, that they were born in the same century, in the same country, and that they have similar reservations about eating live worms, or the practice of hurling oneself out of second-story windows to get the exercise of walking back up the stairs. But none of these things could properly be called coincidences."

"They couldn't, eh?"

"No. They are merely the normal, random, incidental identities that one finds in any encounter. Indeed, if there weren't even one single identity in the circumstances of their meeting, *that* would be a coincidence. You understand?"

"Ah-h...almost."

"I hold that the fact that we both are in theater is one of those normal, mathematically probable identities without which our meeting would have been truly coincidental, and therefore not, in itself, a coincidence at all, but indeed quite the opposite. And there you are."

He looked at her levelly for a long moment. "Did you go to a Jesuit school, by any chance?"

"Girls are not admitted into Jesuit schools. Yet another instance of mindless prejudice."

"So, if I understand correctly, you're saying that if I were to write a play based on the circumstances of our meeting, I couldn't be accused of relying on cheap, unlikely coincidences, am I right?"

She frowned. Wait a minute, hadn't she been arguing the opposite way? And somehow twisting everything until... Hm-m.

He smiled. "I considered ending the play with a quintuple wedding including the playwright character and the actress character."

"Oh?"

"But, of course, that would be ridiculous."

"Yes, of course....Why?"

"*Five* marriages at once might seem a bit much. Then too, the playwright and the actress are what we dramaturges call 'the agents'— and they couldn't possibly get married."

"No, of course not....Why not?"

"Well, for one thing, it would be too predictable. The audience would see it coming the minute he jumps into her cab. Then too, there are the medical and religious implications."

"Medical—?"

"—and religious. When their brothers and sisters marry, they'll be brother-in-law and sister-in-law twice over. And when their parents marry, they'll also be stepbrother and stepsister. The Bible frowns on unions of that sort. And the biologists warn us against them pretty sternly. But whether or not I decide to marry them off isn't my greatest problem."

"It isn't?"

"No, no. My greatest problem will be finding a cast. The role of the young playwright doesn't present insurmountable problems. It could be played by any clever, charming, intelligent, reasonably good-looking actor—provided he has a quick wit and a winning personality. But a young woman who goes around wearing short dresses and agitating for social change and chucking stewards out of compartments and jumping onto trains with strange men and threatening that her granddaughter will one day rule Europe—it won't be easy to find an actress who can pull all that off, and still be charming and lovely and desirable and winning and bright and entertaining and—well, all the qualities that I admire in—in this character I've invented. No, I'll have to search long and hard for an actress who can do the role justice. This is no job for a beginner. I'll need an actress with a long list of successes to her cred—Ai-i-i!"

She nearly twisted the skin off the back of his hand. After which totally unjustified but infinitely gratifying assault, she left her hand on the table, the tips of her fingers accidentally brushing the backs of his. They were not holding hands. No one could say they were in any way holding hands. No. It was just that her hand was resting on the table near his because...well, it had to rest somewhere, didn't it? He was intensely aware of her soft touch, and he didn't dare move his hand even a fraction of an inch lest she suddenly realize that their hands were in contact and withdraw hers. In fact, he needn't have worried.

The waiter brought their desserts, and she began to eat hers slowly, her thoughts turned softly inward. He could not eat his, because it was his right hand she had accidentally rendered immobile, and he would rather have died than move it.

"Aren't you going to eat your dessert?" she asked.

"I don't seem to have any appetite." This was a lie; he was seething with appetite, but not for food.

"Well...if you're sure." She took his crème brûlée, and his heart was lifted by the symbolic significance of it all, as he watched her finish his last spoonful. Then they both spoke at once.

"By the way, what's—?"
"May I ask—?"

"I'm sorry, what were you—?"
"No, you first."

"Well, I was just wondered what your name was."
"I was going to ask you the same thing," she said.
"Now, surely *that's* a coincidence."
"Not at all."

This tale borrows a narrative device from a story by Robert W. Chambers that appeared in the bound European version of New Harper's Monthly Magazine, *August, 1903 (Volume CVII, no. DCXXXIX). I gratefully acknowledge my debt to Mr Chambers, and I should be delighted to hear from his descendants.*

THE APPLE TREE

The Widow Etcheverrigaray took great comfort and pride from the splendid apple tree that grew on the boundary of her property, just beyond the plot of leeks that every year were the best in all the village; and her neighbor and lifelong rival, Madame Utuburu, drew no less gratification from the magnificent apple tree near the patch of *piments* that made her the envy of all growers of that sharp little green pepper. Unfortunately for the tranquillity of our village, we are not speaking of two trees here, but of one: a tree that grew exactly on the boundary between the two women's land and was, by both law and tradition, their shared property. It was inevitable that the apples from this tree should lead to dispute, for such has been the melancholy role of that disruptive fruit since the Garden of Eden.

As all the world knows, neither pettiness nor greed have any place in the Basque character, so one must look elsewhere for the cause of the Battle of the Apple Tree that became part of our village's folklore. The explanation lies in the bitter rivalry the two woman cultivated and nourished for most of their lives. When young, one of them had been accounted the most beautiful girl in our village, while the other was considered the most graceful and charming—although in later years no one could remember which had been which, and, sadly, no evidence of these qualities remained to prompt the memory. As mischievous Fate would have it, both the young women fancied that handsome rogue, Zabala, who was not yet called Zabala-One-Leg, for he was still to commit the unknown (but doubtless carnal) offence for which the righteous God the Father punished him by taking one of his legs in the Great War, while His benevolent Son, Jesus, revealed His mercy by leaving him the other to hobble along on. All the village knew that the young women admired Zabala because neither of them would deign to dance with him at fêtes, and both would turn their faces away and sniff when the cheeky rascal addressed a word to them, or a wink. If further proof of their attraction were needed, both village belles were heard to vow upon their chastity that they would not marry that flirting, two-faced scamp of a Zabala if he were the last man in Xiberoa. They would become nuns first. They would become prostitutes first! They would become *Protestants* first! (Of course, nobody believed they would go so far as *that*.)

Now, being every bit as crafty as He is good, God knows how to punish us, not only by withholding our wishes, but by granting them. In this case, He chose to cut with the back of His blade. He willed that neither of the young women would have Zabala, for he went from the village to punish Kaiser William, who was at that time raping nuns and spitting Belgian babies on his bayonet, the enlistment posters informed us. Zabala returned three years later, without one leg, but with such worldly sophistication that he could no longer remember the Basque word for many things and used the French instead. He bragged about the wonderful places he had seen and the many sinful and delicious things he had done, but he was astonished to learn that in his absence both the women had married simple shepherds far beneath their expectations, that both their weddings had occurred within two months of the exciting and heady fête that marks the harvest of the hillside fern, and that both women had born babies after only seven months of gestation. Short first pregnancies do not occasion criticism in our valley, for it is widely known that the good Lord often makes first pregnancies mercifully brief as His reward to the girl for having preserved her chastity until marriage. Subsequent pregnancies, however, usually run their full terms, which only makes sense, as the very fact that they are not first pregnancies means that the mother was not chaste at the moment of conception. Is it not marvelous how one finds justice and balance in everything? Yet further proof of God's hand in our daily lives.

Over the years, the shepherd Etcheverrigaray slowly increased his flock until he was able to buy a small house on the edge of the village with an overgrown garden that his wife tamed and tended until it was the pride of the village and, it goes without saying, also the envy. But the husband fell into the habit of spending time he ought to have given to the care of his sheep in the café/bar of our mayor, squandering his money on so many small glasses of wine that, after he died suddenly of no disease other than God's will, his widow would have had a hard time making ends meet but for the productive garden she had enriched over the years with her sweat and her loving care.

As for Madame Utuburu's husband, he was plagued by something worse than drink: he was unlucky. And there is an old Basque saying that teaches us: Unlucky indeed is he who is burdened with bad luck. If there was a thunderstorm in the mountains, you could bet that some of Utuburu's sheep would be struck by lightening. If, upon rare occasions, his ewes had a fruitful season, the price of wool was sure to drop. Nor was the village very sympathetic with his misfortunes, for it is well known that bad luck is the lash with which the Lord chastises those who have sinned, however cleverly and clandestinely. And there was another thing: when the price of wool fell for Utuburu, it fell for everybody—even for us, the lucky and the innocent.

You can imagine how surprised we all were when we learned that Utuburu-the-Unlucky was to receive an unexpected inheritance from a distant uncle. But the Lord's subtle ways were revealed when, staggering home after celebrating the only bit of good fortune in his life, Utuburu fell into the river and drowned.

With what was left of the inheritance after grasping lawyers had gorged on it, Madame Utuburu bought the small house next to the Widow Etcheverrigaray's, and there she eked out a modest annuity by toiling morning and evening in her garden, which became either the best or the second-best garden in the village, depending on whether one measured a garden by the quality of its leeks or that of its *piments*.

Thus it was that ironic Fate brought the two rivals to live and grow old side by side on the edge of the village, each with no husband, and each with only one son to absorb her love and color her expectations.

The Widow Etcheverrigaray's son soon revealed himself to be a clever and hard-working scholar, first at the village infant school, then in middle school at Mauléon, later at the lycée at Bayonne, and finally at university in Paris. With every advance in his education, he moved farther and farther from his village, so in proportion as his mother had ever greater reason to be proud of him, she had ever fewer opportunities to show him off to her less fortunate neighbor. At first he wrote short letters that the village priest read to Widow Etcheverrigaray over and over until she had them by heart, then she would share them with the women beating their laundry clean at the village lavoir, her eyes scanning the paper back and forth as she recited from memory. And once her son sent a thick book full of tiny print with his name on the cover, which the priest told us was proof that he had written it: every word, from one end to the other. The book said such clever things about tropical agriculture that not even our priest could read it for long without nodding off. Eventually, the son gained a very important position in some Brazil or other, and the village never saw him again.

As for Madame Utuburu's boy, the best that can be said of his educational performance is that the damage he did to school property during his brief stay was not nearly so great as some have claimed. His native gifts lay in another direction: he developed into the most powerful and crafty jai-alai player our village ever produced—and this is saying something, for it was our village that gave the world the fabled Andoni Elissalde, he who crushed all comers from 1873 to 1881, when a blow of the ball to his head made him an Innocent: one so beloved of God that he was no longer tormented by doubts or led astray by curiosity. After young Utuburu made his reputation with our communal team, he went on to play for Bayonne, where he was selected for the team that toured Spain and South America, humbling all before them and making every cheek in Xiberoa glow with pride. Thus, as the lad became more and more famous in that noblest of sports, he played ever farther and farther away from our village and from his proud mother, who nevertheless saved newspapers with pictures of him and words of praise. She saved the whole page, lest she cut out the wrong part because, like her neighbor, she was not exposed to the threats to simple faith that an ability to read entails. While touring South America the son was offered vast fortunes to play in some Argentina or other. Twice he sent photographs of himself in action, and once he sent a magnificent cushion of multi-colored silk with a beautiful (if rather immodest) woman painted on it and the words 'Greetings from Buenos Aires'. On the back, in a rainbow of embroidery, was the word 'Madre', which the priest said referred either to Madame Utuburu or to the Virgin Mary, in either case a good thought. After this gesture of prodigal generosity, the son was heard of no more.

In the normal course of things, the two widows would have lived out their years lavishing on their gardens the care and affection their husbands no longer needed and their children no longer wanted, go-ing frequently to early morning mass in their black shawls, certain that their piety would not go unrewarded, and little by little slipping from the notice of the village, as old women should. But such was not the destiny of Widow Etcheverrigaray and Madame Utuburu, for the ever-increasing rivalry between them kept them much in the eye and on the tongues of the women of our village. At first this rivalry was manifested in looking over the stone wall at the other woman's garden and murmuring little words of condolence and of encourage-ment for next year. Over the years, these drops of sweetened acid matured into fragments of praise or sympathy that each woman would express in the course of her morning marketing rounds. Madame Utuburu constantly lauded her neighbor as a saint for having put up with that slovenly drunk of a husband. But of course, if the old sot hadn't been drunk when first they met he would never have—Ah, but why bring that up now, after all these years?

And Widow Etcheverrigaray often let escape heartfelt sighs over her neighbor's misfortune in having a husband cursed with bad luck. The poor man had been unlucky in everything, most of all in having to live with a woman who...but enough! He was dead now, and suf-fering yet greater punishment!...if that is possible.

If there was anything that made Madame Utuburu's mouth pucker with contempt, it was the way some people brought a stupid old book along with them to the lavoir every Tuesday, and looked at it and fondled it and sighed over it until others were forced to ask about it out of politeness, only to be drowned in a flood of nonsense about the brains and brilliance of some four-eyed weakling who couldn't catch a *pelote* in a *chistera* to save his life, and who never even had the decency to send his poor mother a little something for New Year's! She who had stayed awake nights trying to save the scrawny runt's life when he was sick...which was pretty often!

And if there was one thing in this world that made Widow Etcheverrigaray's eyes roll with exasperation, it was the way some people forever lugged about a dusty old cushion, shoving it under your nose until you were forced to ask what on earth it was. Then they would dump a cartload of drivel on you about the strength and speed of some ignorant brute of a wood-for-brains who lacked even the common politeness to send his mother a little gift on her saint's day. She who had carried the oversized beast under her heart for nine months!....Well, seven.

Seasons flowed into years. A paved road penetrated our valley, and soon the wireless was inflicting Paris voices on our ears, and planting Paris values and desires in the hearts of our young people. There is a sage old Basque saying that goes: As youth fades away, one grows older. And thus it was with the two women. Stealthily at first, then with a frightening rush, what had seemed to be an inexhaustible pile of tomorrows became a vague little tangle of yesterdays. But still they toiled in their gardens to produce the finest, or second-finest, vegetables in our village, and still they honed and refined their rivalry, urged on in no small part by their neighbors, who were amused by the endless sniping until our peace was shattered by the Battle of the Apple Tree. The tree in question was very old and gnarled, but it never failed to produce an abundant crop of that crisp, succulent fruit with specks of red in the meat that used to be called Blood-of-Christ apples. One never sees a Blood-of-Christ apple anymore, but they are still remembered with pleasure by old men who never tire of telling the young that everything modern is inferior to how things were back in their day: the village fêtes, the weather, the behavior of children....Even the apples, for the love of God!

Because the tree stood exactly on the boundary between their gardens (indeed, the wall separating them touched the tree on both sides and was buckled by its growth), they had always shared the apples, each picking only from branches that overhung her property. To avoid appearing so petty as pointedly to ignore the presence of the other, they picked on different days, although it could be a tooth-grinding nuisance to have planned for weeks to harvest on a certain morning, only to look out one's window and see that hog of a neighbor picking on that very day! Not to mention the fact that young Zabala would surely have asked one to marry him if someone else had not always been throwing herself at him in the most scandalous way!

The fate of the apples on the disputable branches running along the boundary wall was a source of tension each year. Neither woman would run the risk of picking apples that did not indisputably overhang her own property lest she give the other a chance to brand her a thief at the lavoir so they were obliged to wait until God, disguised as the Force of Gravity, settled the matter at the end of the season, causing the apples to drop on one side or the other of the dividing wall. There were years when the Devil, disguised as a Strong Wind, stirred up strife by causing most of the debatable apples to fall into one garden. And every year a heart-rending number of apples fell onto the wall itself, only to rot away slowly on that rocky no-man's-land under the mournful gaze of the women, both of whom muttered bitterly over the shameful waste caused by that back-biting, gossiping old— May God forgive her.

Even if mankind cannot.

Now, the baker from Licq who drove his van from village to village, sounding his horn to bring out the customers, had a sharp eye for profit, like all those coin-biting Licquois. He knew that everyone liked the rare Blood-of-Christ apples and would be willing to buy some...at a just price, of course. Aware of the competition between the two widows, the baker was careful to offer each of them a chance to make a little extra money. After much hard and narrow negotiating, he arranged to buy five baskets of apples from each.

Early the next morning, Widow Etcheverrigaray went out to her tree carrying five baskets that she intended to fill before—what's this?! Madame Utuburu was on the other side of the stone wall, filling *her* baskets with the fine, plump fruit. Under normal circumstances, the widow would never pick at the same time as her greedy neighbor, but as the baker was coming that afternoon to collect his apples, without a word she set grimly to her task. It was not long before she realized that she was unlikely to fill all five baskets, for this year the apples, while especially large and beautiful, were less abundant than usual (thus does God, in His eternal justice, give with one hand while taking with the other). Indeed, when she had picked all the apples from the branches indisputably overhanging her garden, Widow Etcheverrigaray found that she had filled only four baskets. And even this had required a most liberal definition of the term 'full' as applied to baskets of apples. A covert glance over the wall revealed that Madame Utuburu was in precisely the same state: her branches stripped and still an empty basket left. And *her* idea of a 'full' basket was obviously one that was not totally empty! At this moment, Widow Etcheverrigaray was shocked to see her neighbor lean over the wall and squint down it, estimating whether some of the branches along the no-man's-land between them might, upon reconsideration, be judged to be on *her* side of the wall. The widow's eyes grew round with indignant disbelief! This covetous old greedy-gut of an Utuburu was actually contemplating breaking the unspoken truce that had permitted them to share the apple tree! She stepped forward to forestall her neighbor's iniquity by picking the apples that might just as well be judged to be on her side of the disputable branch. "So!" hissed Madame Utuburu to herself. "This grasping hussy of an Etcheverrigaray wants to play *that* way, does she? We'll see about that!" And she vigorously set herself to harvesting the apples that were erstwhile dubious but had now become clearly her own by right of self-defense—to say nothing of revenge.

They were furiously picking on opposite sides of the same branch, when Madame Utuburu happened to tug it towards her just as her rival was reaching for an apple! "What?" muttered Widow Etcheverrigaray between her teeth. "Well, *two* can play at that game! And one even better than the other!" And she boldly grasped the branch and steadied it while she picked frantically with her free hand. "God-be-my-witness!" snarled Madame Utuburu. "Is this shameless strumpet prepared to rip the branches off the tree to satisfy her greed?"

And she jerked the branch back to her side, dragging the unprepared widow halfway over the stone wall. "Ai-i-i!" screamed the widow. "So the brazen harlot wants to play rough, does she?" And she was reaching out to wrench the branch back to her side when Madame Utuburu, having picked the last apple, released it, and it sprang back, striking the ample bosom of the astonished widow, who staggered and ended up sitting with a *squish* in the middle of her prized leeks. There was no time to allow her fury to seethe and ripen, or to communicate her indignation to the villagers who had begun to gather along the road to watch the fun, for her neighbor was already picking at a moot branch on the far side of the tree. Grunting to her feet and slapping the mud from the back of her skirt, Widow Etcheverrigaray returned to the fray determined to punish this outrage. Crying out every vilification that years of rivalry had stored up in their fertile imaginations, they clawed at apples and ripped them from the branch, all the while decorating one another's reputations with those biologically explicit calumnies for which the Basque language might have been specifically designed, were it not universally known that it was invented in heaven for use by the angels. There was a moment when, as each of them reached for the same apple, their hands touched, and each cried out and recoiled as though defiled by the contact. Still fuming over the way Madame Utuburu had underhandedly released the branch, Widow Etcheverrigaray decided to repay the insult in kind. She set all her weight against the branch, bending it back to her side so that when Madame Utuburu reached out for the fruit, she could let it go, and it would snap back and give—

—the branch broke, and the widow found herself sitting once again in her leek bed, the hoots and jeers of the spectators flushing her cheeks with rage and embarrassment. She sat there snarling descriptions of Madame Utuburu's character, ancestry, practices, and aspirations, while that thoroughly slandered woman, finding her last basket still not filled and the branch bearing the remaining apples broken off and lying out of reach in her neighbor's garden, lifted her palms to heaven and called upon God to witness this plunder! This larceny! This piracy! And she hastily crossed herself and begged Mother Mary to put her hands over the ears of the baby Jesus, that

He might not be offended by the obscenities gushing from the foul mouth of this scurrilous, vulgar, low-born Etcheverrigaray!

Which description impelled the widow to make a gesture.

Which gesture obliged Madame Utuburu to throw a lump of mud.

Which assault forced half a dozen villagers to rush up from the road to prevent bodily damage from spoiling the innocent pleasure of their entertainment.

In the final accounting of the Battle of the Apple Tree, it was the Widow Etcheverrigaray who was able—just—to fill her baskets from the last of the apples, while Madame Utuburu had to bargain long and hard before the tight-fisted Licquois baker accepted her scantier baskets with much sighing and many martyred groans and predictions that his children would die in the poorhouse. But many villagers judged Madame Utuburu the victor for, after all, it wasn't *she* who had twice had her broad bottom dumped into her leeks.

For the next few weeks, every time the women in the marketplace asked about the battle (which they did with wide-eyed innocence and cooing tones of compassion), Madame Utuburu threatened to bring legal action against the vicious vandal who had damaged her tree! And Widow Etcheverrigaray made public her suspicions concerning what her neighbor had offered the baker to make up for her missing apples; although, in the widow's opinion, that commodity had been worth little enough when it was young and fresh and would now be accepted by the baker only if he were attempting to shorten his time in purgatory by mortifying his flesh.

During the next year, they fought out their rivalry on the battle-field of their gardens, each working from dawn to dark to produce vegetables that were the pride of the village and the despair of other gardeners. The work in the open air kept their bodies strong and flexible, and the praise of passersby kept their spirits alive, particularly if this praise could be interpreted as a slighting comparison to the other woman's crop.

Then, one cold, wet, autumn day, Zabala-One-Leg died. Not of anything in particular; he simply ran out of life, as all of us eventually must. Zabala had no family, but he was of the village, so we all went to his burial and stood in the rain while the priest took the opportunity to promise us that death was the inevitable portion of each and every one of us, so we had better start preparing for it, and particularly certain people he could name, but he wouldn't mar this solemn occasion with accusations...however just! Everybody left the cemetery, the women to home and work, the men to the café/bar of our mayor to have a little glass in memory of Zabala. ...Perhaps two.

Only Madame Utuburu and Widow Etcheverrigaray remained in the churchyard, standing in the rain on opposite sides of the scar of fresh earth, their eyes lowered to the rosaries they held between work-gnarled fingers. For an hour they stood there. Two hours. Although their shawls became sodden with rain, and they had to clench their teeth to keep them from chattering, neither was willing to be the first to leave, for to do so would be to relinquish the role of chief mourner and admit that the other had the most reason for grief.

Their thick, black skirts became too heavy with damp to stir in the wind that began to drive the rain diagonally across the grave, but still neither would leave the field in the possession of one for whom that handsome rogue of a Zabala had never cared a snap of his fingers. To do so would be an insult to his memory. ...To say nothing of his taste!

In the end, the priest came trotting out from his house beside the church, sleepy-eyed and grumbling about being torn from his meditation by a couple of stubborn old women. He stood at the head of the grave, the wind tugging at his big black umbrella, and angrily ordered them to come away with him. At once! As it is rash to disobey the messenger of God, especially when one is standing so conveniently in a graveyard, they allowed him to shepherd them home, but only after each had made a brief attempt to lag slightly behind. They walked home, one on each side of the priest, each with one shoulder protected by the umbrella while the other shoulder was drenched by rain running from its rim. Without a word, they left the priest at the bottom of their gardens and trudged up their paths, each to her own house.

The next morning dawned with that cold, brittle sunlight that signals the end of autumn, and Madame Utuburu knew it would soon be time to harvest the apples, which had been plentiful this year, but small and not as sweet as usual. (Is not God's even-handed justice everywhere revealed?) As she worked putting up jars of *piperade*, she glanced from time to time out her kitchen window to see if that greedy Etcheverrigaray was already stripping the tree. But the widow did not leave her house all day, and Madame Utuburu wondered what sort of game the old hag was playing. Oh-h, wait a minute! Was she pretending to be too stricken with grief to attend to garden chores? Was this her sly way of implying that *she* had the greatest reason to mourn young Zabala, who had never cared a fig for her? What an underhanded trick!

After mass the next morning, the priest asked Madame Utuburu why her neighbor had not attended service, and she replied that she was sure she didn't know. Perhaps she had given up going to mass, realizing that although God's mercy is infinite, it might not be infinite enough to save certain people who are forever parading their pretended grief! The same kind of people who always go about carrying thick books written by spindly legged sons who are so feeble they couldn't throw a *pelote* against a *fronton!* No, not if the child Jesus Himself begged him for a game! The priest shook his head and sighed, sorry he had asked.

That afternoon Madame Utuburu looked up from mulching her garden against the coming winter to see the priest plodding dutifully up the widow's path. He was inside no more than two minutes before he came out, a leaden frown on his brow. When Madame Utuburu called over the wall, asking what old Etcheverrigaray was playing at, the priest picked his way across to her, holding his skirts up so as not to muddy them. "Your neighbor has been summoned to judgment," he said in that ripe tremolo one associates with calls for funds to reroof the church.

Madame Utuburu could not believe it! That healthy old horse of an Etcheverrigaray? She who was strong enough to rip a branch off another person's apple tree? It couldn't be!

"No doubt her bone marrow caught a fever from standing in the rain at poor Zabala's burial," the priest said. "I found her sitting in her kitchen, her feet in a bucket of water that had gone cold."

The priest went off to make the usual arrangements, and soon four women of the village came down the road wearing hastily-put-on black dresses; their heads bowed, their palms pressed together before them, their tread slow, but each radiating a tremor of restrained excitement at being part of the great events of Life and Death. They turned into the Widow Etcheverrigaray's to wash, dress, and lay out the body, first opening the bedroom window to let her soul fly up to heaven. Then the First Mourner—who merited this privileged title because, as the oldest of the watchers, she was probably 'next in line', though this was never mentioned aloud—went out back to announce the death to the chickens, so they wouldn't stop laying. In other parts of the Basque country, the custom is to go to the Departed One's beehives and whisper that their keeper has died, so that sudden grief will not cause the bees to swarm and abandon their hives. No one in our village keeps bees, so we tell the chickens instead, and it must work, because none of them have every swarmed and abandoned their roosts.

Back in Widow's Etcheverrigaray's kitchen the mourners sat gossiping in felted voices, thrilling one another with pious reminders that any one of them might be called unexpectedly to God, so they had better be ready with clean souls. ...And clean underwear.

The First Mourner suggested that they invite Madame Utuburu to watch with them. After all, the two women had been neighbors for more years than boys have naughty thoughts. But the Second Mourner wondered if it might not offend the Departed One to allow her lifelong rival to nose about in a kitchen she hadn't had time to clean. After some deliberation, it was decided that they would tidy up carefully, *then* invite Madame Utuburu to join the wake.

Stiff and very, very proper, Madame Utuburu sat in her neighbor's kitchen for the first time in her life. Awkward silences were followed by spurts of forced conversation that collapsed into broken phrases, then faded into feeble nods and hums of accord. None of the mourners wanted to praise the widow in the presence of her rival, and no one dared to gossip about her in the presence of her spirit, so what was there to talk about? Finally, to everyone's relief, Madame Utuburu rose to go, but the First Mourner urged her to follow the ancient tradition and take some little trifle from the house as a memento of the Departed One. At first she declined, but finally—more to get away without further embarrassment than anything else—she allowed herself to be prevailed upon. After she left there was a long moment of silence, then a gush of repressed talk burst from all the

Watchers' lips at once. Why on earth had she chosen *that* as a memento?

The whole village came to see the widow off to her reward. Only after standing beside the grave for a respectable amount of time, shivering in a wind that carried the smell of mountain snow on it, did we begin to drift away, the women to their kitchens, the men to the mayor's café/bar to take a little glass as they discussed the priest's warning that every hour of life wounds, and the last kills. ...All right, maybe two glasses.

Madame Utuburu had not intended to linger beside the grave; it was simply that she didn't notice the departure of the others. Fully an hour passed before she lifted her eyes and, with a slight gasp of surprise, realized that she was alone. Alone. With nothing to mark the passage of her days. No one to prompt her to greater efforts at gardening and greater praise from the village. No little victories to warm her throat with flushes of pride, no little defeats to sting her ears with flushes of shame. Nothing left to talk about but her expensive, beautiful, hand-embroidered silk cushion from Buenos Aires.

Winter descended from the mountains, and when its task of purifying the earth with cold was accomplished, retreated slowly back up the slopes, allowing spring to soften the ground and melt-water to fill the rushing Uhaitz-handia with waves that danced beneath the earth-colored foam. This was the season when Madame Utuburu usually set out her *piments* under cloches to get a month's headstart on the rest of the village, but somehow she did not feel up to it. What was the point? She had no husband to feed, no son to praise her spicy *piperade*, and now no neighbor to vex with her superior crop. Maybe she wouldn't bother with the *piments* this year. Indeed, the task of planting a garden at all seemed terribly heavy and unrewarding.

She began to—I must not say 'to understand', for she never submitted the matter to the processes of reasoning. She began to *sense* that her rival had been...not something to live for, but maybe something to live *against*: a daily grievance, an object of envy, a reason to get up each morning, if only to see what villainy she had been up to.

Down at the lavoir, a woman brushed a lock of hair from her forehead with the back of her soapy hand and commented that three wash days had passed without Madame Utuburu showing up. Her neighbor at the next scrubbing stone set aside the paddle with which she had beaten her laundry clean and said that perhaps a couple of them should go down to the edge of the village and see if anything untowards had befallen. After all, she's no longer young and—But look! Here she comes!

And indeed, she was approaching the lavoir with a stately tread, her few scraps of dirty laundry tied into a bundle in one hand, while in the other she carried her famous cushion from Buenos Aires, and there was something balanced on top of it.

Oh no, it can't be!

But it was. The Book. And the women were obliged to listen while Madame Utuburu divided her praises between her own son's remarkable strength and the Etcheverrigaray boy's phenomenal brilliance.

And in this way Madame Utuburu kept the Widow Etcheverrigaray alive for several years longer. And herself, too.

HOT NIGHT IN THE CITY II

There were only three passengers on the last bus from downtown: a woman, a man, and a bum. The young woman sat close up behind the driver because she instinctively trusted men in uniform, even bus drivers. She clutched her handbag to her lap, pressed her knees together, and fixed her gaze on the nippled rubber floormat to avoid making eye contact with the old drunk who sat across from her, smelling of pee and BO and waking up with a moist snort each time the bus hit a pot hole or lurched to miss one. The slim young man sitting alone at the back of the bus had been unable to sleep because of the heat and a relentless gnawing in the pit of his stomach. After squirming for hours, he had left the flophouse and deposited his bindle in a bus station locker so he could wander the streets unencumbered.

An oppressive heat wave had been sapping the city for over a week. Not until after midnight was it cool enough for people to go out and stroll the streets for a breath of air. In the stifling tenements that separated air-conditioned downtown from the breezy suburbs, kids were allowed to sleep out on fire escapes, sprawled on sofa cushions. On the brownstone stoops down below, women in loose cotton house dresses gossiped drowsily while men in damp undershirts sucked beers. At the beginning of the heat wave, people had complained about the weather to total strangers with a grumpy comradeship of shared distress, like during wars or floods or hurricanes. But once the city's brick and steel had absorbed all the heat it could hold and began to exhale its stored-up warmth into the night, the public mood turned sullen and resentful.

The bus crawled through tenement streets that were strangely dark because people left the lights off to keep their apartments cooler, and many streetlights had been broken by bands of kids made miserable and mutinous by the heat. But the interior of the bus was brightly lit, and it made the young woman feel odd to be moving through dark streets with everyone looking at her from out there in the dark. All the bus windows were open to combat the heat, but the breeze was so laden with soot that it was gritty between her teeth, so she reached up to close her window, but it was stuck and she couldn't, so she turned her head away. She saw a familiar advertising placard in the arch of the roof that assured her that she could improve her chances of success by 25%, 50%, 75%...Even More!...by learning shorthand. Money Back If Not Totally Delighted! Don't Wait! Start on the Road to Success Today! The placard showed a handsome boss smiling on an efficient, pretty woman with an open notebook. That would be her, one of these days.

She reached up and tugged the slack cord, and a deformed *ding* brought the bus to a lurching stop. As she thanked the driver and stepped down from the front of the bus, the young man slipped out through the back accordion doors. With a swirl of dust and litter, the bus drove off, carrying the snorting drunk into the night.

She walked towards the only unbroken streetlight on the block, tottering a little because she was unaccustomed to high heels. When her ankle buckled, she looked back at the sidewalk with an irritated, accusing frown, as though she had tripped over something. That was when she noticed him.

It occurred to the young man that she might think he was following her, and the last thing he wanted was to frighten her, so he put his hands in his pockets and began to whistle to show that he wasn't trying to sneak up on anybody or anything. It was the theme from *The Third Man*, a film she had seen one afternoon when she'd gone into a second-run movie house to get out of the rain. She hadn't liked it all that much, particularly the sad ending where this Italian actress just walked right on past Joseph Cotton, who loved her. She knew that people thought films with sad endings were more 'artistic' than those with happy endings, but she went to the movies to shake off the blues, and she wanted them to make her feel good.

The young man stopped whistling when it occurred to him that she probably listened to the eerie tales of *The Whistler* on the radio, so the last thing that would put her at ease would be some man whistling in a dark street. She gave him a real surprise when she reached the streetlight and turned on him. "You better not try anything!" Her voice was reedy with tension. "This is an Italian neighborhood!"

He held up his palms in surrender. "Whoa there, ma'am," he said in a moist, toothless voice, like that western sidekick, Gabby Hayes. "You ain't got no just cause to go chucking a whole passel of I-talians at me." But she didn't find that funny. The streetlight directly overhead turned his eyes into gashes of shadow beneath vivid brows; only the tips of his lashes shone, mascara'd with light, as he smiled and said in his stammering Jimmy Stewart voice, "Look, I'm...I'm just terribly sorry if I frightened you, Miss. But I want you to know that I wasn't following you. Well, yes, yes, I *was* following you, I suppose. But not on purpose! I was just, sort of, well...walking along. Lost in daydreams. Just...just lost in daydreams, that's what I was. Look, why don't I just...just...turn around and go the other way? It's all the same to me, 'cause I'm not going anywhere special. I'm just...you know...sort of drifting along through life."

She still didn't smile, although it was a pretty good Jimmy Stewart, she had to admit. She continued to stare at him, tense and angry, so he made a comic little salute and walked up the street, away from her. Then he turned back. "Excuse me, my little chickadee, but you said something that tickled my cur-i-osity." He dragged out the syllables in the nasal, whining style of W. C. Fields. They were talking across a space of perhaps ten yards, but it was well after midnight and the background growl of downtown traffic was so distant that they could speak in normal tones. "Pray tell me, m'dear. Why did you warn me that this is an I-talian neighborhood. Just what has that—

as the ancient philosophers are wont to wonder—got to do with anything?" W. C. Fields tapped the ashes from his imaginary cigar and
waited politely for her answer.

She cleared her throat. "Italians aren't like most city people. They
have family feelings. If a woman screams, they come running and
beat up whoever's bothering her."

"I see," W. C. drawled. "A most laudable custom, I'm sure. But
one that would be pretty hard on a fellow unjustly accused of being
a mugger, like yours truly." She smiled at the W. C. Fields, so he
kept it up. "You are, I take it, a woman of I-talian lineage?"

"No. I live here because it's safer. And cheap."

He chuckled. "You've told me more than you meant to," he said
in his own natural voice.

She frowned, and the steep-angled light filled her forehead wrinkles with shadow. "What do you mean?"

"You've told me that you live alone, and that you don't have much
money. Now, I wonder if you'd be kind enough to tell me one other
thing?"

"What's that?" she asked, still cautious, although the first spurt of
adrenaline was draining away.

"Is there someplace around here where I could get a cup of coffee?"

"Well...there's a White Tower. Four blocks down and one over."

"Thanks." His eyes crinkled into a smile. "You know, this is a
strange scene. I mean...really strange. Just picture it. Our heroine
descends from a bus, right? She is followed by a young man, lost in
vague daydreams. She suddenly turns on him and threatens to Italian
him to death. Surprised, bewildered, dumbfounded, nonplussed, and
just plain scared, he decides to flee. But curiosity (that notorious cat
killer) obliges him to stop, and they chat, separated by yards of sidewalk that he hopes will make her feel safe. While they're talking, he
notices how the overhead street lamp glows in her hair and drapes
over her shoulders like a shawl of light. ...A shawl of light. But her
eyes...her eyes are lost in shadow, so he can't tell what she's thinking,
what she feels. The young man asks directions to a coffee shop, which
she obligingly gives him. Now comes the tricky bit of the scene. Does
he dare to invite her to have a cup of coffee with him? They could

sit in the Whitest of all possible Towers and while away a few hours of this stifling hot night, talking about...well, whatever they want to talk about. Life, for instance, or love, or maybe—I don't know— baseball? Finally the drifter summons the courage to ask her. She hesitates. (Well, come on! What young heroine wouldn't hesitate?) He smiles his most boyish smile. (I'm afraid this *is* my most boyish smile.) Then the girl— Well, I'm not sure what our heroine would do. What do you think she would do?"

She looked at him, mentally hefting his intent. Then she asked, "Are you an Englishman?"

He smiled at her abrupt non sequitur. "Why do you ask?"

"You sound like Englishmen in the movies."

"No, I'm not English. But then, you're not Italian. So we're even. Well...*I'm* even. Even-tempered, even-handed, and even given to playing with words. But you? You, you're not even. You're most definitely odd."

"What do you mean, odd?"

"Oh, come on! Accepting an invitation for coffee with a total stranger is pretty goshdarned odd, if you ask me."

"I didn't say I'd go for coffee with you."

"Not in words maybe, but...say, which way is this White Tower of yours, anyway?"

"Back the way we came."

"Four blocks down and one over, I believe you said."

They walked down the street side by side, but with plenty of space between them, and he kept up a light trickle of small talk, mostly questions about her. She liked that, because nobody was ever interested in her, in who she was, and what she thought or felt. She told him that she had been in the city only six months, that she had come from a small town upstate, and that she had a job she didn't like all that much. No, she didn't wish she'd stayed in her hometown. Oh sure, she got the blues sometimes, but not bad enough to want to go back there. At the next corner, she turned unexpectedly in the direction of the all-night coffee joint, and their shoulders touched. They both said "Sorry", and they walked on, closer now, but she was careful not to let their shoulders touch again as they approached the White Tower, a block of icy white light in the hot night.

It was pretty full, considering the late hour. The air-conditioning had attracted people driven off the street by the heat. In the booth next to theirs, a young couple fussed over three kids wearing pajamas and unlaced tennis shoes. The baby slept in the woman's arms, its mouth wetly pressed against her shoulder. The other two made slurping noises with straws stuck into glasses of pale tan crushed ice from which the last bit of cola taste had long ago been sucked. Among the refugees from the heat wave, the boy recognized several night people by the way they hunched defensively over the cups of coffee that represented their right to stay there. They were his sort of people: the flotsam that collects in all-night joints; the losers and the lost; those on the drift, and those who'd been beached; nature's predators, nature's prey.

Mugs of coffee between them, the boy and the girl talked; and when their talk waned or their thoughts wandered inward, as sometimes they did, they gazed out onto the empty street lit only by the bright splash from their window. Once she saw him examining her reflection in the glass, but when his eyes caught her looking back at him, they flinched away. She felt sure he hadn't had a real chance to see what she looked like out in the darkness and was making a quick appraisal of her reflection. She was young and slim, but she knew she was not pretty. Still, people sometimes said she had nice eyes, and when she examined them in her mirror, she found them, if not exotic or sexy, at least kind and expressive, and they were set off by long, soft lashes...her best feature. She was afraid he was going to compliment her on her eyes, and she was glad when he didn't because saying a girl has nice eyes is an admission she isn't good-looking, something like describing a person with no sense of humor as 'sincere', or saying a really dull girl is a 'good listener'. Her shoulder-length hair was curled in at the ends, forming, with her short bangs, a frame for her face. She had gone out that night in a stiff cotton frock with little bows at the shoulders, a full skirt held out by a rustling crinoline, and a matching bolero jacket...her 'June Allyson dress'.

Every major film actress had her characteristic makeup, hairdo, and wardrobe that girls imitated, each following the style of her 'favorite movie star': meaning the actress she thought she most closely resembled. For girls with too much face, there was the 'Loretta

Young look'; for hard-faced girls, the 'Joan Crawford look'; for skinny-faced girls, there was Ida Lupino; for chubby-faced girls, Mitzi Gaynor or Doris Day; for very plain girls there was always Judy Garland, with her moist-eyed, hitch-in-the-voice earnestness. And for girls who weren't pretty in a showy way, there was June Allyson, who was always nice and kind and understanding, and almost always got the man, even though she wasn't all that sexy.

"That's a lovely dress," he said with gravity.

She smiled down at it. "I got all dressed up and went to the movies tonight. I don't know why. I just..." She shrugged.

"A June Allyson movie?" he asked.

"Yes. I'd been waiting to see—" Her eyes widened. "How did you know?"

He slipped into a Bela Lugosi voice. "I know many things, my dear. I have powers beyond those of your ordinary, everyday, run-of-the-mill, ready-to-wear, off-the-shelf human being."

"No, come on, *really*. How did you know I went to a June Allyson movie?"

He smiled. "Just a lucky guess." Then he popped back into the Lugosi voice, "Or maybe not! Maybe I was lurking outside the movie house, and I followed you onto the bus, stalking my prey!" He shifted to Lionel Barrymore, all wheezy and avuncular, "Now you just listen to me, young lady! You've got to be careful about letting bad boys pick you up and carry you off to well-lit dens, where they ply you with stimulants...like caffeine."

She laughed. "Well, you're right, anyway. I did go to a June Allyson movie. She's my favorite."

"No kidding?"

"It was *Woman's World*. Have you seen it?"

"Afraid not."

"Well, there's these three men who are after this swell job, but only one of them can have it. And their wives are trying to help them get it, and..."

"...and June Allyson is the nicest of the wives? A small-town girl?"

"That's right, and she— Wait a minute! You said you haven't seen it."

"Another lucky guess." Then back into the Lugosi voice. "Or was it? You must never trust bad boys, my dear. They may smile and seem harmless, but underneath...? Churning cauldrons of passion!"

She waved his nonsense away with a flapping motion of her hand: an old-fashioned, small-town, June Allyson gesture. "Why do you call yourself a bad boy?"

"I never said that," he said, suddenly severe.

"Sure, you did. You said it twice."

He stared at her for a moment...then smiled. "Did I really? Well, I guess that makes us a team. I'm the bad one, and you're the odd one. Riffraff, that's what we are. Tell you what: you be riff, and I'll be raff, okay?" Then Amos of 'Amos 'n' Andy' said, "So elucidate me, Missus Riff. What am yo' daily occupational work like?"

She described her work at a JCPenney's where Weaver Overhead Cash Carriers zinged on wires, bringing money and sales slips up to a central nest suspended from the ceiling, and the change came zinging back down to clerks whom the company didn't trust to handle money. She worked up in the cashier's cage, making change and zinging it back down. "...but most of the stores have modernized and gotten rid of their cash carriers."

"And what if your store modernizes and gives up Mr Weaver's thingamajig—"

"Overhead Cash Carrier."

"...Overhead Cash Carrier. What happens to your job then?"

"Oh, by then I'll be a qualified secretary. I'm taking shorthand two nights a week. The Gregg Method? And I'm going to take a typing course as soon as I save up enough money. You know what they say: If you can type and take shorthand, you'll never be out of a job."

"Yeah, they just keep on saying that and saying that. Sometimes I get tired of hearing it. So, I suppose that what with your job and your shorthand classes and all, you don't get out much."

"No, not much. I don't know all that many people. ...No one, really."

"You must miss your folks."

"No."

"Not at all?"

"They're religious and awful strict. With them, everything is sin, sin, sin."

He smiled. "they do a lot of sinning, do they?"

"No, they never sin. Never. But they...I don't know how to describe it. They're always *thinking* about sin. Always cleansing themselves of it, or strengthening themselves to resist it. I guess you could say they spend all their time *not* sinning. Sort of like...well, you remember when we were walking here and I bumped into you and we touched shoulders, then we walked on, making sure not to touch again but thinking about it every step of the way? Well, with them it's sort of like that with sinning, if you know what I mean."

"I know exactly what you mean."

She suddenly had the feeling that he hadn't even noticed the moment when their shoulders touched, but he didn't want to admit it.

They fell silent for a time; then she emerged from her reverie with a quick breath and said, "What about you?"

"How do I feel about sin?"

"No, I mean, tell me about yourself and your job and all."

"Well...let's see. First off, I have to confess that I don't work in a JCPenney's, and I've never taken a shorthand course in my life. I haven't the time. I'm too busy lurking around movie houses and following girls on buses."

"No, come on! How come you talk with an English accent if you're not English?"

"It's not an English accent. It's what they call 'mid-Atlantic'. And it's totally phony. When I was a drama major in college, I—"

"You've been to college?"

"Only a couple of years. Then the Korean Police Action came along and I—" He shrugged all that away. "No, I'm not English. I just decided to change my voice because I hated it. It was so...New York. Flat, metallic, adenoidal, too little resonance, too much urgency. I wanted to sound like the actors I admired. Welles, Olivier, Maurice Evans. So I took courses in theater speech and I practiced hours and hours in my room, listening to records and imitating them. But it turned out to be a waste of time."

"No it wasn't! I *like* the way you talk. It's so...cultured. Sort of like Claude Rains or James Mason."

"Oh yes, my dear," he said as Claude Rains, "the phony speech eventually became habitual." He shifted to James Mason, a slightly lower note with a touch of huskiness. It was wonderful how he could sound like any actor he wanted to! "But even with a new voice, I was still the person I was trying not to be. Damned nuisance!" Then he returned to his everyday voice. "For all my correctly placed vowels and sounded terminal consonants, I was still a bad boy running away from...whatever it is we're all supposed to be running away from."

"So you left college to join the army?"

"That's right. But later they...well, they decided to let me out early."

"Why?"

He shrugged. "I guess I'm just not the soldier type. Not aggressive enough. Are you cold?" She had been sitting with her arms crossed over her breasts, holding her upper arms in her hands...the way she sometimes did when she was thinking about how small her breasts were. He reached across the table and touched her arm above the elbow. "You *are* cold."

"It's this air-conditioning. I don't know why they turn it up so high."

The refugees had been steadily thinning out, and now the family in the booth behind them left, the mother with the wet-mouthed baby in her arms, the father carrying one child and pulling a sleep-dazed little girl along by the hand, her untied shoes clopping on the floor. Soon the place would be empty, except for the night people.

She looked up at the clock above the counter. "Gee, it's after two. I've got work tomorrow." But she didn't rise to leave. He drew a deep sigh and stretched, and his foot touched hers beneath the table. He said, "Excuse me," and she said, "That's all right," and they both looked out the window at the empty street. She watched his eyes refocus to her reflection on the surface of the glass, and he smiled at her.

"What about you?" she asked. "Don't you have to be at work early?"

"No. I don't have what you'd call a steady job. I just drift from city to city. When I need money, I go to the public market before dawn and stand around with the rest of the drifters and winos. Job brokers come in trucks and pick out the youngest and strongest for a day's stoop labor. I almost always get picked, even though I'm not all that hefty. I give the foremen one of my boyish smiles, and they always pick me."

"It's true, you do have a boyish smile."

"And when the boyish smile doesn't work, I fall back on my 'look of intense sincerity'. That's a sure winner. Stoop labor only pays a buck or a buck ten an hour. But still, one thirteen- or fourteen-hour day gives me enough for a couple of days of freedom."

"But there's no future in that."

"*What?* No future? I've been tricked! They assured me that stoop labor was a sure path to riches, fame, success with the women, and a closer relationship with my personal savior. Gosh, maybe I'd better give it up and take a course in shorthand. The Gregg Method."

He meant to be amusing, but he evoked only a faint, fugitive smile. She didn't like being teased. She'd had a lot of teasing in her life.

"I'm sorry," he said. "I wasn't poking fun at you. If I was poking fun at anybody, it was myself. You are absolutely right! There's no future in stoop labor. I've got to start taking life seriously!" His eyes crinkled into a smile. "Maybe I'll start next Thursday. How would that be?"

She didn't answer for a time, then she said she really had to be getting home.

He nodded. "You want me to walk you? Or do you feel pretty safe in your Italian neighborhood?"

"What about you? Don't you have to get some sleep?"

"They won't let me in. It's too late. So I'll just roam the streets. Cities are interesting just before dawn when everything is quiet, except for the occasional distant siren announcing a fire, or a crime, or a birth—which is a sort of crime, considering the state of the world. There's something haunting about a distant siren. Like when you hear the whistle of a freight train at night, far off down in the valley, and you'd give anything in the world not to be the kind of..." He stopped speaking and his attention turned inward. He seemed to be listening to a distant freight train in his memory.

She cleared her throat softly. "Gee, it must be interesting to travel around on freight trains and see things. Lonely, I suppose. But interesting."

"Yup!" he said in Gary Cooper's lockjaw way. "Real interesting, ma'am. But real lonely, too."

She pushed her coffee mug aside. "I've really got to get some sleep." But she still didn't rise to go. "You said something about not being able to go to bed because they wouldn't let you in. Who won't let you in? Why not?"

"Obviously, you're not *au fait* with the protocol of your friendly neighborhood flophouse. They're all pretty much the same. You sleep in wire cages that you can lock from the inside to protect your bindle from thieves and your body from men who— They're not exactly homosexuals. Most of them would rather have a woman. Most of them fantasize about women. But..." He shrugged and glanced at her to see if this was embarrassing her. But no. She was listening with a frown of concern, trying to understand with a total absence of coyness that he admired. "The flophouse routine is simple and rigid. You aren't allowed in until ten at night, and by eleven the lights are turned off. Early in the morning, usually five-thirty or six, the alarms go off and you've got half an hour to get out before they clean the place with a fire hose, shooting it through the wire cages. The mattresses are covered with waterproof plastic so they don't get soaked, but they always feel clammy, and the place always smells of urine and Lysol. But the price is right! Four bits a night. A dime more if you want a shower. Tonight I took a long cold shower, then I lay on my cot, reading a paperback until the lights went out. But it was so hot! The plastic mattress stuck to my back and made a sort of ripping sound every time I rolled over. And the sweat was stinging my eyes. So finally I decided to get out and wander the streets. But then..." He shifted to a Peter Lorre voice, nasal and lateral with dentalized consonants. "...what should I see but June Allyson coming out of a June Allyson movie, so naturally I followed her. You think that was evil of me, don't you, Rick. You don't like me much, do you, Rick." He smiled and returned to his street voice. "And now here I am, talking to a very, very sleepy girl in an almost empty White Tower. Ain't life a gas?"

She shook her head sadly. "Gosh, what a terrible way to live. And for a person who went to college, too."

He let W. C. Fields respond, "That's the way it is out there, my little chickadee. It's not a fit life for man nor beast!"

"You must be lonely."

"Yup," he said. "Sometimes a fella gets lonelier than one of those lonely things you see out there being lonely." Then he suddenly stopped clowning around. "I guess I'm nearly as lonely as a girl who gets all dressed up on the hottest night of the year and goes out to see a movie...all alone."

"Well I...I don't know many people here. And what with my night classes and all..." She shrugged. "Gee, I've really got to get home."

"Right. Let's go."

She glanced again at the clock. "And you're going to walk around until dawn?"

"Yup."

She frowned down into her lap, and her throat mottled with a blush. "You could..." She cleared her throat. "You could stay with me if you want. Just until it gets light, I mean."

He nodded, more to himself than to her.

They stepped out of the cool White Tower into the humid heat of the street. At first, the warmth felt good on their cold skin, but it soon became heavy and sapping. They walked without speaking. By inviting him to her room, she had made a daring and desperate leap into the unknown, and now she was tense and breathless with the danger of it...and the thrill of it. 'Is this it?' she said to herself. 'Is he the one?'

He felt a thrill akin to hers, and when he smiled at her she returned an uncertain, fluttering smile that was both vulnerable and hopeful. There was something coltish in her awkward gait on those high heels, something little-girlish in the sibilant whisper of her stiff crinoline. He drew a long slow breath.

She led the way up three flights of dark, narrow stairs, both of them trying to make their bodies as light as possible because the stairs creaked and they didn't want to wake her landlady. She turned her key in the slack lock, opened the door, and made a gesture for him to go in first. After the dark of the stairwell, the room dazzled and deluded him. The streetlight under which they had first met was just beneath her window, and it cast trapezoidal distortions of the window panes up onto the ceiling, filling the room with slabs of bright light separated by patches of impenetrable shadow. His eyes had difficulty adapting to this disorienting play of dazzle and darkness because the brightness kept his irises too dilated to see into the shadows. The oilcloth cover of a small table was slathered with light, while the iron bed in the corner was bisected diagonally by the shadow of an over-sized old wardrobe that consumed too much of the meager space. The only door was the one they had entered through, so he assumed the toilet must be down the hall. Actually, it was on the floor below. The room was an attic that had been converted at minimal cost, and the metal roof above the low ceiling pumped the sun's heat into the small space all day long.

"It's awful hot, I know," she whispered apologetically. Standing there with her back to the window, she was faceless within a dazzling halo of hair, while the light was so strong on his face that it burned out any expression; she wore a mask of shadow, he wore a mask of light.

"I'll open the window so we can get a little breeze," he whispered.

"You can't. It's stuck."

"Jesus."

"Sorry. Would you like a glass of water? If I run it a long time, it gets cold. Well...cool, anyway."

"Do we have to whisper?"

"No, but I..."

"But you don't want your neighbors to know you have someone up here?"

She nodded. "You see, I've never..." She swallowed noisily, and the noise of it embarrassed her.

"Yes, I would like a glass of water, thank you," he said, not whispering, but speaking very softly. He sat on the edge of the bed, sunk up to his chest in shadow.

She turned the single tap above a chipped sink and let the water overflow the glass onto her wrist until it got cool, glad to have some-thing to do—or, more exactly, to have something to delay what they were going to do.

The harsh streetlight picked out a two-ring hot plate on the table.

Its cord ran up to a dangling overhead light. The bulb had been taken out and replaced by a screw-in socket. Cooking in the room was forbidden, but she did it anyway to save money. She unplugged the hot plate and hid it when she left for work. There was an open workbook and a pad of paper beside the hot plate: the Gregg Method. These everyday objects were abstracted, caricatured, by the brittle streetlight that set their edges aglow but coated them with thick shadow. The room had a shrill, unreal quality of a bright but deserted carnival lot.

She brought him the glass of water; he thanked her and drank it down; she asked if he would like another; he said he wouldn't, thank you; she told him it wouldn't be any trouble; he said no thanks, and she stood there awkwardly.

"Hey, what's this?" he asked, holding up a glass sphere that his fingers had discovered beneath her pillow where they had been unconsciously searching for that coolness that children seek by turning pillows over and putting their cheek on them.

"That's my snowstorm."

He shook the heavy glass paperweight and held it out into the band of light across the bed to watch the snow swirl around a carrot-nosed snowman. "Your own private snowstorm. A handy thing on a hot night like this!"

"I won it at the county fair when I was a kid. I used my ride money to buy a raffle ticket, and I won third prize. I told my folks I found it at the fairground, because they're dead against raffles and bingo games and all kinds of gambling. My snowstorm's the only thing I took with me when I left home. Except my clothes, of course."

"So your snowstorm's your friend, eh? A trusted companion through the trials and tribulations of life."

"I keep it under my pillow, and sometimes at night when I'm feeling real blue I shake it and watch the snow whirl, and it makes me feel safer and more...oh, I don't know." She shrugged.

"Back to your sentry post, loyal snowstorm." He returned the paperweight to beneath her pillow and patted it into place; then he reached up, took her hands, and drew her down to sit beside him.

"Please..." she said in a thin voice. "I'm scared. I really shouldn't of...I mean, I've never..." She knew her hands were clammy with fear, and she wished they weren't.

He spoke softly. "Listen. If you want me to go, I'll just tiptoe down the stairs and slip out. *Is* that what you want?"

"...No, but...Couldn't we just..."

"You know what I think? I think I'd better go. You're scared, and I wouldn't want to talk you into anything you don't want to do." He rose from the bed.

"No, don't go!" Her voice was tight with the effort to speak softly.

He sat down again, but left a distance between their hips.

For a moment she didn't say anything, just sat there kneading the fingers of her left hand with her right. Then she squeezed them hard. She had come to a decision. She began speaking in a flat tone. "I was sitting at the table, like I do every night. Practicing my shorthand by the light of the street lamp because it's too hot to put on the light. And suddenly I was crying. I just felt so empty and lonely and blue! I wasn't sobbing or anything. The tears just poured out and poured out. I didn't think I had so many tears in me. I was so *lonely*." Her voice squeaked on the word. "I don't know a soul here in the city. Don't have any friends. Even back home, I never went on a date. My folks wouldn't let me. They said that one thing leads to another. They said boys only want one thing. And I suppose they're right."

"Yes, they are," he said sincerely.

"After a while I stopped crying." She smiled wanly. "I guess I just ran out of tears. I splashed cool water on my face and tried to work at my shorthand some more, but then I just closed the book and said no! No, I won't just sit here and mope! I'll dress up in my best and go out and *find* someone. Someone to talk to. Someone to care about me and hold me when I'm feeling blue."

"You decided to go out and just...let yourself be picked up?"

"I didn't think about it that way, but... Yes, I guess so."

"You wanted to make love with a total stranger?"

"No, no. Well...not exactly. You see, I've never..." She shook her head.

"Shall I tell you something? I knew you were a virgin when I first saw you. Yes, I did. You had that Good Girl look. Like June Allyson. But somehow—don't ask me how—I could tell that the good girl was looking for a bad boy to make love to her. Funny, how I could tell that, eh?"

"But you're wrong. I was just looking for someone to talk to. Someone who might care about me."

"Oh. So you didn't want to make love, is that it?"

"I don't know. Maybe I did. Sort of, anyway. I didn't think it out or anything, I just took my towel and went down to the bathroom and had a long cool bath, then I put on my good dress, and out I went. Just like that."

"...Just like that."

"I took the bus downtown, and I walked around. Boys on street corners looked at me. You know, the way they look at any woman. But none of them...I guess I'm not...I know I'm not pretty or anything..." She paused, half hoping for a contradiction. Then she went on. "They looked at me, but nobody said hello or anything, so..." She shrugged.

"So you decided to go to the movies. *Woman's World.*"

"Yes." Her voice had a minor key fade of failure.

"But hey, wait a minute! You did meet someone! Not much of a someone, maybe. Just your common garden variety drifter. But you talked to him for hours over coffee. And now...here we are."

"Yes, here we are," she echoed. "And I'm afraid."

"Of course you're afraid. That's only natural. It isn't every day that a virgin sits in the dark with a bad boy she hardly knows." She didn't respond, so he pursued. "Even though you're a virgin. I suppose you know about how two people...love, and all?"

"Yes. Well, sort of. Girls used to giggle about it in the school locker room. They talked about how people...did it. I didn't believe them at first."

"I know just what you mean. To a kid, it seems such a silly thing to do. Putting your peeing equipment together. How could *that* be fun? And when you think of your own folks doing it...! It's enough to gag a maggot, as a folksy old tramp might say."

"The girls at school used to make up terrible stories about...it. Just to see me blush. I was easy to tease because I was shy, and I didn't know anything. My mother never told me anything. Once the girls played this joke on me? They gave me a folded piece of paper and asked me to write down my favorite number, then on the next line my favorite color, then my second favorite color, then—oh, I don't remember all the things; but the last question was whether I bit ice cream cones or licked them. Then they unfolded the paper and read it out loud. And there in my own handwriting I had written how many times a day my boyfriend and I *did* it, and what the color of his...thing...was when we started, and what color it was when we ended, and stuff like that."

"And finally, your confession that you licked it."

She nodded miserably. "I didn't go back to school for the rest of that week, I was so embarrassed. I pretended I was sick. And then I really did get sick. I mean...that's when my periods started."

"But, of course, that couldn't have had anything to do with the girls' teasing."

"Oh, I know that, but still...coming right after and all..."

"Yeah, I understand. Kids can be rotten to one another."

"That was years ago, but I still get tears in my eyes when I think about it."

"Yeah...tears of rage. I have that sometimes. The rage just wells up in me and I blub like a kid."

"You do? Really?"

"Sure. So you saw all those embarrassing things written in your own handwriting, and now you're learning to write in a different way. In shorthand."

She frowned. "That's not why I'm taking shorthand."

"Could be part of it. Psychology is a screwy business. Like me playing all sorts of roles because I don't want to be—" He shrugged. "So, you've never made love. Gee. Still, I suppose you've necked with boys. Been caressed and...you know...touched."

"No, never. I've never had a...boyfriend." She said the word in a tone of gentle awe. "Boys never found me attractive in that way." She made a dismissive half-chuckle. "Or in any other way, really. My mom used to say it was a blessing, me being plain. At least my looks wouldn't get me into trouble."

"But you've had dreams about lovemaking. That's only normal."

She didn't answer.

"And I suppose you've made love to yourself."

She didn't speak.

"I mean, you've...you know...played with yourself and caressed yourself. There's nothing more natural."

"My folks wouldn't think it's natural. They'd say it was a sin."

"Well, of course they would. But do you think it's a sin?"

After a moment she said, softly, "...yes."

"But you do it anyway?"

"...yes..."

"Hm-m. Well, that's mostly what our making love would be like. Only I'd be doing...you know...what you do for yourself. I'd be touching you and caressing you and bringing you pleasure. Unless, of course, you don't want me to."

She concentrated on the fingers she was twisting in her lap.

He took her hands and kissed them. She wished they weren't so cold and rough. He lifted her face by her chin and gently kissed her closed lips. When he drew back he saw that her eyes were closed, and there was a teardrop in the corner of one, so he shifted to his W. C. Fields voice. "The hardest part, my chickadee, is getting started. If we were already in bed and I was holding your dee-lightful chassis in my vee-rile arms, everything would just happen naturally." Then he changed to a gentle, understanding voice with a smile in it. "I know exactly how you feel. Even with us worldly bad boys it's always awkward. In the beginning."

"It is?"

"Yup. Look, I'll tell you what. Why don't I go stand out in the hall for a few minutes while you slip into bed. Then I'll come back and look around." He donned his Lionel Barrymore voice. "Great land o' Goshen; who's that under those blankets, Dr Kildare? Why, I do believe it's June Allyson. I'd better just slip in and keep her warm. It's my medical duty."

She sniffed the tear back and waved away his nonsense with that flapping gesture of hers.

"I'll be back in a couple of minutes." He made a broad burlesque of shushing her with his finger to his lips as he tiptoed across the room, eased the door open, then closed it behind him.

For a moment she sat on the bed, knowing he was waiting out in the hall, maybe listening. With a sigh she rose, took off her jacket and dress and carefully hung them in the wardrobe. At the sink she washed under her arms with cold water and dried herself, then she stepped out of her rustling crinoline underskirt, hung it over the chair and tiptoed back to the bed. She winced when the bedsprings twanged as she lay down, her heart pounding. Her nervous fingers found the cool snowman under the pillow and she stroked it for reassurance. Then the door opened slowly. He pressed it closed behind him with a soft click.

"This is so..." She sought just the right word to describe the beautiful moment. "...so *nice*. Lying here like this...talking...being close." He had guided her hand to his soft penis, and she was holding it tentatively, dutifully ('politely' might be more exact) while her mind fondled the words: 'boyfriend...my first boyfriend'. Her hand on his penis was the only place their bodies were in contact because it was so hot. After bringing her to climax first with his hand, then with his tongue, he had lifted his head to find her belly wet with sweat, so he had blown across it gently to cool her. And now they lay side by side, looking up at the splayed shadow of windowpanes cast onto the ceiling by the streetlight.

"That was just wonderful," she said dreamily.

"Hm-m, I could tell it was from the way you moved. And the sounds you made."

"Gosh, I hope the neighbors didn't hear." She pulled her shoulders in and laughed silently into her hand.

"How many times have you...?" She didn't know how to put it.

"Have I what?"

"How many women have you...you know."

"You really want to know?"

"No, don't tell me!" Then, after a moment, "Yes, tell me. How many?"

"You're my fifth."

"The fifth time you've made love? Or your fifth woman?"

"Both."

"Both? You mean you've made love only five times, and each time with a different girl?"

"Exactly, Watson," he said in Basil Rathbone's arch drawl. "Five girls...five times. Curious business, what?"

"Were they like me, your other girlfri— These women?"

He squeezed his temples between his thumb and middle finger to ease the pressure. "No, nothing like you. The first one was when I was in college. She was old. About as old as my mother. I met her in a bar that was off limits for college kids. She was always there, sitting at the end of the bar, drinking gin. Her thick makeup and fake ritzy voice were sort of a joke. People called her 'the Countess'. We drank and she talked about when she was a young woman in high society, and how all the men used to be crazy about her, but they were not of her social standing—crap like that. The bar closed, and we went walking down along the railroad tracks. I was pretty drunk. I suppose I thought we were going to her place. She had trouble keeping her balance because the ground was rough and broken. She fell against me, and I caught her, and she kissed me, a big wet kiss, and I laid her back on a muddy bank. And that, ladies and gentlemen, was my introduction to the splendors of romance! That night, I quit college and joined the army to defend American democracy and apple pie against the menace of international communism and borscht. After basic training, I was given leave before being shipped over to Korea. It was Christmas, and I took a bus to Flagstaff, Arizona. Why Flagstaff? I had to go somewhere, and Flagstaff counts as somewhere...well, nearly. Not far from the bus station, I saw a girl in this all-night coffee joint, and from all the way across the street I could tell she was lonely. I have an instinct for loneliness."

"Like you could tell I was lonely?" she said softly into the dark.

He was silent for a moment. "Yeah, like I could tell you were lonely. Well, I joked with this girl, talking in one actor's voice after another, and the next thing you know we were walking towards her place. She was an Indian, and an orphan, and lonely, and just about as far as you can get from pretty, and... Well, anyway." He pressed his thumb into his temple, hard. "I decided not to return to the army. That meant I had to go on the drift. Casual pick-up jobs here and there, following the fruit crops north, flophouses, stoop labor, freight trains. Then there was this woman in Waco, a born-again fanatic who wanted to save me. And later a black hooker in Cleveland who'd been beaten up by her pimp. I couldn't kiss her while we made love because she had a split lip. And that's it. My total love life. Not much of a Romeo. But then, people don't like to get mixed up with someone like me. Damaged boys end up damaging other people. You understand what I'm saying?"

"Sort of. Well...no, not really."

They were silent for a time, then she said, "I thought it was going to hurt, but it didn't."

He tugged himself from his tangled thoughts. "What?"

"When we...you know. The girls at school said it hurts the first time, and you bleed."

"Well, we didn't do the part that hurts."

"Yes, I know. Didn't you...don't you want to?"

"Do you want me to hurt you?"

"No. No, of course not, but I want you to have...you know... pleasure. I wish I knew how to..." She shrugged. "I'll do whatever you want." She snuggled her hot body to his and whispered into his ear. "How can I make you feel good? Tell me. Please."

He was silent.

"I'll do anything."

He chuckled. "Lick me like an ice cream cone?"

He felt her tense up, so he quickly said, "I'm sorry, I was just joking. No, there's nothing I want you to do. There's nothing you *can* do."

"What do you mean?"

"I suppose you've seen drawings on bathroom walls in school. Do you remember what the men's penises looked like?"

She shook her head.

"Oh, come on now. Of course you remember. Describe them to me."

"Well...in the drawings they're always huge. As big as arms. And sometimes there are drops of sap squirting out of them."

"Sap?" He laughed. "*Sap?*"

"Well, whatever it is. The stuff that makes—Oh, I see! You were afraid I'd have a baby. That was why you didn't...." She hugged him.

"No, that wasn't why. I didn't do the part that might hurt you because I...can't."

"You can't?"

"My penis can't get erect."

"Oh." Then, after a longish silence: "Were you hurt? Wounded or something?"

"No, I wasn't wounded." Then, after a moment: "but yes, I was hurt."

"I don't understand."

He drew a sigh. "Well, when I was a kid (actually, it started when I was a baby) my mother used to...she used to play with me. Mostly with her mouth. That's the earliest thing in my memory, her playing with me. Of course, I didn't know there was anything wrong with it. I thought it was just the way things are with mothers and their little boys...kissing and cuddling and all that. Then one night she told me that I must never, never tell anyone what she did, because if I told, then mean people would come and spank me *hard* and put me into a deep, dark hole forever and ever. That's when I realized that we were doing something wrong. And being a kid, I naturally thought that it was my fault somehow. I used to have nightmares about being thrown into that deep, dark hole, and I..." He stopped short and shook his head.

"You don't have to tell me about it if you don't want to," she whispered.

"No, I want to. In fact, I have to, because that's the only way..." He shrugged, then he took several calming breaths before telling the shared darkness above them the things he needed her to know. "While my mother licked and sucked me, she would play with herself, and after a while she'd moan and squirm, and she'd suck faster and harder, and sometimes it would hurt, and I'd whine and tell her that it hurt, but she'd keep on until she was gasping and crying out! Then she'd lie back on the bed panting, and I'd be cold down there where I was all spitty with her licking and sucking. And sometimes it hurt real bad. Inside."

"Your mother...! She was crazy."

"Yup. She was always drunk when she did it. To this day, the smell of gin reminds me of being a little kid, and I can feel the pain inside, behind my penis."

"I'm sorry. I'm really sorry." She slipped her hand away from his soft penis, as though to avoid hurting him more.

"Then, when I was about five or six—I don't know exactly how old, but I hadn't started school yet—she was playing with me this night, tickling and sucking, and suddenly she lifted her head and smirked—I can still see the smirk—and she said, 'Well, well! Aren't *you* the naughty little boy! You want it, don't you, you bad, bad boy?' You see, my penis had got stiff. That can happen, even when a boy is too young to...well, too young to know what's happening. And from that night on, for the next couple of years, she'd make me stiff, and that would drive her wild, and she'd suck me hard while she played with herself, and she'd say I was a bad boy because I wanted it. I wouldn't get stiff if I didn't want it, she'd say, and she'd suck me until it hurt down in my testicles. Then this one night...this one night the hurt didn't go away after she stopped. It got worse and worse. And the next morning I couldn't go to school because it hurt so bad. She told me it was nothing. The pain would go away pretty soon. But I could tell she was scared. She said that if anyone found out what we did, they'd put me in that deep black hole and leave me there forever and ever. And everyone would know it was all my fault, because I got stiff, and that meant I wanted it, and they'd know I was a naughty, bad boy. By the time night came, my side was swollen and I had a fever. All night long I tossed in my bed with pain. The next morning, I found myself all alone in the house. My mother had gone. I had to pee real bad, but I couldn't because it hurt too much. I was afraid I was going to die. So I called the emergency number I found on the back of the phone book. It was the first time I ever used a phone. An ambulance came and took me to the hospital. I had ruptures. Two ruptures. There was an operation, and they kept me in the hospital for a long time. When I was feeling better, a social worker visited me in the children's ward. They couldn't find my mother anywhere. She'd run away. Abandoned me."

She turned onto her side and looked at his profile. He could feel her eyes on him, could feel the weight of her pity, and it felt good.

"What about your father?" she asked. "Why didn't he stop your mother from...Why didn't he do something?"

"There was no father."

"Oh." After a silence, she asked, "Did you tell the doctors what your mother had done to you?"

He shook his head.

"Why not?"

"Because I didn't want to get her into trouble. After all...she was my mom." His jaw muscles worked, and she could hear the grinding of his teeth.

"It isn't fair!" she said.

"No, ma'am, it's not," his Gary Cooper voice agreed. "Not even a little bit fair." Then his own voice continued, "The doctor told the social worker that I had damaged myself by masturbating, and she told me I'd done a terrible thing and I would hurt myself badly if I didn't stop."

"So...what happened then?"

"They put me into an orphanage run by Catholic brothers. I got long lectures about how sinful masturbation was, and my earlobes would burn with embarrassment...and rage...at the injustice of it. Kids have a painfully keen sense of injustice. The brothers made me take cold showers, even in winter. They said it would keep me from abusing myself. The cold showers gave me an ear infection that put me back in the hospital. And that was the end of the cold showers. But not of the lectures." He fell silent, and he lightly rubbed his stomach to quell the gnawing. Then he used his Bela Lugosi voice. "And there you have it, my dear. The blood-curdling tale of...The Limp, Penis!"

"I'm awful sorry."

She could tell from the depth of the silence outside that they had reached that last dead hour before dawn. She felt that they ought to talk about their future. Well...at least about meeting for coffee tomorrow night after work. They could meet at the White Tower...their place.

"You must have been a real smart kid. I mean, you got into college and all." She was determined to find a silver lining in all his troubles: a Hollywood happy ending.

"Yes, I was smart. A bad boy, but a smart one. But I quit college and joined the army. Then I quit the army to become a full-time drifter."

"But a person can't just quit the army, can they?"

"Oh, the army wasn't all that happy about my taking off. They're out there looking for me even as we lie here, sharing secrets."

"Aren't you afraid they'll catch you?"

"I'm afraid of all sorts of things."

She drew a long sympathetic sigh and said, "Gosh."

"Gosh, indeed. While I was in the army, I sort of went wild this one night. I ended up sobbing and screaming and beating up this Coke machine. I might have gotten away with it if it had been a Pepsi machine, but Cola-Cola *is* America, and beating one up is a matter for the UnAmerican Activities Committee, so they put me in the hospital. The loony bin. This doctor told me..." He slipped into his Groucho Marx voice. "...Your problem isn't physical, son. It's psychological. That'll be ten million dollars. Cash. We don't take checks. For that matter, we don't take Poles or Yugoslavs either."

"And now you can't feel any pleasure? Like the kind you made me feel?"

"Yes, I can feel pleasure. And, sometimes I need it very badly. But it's not easy for me to get pleasure. It's difficult and...sort of complicated."

"Is there anything I can do? To help you, I mean?" Her voice was thin, and so sincere.

"Do you really want to help me?"

"I do. Honest and truly, I do."

"Cross your heart and hope to die?" He sighed and closed his eyes. "All right." He sat up on the edge of the bed. "You scoot over here and turn your back to me. And I'll bring myself pleasure. Is that all right?"

She slid over to the edge of the bed, awkward and uncertain. "Will it hurt me?"

"Yes," he told her softly. "But not for long."

She was silent.

"Is that all right? The hurt and all?" he asked. "I won't do it, if you don't want me to."

She swallowed and answered in a small voice. "No, it's all right."

He reached down and trickled his fingers up her spine to the nape of her neck and up into her hair. She hummed, and he felt her skin get goose-bumpy with thrill. His hands slipped under her hair and he stroked the sides of her neck up to the ears, then he reached around and gently cradled her throat between his hands. She swallowed, and he felt the cartilage of her windpipe ripple beneath his fingers. He bared his teeth and he closed his eyes and squeezed and let the up-welling of pleasure sweep him towards...

She gagged and struggled. Her arms flayed about wildly, but his hands were too strong. Her desperately clutching fingers clawed at the rungs of her iron bedstead, then grasped the edge of her pillow, then her snow—

She crouches in the far corner of her bed, trapped. One of her shoulders is pressed against the cool iron bedstead, the other against the gritty wall. She hugs a snatched-up pillow to her naked chest, unable to move because she's afraid of touching the thing that sprawls diagonally across the bed, split down the spine by a shadow that leaves one shoulder, one buttock, and one dangling leg in the bright light.

When she swallows, her bruised throat hurts. After hitting him...and again...and again...she scuttled into the dark corner and stared at the paperweight lying next to him until the swirling snow-storm ebbed and settled to one side of the sphere. There was stuff from his head on it.

She stares at it still, her insides fluttery and cold. Her hip feels slimy. He squirted while they were struggling. She wipes it off with the hem of the sheet, shuddering.

The faucet drip-drip-drips into the sink.

Suddenly the streetlight goes off, and the ceiling is dark. A thin metallic dawn seeps into the room and she whispers to herself that she has to find help...has to tell somebody what happened.

But first she has to get past him.

Down in the street beneath her window, the air is almost cool. Milky tints began to stretch the morning sky, and already the air is stale and dusty in the nostrils.

It's going to be another scorcher.

ACKNOWLEDGMENTS

Trevanian has previously published several of these tales under various pseudonyms. He gratefully acknowledges: *The Yale Literary Magazine; B. B. Uitgerversmastschappij*, Amsterdam; *The Antioch Review; Harper's* magazine; *Playboy* magazine; Clarkson N. Potter, Inc.; *Redbook*; and *The Editors' Choice (The Best Short Fiction for 1985)*, published by Bantam Books.